D0067138

Also by Louis Auchincloss

FICTION

Praise for Louis Auchincloss

"One of the century's very best American writers."
— *Los Angeles Times*

"Louis Auchincloss . . . has established himself as the undisputed heir to the literary turf staked out by that grande dame of American letters, Edith Wharton."
— *New York Times Book Review*

"Louis Auchincloss is one of the best writers alive. He has probed the American character more boldly and more intelligently than many of his more celebrated contemporaries . . . He writes . . . in a prose so deft, so clear, that it's often only after you finish an Auchincloss novel that you think about it—before that you've been caught up in the pleasure of reading it."
— Susan Cheever

"Auchincloss has never been a mere observer; his fiction has always examined what makes life worth living."
— *Washington Post Book World*

"Some writers inform, some instruct, and some tell how rewarding good prose can be. Louis Auchincloss does all three."
— John Kenneth Galbraith

"When it comes to the minute social differences and unexpected human conflicts that can be the life of fiction, there is simply no one else like him."
— Alfred Kazin

"Louis Auchincloss remains our most astute observer of moral paradox among the affluent."
— Arthur M. Schlesinger, Jr.

"In the literary history of New York, it's a rule of thumb that the three chief chroniclers of life among the city's upper crust are . . . Henry James, Edith Wharton, and Louis Auchincloss."
— *Seattle Times*

"[Auchincloss is] a natural storyteller and an artful historian of New York's ruling class."
— *New York Observer*

The Rector
of Justin

LOUIS AUCHINCLOSS

A MARINER BOOK

Houghton Mifflin Company

Boston New York

FIRST MARINER BOOKS EDITION 2002

For information about permission to reproduce selections from this
book, write to Permissions, Houghton Mifflin Harcourt Publishing Company,
215 Park Avenue South, New York, New York 10003.

Visit Our web site: www.hmhco.com.

Library of Congress Cataloging-in-Publication Data is available.

ISBN 0-618-22489-0

ISBN 978-0-618-22489-0

Printed in the United States of America

DOH 10 9 8 7 6 5

For Two John Winthrops
My Son and Brother

THE RECTOR OF JUSTIN

I

SEPTEMBER 10, 1939. I have always wanted to keep a journal, but whenever I am about to start one, I am dissuaded by the idea that it is too late. I lose heart when I think of all the fascinating things I could have described had I only begun earlier. Not that my life has been an exciting one. On the contrary, it has been very dull. But a dull life in itself may be an argument for a journal. The best way for the passive man to overtake his more active brothers is to write them up. Isn't the Sun King himself just another character in Saint-Simon's chronicle?

In Europe a world war has started while in this country Brian Aspinwall is about to go to work in his first job. Surely if I am ever to keep a journal, now is the time. A first job at twenty-seven! I shall be an instructor of English at Justin Martyr, an Episcopal boys' boarding school thirty miles west of Boston. The telegram from a Mr. Ives came in only yesterday. One of the masters wants to go to Canada to enlist in the RCAF which is why I have been taken on without interviews. It makes me feel better about my rejection by the British Army before I left Oxford in July. Naturally, they were not keen about an untrained Yankee student with a heart murmur! Perhaps had I stayed over there, now that war has actually come, they might have lowered their standards, but at least this way I can feel that I am releasing an able-bodied man to fight the antichrist in Berlin.

It is the obvious moment for stock-taking. In the questionnaire that was sent out this year by my class secretary at Columbia, I had nothing to contribute but the meager fact that I had gone abroad to study for a master's degree. And now because I was too sensitive to stay in Oxford out of uniform I will not even get that! I suppose all I have basically done since my seventeenth year has been to seek refuge in literature from the agony of deciding whether or not I am qualified to be a minister. Perhaps life in a church school will help me. Please God it may.

But I must try not to be too hard on myself. That is, after all, another kind of conceit. It is a fact that I suffered all during my boyhood from ill health. It is another fact that as the only child of elderly parents I had to spend a great deal of time with them in their last illnesses. It was a joy — and I write the word sincerely — to be able to help them, but it was still time out of a career. So it is not altogether my fault that I have made so late a start — if it can be said I have even yet started.

With God's grace I shall learn my true capacities at Justin Martyr. It is a good size for a school (450 boys), and its headmaster and founder, the Reverend Francis Prescott, D.D., is probably the greatest name in New England secondary education. He is old now, nearly eighty, but he is a minister, and may have much to teach me. It may even turn out that I have been "called" to Justin.

I am shy and lack force of personality, and my stature is small. I stammer when I am nervous, and my appearance is more boyish than manly. All this will be against me. But I am not afraid to say what I mean, and I think in a real crisis I can be counted on to stand up for the right, if only because I have such a horror of letting God down. Let us hope I add up to a teacher.

September 16. Justin Martyr. I arrived the day before yesterday, a week ahead of the boys, to work up my courses with Mr. Anders of the English department. It is all very rush, but everyone knows I am an emergency replacement and Mr. Anders is kindness itself.

I am not yet entirely sure what I think of the looks of the school. On Monday it depressed me; on Tuesday I felt better about it; today (in glorious weather) I like it. It is fairly consistently in the H. H. Richardson tradition, with masses of dark red brick, Romanesque arches in rock-faced granite, rotundas and long colonnades. A certain leaning to heaviness, suggestive of some medieval monastery in southern France, or, less remotely, of some solid New England summer colony at the turn of the century, is lightened by the profusion of verdurous lawns and hedges and by the glory of elm trees. God, as usual, has done a better job than man.

To be more particular, the school is built around an oval campus at whose northern end stands Lawrence House, the main building, which contains the library, the dining hall and the headmaster's residence. Moving clockwise next comes the schoolhouse, with high Gothic windows in its great assembly hall and an octagonal open bell house from which the "outside" tolls each morning at seven; then the gymnasium, with a Florentine note of large stones and small windows, then the dormitories: Depew, Griscam and Lowell, and finally the brownstone chapel, a relief after so much red and grey, with its square craggy tower rising to dwarf the academic community huddled at its feet.

It is a remarkable tower. The eye travels upward to follow its mighty thrust past the narrow open window slits to the castellated top over which a shingle pyramided roof rises and then climbs yet dizzily further into a pointed round angle turret. Mr. Anders says it is like Dr. Prescott's faith, bold and big, beautiful in its disdain of beauty.

I suppose that many people today would find this architecture ponderous, even banal. They would insist that youth should be educated in modern buildings with plenty of glass to let in God's out-of-doors. Yet I wonder if it is altogether sentimentality that makes me begin to find this campus a heartening place. It seems to me that Dr. Prescott must have recognized from the beginning that boys have no eye for architecture and yet are influenced by it. I imagine that he may have wanted a style that would suggest ruggedness and strength while offering at the same time a certain solid comfortableness, and how better could he attain it than by going back to a Christian tradition of days when the faith was not wholly secure from pagan assault?

For there are aspects of the fortress everywhere: in the machicolated roof of the infirmary, in the grey walls and slit windows of the gymnasium, even in the great tower of the chapel itself. It was this that initially depressed me. Now I see that the sweeping lawns and shady elms make the idea of war retreat into a past of muffled drums. Peace prevails on the campus, and on a brilliant fall day like this one it seems almost a sleepy peace, at least while the boys are still away, and only the hum of an automatic lawnmower breaks the stillness. But it is a peace of dignity, a peace of honor, against the quiet pageant of pinkish red and grey, a peace in which strife has not been forgotten, nor toil neglected, the peace of the Church Militant.

Yes, I think I shall like Justin Martyr.

September 17. Perhaps I have spoken too soon. Yesterday I had not met the headmaster.

He has been here all summer as his wife is very ill, and I ran into him quite by chance as I was passing his front door. I say "ran into him." Let me correct that. One does *not* "run into" Dr. Prescott.

My pen is a poor substitute for the camera to describe a man so magnificently photogenic and so often photographed. He is short for one that dominating, about five feet six, which is accentuated by the great round shoulders, the bull neck, the noble square head, the thick shock of stiff, wavy grey hair. I wonder if he is not a bit vain about his hair, for they say he never wears a hat — even in seasons when it is required of the boys. This afternoon he had on a blue opera cape with a velvet collar fastened by a chain, and he carried a black ebony walking stick, a combination that might have seemed theatrical had it not been so exactly right for him.

His face is remarkably clear for his years, except for deep lines at the corners of his mouth; he has a wide pale brow, thick bushy eyebrows, a straight nose with an almost imperceptible hook at the end, and large eyes, far apart, of a dark brown streaked with yellow. Mr. Anders says that his critics claim that he looks too much like a great man to be one.

I paused when I saw him coming down the steps, not wishing to intrude upon his privacy, but when he paused also, I realized that he was waiting for me to come up to him. He can summon one to his side without a word or a twitch of his great eyebrows.

"You are Aspinwall?" His voice has a deep, velvety melancholy. "We were happy to get you at such short notice. Have you been assigned a football team?"

I assumed that he had mistaken the nature of my duties. "I believe I'm to be in the English department, sir."

His stare was cold. "I'm quite aware of that. But it is our custom at Justin — as you will find it is at other schools — for the younger masters, particularly the unmarried ones, to take part in the athletic program. We might find you a team to coach in one of the lower forms. The Fourth Monongahelas."

"The fourth what, sir?" I dared not confess that I did not even know the rules of football.

"The whole school is divided into two teams for the purpose of intramural sports," he explained in the deliberate, patient tone of one who never repeats. "The Monongahelas and the

Shenandoahs." There was not even the hint of a smile as he brought forth these wonderful Indian names. "Of course, the varsity team which plays other schools is made up of both. The Monongahelas wear blue jerseys and the Shenandoahs red. A boy is assigned to one or the other in his first week at the school and remains in that team until his graduation."

When I am nervous I should be silent. I was appalled to hear myself answer: "That's nice." Would he think I was making fun of him? But he took no note of it.

"You were at Oxford?" he inquired.

"Yes, sir. Christ Church."

"I'm a Balliol man myself." He pursed his lips in a way that pulled his cheeks down and turned the square of his countenance into a triangle of speculation. "We must have a talk one of these days. Poor old England, she's in for it now." And he turned away to proceed on his walk.

So this is the famous Rector of Justin! Not a word about the subject that I am hired to teach; only a lecture on intramural sports. I had not realized that the god of football had conquered even the church schools. It is a dim augury.

September 28. The boys have been here now for five days. I did not wish to record my impressions of the school in session before, as I have learned to make allowance for the timid and apprehensive side of my nature which has a way, like a ghostly and mischievous extra brush, quite beyond the painter's control, of dubbing clouds and rain squalls into the sunniest landscape. If I am ever to be a minister, with God's help, I must learn joy. But now, after more than a hundred hours of boys, when my spirits are still in my boots, I begin to wonder if I will ever be able to adjust my trudge to the noisy march of Justin. I had not imagined there could be so much noise. I have a constant sense of being about to be overwhelmed.

The other masters have been kind, but in the way people are

kind who expect you to swim after the first plunge. Mr. Ives, the senior master, whose relation to Dr. Prescott is that of an executive officer to a ship's captain, a small, delicate birdlike man with a yellow stare that seems to take in everything, patiently briefed me in my duties the first day, but as he obviously expected me to take it all in the first time, I was seized with panic and could only nod stupidly to the meaningless flow of his perfectly organized sentences. It is a sad feeling to stand on the threshold of the school year and know that one's day of reckoning may be tomorrow.

I have seen almost nothing of Dr. Prescott. Thank God he has forgotten the football team! His poor wife is not expected to live, so he has been spending much of his time with her. However, he conducts the chapel service every morning and presides at assembly in the Schoolhouse. The awe which he inspires among the boys and faculty has to be seen to be credited. The masters are always telling tales of his prodigious memory, his uncanny perspicacity, his terrible temper. To hear them go on one would assume that he still handles every detail of school administration, yet in sober fact I suppose it is the ubiquitous Ives who really runs the school. A headmaster, particularly one so venerable, must be like a constitutional sovereign. He performs his function by being seen.

September 30. Worse and worse. My fourth form dormitory has been sizing me up, and now they have decided they can ride me. There were terrible squeals after lights tonight, and I was in a wretched quandary. How does one cope with forty fifteen-year-olds in the dark? Finally in a panic lest the sounds would come to the all-hearing ears of Mr. Ives, I strode to the door into the dormitory, turned on the overhead lights by the switch and called out in what I fear was a trembling falsetto: "Who is talking in this room?" Someone shouted back: "You are!" and the roar of laughter that followed must have been heard all over Lawrence House. In desperation I cried: "'I am going to report the whole dormitory to the headmaster!" and slammed the door. Sitting at my desk again, my hands clasped to my throbbing temples, I took in gradually that the dormitory at last was silent. But what good does it do when in the morning they will all realize I have not carried out my threat?

For I never will. How can I? How can I afford to admit that the boys were out of control? I can only pull out this journal and foolishly wish that I could climb inside of it and pull its covers close over my shamed and ridiculous head. Oh, Journal, if you could only hide me, if I could only turn myself into ink! Dear God, will I ever make a go at teaching? And if I can't handle a few boys, is it feasible that I can ever be a missionary? Or even administer a parish? Perhaps all I am good for is to embrace the Roman Church and join a contemplative order. Please, dear God, keep my dormitory quiet.

October 4. I had my second talk with the headmaster this afternoon. Like the first, it arose from a chance meeting. I was on my way to the river, walking past the athletic fields, when I encountered the stocky figure in the sweeping blue cape. He was crossing the road from the first squad field where he watches the football practice for a daily half hour, leaning silently on his walking stick. When he saw me, his expression was not friendly.

"Good afternoon, Aspinwall. Whither are *you* bound?"

"To the river, sir," And with the instinctive good manners of the nonacademic world I inappropriately added: "Would you care to join me? It's such a beautiful day."

His stare dismissed the irrelevance of weather. "Don't you have one of the lower school teams to coach? I thought Mr. Hinkley was going to assign you one."

"He was, sir. But when he found I didn't know the rules, he gave it up as a bad job."

"Then I suggest you come with me and learn them," he said sternly. "Football is more than a game, you know. It's a combination of training body and character. If you want to understand the boys here, you must understand it. Let us see what the second squad is up to."

For forty miserable minutes I stood dumbly by the empty bleachers and watched the play as Dr. Prescott explained it. At first he was gruff and short, but as the forward passes of one fifth former, evidently a rising star, began to arouse his enthusiasm, he became more friendly, and after a particularly long one, successfully completed, he actually hit me on the shoulder. "By Jove, that Craddock can throw like an angel! Do you begin to see what I mean, Aspinwall?"

When he left me at last, he suggested that I should remain and continue to study the play. I thanked him and murmured that I hoped Mrs. Prescott was better. He shook his head, as if it were not my place to ask. "She is doing as well as can be expected," he said gloomily. "I shall see that Mr. Hinkley gives you a football manual. Good day, Aspinwall."

And this is the man with whom I had meant to discuss my hopes for the ministry! This is the spokesman for the Church of Christ at Justin. Who, spotting my one poor rag of consolation, my free hour in the afternoon, strips it off that my whole pelt may be exposed to the pricks of his institution.

October 10. A new low. In my third form English class this morning the five boys in the back bench managed with their feet to move it completely around while I was writing the test questions on the blackboard so that they had their backs to me when I turned. I gave each a black mark, but the three in the middle protested so vigorously that only the two on the ends had perpetrated the revolution of the bench that I cravenly gave in and suspended all five marks. I noticed that the faces of the rest of the class were now frankly contemptuous. Dear

God, if I become a pitiable creature, spare me at least from the sin of self-pity. I have a terrible leaning to it.

October 12. I found a dead frog in my bed last night, and the touch of it against my bare foot scared me so that I was sick to my stomach. I wonder if such a trick has ever before been played on a master at Justin. But obviously I'll never know, as I shall never dare admit that it happened. Dear God, will it ever be over?

October 14. Mr. Ives is a small man, with hands and feet that are proportionately even smaller, and he wears shoes without laces or buckles that look like fairies' slippers. He has yellowish-white hair which descends over his high, egglike forehead in a soft, neat triangle and yellow, stary eyes which, with his small hooked nose, might give him the appearance of a sparrow hawk, did not his habit of wearing thick fuzzy suits and of moving his head forward and backward as he walks suggest a less distinguished bird.

In character as well as appearance he seems the opposite of Dr. Prescott, which perhaps a good executive officer should be; his glory is in detail, and he makes no secret of it. To the headmaster is left the field of intangibles: God, a boy's soul and school spirit; Ives reigns over the minutiae of the curriculum and infractions of discipline. The boys credit him with second sight in such matters; he seems to know by instinct who is smoking in the cellar and who has gone canoeing on the Lawrence without leave. Yet for all his deviousness, for all his biting sarcasms, for all his lilting reprimands and snapping fingers, this epicene martinet is extremely popular, and to be asked to play bridge in his study on a Saturday night is deemed the highest social honor that a sixth former can attain.

But for the younger boys and, alas, for the younger masters he is Mephistopheles, and he has been eying me as a coyote might eye a wounded cow. I am sure that nothing has happened that has not been brought instantly to his notice, and I imagine that he must be debating whether to let me go now, with all the trouble of a midterm replacement, or to patch me up so that I'll last the school year. He summoned me this morning to his office in the Schoolhouse and told me that there had been complaints about noises in my dormitory after lights.

"Surely, Mr. Aspinwall, you have not left the boys unsupervised?"

"Oh, no, sir. I'm always there."

"Have you been having any trouble with your hearing?"

"No, sir. I shall try to do better."

"Do so, Mr. Aspinwall." Here he snapped his fingers. As he always spoke in the same mocking tone he must have adopted this mannerism to put his hearer on notice when he was serious. "Do so, I beg of you. You will find that you have my full backing and that of Dr. Prescott in any disciplinary measures that you seek to impose. The law of a boys' school is the law of the jungle. When you're strong, we're behind you, but if you're weak, we throw you to the boys."

As if he had to tell me. As if I didn't know that the whole lot of them, boys and masters, were part of the same pack! But perhaps now reading the despair in my eyes and not wishing to overwhelm me, he added: "What about your prefects? Where have they been?"

"I haven't wanted to interrupt their studies at night. I thought I should be able to handle the dormitory myself."

"Sometimes it's hard to get started," he said more kindly, looking at me as he appeared to debate something. "I shall see that you have one prefect on duty every night for the next two weeks."

And as I am making this entry at my desk tonight, Bobbie Seymour, one of the football team, is seated on the sofa opposite, reading a movie magazine which is supposed to be banned from the school grounds. But never mind. In the ominous black of the dormitory beyond the open door an absolute silence reigns. I may have been humiliated by the calling in of extra police, but it is better to be humiliated than lynched. I shall now be able to read in peace another delightful chapter of *Clarissa*. Escape? Who calls it escape? It's salvation!

October 17. I have at last met Mrs. Prescott. Every Sunday after lunch the faculty and their wives foregather for coffee in the headmaster's study, a large, square, book-lined room added like a box to the back of the Prescotts' house. Today, Mrs. Prescott's nurse wheeled her in in her chair and stationed her in a corner, and we all stood about, in a respectful half-circle, while Dr. Prescott, in what must have been for him the unaccustomed role of court chamberlain, brought people up, one by one, for a half minute's conversation.

The poor woman is terribly emaciated and gaunt; her face seems to have been absorbed into her great aquiline nose so that with her dyed thin hair and half-closed eyes she suggests a turkey buzzard sleeping on a dead limb. Yet there is still something rather magnificent about her, something that suggests the grim character and determined intellectualism of an earlier New England. Or is it just that I happen to know she is a great-niece of Emerson?

I was surprised when the headmaster took me by the elbow to propel me to his wife's corner, having assumed that her brief visiting time would be taken up by my seniors, but he explained that she always wanted to meet the new masters. Harry Ruggles, of the history department, one of those wiry fellows with thick black curly hair who are always smiling, was talking to her as we came up, but he did not have the tact to rise, so I was left standing awkwardly between the wheelchair and the sofa arm on which Ruggles was familiarly perched. He was being tedious on the subject of what he called "labor novels," and I was glad to see that Mrs. Prescott was obviously bored.

"There's a great deal of solid fiction being written today," he was telling her, "by men who understand that the fundamental structure of our society changed with the New Deal. You may not like it, Mrs. Prescott, but I don't see how you can deny it."

"Why do you assume I don't like it?" she asked in a tone that would have warned anybody but Ruggles.

"Well, I thought, ma'am, a lady of your background and generation would be instinctively opposed to F.D.R."

"I'm not a background or a generation, thank you very much. I happen to be a human being, and I was a democrat before you were born, young man."

"Well, fine! Then you will sympathize with my idea of having the boys read some of our more important labor novels. It ought to be fun to see their self-satisfied bubbles pricked."

Mrs. Prescott glanced at me here, and I had a distinct feeling that she had somehow divined my sympathy. "Labor novels?" she demanded. "What are labor novels? I know only good novels and bad novels."

"What do you consider a good novel?"

"*The Egoist.*"

"Meredith?" Ruggles' smile just acknowledged him. "He was all very well for his day, I suppose. People had time for him then."

"I have time for him now," Mrs. Prescott insisted. "Don't you, Mr. Aspinwall?"

I do not know if it was the surprise that I felt on her remembering my name or the unexpected tremor of real feeling that I may have imagined in the old woman's flat tone that made me think I might at last have found an ally at Justin Martyr. All I know is that in that minute I fell in love with Mrs. Prescott, and that my love made me bold. "I will always have time for Meredith," I responded warmly. "I will always have time for good novels. And I agree that there are only good ones and bad ones. In art the subject can make no difference."

"There speaks the English department," Ruggles said sneeringly. "I suppose Aspinwall would rate Jane Austen with Tolstoy."

"Higher!"

Dr. Prescott came up now to take us away, but his wife reached out to put her hand on my wrist. "Leave me Mr. Aspinwall, Frank. He and I have something to say to each other." When Ruggles had departed with the headmaster, she shrugged. "What an ass that fellow is. Can you imagine the pricking of *his* self-satisfied bubble? It would be like the explosion of the *Hindenburg*. Why does teaching always seem to attract the intellectually flabby?"

"Perhaps because we want to seem infallible and think that little boys may find us so. How wrong we are."

Mrs. Prescott grunted. "How wrong indeed. The only people Mr. Ruggles could hope to fool would be his contemporaries. But don't worry. He won't last. I can tell by the way Frank holds his elbow that he's seen through him."

I had heard that Mrs. Prescott had become embarrassingly candid with old age, but this still struck me as excessive. After all, I was the most junior of the faculty and she was the headmaster's wife. "I fear he held mine the same way," I ventured.

"No, there was a difference. I can always tell." Her nurse was approaching; it was time to go. "Tell me, Mr. Aspinwall, would you come to see me some afternoon? I'm at my best in the afternoons, though I'm afraid my best isn't much these days. But perhaps we could talk. Or are you a brute, to prefer football to philosophy?"

"Oh, no, I should love to come!"

"Maybe tomorrow then. Any time after three. Only don't tell my husband. He would undoubtedly set you to some violent form of exercise."

At this she was wheeled away, head down, staring at her knees, acknowledging none of the bows or greetings from the faculty on either side. I wonder, when I present myself to-morrow, if she will even remember her invitation. Surely the thread that holds her strong spirit to this world is of gossamer, and I could well sympathize if she identified all other humans with her own body which, decaying, has ceased to be her friend.

October 21. I have had two visits with Mrs. Prescott this week, one on Monday and the second today, each of about forty min-utes in length. The second went better than the first because I at last divined what it is she wants of me. She wants to be read to, and by someone whom she doesn't regard as a total simple-ton. On my first visit I tried to talk of some of my passions: Balzac, Daudet, George Eliot, Virginia Woolf, but I soon found out that talking tired her. Besides, whereas my education — if it can be called that — is almost entirely in poetry and fiction, hers is vastly broader, encompassing philosophy and history and the visual arts. George Eliot leads her immediately to John Stuart Mill and Virginia Woolf to Bertrand Russell. She smiled tolerantly, her eyes half closed, as I chattered on, interrupting me with an occasional grunt or brief comment, but when I men-tioned Henry James she stopped me.

"You know he dictated the later novels," she said. "People think that odd for so accomplished a stylist, but of course it's not odd at all. He always wanted to be read aloud, and how could he know how it would sound unless he thought aloud?" She paused here and seemed to be studying me. "Of course, now that my eyes are so bad it's the only way I can know James."

"Do you have him on records?" There was an old gramo-phone in the corner of the living room, but it had an air of not having been played in years.

"There are records, of course, for the blind," she muttered, "but very little of what I want. Those unfortunates seem to be an uncultivated lot."

"I'd be only too happy to come in and read to you, but I fear I'm not very good at it. The boys get quite restive in the reading period before their bedtime."

"I'm not the boys, Mr. Aspinwall," she said with the ghost of a smile. "I should be grateful. But don't you have athletic duties?"

I thought of the headmaster's injunction and shuddered. "Not really."

It was touching how eagerly she caught me up. "Perhaps we could start next time you come. Do you like *The Ambassadors?*"

"It's my favorite!"

And indeed we did. Today I read for three quarters of an hour before the nurse came in. I thought I did very well, but I had read over the chapter in advance and was prepared. Mrs. Prescott seemed to sleep during part of it, but even that may be good in her present state of health. At least I can hope that I am finally doing something for *somebody* at Justin Martyr.

October 30. It is curious how much my readings to this silent, still old woman mean to me. She offers a contrast to the noisy, active school that is like a little chapel by a thronged highway. Some tiny fragment of her dauntlessness may have shaken off upon my frail shoulders for I actually believe that I am more at ease with my dormitory now and in my classes. Not much, surely, but a little. It helps to know that there is one other soul in this dark male world that cares about beautiful things.

My admiration extends to her surroundings. The big, square parlor in which poor Mrs. Prescott now spends all of her long days is to me everything that a room should be, probably because it *is* everything. By that I mean there seems to be nothing either of the Prescotts or of Justin Martyr missing from it. The school is represented by the number of chairs and small round tables, some of simple porch wicker, used for games on "parlor" night, by the big mahogany chest in the corner that will never quite close, crammed as it is with sets of parchesi, halmar and checkers, by the snapshots everywhere of beloved graduates, by the citations of those gloriously dead in war. The Prescotts are represented by an oval portrait of the three dark-eyed daughters as rather formidable children, inappropriately clad in white silk with big blue ribbons in their hair, by a wonderful sketch of Emerson in profile, by a watercolor of Dr. Prescott's father as an officer of the Union Army, and by Mrs. Prescott's books, in German, French and English, in old bindings, in modern, and in paperbacks, filling the cabinets, piled on tables, even stacked on the floor. True, the room is cluttered and the furniture is of every period, yet over the whole there reigns a certain harmony, a curious dignity, an even more curious simplicity.

One begins to note fine things among the junk; a superb little Boudin under a framed cartoon from *The New Yorker* with a joke about the school, a first edition of Johnson's diction- ary looming over the bound volumes of *Punch*, a gleaming Sheraton breakfront full of mediocre China-trade porcelain. But the real reason for my net impression that the room is so innately civilized is in Mrs. Prescott herself. It is not only the inner temple of the school; it is at the same time her refuge from the school. She knows where to lay her fingers at once on even the smallest item, nor is there any object without its func- tion of present utility or fond association. What seems at first a pot-pourri is in fact the perfectly catalogued and constantly functioning collection of her life.

November 1. Mrs. Prescott surprised me today by asking me to skip to the great chapter in Gloriani's studio where Strether warns Little Bilham not to waste his life as he has done. She told me, in the most matter-of-fact of tones, that in her physical condition she had to pick the high spots of a long book. But, of course, I was not prepared, and James is difficult to read at sight. I would rush into the sentences only to find myself caught up by the undertow of an unexpected construction and cast back, breathless, on the sands of my unfamiliarity. On one of these occasions, observing Mrs. Prescott's closed eyes and motionless head, I decided it would be safe to push on without rereading the passage.

"You'd better try that sentence again," she interrupted me, without opening her eyes. "I think you'll find the second 'he' refers to Chad and not Strether."

Not a nuance escapes her. She is one of those rare people who can read James with the whole magnificent forest constantly in mind and yet not miss a single tree. Her husband, apparently, does not share her admiration for the master. One of the take-offs that he sometimes performs on "parlor night" is called "Mr. James Takes the Shuttle at Grand Central." But then one cannot imagine Dr. Prescott troubling his head over the refinements of moral choice open to James or Strether. Obviously, had *he* been sent to Paris to collect the erring Chad, he would have had the young man back in Woollett by the end of the first chapter!

November 5. The dissension between Dr. Prescott and his wife in their estimates of Henry James resulted in a scene this afternoon that I found embarrassing. Towards the end of my hour with Mrs. Prescott the headmaster made an unexpected appearance. Immediately I closed the book. He had never come in at other readings, and I could not but speculate uncomfortably that this visit was more to check up on me than on his wife. Was it not implicit in the whole Justin tradition that a young master should find more vigorous employment on a glorious fall afternoon than sitting in a close room with an old woman reading *The Ambassadors?* Indeed, when I saw the glance with which he took me in, I assumed that a final judgment of my poor case had already been made.

"Let me not interrupt the reading," he rumbled. "Let me slip quietly into a seat over here and enjoy it."

"No, no, nobody could read James in front of you, Frank," Mrs. Prescott said testily. "You'll just sit there and make faces. Go away and leave us be."

"There's a friendly greeting," he replied imperturbably, settling himself on a small straight armless chair. The very bareness of the seat belied the sincerity of his intention to remain. "I promise I shall make no faces. Proceed, Aspinwall. Which of the novels are you reading?" I murmured the title. "Ah, yes, the fine flower of the later style. It has all that is gorgeous in the master, all that is sublime. And all that is ridiculous."

"What do you mean, ridiculous?" Mrs. Prescott demanded at once. "What is ridiculous about *The Ambassadors?*"

"Simply that it has nothing whatever to do with life on this poor planet of ours."

"It has a great deal to do with *my* life."

"Do you see yourself, my dear, as a Lambert Strether?"

"Certainly I do!" his wife exclaimed with sudden violence. "Strether didn't know until he saw Paris that he'd wasted his life. Well, it took more than Paris to teach me that. It took this abominable wheelchair!"

The moment that followed this outburst was almost unbearable. I clenched my fists and stared at the faded old Persian rug and prayed idiotically that it would sweep me up in the air and carry me far away from all the terrible things in Justin Martyr. In that moment I think I learned the real tragedy of living too long. It is not losing one's health or one's memory or even one's mind; it is losing one's dignity. For I am absolutely sure that Mrs. Prescott's outburst was uncharacteristic. The woman who could throw that reproach in her husband's face was a different woman from the proud creature that she had so obviously been all her life.

If I dared not look at her husband's face to see the pain that I had no doubt he was concealing, I could not avoid his voice. He was talking now, in a quiet tone, filling in a pause that had to be filled in, addressing me in the knowledge that after what his wife had just said, any further reading aloud was out of the question.

"My wife, Aspinwall, takes Mr. James too seriously. That is not to say that one should never take him seriously. But I'm a great believer in safety valves, particularly where art is concerned, and one cannot read James properly without bearing in mind that for every three parts genius he is one part ass."

"Oh, Frank! What utter rot you're talking."

"Let Aspinwall be the judge between us, my dear. Take this very novel you're reading. Strether, an elderly, provincial widower, is dazzled out of his senses by the sudden apparition of Paris. Certainly his creator knows how to evoke the city. Oh, I own that! Renoir himself could not have conveyed a more vivid sense of the greens and greys of the boulevards or of the stately stillness of Louis XV interiors. Strether imbibes Paris through every pore. He is revived and rejuvenated. Yet what spoils it all for him? The simple fact that Chad Newsome, the young blade whom he has come to bring home, turns out to have a French mistress. Which everyone under the sun, including the reader, knew from the beginning and which was indeed the very reason for Strether's mission! What in the name of Gallia did he *expect* the young man to be up to? Yet he finds his vision of Paris incompatible with this simplest of biological facts, and all is wrecked for him. Tell me, Aspinwall, is poor old Strether, like poor old James, not a bit of a dunce?"

"But it is *not* all wrecked for him!" Mrs. Prescott exclaimed passionately. "Chad and Strether may both be going back to Woollett, but Strether is going back with his vision, and his vision will sustain him."

"His vision of what?"

"His vision of Paris. Of life!"

"But *is* it life? Isn't it rather, a vision of the bits and pieces of Paris that he didn't find too sordid? Would you recognize any part of it as the Paris of *L'Assomoir?*"

"It's a vision of beauty. And James transmits it. That is art. And therefore it must be life."

"Or dope!"

"What a Philistine you really are, Frank. Scratch a headmaster, and you'll find one every time. And when I think that you complain about the others!"

At this point it was evident that Mrs. Prescott was becoming too excited, and with the smallest motion of his head her husband indicated that it was time for me to go. I rose and murmured my farewell, but he followed me out and closed the door behind us.

"Aspinwall," he said, taking my elbow as he guided me to the front door, "you are very kind to devote so many afternoons to my wife."

"Oh, it's my pleasure, sir. Truly, I love it."

"It can't be very gay for a young man," he pursued, "and I want you to know that I am not ungrateful. Allow me to see that you are compensated with extra time off."

"Oh, sir, that won't be necessary," I exclaimed, shocked. "Mrs. Prescott is the most wonderful woman I've ever known!"

The grip tightened on my elbow. "Bless you, my boy. Bless you for seeing that."

Outside I almost ran back to the main door of Lawrence House, so full of emotion that it was all I could do to keep from skipping. What a man was this! A man who could read the later James and love his wife so tenderly, a man who could appreciate what a silly mite like myself, the reverse of all he expected in a master, could offer her and not hesitate to ask that mite to continue his offering. This was magnanimity on a scale for the gods. Looking up at the formidable dark tower of his chapel I laughed aloud in jubilation at the thought that there *might* at last be a place for me in Dr. Prescott's Justin.

2

NOVEMBER 6, 1939. I was reading aloud to my dormitory tonight when I received an unexpected visit. This reading period,
incidentally, has not been any more of a success than my other
activities. I read too fast and too low, and I tend to become so
absorbed in the matter that I hardly notice that I have lost my
audience. It is different with Mrs. Prescott where the reading
is so much more a shared experience. The boys whisper and
giggle and even play games. I know that I should reprimand
them, but I cannot help feeling that it is supposed to be their
time off and that they should be allowed to do as they choose.
Tonight, even in my abstraction, I became gradually aware of a
deepening silence about me, the silence of songbirds in the sudden shadow of a hawk, and looking up, I saw the headmaster
himself standing in the doorway.

"Go on, please, Mr. Aspinwall," he directed me with a
friendly wave of his arm as he came slowly forward to take the
nearest seat, from which a boy now jumped. "You must think
I have nothing better to do than interrupt your readings. I
shall listen a bit, if I may. What is it tonight? Not *The Ambassadors* again?" He smiled as he glanced about the room.
"I suppose not for this crowd."

"Oh, no, sir. *The Moonstone.*"

"And a corking good yarn." His approving nod was decisive.
"Let us get on with it."

I read for several minutes in a silence which I found as disturbing as it was unusual. Then the rich level voice interrupted me again. "Excuse me please, Mr. Aspinwall, but what do I see there? Over there by the fireplace? Is that a checkerboard? Good gracious me, I believe it is. Were you two boys actually *playing* while Mr. Aspinwall was reading?" I was aware in the silence of two small moons of dismay over the half-concealed board. "Have you lost your tongues, sirs? *Were* you?"

"Yes, sir."

"Then go to bed. Go to bed right away. And mind you make no noise undressing to disturb the reading. Pray proceed, Mr. Aspinwall."

I kept my eyes fixed on the print to avoid stammering, glancing up only once to see if the minute hand of my clock would *ever* reach nine.

"Carstairs!" the dreaded voice boomed out again. I had learned that one could never tell when Dr. Prescott would address a boy by his name or simply as "boy." It apparently had nothing to do with his memory. "Are you chewing *gum?*"

"Well, sir, I — er —"

" 'Er?' " demanded the headmaster. "What does 'er' mean? Don't say 'er.' Keep your mouth closed until you have the words ready that you want to use. Now I repeat. Are you chewing gum?"

"Yes, sir. But I started before you came in."

"What difference does that make? Do you think the rules operate only when I am present? You must know it is not allowed to chew gum inside any building on the campus. Spit it out. Yes, now. Spit it out in your hand, boy." But when poor Carstairs complied with his order, it seemed only to make Dr. Prescott angrier. "Ugh! What a disgusting sight. Go to bed, boy, right away. We don't want to see you any more tonight. All right, Mr. Aspinwall. We may proceed again."

In a trembling tone I continued the now shattered reading session, knowing that I was but marking time before the next outburst. In two more minutes it came.

"I'm afraid you must excuse me once more, Mr. Aspinwall. I can hardly credit my eyes, but it seems to me that the two boys crouching on the other side of your desk have no ties on. Can it be? Stand up you two, Morgan and the boy next to Morgan. Gracious me, these old eyes were right again. But I fear this time being sent to bed will not be enough. No, I fear I shall have to give you each a black mark. See that the black marks are recorded, Mr. Aspinwall."

"I'm sorry, Dr. Prescott, I'm afraid it's my fault. I allowed them to remove their ties." I hadn't at all, but I had known they were doing it, and I could not have them punished for my own laxness in enforcing the rules.

"Have you indeed, sir?" the headmaster queried, with soaring eyebrows. "How very singular. Then I shall, of course, rescind the black marks, but let it be clearly understood by all present that ties are *not* to be removed nor shoes unlaced until it is time to retire. When a gentleman undresses, a gentleman goes to bed. And as I do not wish to continue to gaze at Morgan's bare neck or at the bare neck of Morgan's friend, I suggest that the whole dormitory go to bed right now, even though it is still ten minutes before the hour."

He remained in my study while the boys prepared for bed and then accompanied me on my round of the cubicles as I pulled each curtain and bade good night to each occupant. His mood seemed to have softened for he paused to banter Carstairs about the chewing gum. After lights, however, he became grave again, and in my study he motioned me to close the door to the dormitory as he took a seat by the fireplace and lit his pipe.

"I want to give you a little lecture about discipline, Brian," he began, using my Christian name for the first time. "You are obviously having trouble with it, and the reason is twofold. In the first place you think it's some kind of trick with which you do not happen to be endowed. That is nonsense. If you were a missionary facing a crowd of cannibals or a lone sheriff facing a lynching mob, you would need what the army calls 'command presence.' But a schoolmaster does not need that. Oh, it's a useful thing to have, certainly, but it's not *necessary*. You have the power of the black mark, and that is all you basically need. When the boys begin to get the idea that the least impertinence to Mr. Aspinwall means missing the Saturday afternoon game or the Saturday night movie, they will give up their impertinence. It's as simple as that."

I realized that he was being kind, which gave me the courage to appeal to him. "But I hate being unjust, sir, and sometimes it's difficult to know who's the culprit. If a boy, for example, makes an insulting noise when my back is turned in class, what am I to do?"

"You can give six black marks to the boy you first suspect. If you are wrong, this will often have the effect of making the true culprit confess. Or you can give the whole class a black mark apiece. This will put the innocent against the guilty, and you can be sure the former will make life so miserable for the latter that the episode will not be repeated. The big thing is not to worry too much about guilt or innocence. A class where an impudent noise is made is apt to be an impudent class. Your dormitory is now a bad dormitory. If you gave every boy in it six black marks on the spot, I wager the great majority of them would be deserved."

"You wouldn't have me do that, sir?"

"No. But I would have you establish your authority. A week after that is done, you'll have a good dormitory. Which brings me to the second reason for your trouble. You want to be popular."

"Oh, surely not, sir!"

"Well, then, you're afraid to be unpopular which comes to the same thing. I've watched you, Brian. I have my spies. Now what I want you to do is this. I want you to give out twelve black marks before the end of next week. Don't worry. There will be plenty of occasions if you keep your eyes open. I shall consult the Black Ledger a week from Saturday at noon and see what you have entered. Is that fair?"

He stood up now, his pipe clenched between his teeth, and I stood up after him, trembling in the knees. "I'll try, sir."

"Good boy." He reached out to pat my shoulder. "You will be unpopular, but you will be respected. And in time you will build a more solid kind of popularity on respect. Take my word for it. I'm an old hand at this game, and I know what I'm doing." Here he suddenly raised his voice to a roar. "I know, for example, there's a boy listening on the other side of that door." In the silence that followed we both could make out the patter of rapidly retreating feet. "There you are, Brian," he said grimly. "The whole dormitory will know of our conversation in the morning. But that's fine. Let them know what you're going to do and then *do* it. Good night, my boy." And he left me to the ominous silence of that dark, awake dormitory and to the blessed anodyne of this journal.

November 14. Well, I made up my twelve black marks. It almost killed me, but I did it. I have been so nervous that I couldn't write a word in this journal until it was done. I gave two to a boy whose voice I thought I recognized after lights. He protested bitterly that it had not been he, and I wavered, but than I remembered Dr. Prescott's warning and told him firmly that he would have to accept my verdict and that I was sorry if it was a mistaken one. He accepted this so philosophically that I realized he must be guilty.

I next gave a black mark apiece to two boys whom I caught fighting in the shower. This was clearly fair, and I began to gain confidence. Four out of twelve. But already the dormitory was becoming orderly, and the week was going by. I then gave one each to two boys who took their ties off during my reading period. Unfortunately this touched off a real test of my authority, as the whole dormitory burst into protest, clamoring that the offense called only for a demerit. Again I wavered, sick at heart, fearing an actual riot, and again I remembered the headmaster's reminder that my power was absolute. I picked up a lead paperweight and banged it down on my desk with all my might. There was instant silence.

"Spruance!" I cried at the ringleader. "You started all this, and I'm giving you six black marks. If I hear a single word more from you, I shall send you to Dr. Prescott. And the entire dormitory is going to bed. *Now*."

It was a terrible moment, and I knew that my career in Justin hung in the balance. When the dormitory rose at last and sullenly filed past me to their cubicles, I had to strain every muscle not to let the surging tide of relief flood into my silly face. I might be a monster, but I had won! And dear God, let my journal be witness that I am humbly grateful for all your help in my foolish crises and for sending to my aid the strong arm of Dr. Prescott. Let me not be proud at petty victories, and let me remember that if I *should* ever become respected by the boys, it will be my task to be merciful and gentle and kind. I am here, after all, to serve *them*.

November 16. Dr. Prescott has played a very mean trick on me. He has doubled all my black marks except Spruance's, telling each boy that I am of such a notorious leniency that he is exercising a headmaster's prerogative of bringing my punishments in line with those more generally meted out. My dormitory is sullen, silent and obedient. I am really unpopular now, which I hate, but I have to confess that it is not a disagreeable sensation to give an order and know that it will be carried out. It is like driving a new car after struggling with a stalling jalopy. Am I being corrupted by power? Please, God, forgive and help me if this is so. At least Dr. Prescott has not given me a new stint of black marks to hand out. I do not think I could have borne it if he had.

November 18. Poor Mrs. Prescott is beginning to go downhill rapidly now, and there are signs that her mind is failing. Twice last Monday it was evident that she thought I was reading William and not Henry James, and yesterday afternoon she seemed to have forgotten all about our project and only wanted to talk. She dwells in the past, as I believe is natural in such cases, except that in hers there seems to be a strong drive to reduce isolated incidents to some kind of pattern. It is difficult to make out, but I believe she is trying to give me an oral memoir of memorable events in her life. It is as if, at the end of a long existence of intelligently receiving impressions, by eye and ear and even touch, she wants at last to give something back, to leave some little record of what Harriet Prescott has observed.

It is pathetic, even agonizing, to see this remarkable woman thrash about in her memories for some bit of tangible evidence that she has been, after all, remarkable. And now it is too late. She told me of her visit to Proust's cork-lined chamber with an old bachelor friend of Dr. Prescott's and of a talk she had had with Mrs. Jack Gardner at the time of her purchase of the great Titian "Europa." But as our vivid memories of sights abroad, of Chartres or the Parthenon, merge in time with the most banal of postcards, so have Mrs. Prescott's impressions become more ordinary than she suspects. I wanted to tell her to stop, to talk only about herself; I wanted to convince her that her life itself had been a work of art and that even the memory of her in my puny mind would be a greater memorial than the observation that Proust was a snob or Mrs. Gardner a sensationalist. But what can I do? She is way past my helping.

November 21. There is certainly no question that the head-master's approbation has made a great change in my campus status. In a word, I am become respectable. So strong is the power of Dr. Prescott's personality in this little world of his creation that his special favors are accepted by all without overt resentment. Mr. Ives himself now asks me to coffee gatherings in his bachelor's wing of Lowell House. I sometimes wonder what is behind those yellow-streaked eyes, but he is certainly pleasant. Best of all, my dormitory seems to have accepted me. When I offered to give up reading in the evening and let them play games instead, the boys actually voted to have me finish *The Moonstone*. Henry James and Wilkie Collins have been my sponsors in Justin! Even the once formidable red and grey stones of the architecture have softened in color, and the dark craggy chapel tower seems occasionally to wink at me. I see what up until now has escaped me: that the common denominator of the heterogeneous faculty is an extraordinary devotion to the headmaster. I am actually happy, however precariously. Have I sold out, and if so, to what? Help me, dear God, not to be puffed up.

November 24. Mrs. Prescott took such a bad turn on Monday that the daughters were summoned, but she has improved again, and they have gone. I saw them all at lunch with Dr. Prescott at the head table and was struck by their resemblance to him. They look much alike, with pale skins and squarish faces and dark hair, and they are all very animated. In fact, there was rather more laughter at the head table than seemed to me quite appropriate under the circumstances. But then in these days the smallest display of grief is considered morbid. I must try to avoid the sin of judging others. Perhaps I wish to denigrate the filial feeling of Mrs. Prescott's daughters so that I may pose to myself as her only true friend. Count on the devil to work overtime!

November 25. I saw Mrs. Prescott this afternoon but only for a minute. She seemed very weak but clearer than before, and she told me that nothing rallied her "old carcass" like a gathering of the clan.

December 1. Mr. Ives fell in with me today, walking after breakfast from Lawrence House to morning chapel. One never feels that anything with him is a coincidence. I am sure that every minute of his day, every colloquy, every walk, every meal is somehow put to the service of Justin. He seems to have no interest in anything beyond the campus and, within the boundaries of the latter, only in matters corporeal. When I confided in him that I had a strong but still unmatured drive towards the ministry, he looked faintly surprised as if I, a nice young man of irreproachable manners, had suddenly told an off-color story. Yet in his narrow field he can be wonderfully illuminating.

"I hear that you have become the official reader to the headmistress," he began this morning in his lilting, half-mocking tone. Now that I know him better, I realize that this tone has merely become a habit and does not reflect, as I had first assumed, an attitude of sustained contemptuousness. "In the court of France it was a coveted position."

"It was a career open to humble gentlewomen," I retorted mildly. "I trust I do not seem presumptuous in aspiring to it."

Mr. Ives glanced sidewise at me as he had a way of doing before changing his emphasis. "My dear fellow, we're all very happy indeed that you're able to do anything to amuse poor Mrs. Prescott. We others have tried and failed."

"But I do nothing!" I exclaimed, embarrassed by his novel note of gravity.

"In a sense, of course, there is nothing one can do," he agreed. "But that makes the tiniest thing loom large. Harriet Prescott is dying, and she resents the process. When you reach my age, you'll know how common it is to resent death. At the same time she has come to resent most of her old friends. We can only love her in silence. But to you, a newcomer, has fallen the privilege of amusing her. Some of us may be jealous, but I assure you that all of us are grateful."

"I'm glad that you call it a privilege, for that is certainly the way I look upon it. *If* it is true that I have amused her, which I very much doubt."

"Oh, she likes you. You have not yet become identified with the school. It is natural that as the end draws near, she should have a jaundiced eye for the institution which has been her greatest rival and which will soon have her husband all to itself. You must have noticed how impatient she is with Dr. Prescott."

"I have indeed. And I've found it very painful."

"You needn't. He understands. Few husbands, Brian, can have been loved as that man has been. And yet she must have always known, as *I* have always known, that for every gram of love that comes back from Francis Prescott, a pound goes to the school. That is the way things are." He looked at me now with his hard, birdlike stare, and I had my first sense of how much emotion it might curtain. "That's the way things always are with great men. But sometimes, for aging wives and senior masters, it's a bit hard."

I made no answer, for we had reached the steps of the chapel doors, and I could hear the tumbling notes of the organ in a Bach fugue.

December 5. My heart is low tonight for I fear I have seen the last of my dear new friend. Please, God, make her parting swift and painless. She will indeed be one of thy ministering angels. I received word at three o'clock that she wanted to see me, and I went for the first time to her bedroom where I found her very feeble and gaunt, but still inclined to talk. The nurse told me I must stay only ten minutes, but when my time was up and the warning white figure appeared in the doorway, Mrs. Prescott sent her away, saying sharply: "I have all eternity in which to rest, Miss Mitchell. Leave us be."

I was uncomfortable about this, but it seemed to me that it would probably be worse for her to be frustrated than tired. She was lying back on the pillow with her eyes closed and talking more to herself than to me. Her thoughts seemed to dwell no longer with famous personalities of the past but with her own youth. I made as few comments as possible, just enough to steer her drifting craft down that quiet stream.

"Oh, that was before I was married," she murmured. "That was when I was only twenty and spending the winter in Paris. We had a tiny apartment in an old *hôtel* on the Rue Monsieur, I and my sister and a maiden aunt. I shall never forget the uproar in the family when it was discovered that we had a sofa in the living room."

"A sofa? What was wrong with a sofa?"

"Why, can't you see what unimaginable intimacies it suggested?" Her eyes were still closed, but the hint of a smile passed over her thin white lips. "There had to be only stiff little chairs for our nonexistent callers. And there were rules about these, too. Oh, yes, those were still the days of *maintien*. One could never, for example, offer a guest a chair in which one had been sitting."

"You mean he always had to have a fresh one?"

"If there was one. Of course! Can you think of anything more horrid than a warm seat? *Voilà qui serait dégoutant!*" She was silent after this so long that I thought she might be unconscious. When she spoke again her voice had a trace of thickness. "Ah, those innocent, happy days. How I rebelled and loved rebelling. My daughters have suffered terribly from frustration because they couldn't shock me. How mean of me it was, as I look back. I wonder if it hasn't been the thing that has hurt them most in life, that desperate, unsatisfied need for a convention to hit at." Here she seemed to be trying to catch her breath. "The mealy nothingness of a civilization that has no hates or loves!"

"But should a parent pretend to be stuffy?" I protested. "Should a mother assume a prejudice if she has it not?"

"Perhaps. Perhaps indeed she should." Again she was silent for at least a minute, and when she talked her voice was very low, and her thoughts seemed to linger in the French past already evoked. "It's all so — so hopeless to convey. Like Paris then. Not a Renoir, no. Not a Pissarro." The pauses between her phrases increased. "No, it wasn't that. I see it more brightly. More lighted. It's funny, isn't it? More like a bad academy picture. A Meissonier. A Gérôme. Rose-cheeked girls with dogs. The Bois. A carriage. And all those market scenes." She smiled again. "How funny if the impressionists were wrong. How — how — funny. And Mother would never let me — Mother would never —" Here I could no longer make out her words, and I rose in alarm to get the nurse whom I found just outside the door.

"Go now," Miss Mitchell whispered angrily. "Please go."

But I was beyond Miss Mitchell's anger now. I went to the bed and leaned down to kiss my poor dear friend's bony withered hand.

"Crébillon," she murmured, very distinctly, and I left the room. I had thought she was wandering, and only just now, as I wrote the word, did I remember that he was the author of *Le Sopha.*

December 6. Mr. Ives told me this morning as we were going into breakfast that Mrs. Prescott had died just before midnight. I had to go back to my study because I could not have the boys at my table see my tears. But after a few minutes I was under control, and I came down. Would I have wanted her to live longer? No. Dear God, she is one of thy angels now, and I have no doubt one of the most beautiful. A bell in the chapel tolled a deep note every minute for an hour this morning from eight to nine. In a curious way the notes seemed to accumulate and spread, as in a basin slowly filled by drops, until a rich deep grief overflowed and saturated the campus. It was quite wonderful to me that a sense of death should sit so easily and nobly on a school dedicated to youth. It was as she would have wished it.

December 8. I have seen Dr. Prescott for the first time since her death. I was summoned to his study where I found him at his desk in an attitude of deep contemplation. He did not even look up at me as he asked in a low voice: "It occurs to me, Aspinwall, that you must have been the last person to hear my wife speak. Would you be good enough to tell me what were her last words?"

There was an odd chill in his tone, almost as if he were jealous of this final intimacy. It was noticeable that he did not call me "Brian" as he had before. I had heard something from Mr. Ives of the "hard" period of his life, before the benignity of his old age, and I wondered if his present demeanor might not be a vestige of it. But I was too full of sympathy and love to bear the least resentment. "Crébillon," I murmured. "Crébillon was the last word I heard her utter."

"*What?*"

Stupidly, I repeated the name.

"Surely, you don't mean the French eighteenth century author of salacious novels?"

Haltingly, wretchedly embarrassed, I explained the context while he stared at me with total gravity. When I had finished he was silent.

"How peculiarly unfitting," he said at length in the same solemn tone, "that the last recorded utterance of the woman who contributed more than any other person to this school should be the name of a writer whose books are not even allowed in the library." Then, without smiling, he winked at me. "How like Harriet. How gloriously like her. To go out on such a note of protest. Thank you, my dear Brian. Thank you for telling me that." He rose and reached his hand across the desk to me. I grasped it and then to my horror I began to sob. I covered my face and sobbed. "It's all right, dear boy," I heard him say in the kindest of tones. "You loved my wife, and I deeply appreciate it."

"Oh, I did, sir," I murmured, "but what a shocking scene I'm making." I looked up at him, in sudden beseeching despair. "Do you suppose a man with so little control could ever become a minister?"

"Is that what you want to be?"

"Oh, yes!"

Dr. Prescott came around to my side of the desk and put a hand on my shoulder. "It's a good thing to have feeling, Brian. One can't really control it unless one has it, can one? You'll be all right. You have a great deal to give to others, and I think your calling may be a true one. But I don't think you're ready yet. I think maybe a year or two at Justin may be precisely what you need."

I rubbed my eyes, grasped his hand again and hurried from the room. I, who should have been consoling, had asked consolation and had received it munificently! Will a lifetime of good works make up for the blessings I have received? Help me, dear God, to be worthy.

3

MARCH 8, 1940. I have made no entries now for three months, not because nothing has happened but because so much has. When I started this journal last September it served no definite purpose, but as time went on it came to serve two. I had a confidant in the first lonely weeks of teaching and a record of my prayers and aspirations from which I hoped to assess my qualifications for the ministry. But now I am not only happy at Justin; I am beginning to be boldly and wonderfully convinced that if God continues willing I shall one day be ready to enter divinity school. And yet I still feel a mysterious compulsion to continue these entries.

I think I know what this compulsion may be, and I am going to write it down now. I am going to make myself do it, no matter how presumptuous it may sound. After all, what is more seemingly presumptuous than the act of becoming a minister? It is robbed of its presumption only by the fact that one is called, and one must learn to distinguish between true and false calls.

What I am trying to say is that I may have a call to keep a record of the life and personality of Francis Prescott.

There, I have said it.

Was it not thus that the gospels and the lives of the saints came to be written? It is not, of course, that there will be any lack of lives written of Dr. Prescott. But since Mrs. Prescott's death I have had opportunities to talk to some of the graduates who have visited the school to offer their sympathies to the headmaster, and it has struck me that they do not see him as I see him. The legend has begun to obliterate the man, and I have the temerity to wonder if the truer vision may not rest with the newer eye, if Dr. Prescott may not be most closely revealed to a non-Justinian.

Mr. Ives, I think, may see him clearly and see him whole, but I wonder if Mr. Ives isn't satisfied with his private vision. Somehow I do not see him memorializing it. He strikes me as a man who has no faith in anything *but* Dr. Prescott and hence who would not see the point in writing anything that survived Dr. Prescott. I do not mean by this that I am trying to make this journal a biography of Dr. Prescott. I am simply seeking to capture something that may ultimately save him from the obliteration of the "official" biography.

If again I am not presumptuous. But then I must learn not to be so afraid of presumption. Such fear may be temptation.

To resume: after his wife's funeral there was a great deal of pressure on Dr. Prescott from friends and family to take the winter off. Each of his daughters wanted him to come to her, but he insisted on going on with his duties. Mrs. Turnbull, the youngest, firm of flesh and manner and loud of voice, with a goodly remnant of the dark looks that won her two husbands, and of the temper that must have driven them away, came up from New York to settle in the headmaster's house and cheerfully to patronize us all, but after a month of paternal snubs she departed. Dr. Prescott was finally to be allowed to handle his grief in his own fashion.

It was then that Mr. Ives called me to his study to tell me his proposition.

"The only way we can help Dr. Prescott is to lighten his load, and the only master who can accomplish this is you. Your stock is high at the moment because of your friendship with Harriet. I am therefore creating a new faculty position for you: assistant to the headmaster. You will help him with his mail and correct the themes of his sacred studies classes. You will be available to walk or drive with him in the afternoons. It's a job, of course, that you'll have to play by ear as you go along. If he lets you, there'll be plenty to do."

"But will he let me?"

"I don't know. When I told him about it, he simply grunted. But he didn't refuse. He didn't knock my head off, as I thought he might. All we can do is try. I shall take over your fourth form English, and you will be relieved of study hall periods."

"Oh, sir, that won't be necessary."

"Perhaps not. But in case this plan *does* work, I want you to be free. Don't worry about not carrying your load. If you can be the least help to Dr. Prescott, you'll be doing more for Justin than any other way."

"I will certainly try my hardest."

This conversation took place a month ago, just after the Christmas vacation. The next morning, according to my instructions, I presented myself at the headmaster's office and asked if I could help with his mail. He waved me to a seat and proceeded to read his letters and dictate answers to his secretary, Miss Burns, without paying the least attention to me. I left at eleven, for first form grammar. It was awful.

The next morning, when I again presented myself, he handed me a belligerent letter from a graduate asking how many courses the school gave in "dead languages."

"They're always trying to brand me as a classicist," he grumbled. "Actually, despite my own fondness for Greek poetry, there's less emphasis on the ancient tongues in Justin than in most of the other schools. The older I get the more I realize that the only thing a teacher has to go on is that rare spark in a boy's eye. And when you see *that*, Brian, you're an ass if you worry where it comes from. Whether it's an ode of Horace or an Icelandic saga or something that goes bang in a laboratory."

He made no comment on the answer that I drafted, but he signed it, and thereafter, without further discussion, I found myself in charge of the letters from graduates.

It fascinated me that there were so many of these. At times it seemed to me that Justinians had nothing better to do than write their old headmaster. Some of the letters were childishly boasting. "You will observe from the letterhead that I am now a partner in . . ." or "Did you ever, Dr. P, expect to address me as a fellow doctor?" In others the writers criticized Dr. Prescott bitterly, holding him responsible for unfortunate developments on the national or international scene, even the war itself. There was a shrill note to these, a "Now it can be told," an ultimate twisting, at a safe postal distance, of the old lion's tail. *See* what has come of your emphasis on football, Latin, cold showers, compulsory chapel, grace before meals or stiff collars on Sunday! "Would it interest you to know, Dr. P, how many of my formmates have been swindlers, dope addicts, alcoholics, lechers, pederasts? And whose fault was it, Dr. P?" "Do you know, Dr. P, that I never really felt like a man until I tore up the prayer book you gave me?"

I mention these first because the others, the encomiums, the congratulations, the almost tear-drenched tributes, were in the vast (and ultimately tedious) majority. I concluded that the common denominator of bad and good, favorable and unfavorable, was that in respect to Dr. Prescott most of his graduates had never grown up. They continued to love him or hate him as if they were still at school and to praise or excoriate him as if they were in a "bull session" in the cellar or a canoe on the Lawrence River. He did not seem to dwindle, as childhood figures usually do, and when they came back to visit the school, instead of seeming a sort of quaint Mr. Chips (was *this* what awed me at fourteen, this lovable Meissen granddaddy with his finger athwart his nose?) they saw the same rector, except indeed that he was even more formidable, for the school having dwindled, he suddenly loomed over it, grotesquely large, the manipulator of the puppet show revealed after the final drop of the curtain. The Prescott they had remembered, by God, was the *real* Prescott!

His schedule is phenomenal for a man of eighty. He rises at six, in the tradition of the great Victorians, and reads for an hour before breakfast. He claims that a mind continually soaked in small school matters needs this daily airing to preserve any freshness. He reads speedily and broadly, with an emphasis on philosophy and history, and although he keeps abreast of modern fiction, he is happiest with the Greek poets. He then officiates at morning chapel, presides over assembly and spends a busy morning in his office at the Schoolhouse. Lunch at the head table is followed by a half hour of faculty coffee, known as the "time for favors," when he is at his most easy and affable. The afternoon is devoted to the physical inspection of his plant, and in the course of a week he visits every part of the school grounds, some of them many times over: the playing fields, the infirmary, the gymnasium, the locker rooms, the dormitories, even the cellars and lavatories. Dinner is at home, with guests, usually visiting graduates, but after the meal he retires to his study for two more hours of paper work and conferences with boys. At ten o'clock he has a couple of strong whiskeys and the day is over. During prohibition he gave these up, and he tells me that it was a sore denial.

March 15. This afternoon Dr. Prescott and I watched a great snowball fight between the first and second forms, "new kids" against "old kids." Except in a few individual struggles, the latter prevailed; they were bigger and stronger and had been toughened by an additional year of the rigors of Justin Martyr. The scene was like a battle canvas of the Victorian academic school. At a distance it was picturesque, even cheerful, full of red faces and brightly colored jerseys against a white background cut by stark, slaty elms. But on closer inspection the details were more lurid. I saw one little boy with a bleeding lip cut open by a piece of ice and another carried off the field with what turned out later to be a cracked ankle. Dr. Prescott did not seem in the least disturbed.

"You've got to let the boys be animals once in a while," he answered my protest as we walked away. "Social life was more attractive when gentlemen defended their honor with swords and not with lawsuits."

"You don't mean you're in favor of dueling!"

"No, no, of course not," he growled. "I said that life was more attractive, not better. When every sniveling calumniator knew that he ran the chance of being called out. Just the way boys are more attractive when they're allowed to take justice into their own hands and not squeal!"

I was learning, little by little, not to be overwhelmed by him. "Do you suggest that boys are mollycoddled at Justin today, sir?"

The question obviously irritated him, for he stomped ahead of me and did not answer, but after a few moments, when I had caught up with him, he said mildly enough: "Well, of course, there's no hazing now. All the schools have done away with it, and we had to, too. The snowball fight is the last vestigial remnant of it. You have just witnessed a rare survival, my friend."

"It did not make me nostalgic."

"Perhaps you are right." He had resumed now his more reasoning tone. "Perhaps my bias for things English made me see a moral value in hazing where none existed. There was a great deal of cruelty in English public schools in the last century, but it went hand in hand with a certain intensity of friendship between boys — almost a passion, you might say — that gave a kind of golden glow to Victorian youth. Of course in America this sort of thing was understood only at its lowest level, with the result that we took over the hazing and discouraged the friendships. It may have been this that gave our boarding schools their peculiar dryness. Oh, yes, Brian." Here he paused to nod his head affirmatively. "The hazing had to go."

"But you never discouraged close friendships between boys, did you, sir?"

"Did I not?" He grunted loudly. "I was one of the worst!"

"Why, sir?"

"Because, sir," he exclaimed loudly, driving his stick into the snow, "I did not think a hundred examples of David and Jonathan were worth one of sodomy!"

I was too shocked to say more. But I am beginning to glimpse some of the conflicts in his nature. He is an artist as well as a preacher, an intellectual as well as a man of God. He probably adores Swinburne and forces himself not to read him. In this he differs from the famous Dr. Peabody of Groton who preached here last week. Peabody would not see the beauty in Swinburne or be tempted by the Loreleis of art. His is a simpler path.

March 16. I asked Dr. Prescott this afternoon his opinion of Peabody. He gave me one of his foxy, sidelong looks and snapped: "A man who considers that Theodore Roosevelt was America's greatest statesman and *In Memoriam* England's finest poem is well equipped to train young men for the steam room of the Racquet Club."

"That's not where Franklin Roosevelt ended up," I pointed out.

Dr. Prescott threw back his head and roared with laughter. "No, but ninety percent of the Grotties wish he had! And evaporated there!" His laugh ended in a spluttering cough, and he leaned over until he recovered himself. "Of course, I'm being facetious. Cotty Peabody is a great man, in his way.

What I really resent is that my graduates are not more different from his. For all my emphasis on the humanities and his on God, we both turn out stockbrokers!"

"Oh, come, sir. You're not being fair to yourself. Or to Dr. Peabody."

"And yet it may be just what explains our popularity," he continued in a more speculative tone, ignoring my comment. "Most fathers would rather see their sons dead than either cultivated or devout. They commend our efforts, but even more our failures. Yes, the greatness of the private school, Brian, is not that it produces geniuses — they grow anyway, and can't be made — but that it can sometimes turn a third-rate student into a second-rate one. We can't boast publicly of such triumphs, but they are still our glory."

"I wonder if Dr. Peabody would agree with that."

"Dr. Peabody doesn't believe in laughing at sacred things," he said dryly. "And Dr. Peabody is right. A sense of humor is excess baggage in a boys' school. Except to fight snobbishness." He nodded ruefully. "Yes, we need it to fight snobbishness."

"Is there so much snobbishness at Justin?"

"My dear fellow, we're riddled with it! Every private school is. Snobbishness is a cancer in America because we pretend it's not there and let it grow until it's inoperable. In England it's less dangerous because it's out in the open. In fact, they glory in it. But if a boy can only *see* it, there may be one chance in ten that he'll fight it."

"You mean that ninety percent of Justinians are snobs?"

" 'I have answered three questions, and that is enough,' " he quoted irritably, " 'be off, or I'll kick you downstairs'!"

That was the end of our conversation for that afternoon, and it has taught me a valuable lesson. When he is in one of his destructive moods, it is fatal to try to check him. It is as if on the heath I tried to argue with the raging Lear. My function is to listen, not to console.

April 18. The Reverend Duncan Moore, Rector of St. Jude's Church in New York, was the visiting preacher this morning. I listened with the keenest interest for he is generally regarded as the most likely candidate to succeed Dr. Prescott. I'm afraid I did not like him. He is a big, beaming, smiling, balding, large-nosed man, handsome in an aggressive way and too good a speaker (*I* think) to be truly spiritual. But of course I am horribly prejudiced. I cannot bear to think of anyone succeeding Dr. Prescott.

As a preacher he is drawn to humility like a lemming to the sea. His theme this morning was the war in Europe which he seems to regard as a judgment upon us for the arrogance and materialism of the inter-war decades. Mr. Moore may not actually believe that God sent the war as a scourge, but he seems to think that we should pretend he did, that we should assume a superstition if we have it not.

I walked to Lawrence House after the service with Mr. Ives and found him at his most sarcastic.

"I feel so reassured, don't you, Brian? I have been foolishly worried about the war. Isn't it nice that Mr. Moore has found time to desert his fashionable parish and travel north to give us the good word? To think that all along it has been a blessing in disguise!"

I no longer glanced about to see if any boys were within earshot. I had learned that they never were. Mr. Ives' indiscretions were totally discreet.

"I suppose it's only human to try to make the best out of things," I urged. "Even war."

"Rot, Brian," he retorted sharply. "And you know it, too. Nothing but death and destruction come out of war. England and France are fighting Hitler. If they can put him down, that's all they can expect. The patient after surgery doesn't emerge better than if he'd never had a tumor."

"Even if he has faith that he will?"

"Then it will be the faith that has done it and not the operation."

I shrugged. "I can't argue with you. You know I agree."

"Then will you kindly admit that Duncan Moore is an egregious ass!"

"How can I?" I pleaded in pain. "How can I admit that Dr. Prescott has anointed an ass?"

"Because it's precisely what great men do."

"Moore may improve with responsibility. He will have you to advise him."

"Oh, no, he won't!" Mr. Ives exclaimed in a barklike tone that came closer to expressing fervor than any of his others. "I shall not remain in Justin a minute after Dr. Prescott goes. And I am very much afraid he will go soon."

I stopped to stare in dismay at the small hawklike figure at my side. "What makes you say that?"

"There are signs," he said flatly. "I am very sensitive to signs. There was one, for example, in the sermon today. The new edifice to be erected on the site of the old. The fresh air in stale rooms. Don't you get it? A glittering new Justin Martyr to be fabricated by Duncan Moore out of the rotten timbers of the old."

The calm clear blank sky, the few, almost stationary wispy clouds, the hard pink buds on the dogwood trees by the Schoolhouse, the sudden whoop of a group of boys, the twittering swallows above my head and the deep clang of the Schoolhouse bell that tolled the quarter hour filled me with a sense of sadness at the transiency of good things. My soul seemed to cry out: let me enjoy it, dear God, if this is all there will be to enjoy! The campus of Justin may be a haven from the war, a haven from reality, but when reality is so grim, to be a haven may be a virtuous thing. Soon, only too soon, reality will burst the walls and swell the gutters of the school to boiling livid streams, but the interim is ours and is not the interim as real as reality?

4

MAY 15, 1940. This is my first entry since the catastrophic invasion of the lowlands. Dr. Prescott has great faith in the English and French armies, particularly the English, but I have a sad tendency to identify the "good" side in any conflict with the weak side and to see the war as Brian Aspinwall against a German tank division. It seems curious that I should have such faith in God and so little in man. But then barbarians have prevailed before, have they not? The dark ages *did* exist.

May 18, 1940. The fiend in Europe goes from triumph to triumph. If only I were there. If only I had stayed in Oxford. Surely, even with my heart murmur they would have accepted me now. But there I go again, thinking of the war in terms of what *I* could do in it, even though I'd be a rotten soldier. What would my enlistment amount to but the placation of my own grubby little sense of guilt? Oh, ego, ego, burning like an ember in the conflagration of the world!

May 21. Even Dr. Prescott is beginning to be depressed. "If they get France, it's all over," he told me this morning. "What can England do without a proper army or air force? If she had time, yes, but where is the time coming from? Oh, to be able to fight, Brian, to be able to *fight*. Every useless old man like

myself should be given a rifle and rushed to the front." *He,*
too!

May 22. The fall of Brussels. It's wonderful how little the
boys care. But that must be the hope of the world, indifference.
If we cared, how could we live?

May 23. Disaster has sent a peculiar ambassador into our peace-
ful midst. It is Mr. Horace Havistock, Dr. Prescott's oldest
friend, who has lived in Paris for fifty years and who, with rare
foresight, decided to repatriate himself only two weeks before
the blitzkrieg. He stays shut up in the headmaster's house and
has appeared only once in the school dining room, where he sat
at Dr. Prescott's right. He seems much older than his host,
though they are supposed to be the same age. He is very bent
and brown, with thick snowy hair, and he leaned heavily on
Dr. Prescott's arm as he hobbled in and out of the dining room.
Yet taken as a remnant of the mauve decade he is rather superb.
He was wearing a high wing collar, striped trousers, a morning
coat and black button boots of lustered polish. Mr. Ives tells
me that his valet has to get up every night at two to "turn" him
in bed.

May 25. Stories about Mr. Havistock, who remains secluded,
continue to enliven the faculty coffee hour. A school is like a
small town, and we all need a bit of comic relief in these grim
days. Dr. Prescott's houseguest has the function as the porter
in the second act of *Macbeth;* he keeps the suspense from becoming unbearable.

Apparently he requires constant service. Breakfast must be
on the dot of eight, and when poor old Mrs. Midge, the housekeeper, comes toiling up the stairs with his heavy tray, she is
apt to find him waiting on the landing, his eye fixed to his
great gold pocket watch, demanding: "Pray tell me, Mrs. Midge,

is my watch fast? I have eight-one." A pity he didn't wait in Paris for the Germans. They'd have fixed him!

How on earth did Dr. Prescott ever become intimate with this elegant old dandy? Mr. Ives says it must be a case of opposites attracting.

May 26. Dr. Prescott told me this morning that he was much upset by Mr. Havistock's opinion of the inner state of France. "He says it's rotten right through. That we must anticipate not only defeat but active collaboration with the enemy."

"You don't suppose he's judging it by his own social circle?"

Dr. Prescott looked up with a trace of amusement in his eyes. "What do you know about his social circle?"

"Nothing. But isn't it the same one that Proust wrote about?"

"Or what's left of it," Dr. Prescott conceded with a chuckle. "As a matter of fact, he was a friend of Proust's. He took Harriet to call on him once in the cork-lined chamber. He wouldn't take me; he said I was too noisy. But you mustn't judge Horace's intellect by Horace's social life. He may be a hothouse plant, but he sees a great deal from his hothouse windows. He is wise, Horace. Very wise."

"He is wise, anyway, in his choice of friends," I ventured.

"Oh, Horace only cut his teeth on me," Dr. Prescott said with a laugh. "We were at school together. Since then he has gone way beyond me. But he is loyal. He remembers the old days."

"I shouldn't think a life in the Paris salons was necessarily going so far beyond Justin Martyr."

Dr. Prescott seemed thoroughly amused by my reservations about his friend. "Ah, but Horace did not confine himself to duchesses. He knew your hero, James. He knew Conrad and Hardy. He was intimate with Proust. Redon did the panels in his living room, and Braque the drawings in his study. Horace has an instinctive understanding of the problems of important people. He loves them as our Lord loved little children."

"And how does he feel about little children?"

"Perish the thought!" Dr. Prescott threw up his hands. "I see you have been listening to school tattle about poor Horace. No doubt Justin can make little enough of him. But come and have tea with him this afternoon and judge for yourself."

"What on earth will I talk to him about?" I cried in dismay.

"James! The master," he retorted with mocking emphasis and turned to his mail.

Well, I went. I was nervous all day and my nervousness was not diminished when I came into Mrs. Prescott's old drawing room and found Mr. Havistock seated before her tea tray checking each plate before dismissing the hovering Mrs. Midge. He paid no attention whatever to my entrance.

"Now, let me see. Is my half piece of lime there? Ah, yes, I see it is. And is the toast buttered on *both* sides? It wasn't yesterday." He inspected a piece. "Oh, good. Well, I think that will be all for now, Mrs. Midge. I'll ring if I need anything."

The world in flames and he worries about his toast being buttered on both sides! There must have been five minutes of fussing with the tea things before he finally leaned back in Mrs. Prescott's old chair, touched the tips of his long fingers together before his hawk nose and gazed at me shrewdly.

"Well, Mr. Aspinwall! Frank tells me you were a friend of Harriet's. I can imagine no greater recommendation, for she was a woman of perfect taste. Oh, perhaps not always in clothes . . ." He raised his dark eyebrows which formed a striking contrast to his snowy hair and coughed. "And yet even her clothes, in a wonderful basic Bostonian way, had style."

I looked back now into his small cold grey eyes with a greater sympathy. "It is true. She had great style."

"It is to your credit that you recognize it, young man, for your generation has had little opportunity to observe it. It went out with the last war. Or even before." There was a long pause as he took a sip of his tea and a bite of his doubly buttered toast. "Style," he repeated reflectively. "Odette in the Bois as Proust describes her in *Swann*." He looked up at me now with sudden aggressiveness. "Do you agree there have been no writers since Proust?"

"Not Hemingway?" I protested. "Not Lewis or O'Neill or Fitzgerald?"

"They had talent." His shrug implied that this was to the man what the cravat was to the wardrobe. "I knew Lewis and young Fitzgerald. But they were not presentable. You couldn't depend on what they'd do or say. They bore in their souls the malaise of a dying world. It was art but corrupt art."

I saw there was no purpose in going on with *that*. "Dr. Prescott tells me you knew Henry James."

"My dear fellow, of course I knew him. Don't you know the Lubbock correspondence? There are several letters to me in it."

So he was *that* Havistock, the "dear, dear boy"! Was it possible that this relic before me had once been young? I can quite see Dr. Prescott as a youth, but not Mr. Havistock. Perhaps it was only one of James' hyperbolean compliments.

"Have you ever written your memoirs, sir?"

"Not really. I started a little book that was to be entitled 'The Art of Friendship,' but I never got very far with it, and now I never shall." He smiled complacently. "I'm too old."

"But I would have thought that just the time to write memoirs."

"Also I'm lazy, Mr. Aspinwall." He shook his head solemnly as if he were proclaiming a virtue. "I was born for the oral and not the written word. Some of the pages were all right, but oh, the *work* it took. I have a nice little thing on Réjane and a few good stories about Anatole France. But the only one I completed was the piece on Frank Prescott. About our early days."

My mouth went suddenly dry. "You wouldn't let me see it?"

"Oh, good gracious no. It's highly confidential."

"But if I swore I'd never repeat a word of it?"

He looked up at me, surprised at my eagerness. "Why should you care? When you have Frank in the flesh, what is the fascination of ancient memories?"

"Because I want to know everything about him. How it all started, for example. The whole idea of Justin!"

"You wish to write his life?"

"Oh no, sir. I'm not so ambitious. I simply want to *know*."

"You have no axe to grind?"

"But the very sharpest! I feel . . . how shall I put it? That to know Dr. Prescott is to be enriched. The more I know, the richer I shall be. Oh, yes, I'm quite selfish."

Mr. Havistock smiled almost pleasantly. "But not vulgar. Not yet anyway. You are still uncorrupted. I tell you what, Mr. Aspinwall. When I am settled in Long Island, where I have rented the only Ogden Codman house I could find, I shall go over my papers, and I will consider your request. Yes, I will consider it."

He now tasted a piece of toast from the second tier of the tea stand, one on which marmalade had been spread, and it was evidently not his special brand, for poor Mrs. Midge had to be rung for, and a long discussion ensued. I was disappointed in him. He had taste and perception, no doubt, but the world that he tasted and perceived existed only for his own amusement. He liked marmalade and he liked Proust, which seemed to put them on the same footing. I wonder if the Edwardian era did not contain many such figures in the background, if behind the beauty of James' fiction and of Sargent's portraits there were not a good many limp pieces of toast that had to be buttered on both sides.

May 27. Apparently I passed muster with Dr. Prescott's friend for I was asked to a small dinner tonight at the headmaster's house. It was not a success. Following our host's lead, we all deferred as respectfully to Mr. Havistock as if he had been

Walter Lippmann or Dorothy Thompson, but the old boy was in a foul mood (perhaps his valet forgot to "turn" him last night) and answered our questions about the war in grumpy monosyllables. It was obvious that he has no use for any schoolteachers outside of Francis Prescott. He ended by being positively offensive to poor Mr. Ruggles who had the misfortune to suggest the invincibility of a Frenchman "fighting on his own soil."

"As proved, I suppose, in 1815 and in 1870," he snapped. "Unhappily for Europe the clichés of the American tourist will not save the day. The French peasant may be brave enough; peasants usually are. But in this black century of ours a country is no stronger than its ruling class, and I have known the ruling class of France for forty years."

When the others rose to go, shortly after the silence that followed this outburst, Dr. Prescott winked at me to indicate that I should stay on. Old Horace continued to sit morosely by the fireplace and sip his brandy as he descanted on the horrors of the war.

"Over here you see that things are bad, but you have no conception of how catastrophic they really are. You see that the old world of grace and leisure and art, my world if you will, or the remnants of it, is doomed. Obviously. But what you don't see, Frank, is that your world is doomed, too."

"What do you call my world, Horace?" the headmaster asked in the milder tone that he used with this old friend.

"The world of the private school," Mr. Havistock answered with a snort. "The world of the gentleman and his ideals. The world of personal honor and a Protestant God. When a civilization crumbles, it crumbles all together. The colors run out, the good with the bad. Roman virtue goes with the Roman arena. Voltaire and Watteau with the *lettre de cachet*. Francis Prescott with Horace Havistock. You can't pick and choose in a flood."

"Please! You make me feel like an old piece of antimacassar."

"You may laugh, my friend, but it's just what you are."

I trembled with indignation to hear Dr. Prescott so slighted. For if he was jesting, Mr. Havistock was not. How did this old fop dare to come up to Justin to taunt the headmaster in his bereavement!

"You'll be telling me I should retire next," Dr. Prescott said in a gloomier tone.

"Of course I will," Mr. Havistock retorted promptly. "It's precisely what I've come up to tell you."

"But if everything is going to pieces," I protested in dismay, too upset now to be silent in the presence of my elders, "why does it matter whether Dr. Prescott retires or not?"

They both looked up at me as if they had forgotten I was there, and I had a sharp sense of intrusion upon an ancient intimacy.

"Because there's such a thing as dignity," Mr. Havistock explained coldly. "And dignity requires one not to hang on."

At this I lost all restraint. "What a cruel thing to say!"

"It's a cruel world."

Dr. Prescott, turning from both of us, had arisen and was staring moodily into the fire. "There must be a limit to what is expected of the old," he said in a grave, melancholy tone. "If we do our job, must our years be thrown in our teeth? Where am I weaker, Horace, than I used to be?"

"You read the service now from the prayer book. The time was when you recited it right through by heart."

Dr. Prescott turned on him, stung. "And *you* claimed it was theatrical. Must I be condemned by my own high standards?"

Mr. Havistock seemed to relent a bit at this. He passed his fingertips over his temples in a brushing gesture that made me suddenly realize that for him, too, the scene might be proving a strain. "Do you remember, Frank, when you used to admire Browning? And 'Pheidippides'? 'Never decline, but, gloriously as he began, so to end gloriously'? Don't decline now."

"But the years have taken me from Browning to Tennyson," Dr. Prescott came back at him. "Like Ulysses, I claim that 'old age hath yet its honor and its toil.' How do you know, Horace, that no 'work of noble note' remains for me to do?"

Mr. Havistock shook his head relentlessly. "The work of noble note is to quit while you're still ahead. I've always given you good advice, Frank. You won't get it from your graduates or your trustees. They're all too scared of you. Believe me, my friend."

Dr. Prescott had turned back to the fire, and his face was drawn down in an expression of bitterness. Suddenly he gripped the mantel with both of his hands and kicked a log viciously. "Nobody's scared of me," he muttered. "Sometimes I wish they were."

"Harriet would have told you the same thing."

"Oh, go to bed, Horace, and stop croaking! You just want everyone else's world to come apart because yours has."

Mr. Havistock did not seem to resent this in the least. He asked me if I would be good enough to fetch his valet, and when I returned from the kitchen with Jules, he and Dr. Prescott were actually laughing!

Of course, I know that at eighty Dr. Prescott cannot go on forever, but I doubt if there is a single master or boy at the school who thinks him inadequate for his job. I had hoped that he might continue a few more years and perhaps have the blessed luck to die in office. But tonight I know there is no such chance. Old Havistock is too practiced a vulture to have come prematurely to the scene of demission. It is perhaps his very undertaker's face that Dr. Prescott has awaited.

June 2. Prize Day, and Mr. Havistock's seed have borne bitter fruit. Dr. Prescott made the announcement of his retirement at the close of the ceremonies. It came as a complete surprise and shock to his audience.

The weather, at least, was perfect. The whole school, in Sunday blue, and the parents sat on benches in the middle of the campus facing the dais for the headmaster and visiting dignitaries. I have never seen so brilliant an azure sky, so emerald a lawn. The awakened earth seemed to burst with promises that had nothing to do with disaster across the seas.

When the last diploma had been handed out and the last prize given, the headmaster stood silent for a long moment before the amplifier, both hands in his pockets, his eyes fixed beyond the crowd at the point where the river path disappeared into the woods.

"I have one more brief statement to make. Since the death of my beloved wife I have felt the moral support of every boy and of every master in the school. I have been buoyed up in a difficult time by close to five hundred pairs of arms. With such a backing I have almost fooled myself that I could go on forever. But time is remorseless, and I have passed by a whole decade the biblical limit of threescore years and ten. I shall remain in office for one more year so that my successor may have time to prepare for the transition. In June of 1941 the Reverend Duncan Moore will become headmaster of Justin Martyr. God bless you all. We will now adjourn for lunch."

There was a stunned, staggered silence and then gasps and then cries of "Oh, no!" Dr. Prescott walked abruptly to the edge of the dais, and we heard the quick click of his heels descending the steps. He strode rapidly down the aisle and was almost out of sight before next year's senior prefect, very red in the face, leaped to his feet and screamed hoarsely: "Let's have a long cheer for Dr. Prescott!"

We all rose and roared that cheer. It echoes in my ears as I write this.

June 3. Dr. Prescott has, of course, been surrounded by people since his great announcement. Graduates, parents and trustees

mill about him to try to impress their little pinpricks of sympathy and admiration into his bland, impersonal attention. I
have a discreditable feeling of resentment, as if they were
taking him away from me and had no right to, as if I alone and
not they had any true appreciation of his greatness. Of course
this is nonsense and egotism, yet I cannot help feeling that the
man I see when we're alone is different from the idol of the
crowd.

He sent for me tonight before supper in his study and asked
me if I wished to go to divinity school in the fall. He had
spoken to the Dean at Harvard about me. He was so gentle,
and I was so touched that he should remember my problems
that I stammered too badly to be understood.

"Oh, sir," I protested at last, "I only want to stay and help
you!"

"But I shan't need you now, Brian. I only needed an assistant while I was trying to conserve my energy. Now that I'm
going to retire I can be a spendthrift. I can blow it to the
winds."

"Well, if you don't need me, sir," I pleaded, "then I need
you!"

He coughed with a hint of disapproval. He disliked any demonstration of feeling, particularly with regard to himself. "You
don't need *me*, young man, but perhaps you need another year
at Justin. Particularly if you want to come back here when
you've taken orders. What will you do this summer?"

"I thought I might go to Columbia for a course in Elizabethan
drama."

He laughed. "It's better reading than the papers today. Perhaps I may try a bit of it myself."

August 1. New York. Since the last entry France has surren-
dered, and England has entered her hideous ordeal. I have
been unable to write. I sit in my rented room on upper Broad-

way with windows open on a sultry silent avenue and immerse myself in Beaumont and Fletcher. It has been as if a dark curtain had blessedly been lowered over the agonizing vividness of the past year, over death in Europe and death in Justin Martyr. It has been as if I had died and gone to a seventeenth century spirit kingdom inhabited by jealous sovereigns and crafty nephews, by ambitious cardinals and cynical clowns, by melancholy and madness, bones and diadems.

This morning I received a large brown envelope from Mr. Havistock containing the typescript of his chapters on Dr. Prescott and the following note:

Dear Aspinwall: Here is the "Prescottiana" that you wanted. I make you a present of it. The world is full of asses, but they are particularly abundant among the loyal graduates of New England church schools. Justin Martyr is no exception. Poor Frank is so surrounded that you may be the only chink through which he can be seen. Unless you become an ass, too. Don't.

Your friend from another century,
H.H.

As I read the words I felt again the throb of my ancient faith. God's presence had been suspended, not withdrawn, and I blush for my craven doubts and turn to Mr. Havistock's piece.

5

As I LOOK back upon a long and (I hope) non-useful lifetime over decades devoted to cultivating the luxuries and letting the necessities go scrape for their sordid selves, I am perfectly clear that the greatest and most indispensable of the former has been that of my friendships. The art of making these, distrusted of women, has never been much cultivated in America, and I have had largely to pursue it abroad, but I will always remember and will here gratefully record that my first lesson was taken under the ashen sky of a New England winter.

I met Frank Prescott when we were sixteen, at St. Andrew's School in Dublin, New Hampshire, in the fall of 1876. Had he not been in my form, I should certainly not have been able to last out till Christmas. It was bad enough that I was at once a new boy and a fifth former, an incongruous situation, but it was a good deal worse that I had been brought up exclusively by nurses and tutors and kept safe until well past puberty from the savage competition of my contemporaries. How I happened to be suddenly shorn of my curls and stripped of my velvet suits and isolated with members of my own sex — total strangers every shrieking one of them — involves my telling something of my own beginnings.

I am the youngest child of a marriage of June and January, and, alas, I cost June her life. My father, Gridley Havistock, had children of an earlier match who were older than my mother; he was sixty at my birth and survived to my thirtieth year. He was a huge, big-bellied, bulbous-nosed, pig-eyed be-whiskered old-school New York gentleman, magnificent in his authoritarianism, but testy, snappish and accustomed to obedience. A great deal that he said was banal, and all of his aphorisms were platitudes, but he *looked* like a business leader and certainly acted like one, and in his generation appearances counted for more than they counted later when scalawags like Gould and Fiske had taught New Yorkers to be suspicious of everyone.

I doubt if Father would have been president of the Merchants' Bank and a trustee of New York Central a generation later. He was not in the league, financially, mentally or immorally, with the new magnates of steel and rail, but he had the happy good sense to have learned to get on with them and to be able to make them feel that an invitation to 310 Fifth Avenue or "Gridley Court" in Newport was one of the things they had dreamt of in their log cabins or steerage days. This good sense, I may add, he conveyed to his children, and it has proved the most valuable gift of the few with which he endowed us.

My older brothers of the second bed enjoyed Father's rude health, but I was a rheumatic child, subject to constant respiratory complaints, and was turned over at a tender age to the ministrations of the one person who wanted me, a faded, ailing, old maid half-sister who presided timidly over her terrifying father's table and who, because of the difference in age of more than a generation, was addressed by her demi-siblings as "Sister Sue." She, dear creature, was full of recipes and quaint medicinal superstitions; she ventured out of doors in only the balmiest weather and then swathed in furs and scarfs over the black of her perpetual mourning for perpetually dying cousins. My childhood was spent in upstairs parlors before small well-tended fires, reading English and French fiction while Sister Sue worked on her needlepoint, and in the blur of early memories Grant in the Wilderness, Sherman riding to the sea, my brother Archie winning a tennis match or the bray of laughter from downstairs at Number 310 where Father was entertaining the Hone Club, were part and parcel of a men's world, happily no more real and not nearly as exciting as the romances of Dumas or Jane Porter.

I managed to protract this dreamlike existence to my fifteenth year and might have stretched it to my own maturity had poor Sister Sue not died of a breast cancer. Of course, it was not put that way to me. "She was tired and went to sleep," was the Havistock diagnosis. And I was discovered, or perhaps I should say "realized," by my family for the first time, an ungainly, despairing, dressed up doll, abandoned on top of the pathetic little heap of her possessions. Everyone tried to be kind, but their kindness congealed into something more brittle when the great doctor, from whom Sister Sue had guarded me behind the opaque wall of her quacks, pronounced me to be in fully adequate health for boarding school.

My brother Archie, as oldest of the second bed, now "took me in hand," promising Father that he would have me ready in a few months' time for St. Andrew's where all my brothers had gone. He went straight to work, firmly and I think fairly, with lessons and exercises and instruction in sports, but all his preparations were blown to bits by the first crisp blast of an autumnal New England wind and the terrifying shouts from the football field on the day that he delivered me to and abandoned me at my new abode.

It is important briefly to describe St. Andrew's, as it existed in the seventies, because it later became the model of all that Frank Prescott thought a school should not be. Life there, outside of classes, was totally disorganized. The boys played informally at football and baseball, making up their own rules, but they were quite at liberty, if they pleased instead, to roam the

New Hampshire countryside and fish or trap in their afternoons. They were equally at liberty to haze the weak and to group themselves into fierce little competing clubs. They bathed but once a week and never changed, even when exercising, from their stiff collars and itchy flannel underwear, so that the evening meal after a hard game of soccer was a trial for the sensitive. I will admit that they seemed to have enjoyed themselves, but to me the school was another Dotheboys Hall.

I was always cold, always dirty and generally disliked. I was mocked and chastised, not only by my peers in the fifth form but by boys much younger who quickly grasped the idea that I was hopeless at fisticuffs. I was called "Frenchy" because of my suits and "Willow" because of my walk. Archie's standards of clothes, however Spartan in contrast to Sister Sue's, seemed grossly luxurious to St. Andrew's. From the morning bell and my pail of icy water to evening prayers and the threat of a turtle in my bed, life was a series of hideous apprehensions.

The faculty lived in a world of their own, as remote from the daily problems of the boys as the quaint Gothic gingerbread buildings which gave to the little campus the air of an English college in a puppet show. In this they followed the example of the headmaster, Dr. Howell, a tall, spare, otherworldly cleric, garbed in rather dirty black, who never used any term of address but a vaguely benevolent "my dear" and who made no secret of his low opinion of boys, or "apes" as he blandly called them. He had the iron will of the temperless religious fanatic, and he exercised absolute authority over the small areas of school life that broke through the icy wall of his spiritual preoccupation. He cared for our souls and only for our souls; he took no interest in games or recreations and used to revile the human body as an "unlovely thing." An uncompromising Episcopalian, he would remind boys whose families were known to be friendly with Unitarians or Baptists that members of these sects would occupy a lower social level in the hereafter, and he

was said to have fired a boy who came to his study to confess
that he was suffering from doubts as to the apostolic succession.

Yet the extraordinary thing about America in the last century
was that Dr. Howell was not only revered by graduates; he
was held in respect and awe by the boys. He is a legend in the
vastly expanded St. Andrew's School of this day, and to suggest
that he was a bigot and a tyrant would be regarded as appalling
heresy by a generation which knows him only from the great
Chase portrait in the school dining room, a fabulous study in
the El Greco manner of zealous faith and asceticism.

I myself looked up to him as a creature happily exempted
from my own sordid tribulations. I admired his detachment
from problems that I regarded as inevitably, if humiliatingly,
my own personal doom. Watching him drive his pony cart
about the campus, so blissfully unaware of the cold, the rain,
the horrid little boys and all the horrid things in their horrid
little minds, like a priest in the Middle Ages who has had the
sense to understand that only by the cassock could he escape
the armed strife and dominate the armored figures, I could almost persuade myself that I, too, might one day be a free soul.

Frank Prescott at first seemed as remote as the headmaster.
He was also a fifth former but, unlike me, he had been in the
school for three years, and he led our form, not only in studies
but in athletics. His short, thick figure and broad shoulders
made him a superb tackle in football, a game which he played
with a passion and roughness that was more the way it came to
be played in the nineties than it was then. But Frank, however
respected and admired, was not as popular as one might have
supposed. He cared too little for the opinions of others, and he
could be brutally outspoken in his speech. He was a silent,
moody boy, and there was an air of truculent, rather unlovable
superiority in his pale square handsome face and in those big
calm brooding wide-apart brown eyes.

He was an orphan of small means but of the best Boston connections, a distant cousin of the historian, and even as a boy he had the natural dignity of a New England aristocrat. To me he was a romantic, Byronic figure from the beginning, an impression that was intensified when I learned that he was an orphan, the only child of a father who had died a hero at Chancellorsville and of a beautiful, grief-stricken mother who had quickly followed him to the grave. Frank never joined the others in making sport of me, but then he never seemed to notice me at all.

The episode that brought us together was an attack launched upon me with iced snowballs by three fourth formers one early December afternoon as I was leaving the library. After pelting me unmercifully, they threw me in the snow and would have jumped upon me had not Frank at that moment appeared down the path. When he shouted at them to leave me alone, two of them ran discreetly off a ways, but one, the smallest, stood his ground.

"What business is it of yours, Prescott?" he cried shrilly. "He's a new boy, isn't he? He's fair game. Who the hell do you think you are? God almighty?"

Frank stepped forward quickly and struck the boy so viciously across the mouth that he fell his length on the snow. When he struggled to his feet I saw that his lips were bleeding.

"What did you do that for?" he shrieked, but for all his outrage he dared not make a move to strike at Frank, nor did his two friends, hovering, take any step to come to his aid.

"To teach you a lesson about upperclassmen."

"But he's a *new* boy!" my persecutor insisted again.

"I don't care. He's a fifth former, and you'd better remember it."

When I was alone with my rescuer, I tried to thank him, but in the suffocation of my gratitude I stammered so badly that I made no sense. Frank cut me short with words as brutal as his blow to the other boy's cheek.

"I didn't do it for you, Frenchy, don't worry. I did it for the honor of the form. Pick up your ridiculous hat. You're a disgrace to us, allowing yourself to be beat up by fourth formers. Why didn't you even put up a fight?"

"They were three to one!"

He did not deign to answer this, but strode off, leaving me to the shame that he felt I ought to feel. But I have never wasted much time on shame. I have always freely accepted myself and my limitations. What struck me most as I stared after that broad, retreating back was the vision of how different life would be if I could always count on such a protector. Might it not make life even at St. Andrew's bearable?

Now the reader may wonder how one of my lowly position in the school could possibly aspire to a friendship with such a boy as Frank Prescott, particularly after the rebuff which I had just received. There were two reasons: first, that I was quick enough to grasp that the rebuff had really come from Frank's dislike at being thanked for striking a smaller boy, and second, that I was already unconsciously developing the theory of friendship around which I was to build my life. This theory was simply that any man who wants strongly enough to become the friend of another will succeed if there are no unbridgeable class or racial gaps and if he wastes no time in worrying about his own inferior attainments. The unlovable Boswell pursued and captured Paoli, Rousseau and Voltaire before he even started on Johnson. I am known today as a veteran collector of paintings and bibelots, but the collection of which I am proudest is that of my friends. They are a distinguished and variegated lot, beginning with Frank Prescott, and ending (at least to date) with Scott Fitzgerald.

Two days later I walked as boldly as I knew how down the fifth form study corridor to knock on Frank's door. "I know you don't want to see me," I began, "but one good turn deserves another. I've been thinking of what I could do for you in return for what you did for me, and I've decided the only thing I'm any good in is French. I had a real mademoiselle and used to talk it with her. I can help you, if you'll let me try."

Frank stared at me with unfeigned astonishment for several moments and then broke into a rude laugh. "Well, I'll be damned," he exclaimed. "If Frenchy doesn't want to teach me to be a frog!"

"Very well, if that's the attitude you want to take," I retorted with what I hoped was a chilling dignity. "But I meant it nicely, Prescott."

I went back to my own study, and fifteen minutes later he knocked at the door. "I'm sorry, Havistock. May I sit down? I'm having the devil of a time with this chapter of *Émilie*."

I discovered that winter that I was a first class tutor. Indeed, I could have made my living at it had my situation in life so required. I even gained a small headway against Frank's Boston accent which must be one of the greatest obstacles the Gallic tongue has ever encountered. But the friendship, for all my assiduousness, developed very slowly. Frank had too little time for human relationships. He studied hard, read a great deal and exercised violently. When he did allow me to accompany him on one of his long Sunday hikes, I would be too exhausted keeping up with his quick stride to have the energy to break his silences.

Yet he tolerated me, that was the great thing. I never had to fight with him the usual adolescent's snobbishness which frowns on the least companionship between a popular and an unpopular boy. Frank may have cared little enough for me, but I was quick to note that he cared as little for anyone else.

Gradually, a more personal note came into our colloquies as we walked together to chapel or as we sat side by side at meals. Frank had an aunt, a Miss Jane Prescott, to whom he was very devoted, and I told him about Sister Sue. It was a bond, if a tenuous one. Others followed. We discovered that we both liked Greek drama and despised Lord Tennyson. That we both liked chess and sneered at checkers. That we both revered the shade of Lincoln and deplored a civilian Grant.

But Frank had terrible prejudices which would sometimes make a clean sweep of all the little ropes and grappling hooks that I kept casting up to his decks. He passionately believed that an age of heroes had died with his father in the red clay of Virginia and that a generation of jackals now gorged itself on the bloated carcass of valor. He completely blew up at me when I suggested that the Civil War might have been avoided had more people, like my own father, tried to compromise the issues.

"You New Yorkers would compromise with the devil himself to save your pocketbooks!" he exclaimed bitterly. "You must have all fainted with relief when you found out, after war *did* come, that you could still make money out of it. We Bostonians, poor idealistic fools, went south to fight while you bought substitutes. The Prescotts died poor while the Havistocks filled their cashboxes!"

He was a strange, proud, bitter boy, and he could be very cruel indeed when he wanted. I did not mind his outbursts against New York or my family which I felt were more or less justified, but I minded very much one night, in front of the whole dormitory, when he volunteered a wicked parody of my early ablutions on a cold winter morning. It was such an unexpected blow, so brutally repudiating to what I was just beginning to look upon as friendship, and he did it with such unexpected and fiendish skill, that I burst into tears and embarrassed everybody. Everybody but Frank himself.

In the spring I made my great bid. Archie had suggested to Father that I be allowed to ask a friend to visit us in Newport, and I invited Frank. I had an unfair advantage in that I already knew that his only alternative to a hot summer in Boston with his Aunt Jane was to tutor a rich brat of a Prescott cousin on the Cape. Perfectly fairly, he expressed no gratitude when I made my offer; he simply informed me that he would have to consult his guardian. The latter, fortunately for me, approved of this solution of his ward's summer and even advanced the funds for an outfit that would not disgrace a Prescott amid the

Havistocks, and Frank was delivered to me in early July, bound, so to speak, in summer wrappings. It was a curious reversal of our roles, that he, the athlete and school leader, should become a boy put up, almost as a charity, for the summer to be a playmate for the delicate and difficult Horace. But, needless to say, it did not take him long to put things back in their proper place.

Newport in the seventies was beginning to show signs of turning into the silly jumble of derivative palaces that it later became. The little white hand to which Henry James was to liken the summer colony of his childhood was already filling with gold. But the essence of the old Newport was still there, the Newport of Julia Ward Howe and romantic Gothic and ladies' archery contests on small bright green lawns, the Newport, as James was again to put it, "of a quiet, mild, waterside sense, one in which shores and strands and small coast things played the greater part." It was a Newport that had not yet succumbed to the Vanderbilts and Goelets, and the only Newport I have ever cared for.

Our house, which was grand for those days, stood in the center of a twenty acre plot on Bellevue Avenue surrounded by a huge, beautiful lawn shaded with great elms. It was an Alexander Jackson Davis structure of smooth brown stucco, utterly asymmetrical, with many little balconies and unexpected porches and odd, protruding conservatories. As its arched windows, though multitudinous, were tiny, it was utterly dark within. Father, still magnificent at seventy-seven, with his five young sons, four of whom, at least, were handsome blades, continued to be an impressive figure in the summer colony. His bays were the sleekest, his carriages the most gleaming, and when the six of us, in black coats and striped grey trousers, marched down the aisle to our pew in Trinity Church of a Sunday morning, it must have been a pretty good show.

All of the family were immediately attracted to the silent, handsome boy whose good manners (for Frank's manners with adults were always perfect) never seemed to compromise his rugged independence of thought. He had a bit of a row with Father over the reconstruction of the South, but he won it decisively. Father was one of a small persistent group who, despite the posthumous sanctification of Mr. Lincoln, still regarded the late President in the rail-splitter tradition. He had actively supported McClellan in the 1864 campaign and thought Lincoln "soft" on the South, positions that might seem inconsistent today but which then quite commonly went together. When Frank, one night at dinner, spoke up loudly to condemn the loss by the living of the precious unity for which the dead, including his own father, had been sacrificed, there was no further waving of the bloody shirt.

The summer was a happy one for me. Frank, as a guest, reined in much of his natural sarcasm and took me sailing almost every clear day. He loved to poke about the rocky inlets along the coast and to fish and swim from the boat, and he loved returning in the early evening and watching the spires of old Newport against the setting sun. I was asked to parties now, because all the girls were interested in Frank, and I discovered, not without a pang of adolescent jealousy, that he had a very distinct taste for their company. I wanted to keep him to myself, but I was shrewd enough, even at seventeen, to know that the smallest effort in this direction would be fatal to our still precarious relationship. It had to be my consolation to remember that back at St. Andrew's there would be no silly girls to giggle at his least funny remarks and to lead him on to talk, unbecomingly, of his prowess in sport. I believed then, as I believe today, that men are at their most attractive in the company of other men.

I paid for the entire happiness of that summer in a single incident that occurred after our return to school. I do not know if it happened because of Frank's restlessness under the burden of his imagined duty of gratitude, or because he felt cut off from the other boys at so marked an association with one who was still considered "different," or because he was stifled by the now compulsory blanket of friendship that the summer had seemed to throw over us. At any rate, one night at the sixth form table during a general discussion of our future careers, he answered my innocent question about his own by lashing back at me in a voice for all to hear: "Oh, I'm going to Newport in a red and yellow blazer to court the richest heiress I can find. And when I've married her, I'll lie back in silk sheets like a Havistock and puff at Turkish cigarettes and be so, *so* above the poor old vulgar world."

My eyes filled with tears (I still hadn't learned to repress them), and I abruptly left the table. In my room alone I reviewed the history of my relationship with Frank. I considered each aspect with what I hoped was a minimum of self-pity and decided in the end that the pain outweighed the pleasure. The little bits of kindness that he occasionally tossed me did not compensate for his cruelty. I was not even angry as I came to my sad conclusion. I felt sincerely sorry for him. He would probably go through his life antagonizing everyone who tried to be nice to him, slapping away helping hands and spitting in sympathizing eyes. Well, so it would have to be. It was better to have no friend than the like of him.

I did not speak to Frank for the next two weeks, and he took no notice of it. He was busy with football, and as one of the school prefects he had to act as an assistant to Dr. Howell. But one afternoon, when he had sprained his wrist and was unable to play his favorite game, he appeared at the door of my study and without the least hint of an apology for his past conduct, blandly suggested that we take a walk. When I told him that I did not care to associate with a person who had pretended to be my friend and later made public mock of me, he simply laughed.

"Don't be an ass," he said. "Come along. I thought we might sit in chapel for a bit and then watch the football."

"Why sit in chapel?" I asked in surprise.

"Because it's nice."

He walked down the corridor, and I sat looking after him until it broke in upon me that this was his way of apologizing. I could choose between my pride and Frank, and I have never been one to spite my face by hacking off its features. I hurried after him, and we walked to chapel where we sat for half an hour in adjoining choir seats, absolutely still and silent, while Frank stared up at the big, beautiful altar window that portrayed, in glowing whites and reds, the transfiguration.

I found the experience a bit embarrassing, as if we had happened uninvited into God's house and caught him in his dressing room. Religion to the Havistocks was a formal matter. God and man met only in their Sunday best, and one did not talk about him, any more than one talked about one's hostess at a party, except in terms of perfunctory respect.

I suspected, however, that God meant more than this to Frank, not from anything that he had ever said, but from the way he closed his eyes in prayer. One knew then that he was not thinking of games or girls. In that half hour at chapel he may have been with the father whom he had never known, coughing blood in the mud at Chancellorsville or with the poor little white shadow of a mother, roaming the dark corridors of the Marlborough Street house with crooning moans. Or he may have simply been opening the pores of his soul to the Holy Spirit and passively allowing it to enter. I have never had any faith of my own other than one in that of others, a curious kind of heretical suspicion that God would not abide in such as me but might abide in such as have been my friends. Call it what you will, faith or superstition, it has got me through most of a long life.

Frank nodded to me at last, and we left the chapel. "That was bully, wasn't it?" he asked, and I was embarrassed again by the unexpected adjective.

We walked down to watch the football which bored me but which seemed of unending fascination to Frank. A play had

just ended in a violent scrimmage, involving most of the members of both teams, when an odd thing happened. We suddenly
saw the headmaster hurrying across the field, waving his umbrella and shouting in a shrill tone. I had never seen him on
the athletic field before, much less running. When he reached
the scrimmage heap he tried to pull away one of the boys by
his legs, and I could now make out his high voice exclaiming:
"Don't kill him! Don't kill the boy underneath! What are you
doing? Dear God, what are you *doing* to him?"

All the boys stood up now bewildered, and we heard the
embarrassed but respectful coach explaining to Dr. Howell
that the scrimmage, far from being an organized pogrom, was a
natural, indeed an integral part of the game. Dr. Howell, however, did not seem in the least embarrassed by his mistake and
proceeded on the spot to draw up a new code of rules. Why
was it necessary for the boy carrying the ball to be brought to
the ground? Why should it not be sufficient simply to touch
him? I was thoroughly enjoying the discomfort of the players
when I realized that I was alone, and, turning, saw Frank strid-
ing swiftly away towards the Dublin Lake Road. I ran after him
and caught his arm, but he shook me impatiently off.

"Don't you want to see how they settle it?" I asked. "Honestly, it's a circus!"

"To you it is. You don't care about football."

"Well, if you care so much, why don't you stay and argue
with him?"

"Oh, what the hell, Horace!" he exclaimed impatiently.
"We'll be out of here in the spring. Let's go on to the lake. I
need a walk and some air. Let that old baboon turn it into a
game of tag if he wants."

"You call Dr. Howell a baboon?" I cried, scandalized. "I
thought you admired him."

"Admired him!" Frank stopped and looked at me in perplex-
ity as if he would never come to the end of my quixoticism.

"For what do you take me? Admire that bigoted, sanctimonious jackass?"

I remember distinctly that it was then and there that I decided that I would have to establish limits to the domination of Frank Prescott. "You go too far," I retorted. "You always go too far and get violent about things. Dr. Howell is rather superb, really. He's a kind of symbol, like a sovereign or pope. He's above the vulgar hurly-burly of school competition."

"Above it!" Frank shouted. "What business does he have being above his boys? Football is a tough, hard game, the way life is, except for a few favored souls like the Havistocks. A headmaster ought to be down on that field playing with the boys himself. He ought to be *in* that scrimmage, not whimpering about it!"

"Dr. Howell? Would you want to kill him?"

"Well, he ought to know the rules, then, and what a scrimmage is. You're the most impossible romantic, Horace. You have to visualize him as some kind of Michelangelo prophet with flowing robes and a thunderstorm in the background. You can't bear to see him as a silly, preoccupied old boy in a dirty black suit pulled around the campus in a pony cart because he's too lazy to walk!"

I burst out laughing. "Can you blame me?"

"Oh, to hell with him." Frank gave it up and slapped me painfully on the shoulder. "He's not worth a row. But I can promise you there won't be any Howells in my school."

"In *your* school? Are you going to have one?"

"Maybe some day." He shrugged, but I knew at once by his suddenly averted eyes and the quick set of his jaw that he was entirely serious. "Why not? Don't you think I could manage one?"

"On the contrary, I think you'd manage it very well. Would it be a church school?"

"Certainly."

"But wouldn't you have to be a minister?"

"I'm going to be a minister, Horace." He turned to look at me hard now, and those glittering brown eyes defied me to smirk. "I'm going to be a minister and a schoolmaster. You asked me once what I was going to be, and I put you off. Well, there it is. I'm going to England next year because I think an American schoolmaster should know all there is to know about English schools. My guardian's arranging to get me into Balliol, at Oxford. Would you like to go to Oxford with me?"

"I should love it!" It was all very startling, but I have always made decisions quickly, and this was an easy one. Harvard had loomed before me like an extension of St. Andrew's, and the prospect of a life abroad and shared with Frank seemed almost impossibly glamorous. "Perhaps I could teach at your school, too. You remember I taught *you* French." But a sudden horrid doubt assailed me. "Would I have to play football?"

Frank threw back his head and roared with laughter. "God forbid! No, you could teach French and handle the mothers when they thought I was being too hard on their precious darlings."

I was enchanted that in two minutes' time my entire future, which until then had been such a dreary blank, should now be so cheerfully disposed of. "Where will the money come from?"

"For the school? What about yours?"

"I don't think I have any," I reported ruefully. "Father always tells me I'll have enough to live on 'decently,' whatever that means, provided I stay a bachelor. If I want to marry, I shall have to work."

Frank seemed to find this enormously funny. In fact, his mood was exuberant now, almost hilarious. "Let's hope that no such terrible sacrifice will be required of you. Don't worry about the money. I have some rich cousins. There's always a bit of money to be had for a worthy cause in Boston. For example, my guardian was able to find a trust fund to pay for the education abroad of any descendant of my great-grandfather."

"So that's why we're going to Oxford!"

Frank winked. "Let's put it that I'm killing two birds with one stone."

I realized that the half bantering, half solemn temper of the conversation had been Frank's way of telling me that my long submitted bid for his friendship had been accepted. There was never anything else said to establish this, but nothing else, to a boy of Frank's reticences, was necessary. I had weathered his coldness, his rebuffs, his actual insults; now they would cease. Once admitted to Frank's intimacy — and I am proud to say that very few have been — one found oneself a life member. He expected to be the dominant partner; he expected me, for example, to attend the college of his choice and to help him in the creation of a school of which *he* would be headmaster. But that was the way I wanted it. I was quite willing to settle for the junior position provided only that I was at liberty to speak my mind.

For the rest of the school year we walked together on Sunday afternoons and made elaborate plans for the future. He lectured me about my triviality and sophistry and tried to interest me in sport, while I mocked him when he took himself too seriously and laughed at his moodiness. The element of the female in my nature matched well with the masculine in his; in many ways our relationship was like that of a strong, single-minded husband and a clever, realistic wife. I quite realize that in the days in which I am writing, it will be impossible for a reader of the last sentence not to jump over a Freudian moon, but I belong to a simpler and less polluted generation. I have always gloried in my conception of friendship, and I will insist to my dying day that it has nothing of sex in it.

For a time it seemed that I had everything in life that I could possibly want: a friend whose approval made me at last a respectable figure on the little campus of St. Andrew's and a European future, just around the corner, that loomed, like the great pack on a Santa Claus' back, with spires of old cathedrals and castle turrets jutting out of its open end. I had, for the first time in my life, everything that I seemed to desire, with everybody's blessing, to boot. And what did I feel? Simply a small, half-recognized, vaguely tickling ennui. It was my first lesson from the gift-bearing Greeks.

The trouble, I found, lay in the very core of my supposed happiness: in my intimacy with Frank. He, too, had never had a confidant before, and once he had overcome his initial reticences, he helped himself, in increasingly liberal doses, to my extravagantly offered attention. He would have listened to me, no doubt, had I had confidences of my own of equal value. But I had little to show for my years of loneliness but my daydreams and fantasies, and he had the whole complicated structure of his school, created in his mind over the adolescent years, course by course, master by master, building by building. No wonder he had been a silent and moody boy. Like Frankenstein, he had been locked away in a mental laboratory, creating his monster.

I call it a monster because I had already begun to fear that it would swallow me. To him it was something far, far different. To him it was nothing less than the source of regeneration of a modern world that had been corrupted by carpetbaggers and venal politicians. Frank believed passionately that the maw of civil strife had swallowed all that had been finest in the generation before us and had ended, fittingly enough for such a holocaust, with the assassination of the sainted Lincoln. Grant was to him the body of the hero which has lost its soul, the plight of a nation of ex-warriors grubbing for gold. And God would work through Francis Prescott, a humble instrument selected to reward his father's sacrifice, to raise up new leaders of men.

"I know it is what my father would have wanted of me," he would tell me somberly, over and over. "It is the only way I can give to God what he gave."

I used to visualize Frank's God with a little shudder as a despondent general, sitting, chin in hand, on a campstool by a tent, like one of those lithographs of Napoleon in Russia, surveying the field of that day's defeat and waiting for a miracle in the morning. Frank's father, his own faith and his projected school were all inextricably intertwined, and my early knowledge of this gave me an insight into some of his later peculiarities as a minister which were to baffle and shock so many. Frank was never to be interested in any souls but those of his boys.

Not only did I have to learn more than I wanted about the administration of Frank's still fictional academy; I had to try to improve my own spiritual qualifications to become a member of his imagined faculty. He sought to discover the state of my religious life and asked me questions about my family with the sometimes brutal frankness of one who had none of his own. I have always been the kind of egotist who likes to talk around, rather than about, myself, and I found his probing painful. Our talks on Sunday used to go something like this:

"I'm afraid you must face the fact, Horace, that your family is a peculiarly worldly one. I doubt if I've ever in my life seen such an emphasis on appearances. Indeed, your father seems to believe in nothing but the *appearance* of believing."

"'That's what he calls 'setting an example.' "

"You admit, then, he's a Pharisee?"

"I admit he's a magnificent one! If you're going to be a Pharisee, you may as well do it with style."

Frank would shake his head, whistle and quicken his pace, and I, stumbling after him, would simply pray that the glories and fascinations of old England would soon divert him from his favorite topic. My prayer was to be fully answered in six months' time, and I was again to learn the malevolence of those seeming generous Greeks.

6

FROM HORACE HAVISTOCK'S
"THE ART OF FRIENDSHIP"

OUR three years at Balliol were a happier time for me than for
Frank. I developed my character into the essential shape which
it possesses to this day, while he pursued his down a side street
that dwindled to a dead end. Yet of the two of us he seemed
the more content.

He took immediately to English life and English ways. It
was as if he had suddenly discovered his natural environ-
ment. He was heartier, louder, funnier, more companionable
and far better dressed, for the Prescott trust permitted him to
become a bit of a dandy. He loved the solid masculine comfort of the English gentleman's life, the large cold stone houses
with their roaring fires, the hunting on foggy moors and the
long dinners at long tables glittering with more jewelry and
silver than seemed quite decent.

He had many letters of introduction from Boston, some to
the highest places, and he was much taken up as a Yankee who
could talk back without being rude, who could praise his own
country without seeming shrill and who was a first class oar and
shot. It seemed to me that he spent rather more time visiting
castles than schools and that his talk was more of foxes and of
wines than it was of masters and boys, but I supposed that this
was all part of his education. That is one of the joys of going to
school abroad; whatever one does can be chalked up to the

imbibing of atmosphere. If Frank, however, seemed to be neglecting the project of his lifework, he did not neglect his courses, for he ended up with a first in "greats" and was offered a fellowship.

I was more Yankee than he in that my eyes kept straying in the direction of Paris. On vacations in France I was apt to spend my time in the capital glutting myself on theatres and art galleries, while Frank bicycled alone through the countryside from cathedral town to cathedral town. When he did come to Paris, he was taken up with pursuits where my presence would have been only an encumbrance, or at least so I assumed, for unlike most young men even of that era, we rarely discussed girls. He was always extraordinarily tactful (when he was not deliberately being rude), and knowing my nature less earthy than his own, he must have supposed that I did not like to be reminded of my unearthiness. Actually, however, I would have been delighted to hear of his conquests. I had grown up while in Oxford and had learned to apologize to nobody for taking my pleasures primarily through the eye and ear.

The crisis towards which we were heading and that I was too obtuse to anticipate exploded at the end of our second year when Frank lost his faith. This was an experience not unusual to serious young men in the last century and was treated as a very grave event. Today, of course, it couldn't happen because nobody has any faith, or if they do, they find it unfashionable to talk about it. But Frank had a very deep one and had been confirmed at his own request at the age of fourteen. His idea of teaching was inextricably tied up with the Episcopal Church, and the only kind of school that he could contemplate founding had always been a church school. I knew instantly, therefore, what a serious matter it was when, pacing back and forth before the fire in my room one night, and stopping occasionally to take a somehow wrathful sip from the glass of whiskey on the mantel, he announced to me that he doubted the divinity of Christ.

"You've been reading too much Renan," I suggested.

"I've been reading a great deal besides Renan," he said with a snort. "I've been reading the early Christian fathers. But you can't get away from the fact that Renan has one terribly valid point. Jesus obviously believed that the resurrection of the dead would occur within the lifetime of his contemporaries. 'Verily I say unto you, There be some standing here, which shall not taste of death, till they see the Son of man coming in his kingdom.'" He became very dry of tone now, like a lawyer with citations. "Matthew 16:28. And again in 10:23. And again in 24:34. And again in Mark, 9:1. And again in Mark, 13:30. And again in Luke, 9:27. And again in Luke, 21:32."

I couldn't help smiling at this show-off of memory. "But not in John? Hasn't John always been your favorite gospel?"

"I find it trivial of you, Horace, to describe a gospel, like a magazine, as a favorite."

"Well, whatever you want to call it then. The most spiritual?"

Frank seemed even more pained at this. "I think I may have described it once as the most sophisticated. In any case, you are partially right. The prediction is *not* made in the same words in John. But you will remember that Jesus hinted that John might not have to die. Which could only have meant that he would live to see the second coming." Here he paused and shook his head. "Matthew, Mark and Luke must have meant *something* by all those statements. And certainly the early fathers took them literally. It explains so much of the casting away of the world. The church had to be totally reconstructed when Christians finally realized that they were in for the long pull."

His worries must seem absurd to twentieth century readers. The teachings of a protestant Christ have long been watered down to a gentle ripple of aphorisms about the poor and meek, and nobody troubles his head any more about the question of divinity. It is probably the work of thousands of loose thinkers like myself. I had read Renan and found his pastoral idyll of a mortal Jesus struggling under his messianic illusion and finding relief in death from his impossible, self-imposed mission a charming one. I now suggested this to Frank.

"Charming!" he cried in disgust. "Is there nothing more important to you than charm? Is that all the gospels mean to you? Charm?"

"Well, I don't see the point of getting all worked up about them. Maybe the Catholics are right in not encouraging the reading of the Bible. Look at the funk it's got you in!"

"How can a man *not* be in a funk if his whole life depends on it?" Frank paused to take another fierce gulp of his drink. "Don't you see, I want to be a *minister?* How can I preach the gospel of a deluded mystic who traveled about the countryside foretelling the end of a world that never came? And consider, Horace, the presumption of such a man if he was not God. How did he dare threaten the multitudes with damnation? Oh no, my friend, I tell you, he's God or nothing." Frank shook his head again, slowly and gravely, half a dozen times.

"You call the Sermon on the Mount nothing?"

"You can find the same principles among the Essenes. There's nothing in the least original about them." He shrugged impatiently and continued to pace about, his voice rising sharply as his argument became more violent. "What I cannot stomach, at least in the founder of *my* faith, are the miracles. As the work of God, they are awe-inspiring. As the work of a mortal, they reduce themselves to the slickest kind of sleight of hand. 'Go thou to the sea and cast an hook and take up the fish that first cometh up, and when thou hast opened his mouth, thou shalt find a piece of money.' 'Go your way into the village over against you: and as soon as ye be entered into it, ye shall find a colt tied, whereupon never man sat; loose him and bring him.' No, I tell you, Horace, it won't do. Even the miracle of the loaves and fishes becomes a cheap catering trick."

At last he had shocked me. I have always thought it the worst possible taste to depreciate religious values. One certainly did not have to swallow the Bible, but a great many reputable people had, and out of respect for them, if nothing else, one should maintain a discreet silence. When it came to heresy, I found that I could, after all, be a Havistock.

"You should have more respect," I reproved him. "After all, even if he was mortal, might he not have been divinely inspired?"

"Divinely inspired to say he was something he *wasn't?* How could that be?"

We kept reverting to the subject again and again, all that winter and spring, until, alas, I was fearfully bored with the whole topic. I finally suggested that he take his problem to our master at Balliol, the famous Dr. Jowett. Frank was at first reluctant to do so; he did not share in the popular cult of the "Jowler." I pointed out that at least the master was an acknowledged theologian, and I eventually pushed him through that door out of which, like Omar, after "great argument about it and about," he eventually emerged — with the same doubts. But in his case, unlike Omar's, an important practical decision had been taken. He was bright-eyed and feverishly cheerful, and he discussed his faithlessness no more.

Jowett was certainly never Frank's idea of a great man. The Master's plump, soft figure, his silvery white smooth hair, his pink, clear countenance and treble voice, his cerebral, epicene manner and the intellectual (and at times social) snobbishness of his conversation struck the young American athlete as the epitome of all that was worst in English education, of all that *his* school, if he ever founded one, was not going to be.

I, on the other hand, delighted in Jowett's dry wit and worldly anecdotes and in the great names which so frequently adorned his discourse. I knew that I could qualify under none of the three headings to which his intimates were supposedly limited: peers, paupers and scholars, but I was determined that I would nonetheless attract his notice. He liked funny stories and he liked gossip, and the first time that Frank and I were asked to dine at the Master's House I was full of both.

"Havistock is a bit of an ass," Jowett later told a blunt Yorkshire lad who bluntly repeated it to me. "And an American ass at that. But a dinner party is pleasanter for his company, and how many men can you say that about?"

How many indeed? I should like his encomium on my tombstone.

Jowett took Frank more seriously, as an aggressive and possibly dangerous Red Indian. During that same first dinner Frank actually suggested a correction in our host's famed translation of Plato. Had he been wrong, it would have been the end of their relationship. But he was right, and, as I have said, Jowett liked scholars.

"And to think that such illumination should come to us from the antipodes!" the Master exclaimed, raising his hands. "The Old World can only bow its head." The tone may have been bantering, but he took out a notebook to record Frank's correction.

Did that wise old man feel a tremor of satisfaction when the brash younger one came to him with his doubts? I think not. Jowett was fundamentally kind. Frank's problems, at least in their initial form, were elementary enough, and the Master was about to suggest a dozen explanations of what Christ had meant by the day of judgment. But he soon discovered that his Yankee pupil had a flare for theological disputation that would have made him at home in the Byzantine Court. Jowett's arguments simply stimulated Frank to deeper research, in Latin, Greek and even Hebrew texts, until he was able to challenge the Master on equal ground.

"If you're the kind of man to lose sleep over whether Jonah was actually swallowed by the whale," Jowett retorted at last, "the church is no place for you. You'd better go back to the fresh breeze of your western prairies."

Of course, they had totally opposite religious temperaments. Jowett admired philosophy; Frank cultivated burning zeal. To one Christianity had been better stated by Plato than by Christ; to the other Christ was all. Frank belonged among the disciples of Phillips Brooks and A. V. G. Allen who gave to Jesus the supreme position in the Trinity which, according to Henry Adams, the thirteenth century had given the Virgin. To Jowett such Christology had a distasteful smack of evangelicism and American exaggeration. To him the life and death of Christ was the life and death of Christ in the soul, the imitation of Christ. As a Platonist he saw everything on earth as broken arcs which merely suggested the perfect rounds above. Christ was essentially a larger segment of arc. To insist that he had to be either all God or all man must have struck Jowett as a crudity of youth.

Nonetheless he might have enjoyed indefinitely his theological debates with a mind as keen as Frank's had it not been for bitter memories of the conflict which had torn the Church of England, years before, on the publication of his own views of biblical interpretation. Jowett had come out all right in the end, but the memory of that fuss and feathers over the exercise of a harmless bit of rationalism had given him an abiding distaste for religious controversy. He had little respect for the clergy and barely regarded himself as one of them.

"I wonder if any really great men are ever clergymen," he speculated one afternoon at tea in my rooms. It was his first visit, and I was very proud.

Frank, of course, picked him right up. "Hildebrand? Ximenes? Richelieu?"

"I'm not talking of statesmen in cassocks, Prescott, but of *clergymen*. Why would a great man want to shackle himself with the *gêne* of a creed?"

"Luther was a great man and a clergyman, and *he* did."

"Ah, Luther. I should have anticipated the name of a rebel from the citizen of a separated arm of the Queen's realm."

"But surely, Master," Frank retorted, "a martyr like yourself should sympathize with rebels."

Jowett's face was inscrutable, and I was breathless. I had never heard anyone twit him before with his ancient heresy. But Frank, it seemed, got away with everything. The Master gave him a long, shrewd stare and said: "It's a pity you weren't a young man in 1776, Prescott. I'm sure you would have greatly enjoyed it."

"Would you, Master, have enjoyed the reign of Mary Tudor?"

Jowett grunted. "Perhaps the bar should be your profession. I'm told that lawyers and judges occupy a unique position in your great nation. Can your courts not invalidate laws of congress? Fancy. I propose, then, that you make your fortune at the bar and secure an early appointment to the bench. The judge in this commercial era is the only person who can enjoy the esteem of the worldly with the detachment of the philosopher. Even the proudest burghers dare not yawn when he quotes Latin."

"At home our judgeships are the spoils of politics."

"Be a politician, then!"

"You are full of alternatives, Master."

"They are all the old can offer."

Frank was repelled by this, and though he remained on friendly terms with the Master he did not again seek his advice in personal matters. He had a young man's distaste for compromise; it seemed to him that one must make a clean choice between God and Mammon. At the time it was Mammon, and there was no further talk of his being a minister or a schoolmaster.

What surprised me most was how much *I* minded. One might have thought that the new, more secular Frank would have been closer to the easygoing and worldly Horace. Yet such was not the case. We remained the closest of friends, but something had gone out of the relationship. In my own odd way, if I could get along without God, I could not seem to get on without God in Frank. I felt that he was turning into someone he was not meant to be — a good person, no doubt, but not the person I had visualized. In brief, I suppose I thought myself let down. After all, I, too, had had a stake in that school. I had hitched my modest but well-appointed wagon to a star, and now, looking ahead, I saw it was only another wagon. I could have done as well on my own.

7

FRANK and I came back to America in the fall of 1881, and he visited with my family for several weeks. He had little idea of what to do or where to live and was disconcertingly open to suggestions. My brother Archie, who had always liked him and found unaccountable his intimacy with me, advised him strongly to stay in New York and go into business. He persuaded Father to give him a letter of introduction to Chauncey Depew, and Frank went off to call at the New York Central offices. He came back, dazzled, to tell us that he had been offered a job in his first interview.

"But I daresay it's not very adventurous to start right off in the biggest company," he concluded.

Archie rebutted vigorously what he called the "vulgar" American fallacy that the big fortunes were all made in new ventures. "Stay with the tried and true," he warned Frank. "That's what the big boys understand. The profit is never 'out' of a good business. Central will double again."

So Frank went to work for the Vanderbilts, the "brownstone Medici," as he called them. His heart was certainly never in railroads, but his shrewd intuition and his quick grasp of detail made him a useful assistant to Depew who was later to be the first chairman of the board of trustees of Justin Martyr. Frank's irreverent amusement at the pomp and power of the

railway great was manifested in a series of witty monologues
that he used to perform for his intimates and, years later, for
the boys at school. His best was of William H. Vanderbilt, in-
terviewed by the press on board his Wagner palace car, shifting
in his plush chair, coughing, snapping his eyes, playing with his
watch fob, mumbling, shy and miserable, and ending finally
with a high squeak: "The public be damned!" The companion
piece was of the same gentleman in his art gallery bargaining
with a dealer for a gory Meissonier battle scene. Frank would
stand, his hands behind his back, his nose two inches from the
purported canvas, studying the detail of a helmet. But there
must have been a dose of admiration in so exact an observance.
Frank all his life had a grudging, half-concealed fascination for
big business. He used to say that if you sold out to Mammon,
you might as well get a seat in the Inner Temple.

In his two years at Central he lived in a small room in a
boardinghouse on lower Madison Avenue and spent his salary
on his clothes and pleasures. He continued the habit that he
had acquired in England of being a bit of a dandy, and on
Sundays he hired a horse to ride in Central Park. With his
looks, his name, his confidence, his ease of manner and his amazing general knowledge, he soon became a popular extra man in
society. New York was worldly and Frank was poor, but this
is always forgiven a bachelor, and was he not a Boston Prescott?
Even the mothers of heiresses did not frown at Frank's brown
eyes and broad shoulders.

He and I once again played reversed roles in that period, for
I found (as I always have since) New York society distinctly
tiresome. There was opulence, but it was a heavy, tawdry opulence, blinking out at one from heavily laden dinner tables
where sour, sleepy-eyed magnates and their stertorous, big-
busted wives overate. There were no artists, no philosophers,
no men of science in that bourgeois world. And worst of all,
there were none of those wonderful, worldly-wise, sympathetic

older women, in whom London and Paris abounded, former beauties or demimondaines, who could talk to a young man of love and art and politics and give him a sense of the continuity of charm in the history of civilized men and women.

My health was bad again; I had constant colds and was beginning already to show symptoms of the arthritis that has nagged me all my life. I spent my days in the comfortable fire-warmed third floor sitting room in which I had lived as a child with Sister Sue at 310 Fifth Avenue. All my brothers were married and had moved away, and Father, turning senile, thought only of dinner invitations which were becoming so rare that I had the mortification of having to solicit them from his old friends. There was little to tempt me away from the manuscript of a novel that I was writing about Newport in the Revolutionary War. It was not a good novel, and it was never published, but it was better than many of the novels that were published in those days.

Inevitably, with my sedentary life and Frank's active one, we saw less of each other. He never let a week go by without calling at the house, but the daily intimacy of our English years was gone, and I found that I wanted another confidant, perhaps even a confidant who was more interested in me and in the things I cared about than Frank, for all his kindness, ever could be. Even in his Mammon days, he always leaned to the general while I tumbled head over heels into the particular; he loved ideas and I personalities; he was all for argument and I yearned for gossip. Neither of us, obviously, could be all in all to the other.

It came as a bit of a shock to me, as it undoubtedly will to the reader of these pages, that my new friend should have materialized at last in the shape of a beautiful and popular young woman, a scant year older then myself. I met Eliza Dean at a small dinner given by Ward McAllister, a foolish fellow but a very kind one, who, when not pursuing the old and grand, like

Mrs. Astor, could give charming parties where, over the best of food and wine, something not too far from conversation was occasionally born.

Eliza was a bit in advance of the Gibson girl, but to some extent she anticipated her. She had thick rich auburn hair, a high ivory forehead, hazel eyes that gazed at one unflinchingly, the straightest of noses and a chin that would have been almost too resolute had it not suggested the proud princess of fairy tale. Eliza moved, too, like a princess, but I think she may have done so to offer an effective contrast to her free candor of manner and a laugh that was as hearty as the West from which she came. She was the only child of a widowered father, a gnarled old leathery 'forty-niner who had once purchased a senate seat and who had now come to New York to retire on Fifth Avenue and launch his beautiful daughter in society. People suspected the most terrible things about his past and something worse about his present, namely that his reputed fortune was largely fictional, but it helped that he, a morose old bird, did not want to go out, and everyone was charmed by his daughter.

Eliza was far too clever to try to compete with New York girls in their own specialties; she knew that the out-of-the-ordinary, properly handled, could be an asset, and she introduced into her conversation a directness, a forthrightness, a kind of high honesty that seemed designed to fill the stuffy interiors of Manhattan with a fresh wind from over the Rockies. Instead of playing the mincing little thing who wanted to be shielded — from nothing — by a masculine arm, she appeared to offer herself as a brave, free companion to a man, the kind of woman who could fire her rifle alongside him in the Indian-besieged stockade, an Elizabeth Zane with an apron full of gunpowder.

But there was a pointed difference. Elizabeth Zane had not been playing a role, and Eliza Dean most decidedly was. Nobody smelled the paint or saw that the cardboard fortress trembled in the breeze but Horace Havistock, and nobody guessed that he smelled or saw such things but Eliza Dean. It was our recognition of each other's skill that formed the rock, albeit a slippery one, on which our friendship was based.

Like myself, she needed a friend and confidant, and he had to be not only a man, for she was one of those women who had little use for her own sex, but a man who would not spoil their special intimacy by falling in love with her. Had it not been for this latter qualification, so firmly set forth at the beginning, I think I might have. Certainly I came as near to falling in love with Eliza as I ever came to falling in love. But I knew that I would have repelled her, awkward reedy creature that I was, and I was glad to settle for friendship and to content myself with being fussed over, like a doll in the hands of a very determined little girl.

Eliza had a pale blue open Landau with red leather upholstery and a coachman in red livery. She used to pick me up twice a week at Number 310 and take me driving in Central Park as far north as the terrace and the Bethesda Fountain and sometimes all the way to Cleopatra's Needle. If it was a good day, we would get out at the Mall and stroll. It was part of her act of independence to be always unchaperoned.

"You shouldn't be writing a novel about the Revolution," she told me on one of those excursions. "What's happening today is far more exciting, right here in Manhattan. Why, you could fit all of revolutionary New York into five or six blocks of the city today!"

"I'll take those five or six blocks, thank you. And I'll leave you that." I pointed down to the Angel on the Bethesda Fountain that we were passing. "In fact I'll make you a present of everything north of Union Square."

"You'd make me the richest and most powerful woman on earth!"

"Why do you care so much about power, Eliza? Is it so important to be able to order your fellow men about? Of course, they're all your slaves, anyway."

"Not Horace Havistock. He's safe." There was a tiny glint

in her eyes as she folded her hands in her muff. "You see, we're utterly different, you and I. You can be perfectly happy just watching the pageant of power. And occasionally sneering at it. But I have to be involved. Oh, don't think that I have a mere vulgar craving for money and preferment." Her hazel eyes were turned on me now, full of a fine scorn at such a concept. "When I speak of power, I mean involvement in all the wonderful things that are going to happen here. Politically and artistically and scientifically. Big business is only a precursor. A herald of the Athenian age. And I want to be in the center of that age!"

"I wonder if the only difference between being 'involved,' as you see yourself, and being a spectator, as you see me, isn't in the choice of seats. You want a box."

She considered this carefully, in all fairness to me. "All right, I want a box," she agreed. "Boxholders, after all, can at least be decorative. They're part of the show."

"Like a queen, you mean? In a royal box?"

"Well, you put it very crudely. But, all right, if you must. Let's say a queen."

"And will it just be you there? Will you be a virgin queen, all alone, or will there be a William for your Mary?"

"Oh, there'll be a William," she answered, with a nod. "There will indeed be a William. I think I even visualize him."

" 'Divinely tall and most divinely fair'?"

"He need be neither tall nor fair. It will be quite sufficient if his face shows character. I shall want him, of course, to have brains and imagination, and ambition, of a noble sort. He need not have money, but he should be able to make it if necessary. I have no wish for a dreamer or for a dry academic type. I want a man of intellect who is also a man of action."

"In other words," I suggested with a smile, "a man who is capable of enjoying the success you expect him to achieve?"

"Precisely. Am I presumptuous?"

"Let's say you're optimistic. What fascinates me, Eliza, is that all the things you want are noble things, yet the mere fact of your wanting them is enough to make you . . . well, may I say the most charming of materialists?"

"You may say a materialist. I make no bones about being a materialist." Indeed, it occurred to me, glancing at that fine profile between the chinchilla hat and the chinchilla neckpiece that she was the portrait of what she professed to be. "But it's only fair to myself to add that I consider us all materialists. What do we have to choose from but material? The question is: do we pick the good or the shoddy?"

"Who are your candidates?"

Eliza laughed her loud, smooth clear laugh. It was a remarkable laugh for a woman, so assured and resonant, so chuckling, with just a hint of scorn that was somehow not in the least wounding. I think it was her laugh that made me almost love her. It seemed to warn you that its owner could take you over, but that you might be better off taken over. "You don't expect me to tell you that, do you?" she demanded. "Who are yours? Do you have a man to meet my high requirements?"

"As a matter of fact, I do. You seemed just now to be sketching his likeness."

"Fancy! Do I know him?"

"You've never mentioned him, so I assume you don't."

"Oh, Horace, *who?*"

"I don't think I'm going to tell you. You'd simply grab him, and I may want to keep him for myself."

"Dog in the manger! *You* can't marry him."

"True. Perhaps the woman has the greater right. But I'm a very selfish person. I don't always regard greater rights."

"What an odious pig you are, if I may change my metaphor. You'd better hide your friend very carefully, then, because I warn you, I shall now be on the watch!"

And she was. Nothing could have whetted her curiosity more than my refusal to give her Frank's name. It was comic to watch her maneuvers and machinations, and the pleasure of it came near to compensating me for the realization — one might almost say the prognostication — that she would, of course, meet Frank and capture him. It was much more likely in the smaller New York society of that time than it would have been today. In fact, it was almost inevitable that two young people who dined out as frequently as Frank and Eliza did should ultimately meet. When Eliza discovered one night that her handsome dinner partner was a Balliol man and a friend of Horace Havistock's, the fat was in the fire. As I learned later from Frank himself, she had burst into her vigorous laugh and exclaimed, to his astonishment and mystification: "So it *is* you, at last! Could Horace have *planned* it this way?"

With him it was a case of love at first sight; with her, of love at first foresight. I assumed uncomfortably that my poor personality had been the kindling to set off the torrid blaze of their initial conversations, but I daresay I was soon consumed. I do not mean that they tore me to pieces, but I am sure that they laughed over my foibles and agreed that I was as spoiled as a pampered kitten. And worse, far worse, whether the idea was ever actually articulated or not, there must have been in the air between them the contrast between the puny baby of friendship that I offered to each and the full grown, wonderful glory of the kind of thing that they offered each other. Oh, yes, they made a beautiful couple, Frank and Eliza, Gibson boy and Gibson girl, standing like newlyweds in an insurance poster to represent all the brave new things that life *seemed* to offer. I could not help but be a bit disgruntled; the sexual happiness of others has always an excluding effect.

Frank had first called at Number 310 in an agony of embarrassment, stomping about my third-floor sitting room with darkened countenance, until he had finally managed to stop and blurt out: "Do you care for her?" When he had been assured that I did not, at least not in the sense that he meant, I had been royally and painfully thumped on the back and hugged. Poor fellow, he had been planning to leave New York to get out of my way if he had found that I was courting Eliza, and I believe he would have done so.

But touched as I was by the loyalty and integrity of my friend, I did not find his companionship in the months that followed very stimulating. He was a greater bore on the subject of Eliza than he had ever been on his school, for he assumed that I, as her friend and intimate, was as interested as he in her greater glorification. Did I know that she had the good taste to prefer German to Italian opera? Was I aware that she was an expert horsewoman? Had I ever encountered such a natural generosity of heart or a mind so cultivated and yet so unspoiled? Was she not head and shoulders above the simpering ninnies who cowered behind their growling mammas and waited for some ass of a moneybag to propose?

"It's uncanny, Horace," he would always end. "I never dreamed that I would meet a girl so close to my ideal. Do you realize that she's simply — *perfect?*"

It was even harder on me to be subjected to the same kind of confidences from Eliza. Never have I known a couple who seemed so uncritically enthusiastic about each other, and the remarkable thing was that their enthusiasm seemed to wax with better acquaintance. I understood it with Frank, for at this period of his life, or rather just prior to his meeting Eliza, he had been showing an increasing taste for extremes. He had talked about giving up his job for the Fiji Islands; he had written reams of florid poetry that made very little sense, and he had filled a sketchbook with pictures of the most grotesque monsters. I discovered that he even spent his Sundays at the city hospitals, reading to patients. It was all perfectly all right, but a bit quixotic, a bit bizarre. Eliza, on the other hand, for all her capacity for excitement, had a very level head. I suspected her of puffing her feelings and demonstrations a bit, and this irritated me.

"It's all very well to deify Frank," I told her one afternoon in the Park, "but sooner or later we have to let him drift back down to earth. Granted that he has brilliant gifts, but what has he done with them? What is he so far but a young man at Central who isn't even engaged to a Vanderbilt?"

"He's engaged to me."

"*Is* he? Since when?"

"Since yesterday."

"Well, congratulations! Has your father consented?"

"Oh, I haven't even asked Father. I'm my own mistress, you know. Father's living on an annuity. When he gave me what little I have, he said: 'Here it is, Liza. There ain't going to be no more. You're on your own now, my gal, and make the most of it.' "

"I trust he gave you enough."

"How much do you think?"

I calculated rapidly for a minute and then made a shrewd guess. Eliza burst into her high laugh. "Really, Horace, you old New Yorkers are beyond anything! Where do you get that financial sixth sense?"

"You mean I was right?"

"A bull's-eye! But how did you *know?* I thought I was supposed to be rich." She shrugged her disdain of such things. "Anyway, we won't starve. Frank's going to get ahead in Central. Mr. Depew told me so himself. And he can go from there to anything. The state legislature, congress, an ambassadorship. Oh, you'll see, Horace. Frank may need a little pushing, but look who he's got to push him!"

"He's an unpredictable man," I said grudgingly.

"That's exactly the excitement! But don't you see, with the talents he has, where can he go but up?"

"Do you know he once wanted to be a minister?"

"Of course. And a schoolteacher. And what a good one he'd have been. But he's left all that behind."

"Yes," I said with a little sigh. "He seems to have left it all a good ways behind."

I believed it when I said it. Afterwards, Eliza always thought that I must have suspected something, and she never forgave me for not giving her an earlier warning. But I could not have. I had reconciled myself completely to the idea of Frank as a railroad man. I had fully accepted the notion that the aspirations of his days at St. Andrew's had been mere adolescent religiosity. Frank, to my mind, had simply reverted to the tradition of his family, as I was reverting to that of mine.

But, indeed, his exhilaration of that period was by no means all love. Love seemed to have been rather the catalytic agent that had started the vibrations of every emotional chord in his being, vibrations that boded to be powerful enough to survive even the removal of the agent itself. I made this all-important discovery one night after a dinner meeting of the Hone Club at our house, where Frank and I were guests. After the last of the old boys had left and I had escorted Father to his bedroom, I was very tired, but Frank, who was never tired himself and did not understand the condition in others, suggested that we have a drink of whiskey before he left. I told him flatly that I wanted to go to bed, but he did not even hear me. He was standing by the long table where Father kept his newspapers, turning the pages of one in sheer nervous activity. This was unlike him, as was the odd little feverish glitter in his eye, and I was suddenly attentive.

"Have you something to tell me?"

He did not turn. "Yes."

"About Eliza?"

"No. I mean yes. Yes, in the sense that nothing happens to me that doesn't concern Eliza."

"Something nice?"

"Something that you would call 'charming.'" He turned around with a smile that I can only describe as radiant. No other adjective would fit it. "I've found my old faith again. I'm going to Boston to see Phillips Brooks on Saturday. He thinks he can get me into divinity school in a month's time."

At this I went to the sideboard to pour myself a generous helping of whiskey. It would mean a terrible headache in the morning, but that no longer mattered. I sat on the sofa, tucked my feet under me, and simply murmured: "Tell."

Frank walked about the room as he told me of his reconversion, his voice jagged with a tense excitement, his hands straying over the surface of tables, tapping books and bronzes, his shiny eyes roving and not seeming quite to take me in when they rested on me. I did not move, except when I took a discreet sip of my drink, nor did I speak, even when he paused for a possible comment. His monologue went something like this:

"I've even had a vision, a visitation, whatever you want to call it. I know that sounds like the most incredible arrogance or the most incredible naïveté — perhaps both — but I don't care. I'm way beyond caring! It didn't happen to me without preparation, as it happened to Paul on the road to Damascus. Oh, no, I was prepared. Only the stubbornest kind of ass could have resisted so much preparation for so long. For, you see, Horace, there's something you don't know about me, something I haven't told a soul. Not even Eliza, at least till the other day. And that is that even after I lost my faith in Oxford, I've never stopped reading the New Testament and the early fathers. In the past year I've read the gospels every night when I came in for two or three hours, in Latin, in Greek, even in French, trying to approach them freshly. Do you know, I can recite Matthew right through? Don't worry, I shan't.

"All I'm really trying to tell you is that the figure of Christ became consistent to me. He *is* the same in all the gospels. Indeed, he is the only thing that is. Verses began to ring in my ears at odd times during the day at the office. 'Why callest thou me good? None is good, save one, that is God.' 'The Son can do nothing of himself, but what he seeth the Father do.' 'For I came down from heaven, not to do mine own will, but the will of him that sent me.'

"Oh, yes, Horace, it is divinely assured selflessness. The selflessness that comes from an absolute knowledge that the praise or scorn of the world is a total irrelevance. The mortal part of Jesus, the assumed shell of the Godhead, hardly exists in the gospels, except for a few twinges, the agony in the garden, the cry from the cross. And even here, in Christ's passion, it is the pain of the Father over what men are doing to his son and hence to themsleves. It is the rejection, not the torture that concerns him. And I began to see that the discrepancies and oddities of the gospels are the discrepancies and oddities of mortal writers, mortal witnesses."

He paused here so long that I thought I had to say something. "Was that your vision?"

"Oh, no." He became even graver now. "My vision came a month ago, one night when I had not been able to sleep. I had lain awake, thinking about the passion, until almost dawn. I suppose you will say that I fell asleep, exhausted at last, and dreamed my vision. It doesn't matter. It was equally real, awake or asleep. It was the sudden appearance by my bed of my father. No, not by my bed. He was somehow everywhere in the room, I can't explain. He did not look like the daguerrotypes that I have seen or like Aunt Jane's miniature, yet I knew that it was he. He was very pale, haggard, perhaps unshaven, in uniform, and for some reason he had his left arm in a sling. He shook his head slowly at me and said in a reproachful voice — but, oh, the kindest, Horace, you ever heard, the very kindest! — 'Frank, my poor boy, how many times must you be told before you *see*?' "

Here Frank, overwrought, dropped suddenly into a chair and

covered his face with his hands. "To think I had to have a sign! To think I had to disturb my poor father's spirit before I believed! To think I was worse than Saint Thomas!" His voice rose now to a pitch that made me apprehensive of hysteria. "Unless I could see the print of the nails and put my fingers into the print of the nails and thrust my hand into his side, I would not believe. And Christ was as good to me as he was good to Thomas, his own apostle, and took my fingers and made me feel the print of the nails in his flesh and took my hand and thrust it into his side. Oh, Horace, if only I am spared long enough to make *some* return for that!"

I felt at last that I had to pull him up. "Is there any reason to think that you won't be? Do you interpret your vision as implying an early demise?"

He looked startled for a minute, as if at hearing me talk at all. Then he smiled, his old smile, and he was Frank again. "No, of course not. And forgive me, old fellow, for running so off at the mouth. I've given you a dose of it, haven't I? But that's what friends are for. I had to tell somebody."

"Haven't you told Eliza?"

"Oh, yes. But not in quite such detail. Women hate the abstract, you know. The point she went straight to was my giving up Central to become a minister."

"I can imagine. And how did she take it?"

"She was a brick, Horace. A perfect brick. Which I'm sure comes as no surprise to you." He rose now, looking tired himself at last, and came over to put his hand on my shoulder. "It was a shock to her, of course. She hadn't planned on being a minister's wife, much less a schoolteacher's. She broke down at first and actually wept. Oh, it was hard, I can tell you. But the next day she was much calmer. She said she'd have to think it over while I was in Boston. But I have an instinct that she's going to stick."

"No doubt she is readjusting *her* vision to include an archepiscopal palace."

"Now, Horace, don't be mean. Go to bed and pray that she'll stick. Can you imagine a more magnificent headmaster's wife? And you know she'd love it when she really got into it!"

"Yes," I said bitterly. "I can see it all. *Jo's Boys.*"

At that he left me, good-natured enough to laugh, and I finished my drink, deriving a sour satisfaction by contemplating how wretchedly I was bound to feel in the morning.

Eliza was cool and quiet the next time that she took me driving. She was as beautiful as ever, and everything she did, even pouting, she did with a natural grace, but it was evident that she was thwarted, terribly thwarted, and frustration is the hardest thing in the world for a woman to make attractive. When she did begin to talk, it was to question me closely on how long I had known of Frank's state of mind.

"Well, does it matter," I finally put to her, with some impatience in my tone, "how much I guessed and when? I tell you it came as a complete surprise to me, and you won't accept that. But the important thing is that Frank has found his faith again and is happy. Personally, I'm delighted."

"It's all very well for you to say that. It doesn't affect *your* future."

"On the contrary. If Frank ever starts his school, he may renew his old offer to me to be a master. It could change my whole life."

"*You?* A master?"

"Well, why not?" I demanded, stung by her tone. "Do you think all masters have to be athletes? Do you think there are no sensitive boys who might profit by a cultivated teacher who cares more about art and literature than football? I know I might have been much less miserable at St. Andrew's had there been a Horace Havistock on the faculty."

"I'm sure you would have," she said placatingly, retreating before my sharpened tone. "You must remember that as an only child I've had very little to do with boys. However," she continued with a sigh, looking pensively across the Mall, "it appears that yawning gap is going to be amply filled."

I glanced around. "You mean you're going through with it?"

Her answering look was aloof and steady. "I thought that I had told you. Frank and I are engaged."

"But it hasn't been announced. I should think you were both still free to withdraw."

"What makes you think I want to?"

What indeed? And what made me so sure that she ought to? When I look back upon my decision of that afternoon, it strikes me as sufficiently uncanny. How did I, who had never interfered to the smallest degree in the affairs of others, who had confined myself to chatter over the past and passive speculation as to the future, have the courage, or perhaps I should say the nerve, to betray my best friend by plunging into the troubled tub of his engagement and pulling out the stopper? And how, furthermore, did I manage to do it without any qualms of conscience (besides the shivering from my natural tension at the idea of any action at all) when I knew that my soul was full of a complicated jealousy that Eliza and Frank should each be taking the other from me? Yet I seemed to have had no doubt at all that I was doing the right thing. Could the angel or imp that had sent Frank's father to him have intervened again through me?

"Don't marry him," I said flatly. "Don't marry him, I beg of you."

Eliza did not even blink as she stared at me. Yet she seemed to sense that such impudence must have sprung from a strong conviction, based on something she had yet to learn. "Why should I not?"

"Because you'd make each other miserable."

She drew a quick breath. "I think you underestimate me, Horace."

"Oh, no, I don't! You'd be superb. You'd handle them all

magnificently, the little boys, the mothers, the masters and their wives. You'd be beautiful and gracious and decorative and brave. Oh, you'd do it to the queen's taste. And the better you did it, the worse it would be for both of you. Frank would see that he had taken you from the great world where your talents were meant to shine and squandered them in a New England backwater. And you would see it, too. Oh, you would, Eliza! No matter how desperately you tried to hide it from him. You would both always know that you had been sacrificed."

Eliza ran the tips of her forefingers gently across her eyelashes. I wondered if she was catching a stray, rebel tear. If so, her gesture had made the others retreat. It was difficult to tell such things with Eliza. "Perhaps I should be subtler than you think."

"Impossible."

"Why impossible?" she asked, annoyed. "There's one thing that you discount. That *you*, of course, would have to discount. It so happens that I love Frank."

"Oh, love."

"Yes, love!" she exclaimed angrily. "Don't smile at me in that cool, cynical way. If you could see how immature you looked! Only little boys and old men sneer at love. I happen to love Frank Prescott, and he happens to love me."

"Great lovers have made great sacrifices."

She opened her lips to retort and then closed them. Something about my persistence evidently frightened her. "How *can* you go on that way?" she cried in exasperation. "How can you be so sure about what other people should do and not do?"

"Because I know you, Eliza. I know what we have in common. Something that has nothing to do with Frank. We're hopeless egoists, you and I. We want the nicest things, oh, the very nicest things, for ourselves and others, but the best thing about those nice things is always going to be the little personal touch that *we* can give them. You'd never see Frank's school in any other light than as a backdrop for a beautiful headmistress. An inadequate backdrop, at that. And ultimately it would become a backdrop for the pageant of the splendid good sportsmanship of Mrs. Prescott who has given up the world for her husband. I can see you, Eliza, in maturer years, grey and slim and still so lovely, confiding to some soft, admiring long-haired sixth form Horace Havistock, over tea and crumpets, the secret chagrin of your sacrifice."

Eliza's eyes really blazed at this. "Stop, Tom!" she called to her coachman. "Mr. Havistock is getting out."

"Really, Eliza!" I protested. "In the middle of the Park!"

"Then *I'll* get out!" she retorted, and in another moment she was out of the carriage and walking at a rapid pace eastward along the sidewalk. "Take Mr. Havistock home!" she called back over her shoulder. "I'll walk."

I told Tom to trail her at a discreet distance, and although she must have known we were there, she never turned her head as she strode resolutely forward. At first I was amused, but as I continued to watch her straight, fast-moving figure from the slowly joggling carriage I became uneasy. Could I have been wrong? Had I underestimated that strong, beautiful creature who swept along ahead of me, causing every passerby to turn and stare? For fully half an hour we must have continued our strange procession, while I shifted back and forth between conviction and doubt, until I noticed that she had stopped and was waiting, still without turning, for us to catch up. As Tom brought the carriage slowly abreast of her, she turned abruptly and got in. "Home now," she said and sat in silence, her head averted from me, her brooding eyes taking in the brown sky line to the south.

"I tell you what I've decided," she said at last, still without looking at me. "If I do give Frank up, I shall expect you to do the same."

"You mean, give him up as a friend?"

"No. I mean, give up the idea of being a schoolteacher. In *his* school, at least."

"I doubt if I'd be asked in any other."

"Then there it is. You won't be a schoolteacher."

I had not really thought I had much wanted to be, but now, in the perverse way of humans, I felt that I might be giving up the one occupation for which I was suited. "But why?" I demanded in bewilderment. "Why should you care? Is it just spite?"

"You should know me better," she retorted scornfully. "I don't do things out of spite. I may, as you say, be an egoist, but I hope I'm not a petty one. No, if I give Frank up, it will be because I want him to be free and untrammeled in his new life. If you can sense the corruption in me, it is, by your own admission, because there's a dose of it in you. Let there be none of it at all in Frank's school."

It is odd, but I think I was flattered. I had always been considered such a nonentity where human relations were concerned that the idea that I might have an influence, even a corrupting influence, on one as strong as Frank penetrated my heart with a fierce little sting of pleasure. To be allied with this magnificent girl in a team that might detract Parsifal from his quest of the Grail was to be given at last, was it not, a role in the opera? And wasn't Eliza correct? Had I not felt in my own heart that things were most right with Frank when he had been most alone with his God? I made up my mind in a moment.

"I give you my word," I told her solemnly, "that I will never be a schoolteacher."

"Even if I *should* marry Frank?"

"Oh, particularly not then!" I exclaimed. "I couldn't bear to see a chapter of the gospel turned into a chapter of Trollope." After this, we finished our drive in silence, for I understood, with absolute clarity and for the first time in my life, what a woman was like. I knew then and there that Eliza would never forgive me.

I did not see Frank for several days, but when he called next at the house I was at once aware from his somber face that Eliza must have communicated her decision. Walking about my room as I sat by the fire, he told me about it in harsh, clipped phrases. A life in the church, he said dryly, was evidently not the life for Eliza. He then excoriated New York, its society, its money, its worldliness. We lived in the vilest of ages. By my silence I agreed.

"Oh, what a bloody ass I am!" he cried suddenly, turning on me with a violence that made me jump. "As if a girl like that would want to tie herself up with a shaveling priest who hasn't even taken his orders! I wooed her under false pretenses, Horace. It is *I* who am vile!"

Then he came and sat by the fire and stared into it moodily for five good minutes. When he spoke his voice had a curious softness that I did not remember having heard before, like a sigh after the passage of some terrible pain.

"I thought I was not going to have anything to give up, Horace. I thought I was to have no test. I knew that I could leave the Central and all its rails and the fortune that glittered at the end of them with joy. With *joy!* But I dreamed that I would step forward into the service of God with a strong, beautiful woman on my arm, a helpmate, like an illustration for the last chapter of a Thackeray novel. O God, what fatuousness!" He leaned his head suddenly down in his hands and actually sobbed. "Of course, *she* was the sacrifice you wanted, Lord. So be it. Thy will. *Thy* will. I should be happy to be able to give up something so dear!"

After this outburst, which left me in a rigid shock of embarrassment, he played backgammon with me in morose silence for a full hour and then went home. Never again would he discuss

Eliza with me. In fact, he reverted to the fifth former at St. Andrew's who had had no need to communicate his inner discomforts. But then why should he have? Presumably he had discovered a higher source of consolation.

He resigned from Central the following week with the full approval of Mr. Depew who was much impressed that a call to the ministry should have been heard above the worldly bustle of his office. Frank even received a hand-written letter of good wishes from Mr. Vanderbilt which went far to allay Archie's violent objections to his step. He then departed for Cambridge to commence his divinity studies, which were apparently to be paid for by another of the mysterious Prescott trusts, and for the first time in seven years I ceased to see him regularly. It was a great light out of my life, but I had learned that one had to have spare luminaries.

I visited Frank in Boston on several occasions in the next two years. I stayed with his dear old aunt in Marlborough Street, and he came over from Cambridge to spend the evenings with me. He seemed in good spirits, but preoccupied with his work, and it was no surprise to any of us when he graduated first in his class. He spoke in a kindly tone of his classmates, but I knew him well enough to sense that he was discouraged by the quality of their intellects. He was to struggle all his life to avoid condescension to his fellow clergymen. "If the church," he once told me, "appealed to the kind of young men who went into New York Central, it would soon conquer the world." But, of course, it didn't so appeal. It didn't, if the truth be told, fundamentally appeal to Frank. He took orders only because he wanted to found a church school, and he sought to get his studies and ordination behind him as quickly as possible.

He had one diversion, however, and that was Harriet Winslow. She was totally different from all the girls in whom I had ever observed him to take an interest, but in her own way she was quite as individual and quite as remarkable as Eliza Dean.

She was plain, but magnificently plain, with a high, intellectual brow, a large, thin, very white aquiline nose and green eyes that seemed to look through the toughest barricade of one's own complacency. A grand-niece of Emerson, she could read Latin and speak German, but she had the reticence of a lady about pushing herself forward. She was neat, efficient, quiet, firm and, to my mind, charming. She belonged to the inner circle of Boston society, the only society in America that Frank ever really enjoyed, being like its English counterpart, unpretentious, self-assured, eccentric and, in parts, genuinely intellectual.

Harriet won my everlasting loyalty by understanding from the beginning that, different though we were, Frank had no better friend than I. She proceeded promptly to establish her own independent relationship with me and on two occasions invited me to lunch at her family's without Frank. It was evident to me that in her quiet but unyielding fashion she was determined to marry him and had accepted as entirely natural that his feeling for her was never going to be what hers was for him. I applauded her resolution in my heart (needless to say, we never discussed it), for it seemed to me that she had everything Frank needed in his chosen life, and so indeed it has proven. I think she even had money, but how does one tell with Bostonians?

I have never known how much she knew about Eliza Dean, but, if she did, she always had the heart and the intelligence neither to resent nor to apologize for the fact that she was second best. When, standing at the side of the newly ordained Francis Prescott, I watched his bride approach us down the aisle, I knew that on that afternoon in Central Park by the Bethesda Fountain I had done the best job in my life.

Nor was it only for him. It was for Eliza, too. She gave up the false start of Manhattan and returned to the West when her father died where she married the man who had bought his

mines. He was much older and left her hugely rich. Thereafter she married Byram Shaw, of Wilson's cabinet, and had a
splendid career in Paris when he was ambassador. She lives
today in a Genoese palazzo on Du Pont Circle in Washington
and gives those great diplomatic-political receptions of which
everybody knows. She has aged gracefully, but she has become
even more Western in tone and manner than she was in the
early days in New York. In fact, it has become her distinctive
mark.

She has always been cordial to me, but our intimacy has
never been resumed. When David Griscam was making his big
fund drive for Justin Martyr and asked me for the names of
possible donors, I gave him Eliza's. He wrote to her twice, but
received neither acknowledgment nor contribution. She must
have felt that she had done enough for the school.

8

NOVEMBER 15, 1940. Here I have been back at Justin for two months without a single entry, but the purpose of my journal is Dr. Prescott, and I have not seen him alone more than twice since the term started. However superior I run the risk of sounding, I cannot feel that it is my mission to record what everybody could record and what, it now seems, everybody *is* recording. Poor Dr. Prescott has become a public event.

I am no longer his assistant because Mr. Ives, who is also re tiring in the spring, has turned over his own executive duties to Mr. Anders and now has time himself to help the headmaster. But worse than this, it is difficult even to get near Dr. Prescott. The whole world of Justin's graduates and friends is awake to the fact that it is his final year, and all want a last glimpse of him in office. Every week that goes by contains a "last" something that must be duly commemorated: the headmaster's speech on the school birthday dinner, his "fight talk" before the Chelton game, his halloween monologue on parlor night.

Graduates come up for a look, a handshake, a snapshot, a bit of talk. Dr. Prescott lives as publicly as a monarch at Versailles. But whereas Louis XIV had only one Saint-Simon among his courtiers, the Rector of Justin seems to have as many as he has graduates. I sometimes feel that I'm the only person on the campus who's not actively engaged in "writing him up," and I've only stopped because I want to be the only one.

There is a professional cameraman here now to make a film, commissioned by the trustees, of a typical day in the headmaster's life. A recording has already been made of one of his sermons. And there is a big easel up in his study in the Schoolhouse where an artist paints him as he works at his desk. I feel that if I so much as stop by to bid him good morning, I run the risk of seeming to be trying to encroach my little ego on the glorious illuminated page of his personal history.

Yet he himself has never been more wonderful. He seems totally resigned to the circus of these final months; he is more than philosophic — he is benign. He smiles with unfailing charm at the gaping world about him. The agony of decision is over, and he appears to be reconciled to the prospect leaving his creation in inferior hands. Perhaps he has reflected that those hands, after all, are also in God's. Nothing in his headmastership becomes him more than the leaving it.

January 21, 1941. He sent for me last Monday and suggested that I attend one of his sacred studies classes.

"If you do become a minister and if you decide to go on with teaching, you will have to face the fact that you'll always be stuck with sacred studies. It might not do you any harm to see how I do it. After all, I've been at it half a century."

This morning I sat in the back of the classroom hung with maps of the Holy Land and the Roman Empire which adjoins his office and watched him with the second division of the fifth form. Like all great plans, his is basically a simple one. Fifth formers have had their biblical and church history, and Dr. Prescott tries to tie the church into their other courses. He calls on a boy and asks what he is studying that day in Latin, history or mathematics and takes the discussion from this.

Today he chose history, and Jimmie Abercrombie answered on the day's assignment.

"The Thirty Years' War, sir."

"Dear me, *all* of it?"

"Well, I think, sir, today Mr. Evans was planning to discuss the role of Richelieu."

"Ah. The role of Cardinal Richelieu. Do you know, Abercrombie, what the Pope is supposed to have said when Cardinal Richelieu died?"

"No, sir. I don't believe it was in the lesson."

"Must we limit ourselves to the lesson, Abercrombie? May we not talk, you and I? May we not seek a bit of truth, hand in hand, so to speak?"

"Oh, yes, sir. I suppose so, sir."

"Thank you, Abercrombie. The Pope is supposed to have said: 'If there be a God, the cardinal will have much to answer for. If not . . .'" Here Dr. Prescott gave a monumental shrug. "'Well, if not, he led a successful life.' Have you any comment on that, Abercrombie?"

"Well, of course, *I* believe in God, sir. It seems strange that a pope should say a thing like that."

"Popes in the seventeenth century were in some ways very broad-minded. As to what things popes were allowed to say. Then you would agree that the cardinal had much to answer for?"

"I suppose he did his best, sir."

"For mankind? Or for France?"

"Oh for France, sir. That was his duty, wasn't it? To his king?"

The headmaster's deep brown eyes here fixed on Abercrombie for a moment of silent reverie. "Evidently *he* thought so. Do you know what he said on his deathbed?"

"No, sir, it wasn't . . ."

"In the lesson. I am aware of that. But I will tell you. He was asked if he had forgiven his enemies. 'I have none,' came the serene reply, 'but those of France.' The man who has been called the architect of modern Europe was evidently satisfied with his handiwork. Think of that, Abercrombie!"

"Shouldn't he have been, sir?"

"I see, Abercrombie, that you are not in a speculative mood. Let us return to the letter of the lesson where you may feel more at ease. What *was* Richelieu's policy in the Thirty Years' War?"

"To support the Protestant cause, sir."

"You astound me, Abercrombie. I had thought he was a prince of the Roman Church."

"He was, sir. That's why he had to do it secretly. Sometimes he helped the Catholics, too. He had to keep the civil war going in Germany as long as he could."

"*Had* to, Abercrombie?"

"Yes, sir. To weaken the power of the Hapsburg alliance."

"Do you think that was ethical, Abercrombie?"

"It worked, sir!"

Dr. Prescott laughed cheerfully now. "What a pragmatist we have in our midst! Does it mean nothing to you, Abercrombie, that millions may have died to effectuate that policy?"

"But not millions of Frenchmen, sir. Richelieu made France the first power in Europe. It wasn't *his* fault if people in other countries were stupid enough to fight about religion."

"And would it have been the duty of the British government during our own civil war to support both sides to prolong the conflict?"

"Perhaps that was different, sir."

"Why? We were stupid enough to fight about slavery, weren't we?"

"Very well then, sir, perhaps it *might* have been Britain's duty. From Britain's point of view."

"Bravo, Abercrombie! You have the courage to be consistent. I don't know that I agree with your ethics, but I concede they might have been those of my old master at Balliol, a most esteemed scholar. They are certainly those of the political world. But let me put you one more question. A general question, Abercrombie, having nothing to do with marks or lessons.

As you look abroad today at a Europe in flames, created by just such policies as Richelieu's, does it not occur to you that the cardinal's inspiration may have been something less than divine?"

"Perhaps, sir. Yes, sir."

"Thank you, Abercrombie. I guess I made it sufficiently clear what answer I wanted."

April 2, 1941. I had an experience today which may have been a reminder of my "call." It has certainly added to the little store of material in this folder and restimulated my zeal as a recorder. But before relating what happened I must briefly describe Mr. David Griscam, chairman of the Justin trustees. He has not appeared in these pages before as I had not thought him of such significance in Dr. Prescott's life. His appearance is deceptive.

He is reputed to be a very good friend of the school. He was taken into Justin early in its history as the penniless child of an absconded financier and has ever since rather lavishly demonstrated his gratitude. Despite a brilliant career at the New York bar, a wealthy marriage and two minor ambassadorships, Justin, according to the all-knowing Ives, has always remained his primary interest. But he does not believe that a trustee's function is simply to raise money, nor does he always behave with the subservience that Dr. Prescott has come to expect from his board. Or rather, according to Mr. Ives, he may behave with subservience at Justin but acts otherwise when he gets back to New York. He has distinct ideas of his own, and they are not always the headmaster's.

Certainly, at least, he *looks* acquiescent. That is what first put me off. He makes a great fuss over Dr. Prescott, who doesn't like to be made a fuss over. I suspect Mr. Griscam of being one of those outwardly deferring, inwardly resisting men who care more about the fuss they're making than how it is received. He is of middling stature, with a good head of smooth grey hair, tranquil grey eyes and what he must consider, from the way he keeps turning his profile to the viewer, an aristocratic Roman nose. Everything about him, however, suggests to me the small man who would like to seem larger, the guest who is trying to look like one of the portraits in the club. I do not mean to be uncharitable, but Mr. Griscam is a most enigmatic character.

This afternoon I met him and Dr. Prescott walking back from the river. I nodded respectfully as they were about to pass, but the headmaster reached out and caught my arm.

"Come, Brian, and join two old men who are bored with each other's company. We'll have a look at the baseball and then have some tea."

His firm grip admitted of no refusal, and I obediently joined them. The headmaster was in a curious mood. He was joking, but his jokes were very dry, like his inclusion of Mr. Griscam, who must have been fifteen years his junior, in the term "two old men."

"I have never much cared for baseball," Dr. Prescott continued as we walked, "but that's my generation. I detest all the chatter. Football is my sport, a clean, silent game." As we crossed to a little summit overlooking the diamond, we passed two boys with tennis rackets coming from the courts in back. "Oh, yes, I allow the fifth and sixth forms to elect tennis now," he said, noting Mr. Griscam's stare, "so long as some of them feel they cannot stomach baseball or crew. You see, David, there is no end to my broadmindedness! Despite my great age and imminent retirement I continue, as they say in magazine fiction, to 'grow.' "

"Who persuaded you of that? You used to call tennis a game for mollycoddles."

"This young man here."

"Aspinwall?" I felt the prick of Mr. Griscam's quick suspicious stare.

"None other. Oh, he is quite transforming me. He is my Father Joseph or my Colonel House. Or my John Brown, depending on the point of view."

Mr. Griscam smiled at the picture of me as Queen Victoria's gilly. "Does he spike your tea with whiskey?" he asked.

"No, Brian is too pure. In fact, I may have to spike his." Dr. Prescott paused for a moment as we watched the baseball. "He made a persuasive argument that it might be as developing to a boy's character to stand out against organized sports as to play them. That it takes courage to be a mollycoddle!" He turned on me now in a sudden quixotic reaction against the very argument by which he had allowed himself to be persuaded. "Perhaps we *have* reached the point where we must talk of courage in such terms. Perhaps it *does* take guts to face a frown, a sneer, a clatter of teacups. There was a time when it took courage to have one's tongue branded or one's ears shorn off or to be broken on a wheel. Don't tell me physical courage isn't the greatest!" He walked away abruptly from the diamond, and as we followed him, I heard him mutter: "The war will teach our young men that. Oh, yes, alas, it will."

Mr. Griscam asked where we were going.

"To tea, of course. Or whiskey. Whichever you want. I can see you have no eye for baseball. There's only *one* subject on your mind. Prize Day."

We had tea in a corner of the square study from whose wide west window one could see across the campus to the chapel. The twelve Caesars occupied niches in three walls covered from floor to ceiling with books. Since his wife's death Dr. Prescott never uses the living room or parlor except for large occasions. Mr. Griscam began talking of plans for Prize Day. He said it should be celebrated as a jubilee and not a leave-taking.

"I'd like to see it as a day of thanksgiving, Frank," he explained earnestly, "with as many graduates coming back as can be accommodated. A thanksgiving for Francis Prescott. We could run buses down from Boston. I know all the trustees feel it should be an ovation to your fifty-five years in office."

"You see what they're trying to do to me, Brian?" Dr. Prescott demanded with a wry smile. "They're trying to bury me with praise. To mummify me with laudation. In the next months, or years if I am spared, I shall be choked with testimonials. I'll become like a bad marble statue in a public park with puckered brow and those wrinkled trousers that the Victorian sculptors used to carve so lovingly. Ugh! If I live to be ninety I may catch a whiff of the same kind of horror that Wendell Holmes went through. I may even get to like it. That's the worst of it."

"But it won't be like that, Frank. It will be a simple ceremony, deeply felt."

"Don't tell me what those things are like, David. I've spent my life attending them. I do not wish this Prize Day to be different from any other Prize Day. When I go, I go. That's all there is to it. Is that understood?"

Poor Mr. Griscam looked crestfallen. "But we've made such plans, Frank. You mean it's really no?"

"I mean it's really no." Dr. Prescott allowed his lips to crease into the briefest smile. "I've always said that if a headmaster's vocabulary were limited to a single word, he might still get by with 'no.'" And then he added, as if with a sense at last that he might have been too rough: "Besides, I'm not really leaving Justin. I've rented the Andrews cottage just down the road."

"Oh, *have* you?" Mr. Griscam asked. "I didn't know that."

"I suppose I am entitled to select my own place of abode," Dr. Prescott said dryly. "*After* my retirement, of course."

"I wasn't suggesting the contrary."

"But you don't approve?"

"Did you expect I would? Is it fair to Duncan Moore?"

"Well, he must learn to put up with it!" Dr. Prescott rose now and paced heavily across the room. "There's got to be some limit to what's demanded of the old. We have to step down when we still feel able to go on. We have to keep out of the way of our children. We have to avoid embarrassing youth with the reminder of what it will come to."

"Don't I know!"

"Pshaw, you're a child, David. Sixty-five, isn't that it? Besides, you have a pot full of money. That's the only way to be respected by the young in this country."

"It isn't a question of age," Mr. Griscam insisted. "It's a question of *you*. You don't realize the force of your personality. How can Duncan Moore be anything while you're still here?"

The headmaster seemed now to regret that he had mentioned the matter. There was almost a coaxing note in his voice. "You'll see, David. In my little house I'll be no more trouble than if it were my grave. Anyway, I've already signed the lease. And all three girls approve. I shan't, at any rate, be inflicting myself on them. With or without my hundred knights."

Mr. Griscam obviously saw that further argument would be vain. "Well I didn't come to advise you about your retirement, Frank. I didn't even come, despite what you say, to praise you. I came to . . ."

"Bury me?" Dr. Prescott sat down again at the table and, raising his cup to his lips, drank off half of it rather noisily. "Have the trustees asked you to commission a fitting mausoleum?"

"Nobody has asked me to do anything. This is entirely my own project." Mr. Griscam paused, and my heart jumped when he proceeded to say exactly what I had divined that he was going to say. "I want to write your life."

"Great Scott, man!" Dr. Prescott exclaimed, putting down

his cup with a clatter. "Is Griscam on *Inter-Vivos Trusts* to become Griscam on Prescott?"

"I've known you since I was a child," the chairman continued stubbornly. "I'm one of your earliest graduates, and I've been a trustee of the school longer than anyone. Who else is more qualified? Can't I have a try at it?"

"A try? How on earth can I stop you?"

"By asking me to stop."

The headmaster shook his head impatiently. "I should not dream of giving so small a matter the dignity of a refusal. You may do as you choose."

"But would you cooperate?"

"How?"

"By talking to me about your life with some degree of candor?"

"Never!"

"Then how am I to do it?"

"That's *your* problem. Do you think I will voluntarily assist at my own Stracheyfication?" Dr. Prescott's tone was sharply mocking again. "Do you think I want posterity to know all my foibles through the probing lawyer's eye of David Griscam? No, if you must write a book about me, why not do it in the great Victorian tradition of the two-volume life and letters? With plates of bad portraits covered with onion skin and an index listing my characteristics, such as courage, magnanimity, foresight, judgment, prudence, and so forth?"

"Who would read it?"

"*I* would! If I have lived only to be your subject, David, and you only to be my biographer, why shouldn't we both get some fun out of it?"

"Let's talk of something else," Mr. Griscam said with a sigh. "You're obviously not in a mood for this today."

"No doubt you'll find Duncan Moore an easier headmaster to handle."

I was suddenly sorry for Mr. Griscam. Dr. Prescott's gibes glanced off me as they drove home into his poor trustee who now said in a voice that trembled: "You know how much of my life you've been, Frank. It's bad taste to pretend I won't regret you."

But he should have known that Dr. Prescott was an old hand in dousing sentiment. "That's just why I'm staying!" he cried remorselessly. "That's why I'm taking the Andrews house."

I got up as I heard the "outside" tolling the end of afternoon sports and excused myself to get ready for the Lawrence House study period. Not since my first month at Justin Martyr had I been happy to leave the headmaster's presence. I would not have believed that he could be cruel.

I had not, however, heard the end of it. Tonight, as I was walking down my darkened dormitory after bidding the boys good night and switching off the overhead lights, I saw ahead through the open door to my study that I had no less a visitor than Mr. Griscam himself. He was standing with his back to the doorway, studying the little portrait of Samuel Richardson which hangs over the mantel. This is my one great treasure, given me on my twenty-first birthday by Mother and Father. Painted on copper, it depicts the father of the English novel at the height of his glory, with a seraphic smile on his serene, round face and a black velvet cap on his bald head, holding a manuscript on a board stiffly out before him.

"Which one do you suppose he's writing?" Mr. Griscam asked, without turning, when he heard my step. A frequent visitor, he is at home anywhere in the school.

"Oh, *Clarissa*," I exclaimed. "At least, that's what I like to think."

"He doesn't seem to be undergoing many of the pangs of creation."

"But should he? Shouldn't the man who's writing the greatest of English novels *beam?*"

"*Clarissa!*" He turned to me now, and his smile, if disbelieving, was kindly. "Is it really that?"

"Well, to me it is. I don't think anyone else could have written so wonderfully about a villain without, deep down, admiring him. The way Milton admires Satan. But I feel Richardson *detests* Lovelace."

"You don't think he envies him a bit?"

"Oh, no!" But now at last I pulled myself together. "What am I thinking of, Mr. Ambassador? Won't you sit down?"

"Please don't call me 'Mr. Ambassador,'" he replied as he settled himself in the armchair by my desk and pulled out his pipe. "I no longer am one, and, besides, Panama is a very small country. I hope you don't mind my popping in on you?"

"I'm most honored." As he filled his pipe, I continued, a bit constrainedly: "But you read Richardson? You like him?"

"I know that note of surprise," he answered with a chuckle. "English teachers are always shocked to find that Wall Street can be literate. You think of us as bullying sparrows who peck canaries to death because we cannot sing. As men who may collect but who never read."

"I'm sure you must do both."

"Oh, I've picked up a few nice things. Especially in the Elizabethans whom Dr. Prescott tells me you admire. To me they're all gold and ebony. They light up the sky of our grey world. Don't you find it so?"

I think it was at this point that I began to have a glimmer of sympathy for Dr. Prescott's disputatiousness with the chairman of his board. There is something about Mr. Griscam that makes one want to take issue with him. It may be the implication in his tone that it is a higher thing for him, a busy man of affairs, to have discovered literature than for a poor teacher. Yet his words imply humility. "I find I don't believe in the things they believed in," I replied. "I don't see it's so vitally important for women to be chaste. I mean so much more important than anything else. And I don't think it's so terrible to die. Why were they so obsessed with symbols of transiency: grinning skulls and graveyards? I *know* we have only a few petty moments of mortal time, and I think it's quite enough."

Mr. Griscam nodded his head slowly as he seemed to consider this, as I am sure he always considered everything. "Don't you think Frank Prescott is a bit of an Elizabethan?" he asked. "Not, of course, that Harriet was not chaste." He smiled, and I objected to his smile, even while I speculated that he might be one of those unfortunate persons who always say the wrong thing when they mean to be kind. It would not be so much that he lacked heart as that he feared that he lacked it. "Frank has a bitter sense of mortality," he continued. "He can be as gloomy as Hamlet when the mood seizes him."

"Yet he has faith," I protested.

"Oh, yes, he has faith. It's his keel. No matter how much rumbling and tossing about he does, you can be sure he'll always straighten up in the end. Sometimes I wonder if he doesn't put on the show just to give us a scare."

I shivered suddenly with resentment. Who was this lawyer to condescend to Francis Prescott? Did he think we were his puppets, playing with little crucifixes and ideals up here in Justin Martyr?

"You don't like Dr. Prescott!"

I could hardly believe that I had uttered the words, even while they were ringing in my astonished ears. Mr. Griscam, however, did not blink. He is too practiced an advocate not to take immediate advantage of a witness's emotionalism.

"It's hard to tell, isn't it?" he answered calmly. "All I know is that I worship him. I suppose it's quite possible to dislike one's god."

"I'm sorry," I muttered, raising my fingers to my now burning cheeks. "I spoke too hastily. I had no right."

"You had every right, my dear fellow. Every right in the

world. My trouble may be that having done a good many things for the school, I subconsciously expect more consideration than I get. And what is anything I've done compared to what Frank has done? Nothing. Frank *is* Justin Martyr." He stared into the empty grate of my fireplace and nodded sadly. "Yes, I suppose it's only too possible that I should resent Frank. Just as it's only too painfully evident that he resents me."

"For the same reasons?"

"Oh, there are many reasons for his resenting me. I won't tell you all of them, but I'll tell you one. Frank doesn't like to face the fact that it takes diplomats as well as soldiers to win wars. Even holy wars. Talleyrands as well as Napoleons."

"And you're his Talleyrand?"

"In some ways. Of course, the world loves soldiers and hates diplomats." He shrugged and then looked around at me with that curious little flare of defiance that I had noticed before. "But I'd like to see it get on without us! Frank knows that. Frank, of course, knows everything. But he wants his board of trustees to be like the scaffolding around an edifice under construction and to come off when the building is finished." He suddenly spread his arms wide. "And there is Justin Martyr, bright, inviolate, a shining Valhalla in the sky! Well, I agree with him, that's the funny thing. I make no bid for personal praise or glory. At least not consciously. I realize that the greatest diplomat, by definition, must be the one of whom nobody has heard. And that's the way I would have written Frank's life."

"Tell him so!"

"He'd never believe it." For the first time I heard the naked bitterness in his tone. "He's too afraid that I'd make myself the real hero. But I wouldn't have, Aspinwall. I swear I wouldn't. I wanted to write that book. I wanted to write it more than I've wanted anything in years."

"You can still write it."

"Without his blessing? Would *you?*"

"No. But you might wait until . . . until . . ."

"Until he's dead? He'll never be dead for me. No, Aspin-wall, I give it up. I give it up once and for all. It is *you* who must write the book."

"I?" My voice was a whisper. "But I'm not even a Justinian."

"That may be all to the good. There are those who would say: why should a young man who has known Prescott only as an octogenarian be the person to do his life? Yet I can see that maybe only such a person *could* do it. In any event, I don't want to talk about it." He rose from his chair and knocked the ashes out of the pipe that he had only so recently lit. "The whole subject is very painful, and I'm not going to keep you up talking about it. You will note that I have put an envelope on your desk. It contains my notes for the first two chapters of my life of Frank. It is yours to do with as you wish."

"But, Mr. Griscam," I protested in distress, "what reason do you have to think I even contemplate such a project?"

"Only that Horace Havistock told me he had given you *his* papers. I was terribly jealous for a bit. I had gone to see him in Westbury with the express purpose of raiding his desk. Ah, well." He smiled and held out his hand. "It's a job, anyway, for youth. For youth and faith."

No sooner had I taken his hand than he pulled it away and was gone. Obviously he did not trust to the durability of his own magnanimity. Had I had only myself to consider I would have hurried down the corridor after him and stuffed his manu-script into his pocket. But I had to consider that I might be only an agent. That I might not have the right to refuse.

9

A BIOGRAPHER should commence by stating his prejudices, if he knows of any, and I will undoubtedly antagonize my reader at the outset by affirming that I have none. "But you're a lawyer!" he may object, to which I answer: "Exactly. But a *good* lawyer, such as I claim to be, must be without prejudice."

It seems hard to irritate one's audience at the outset, but as I am bound to do it sooner or later I may as well have it over with. People don't like my type. They resent the fact that I never raise my voice, that I am always reasonable, always willing to hear both sides. Because I am everybody's trustee or on everybody's board, because I have the gift of being able to get any old chestnut out of any old fire, people take for granted that I'm dull.

I, in turn, resent this. I have tried all my life not to be narrow and stuffy. I believe I know as much about Elizabethan drama as any man living, short of the great scholars, and my collection, which I am leaving to Justin Martyr, is full of treasures. I have always been a staunch democrat in the very heart of republicanism, and under Franklin Roosevelt I served as assistant secretary of the Treasury and later as ambassador to Panama. I was enthusiastic for the New Deal when most of my friends were for *laissez-faire,* and as Chairman of the Board of Trustees of Justin Martyr I consistently backed Dr. Prescott in every one of his great forward-looking steps. Yet my son Sylvester, a conservative bank vice-president, and my daughter Amy, who cast her first vote for Herbert Hoover, both regard me complacently as an old fogy. Emmaline, my wife, who has devoted her life to good works, is nearer the mark. She simply regards me as a hopeless materialist, which all of us, except Emmaline, basically are.

I must stop before my introduction dwindles into an old man's querulousness and state the essential prefatory things. I was the only child of a wretched marriage, born to the memory of wealth and the prospect of poverty. I cannot remember my father, Jules Griscam, but I have always been told that he was a dark, flamboyant, charming man, full of wit and brassy impudence, the contemporary picture of a villain and the opposite of myself. He dazzled the Joneses (Mother's family and old New York) during the brief period of his success and dazzled my mother, who had never been dazzled before and never was to be again. After the collapse of his insurance company and the discovery of his peculations he fled to Argentina where, a few years later, he died, leaving to his widow and son a pile of debts which in those days it was considered a sacred duty to pay, so that I started life with a price on my head. Grandpa Jones took us into his old brownstone, full of black walnut and stained glass, paid for my upbringing and supported Mother, and to this day I have never been able to figure out how he was able to make us feel so keenly the load of our obligation without ever even hinting at it. It was a trick peculiar to the family, and I think in time I may have mastered it myself.

Mother was that most irritating of females: the kind who believes implicitly and forever in her male progenitor. No wonder Father told her nothing of his business troubles! She minded the shock of his disaster mostly because of its jarring effect on Grandpa, and she lived thereafter a life of muted apology, acting more as a plain, submissive paid companion to the old man than as a daughter. Even as a child I resented her deference to Grandpa in his testy senility and to my uncles in their youthful arrogance. I wanted to be her champion and take her away from the eternally superior Joneses. I wanted to make a fortune and put her back on top of their world. But my dreams dissolved into slush before the hum of her constant admonitions: "Be sure to tiptoe when you go by Uncle Andrew's room in the morning"; "Be careful not to interrupt your Uncle Timothy when he's reading his paper," and "There's a good boy, fetch your grandfather's shawl." How I hated it all! And the cruelest thing they did was to give me no excuse to hate them.

I went to day school until I was fifteen when I was entered in the fourth form of Justin Martyr. I was sent there because it was a new school and cheaper than the others, and because the headmaster, Francis Prescott, had been a good friend of my Uncle Timothy Jones when they had worked together in New York Central. He often called at the house in those days, and, unlike other family visitors, always took notice of the lonely little boy hiding on a landing, behind a chair or under a table. Prescott would reach out suddenly in passing to grab and haul me forth, tousle my hair or pick me up and swing me about his head. Sometimes he would even bring me a present or take me into the backyard to play at catch. I was dazzled, a bit uncomfortably, to find myself so tossed about by this hearty young man. I suppose I appealed to his sympathy because the shame of my father's disgrace attached itself to my woebegone appearance. When he departed for divinity school, acting on a decision that to me seemed as quick as it was quixotic, I felt sadly abandoned.

Justin Martyr in 1891 was only five years old, with forty boys, six masters and one big yellow barn of a building that stood up barely in the midst of a large field near the village of New Paisley, thirty miles west of Boston. People were already beginning to say it had a great future, but to the hardworking headmaster who combined the functions of minister, teacher, coach, tutor and superintendent, that future must have still seemed a good way off.

For me, anyway, coming from the gloom of the old Jones house on lower Madison Avenue, the first months there were a kind of paradise. The atmosphere seemed more that of a large happy family than of an academy. The masters, including Prescott, were all young and played football with the boys; everybody ate together at three round tables, and the Prescotts entertained the whole school at parlor games and singing on Saturday nights. Discipline was handled by simple reprimand or occasional extra chores, and sick boys were put up in the headmaster's wing and looked after, when a trained nurse was not required, by Mrs. Prescott, who also taught the German classes. But above all there was a comradeship between the boys, even between those of different forms, which inevitably disappeared as the school increased in size. Dawn must give way to morning, but it was still bliss to have lived in that one.

Prescott himself, who later became a somewhat austere figure to the multitudes of students who passed under his all-encompassing brown stare, was then on easy, even bantering terms with the older boys. He had a natural authority and could check the least familiarity with a glance, and he could be terrible in his tempers, but the occasions for them were rare. I was a modest boy and tended to keep myself out of his way in fear that he might think I was presuming on our old intimacy. I determined that I would win his respect independently of the family connection, and to do this I worked hard at my books, paid an almost fierce attention to his sermons in the little church in New Paisley where the school worshiped and flung myself recklessly at the biggest boys on the football field. As I was a rather small fifteen, I got badly battered a few times, and once the headmaster himself picked me up, patted me on the back and said with a laugh: "You're a tough little fellow, Davey, but try to remember it's only a game." How I thrilled at those words!

Human beings, however, cannot be happy together for long; the compulsion to mar a scene of content is, in my now long experience with my fellow men, sooner or later irresistible to the average observer. You may think you're going your own way, inoffensively enough, modestly enough, not even whistling under your breath, but make no mistake. Someone is watching you and watching you with hate. How could it be otherwise? Animals live to kill and be killed, and if our food is supplied at table, the hunting instinct must still be satisfied. Every garden has a snake, and every boys' school a Hal Leigh. Need I describe him? Surely the reader can see him, big and brash and sneering, popular with the boys who preferred the dirty story in the cellar to the clean play of the football field, feared by the weak, suspected by the strong, a brute, a bully and a toady. How I hate him still! It was he, one morning at recess time, when we were eating our crackers and discussing a test in mathematics, who brayed out: "Ask Griscam. His old man was a wizard at all that. He could multiply by a million, divide by himself and come out with zero."

I flew at him with a wild confidence that the wrath of the insane would make up for the difference in weight. It did not. My schooldays were not to be those of Tom Brown. I did not even manage to blacken one of Leigh's eyes before he had knocked me over and kicked me down a stone stairway where I sprained both a wrist and ankle and cut an ugly gash in my head. While I was in the dispensary afterwards, having the cut treated by Mrs. Prescott, her husband came in and asked me how the fight had started. I imagined that he suspected the truth and would have gladly punished Leigh for his cruelty, but I refused to tell him a thing about it. No gentleman could have been more staunchly mute in concealing the indiscreet presence of a lady in his bachelor apartment than was I in shielding the hated Leigh. It was my code of honor, and I gloried in it because I thought it was the headmaster's. I did not realize until years later that he was first of all an eminently practical man.

The glory that I felt, however, was no match for my rancor against the unchastised Leigh. He made no further remarks about my father, it was true, but was his silence the equivalent of my limp or the pain in my wrist? I brooded over my injuries, both to my honor and to my person, until it seemed to me that I could not endure another week at school without some kind of retaliation. For all the power of Prescott's personality and the weakness of Leigh's, it was the latter which now discolored for me the light green of the woods and leered over a pale spring sky. I dared not assault Leigh again, for a second beating would have made me ridiculous and might have exposed me to the headmaster's anger. I could not even complain to my friends about his viciousness without repeating his remark about my father. If I were to have my revenge, it would have to be underhanded, and how then was I ever to look Mr. Prescott in the face again?

Unhappily for me, on a half holiday, the perfect opportunity presented itself. Several boys, including Leigh, had gone canoeing on the river, leaving their schoolbooks and papers in piles just inside the boathouse. I noted that Leigh had carelessly left on top of his pile the paper about the Punic Wars on which he had been working all term. It took only a minute to stuff his thesis in my pocket, all but the last page, and leave the door ajar so that the strong wind scattered the copybooks and notes over the dock and into the water. I then hurried off, unseen, to burn the Punic Wars, knowing that it would all seem an accident, as the discovery of that final page with the rest of the litter would confirm.

And so in fact it turned out, but loud as were the howls of Hal Leigh at the loss of his masterpiece, instead of joy in my heart I felt only a sick depression. Even after the headmaster had agreed to give Leigh a mark for the lost paper higher than the original would have probably received, so that my act of vengeance had actually benefited my foe, I felt no relief. I had proved to myself that I had inherited my father's character, and it could now be only a matter of time before I made this manifest to the world. I could visualize already the nodding heads and deep shrugs of my maternal uncles.

As the spring deepened and the spirits of the boys rose, my own continued to decline until, morose and moody, my marks became affected. I caught a severe cold and in my state of dejection a fever followed, and for some days I was seriously ill in the Prescotts' house with a day and a night nurse. But however much I may have romantically wanted to die, the melancholy spirit could not erode the vigor of my sixteen years, and I soon found myself on the road to a vulgar recovery. It may have been my need for a compensating drama that made me confess to the headmaster at my bedside the whole sorry tale of Hal Leigh.

He was wonderful in that he accepted it with the same gravity in which it was offered. "Of course, you did a very wrong thing, Davey, and one that I would not have expected of you. But on the other hand, I would not have expected you to have received such provocation." He shook his head sadly. "And right here in Justin Martyr, too. Yet perhaps it is all for the good. You have to learn, my boy, to live with your father's reputation. You need not be ashamed of it. Indeed, it would be very foolish of you to be ashamed of it. But you must accept it, because it is a fact."

"It's hard to be the only boy with a father like mine."

"Very hard. I don't minimize it."

"*Your* father was a hero."

"And that has its problems, too, Davey. The good Lord deals us our different hands to play, but don't you suppose he keeps score according to how we play them? I find a hero in mine. Played one way he can set me. Played another he gives me rubber. Your father may seem a liability to you, but he can also be a challenge."

"To what?"

"To a grand slam! Look, my boy: you have a name that is temporarily discredited. So be it. You have had a lonely childhood with uncles who are too afraid of being demonstrative to be properly kind. Oh, I know them." He nodded slowly as I stared, fascinated by this new candor. "You have a mother who has been overburdened with disappointment." I did not know then, but, of course, he did, that Grandpa Jones was at last dying and that Mother had refused to leave his bedside to come to mine. "But look now for your trumps. You have a first-class mind, a well-made body, an aptitude for friendship, high ideals and honesty. Are you to be put out of the game in the first rubber with all that?"

"You really think I'm honest, sir? After what I've just told you about tearing up Leigh's paper?"

"Your telling me proves it. It was wrong, to be sure. But you had great provocation, and now you have made confession. It would be maudlin to dwell on it further."

"And *you* believe in me?"

He smiled, for the first time, at the intensity of my tone. "I do believe in you, my boy," he said and patted me on the head. "Now get some rest."

During the three weeks of my convalescence Prescott tutored me for an hour a day, and when I rejoined my classes I was actually ahead of the others. Even at that age I had some dim appreciation of the remarkable keenness and scope of his mind which could reduce anything, an eclogue by Virgil or the War of the Spanish Succession, to a few vivid terms that would glue the material in all but the stupidest mind at least until whatever test was pending. But Prescott was being far more than a brilliant tutor; he was nursing a sick soul. His kindness was overwhelming, without ever being in the least sentimental, without even, perhaps, being personal. He raised the great beaker of his hope to my lips like a communion cup and watched with grave countenance as I drank, and when he took it away, I knew that it was because I had had enough. There was no question of turning my convalescence into a party.

He talked to me of God and of his early doubts and of the loneliness of his own childhood. He talked of the futility of any action in life that was not service to others. He explained to me and made me believe that happiness had nothing to do with one's outward circumstances, but could be created only within. And then he made me laugh, too, by talking of the past and poking fun at the Joneses and persuading me not only that they were less formidable than they appeared but that they might even be human. When he came to my room with the telegram announcing poor old Grandpa's death we knelt together in prayer by my bed, and I found that I was actually weeping.

I was too clever, and also at this point too well acquainted with the headmaster's character, to make the smallest effort, after my return to a normal schedule, to trade upon convalescent days. I adored Mr. Prescott as I had never adored another human being, but it was a worshipful kind of emotion, and I was able to sublimate it into violent activities and studies. I rose to be second in my form, and in my last year I was one of the school prefects. I was not big enough to be very effective at football, but I played it hard, and I edited the school paper, *The Justinian*. The best part of sixth form year was that the prefects were in constant contact with the headmaster, and we could feel that we ran the school in a sort of partnership. Mr. Prescott treated us almost as equals and even allowed me to share in one of his melancholy moments. We had been out together on a cold winter afternoon, snowshoeing on the crisp surface, and as we came back, it was already dark, and we paused for a moment on the crest of the hill overlooking the school and stared down at the lighted building so far below. My heart was so full that I exclaimed: "I can't bear to have spring come!"

"Why not, Davey? Are you so fond of the winter of our discontent?"

"I'm so fond of Justin, sir. I can't bear the thought of graduation."

"But Justin is only a prelude," he protested. "It is nothing but a simple first course. If I thought I had made it the whole banquet of life for any boy, I should know I had failed indeed."

"But it's the whole banquet of life for *you*, sir."

"It is that, Davey." His smile was grave as he stared down at his school. "It is that indeed."

"And how happy it must make you!"

"Very happy," he agreed in a rather somber tone. "I am most blessed. I have what I wanted. I have what I prayed for. And do you know what I pray for now, Davey?"

"What, sir?"

"That the sin of boredom shall never fall upon me."

I said nothing, awed, for I knew that in that moment we were as intimate as we ever again should be.

Graduation was a sad time for me, although Mother came up for it, urged, no doubt, by Mr. Prescott. My friends thought me very emotional, for there were tears in my eyes, but in those days such emotion was still respectable. I felt that I was emerging from a Garden of Eden that might be artificial by the standards of a world that had first applauded and later persecuted my father, but I was armed with the faith that that garden had nonetheless prepared me for that world.

I went to Harvard and made a good record there, but I was never as happy as I had been at school. Harvard was already the world, and although I could cope with it I had not learned to cope with it joyfully. I went back to Justin, now rapidly expanding, on so many weekends that at length Mr. Prescott had to warn me in a friendly fashion that I might be neglecting the social duties of a college man. It was then that I asked him if he would consider me for the faculty of Justin when I graduated. We were walking to the river, and he grasped my elbow as he debated, too long for my comfort, the answer.

"Are you so sure you want to teach, Davey?"

"If I could teach here, sir."

"No, that won't do. You'd have to want to teach anywhere to be able to teach here."

"Then I want to teach anywhere!"

"It might work out." He removed his hand and strode on. "But not until several years after your graduation. You must see more of the world first, Davey, if you're to teach boys to deal with it. And I can't help but wonder if a life at Justin would be the happiest life for you. Your father's name received its blemish in New York. Isn't it there that you must seek to remove it?"

"Is that so important?"

"Not to my thinking. But I thought it was to yours."

"You mean I should pay his debts?" My question, I fear, was belligerent.

"No, Davey," he said patiently. "I mean you should bury his old reputation under the monument of your new one."

Of course he was being reasonable and kind, and who but I had given him the notion of the importance of my father's crime to me? Of course he saw instantly that Justin was a haven for me, a refuge from a world that I deemed cold, if not actually sneering. He wanted no escapists in his school, and he was right. But at the time I refused to discuss the matter any further, and we reached the river in silence. I had been rejected by too many people in my life to be a good sport about being rejected by Francis Prescott.

10

ONCE I had squarely turned my back on schoolteaching and resolved to become a lawyer, I never wavered again. My poor mother died only a year after Grandpa Jones, and my inheritance was just sufficient to put me through Harvard and Harvard Law. After that I got a job with Prime & Ballard, a small but lucrative "family" law firm, which is now Prime & Griscam and one of the last of its kind on Wall Street. We get our clients everything from theatre tickets to divorces; we file their birth certificates and we bury them. I started as Mr. Prime's law clerk and became in turn his son-in-law, his partner and his executor. It was an old-fashioned success story.

I discovered not only that I enjoyed my law practice, but that I was admirably adapted to it. I am by nature reserved, patient, of even temper and a good listener, and I love the challenge of domestic puzzles. I became a specialist in the multiple prejudices under which Americans suffer in the spending of their money, according to whether it has been earned, married or handed down, and I learned to stay within the framework of the sacred mores surrounding these categories while putting the dollars to work to the greatest advantage of the whole family. I even found that it was occasionally possible to persuade old New Yorkers that money could be used for pleasure.

Once Mr. Prime had made me his partner everything seemed

to go my way. I was even assisted by the kind of windfall that is usually the lot only of fictional heroes. I bought from my father's creditors some supposedly worthless gold-mining stock at the price for which he had pledged it, and it turned into a very good thing. What happier ending could there be to the grim saga of the paternal obligations? Was it not what ought to have happened to the conscientious, debt-assuming Victorian son? Paradise was on this earth, where it belonged, and I thrilled with my first sense of the Midas touch.

But the greatest reward of my successful professional life came with a letter that I received from Mr. Prescott on the occasion of my twenty-ninth birthday. He wrote that he had for some time wanted a younger point of view represented on the school board and that he was suggesting my name to Mr. Depew as the first graduate trustee of Justin! It was like him not even to ask my permission. He knew only too well that I would jump at the chance.

From the very beginning, except for my diplomatic years, I never missed a meeting of the board. These were always held at the school, and it would have been worthwhile to attend them if only to watch Frank Prescott handle my fellow members. He would stare hard at the one who was putting the question, not a muscle moving, his big brown gaze seeming to encompass not only the question but the motive behind it. He would nod briefly, express his satisfaction that the point had been raised, immediately associate himself with the complaint, if any, contained, sometimes even rephrasing the question to give it a sharper lunge, and then proceed to defend his administration, then to counterattack, then to defend it again. It was Prescott against Prescott in a duel whose brilliance distracted the attention of the audience from the fact that Prescott was also the referee. I asked few questions myself for I found it more instructive to gather knowledge on my own.

My great project, which I nursed for a year before I even began to sound out the other trustees, was to double the size of the school. Justin in 1906 had reached an enrollment of two hundred where Prescott had arbitrarily cut it short as the maximum number of boys that a headmaster could get to know personally. I doubted that he could get to know even that many. It seemed to me that the attractive intimacy of the school's early days had been lost forever when the roll call had passed fifty and that having lost that, we might as well push on to four or five hundred. If we went too far, of course, the essential character of the school would be lost. The point was to find the greatest number of boys on whom Prescott's genius could still successfully operate. Otherwise we were wasting him. Could any other conclusion follow?

The trustees, on the whole, were responsive, particularly when I made it clear that I would take charge of the necessary fund raising. I had already discussed this with Mr. Prime who had promptly offered me a leave of absence.

"It's precisely the little push that your career needs at precisely this moment!" he exclaimed, briskly rubbing his hands. "You should see every big man in New York, Philadelphia and Boston. They'll all have heard of the great job that Prescott is doing at Justin, and they'll be glad to see you, even if they don't give you a cent. You'll be identified with a great cause. We lawyers have to take advantage of these things, you know. After all, we can't advertise. Go to it, my boy, with all my blessing!"

"I wasn't thinking so much of what it would do for *me*," I protested, taken aback by such crassness. "I was thinking of Prescott and the school and perhaps a little bit of the rehabilitation of my father's name."

"Well, that's fine, dear boy, that's fine," Mr. Prime said soothingly. "There's no reason you shouldn't knock off several birds with a stone as round and smooth as this one."

It was agreed among the trustees, after the project had been reduced to a simple outline listing the proposed new buildings and masterships, that I should be the one to approach Prescott, and with the paper in my pocket and their blessing on my head, I journeyed apprehensively up to Justin for the first conference.

In his study, leaning over the surface of his large uncluttered desk, a fist in each cheek, Prescott moved only his eyes as I talked: to my face, to the blotter, back to my face again. There was not even a hint of surprise in his own and certainly none of gratification. Obviously, he had been forewarned. I began to feel as if I were making a too lengthy confession of a misdeed that was more unattractive than criminal. When I leaned down to pull the outline from my briefcase he finally raised a hand.

"Whoa, David, whoa!"

"Don't you even want to see it?"

"I don't want to see anything for just a minute, thank you," he said in a cool, gruff tone as he stared, seemingly through me, at the window behind my back that looked out at the chapel. "I need a little time to pull myself together now that your proposition has finally come." As he sighed, some of the frostiness went out of his tone. "I always knew it would, you know. From you or another. No matter how much the conception of a school may be one's own, sooner or later, if it has any use, any currency, it is bound to pass into the public domain. We can keep only our failures. Obviously, I cannot keep Justin."

"But it seems to me, sir," I suggested, for I now called him "sir" and "Frank" alternately, "that with two hundred boys you're already pretty well in that domain."

"I had hoped not, David." He shifted his gaze to me from that imaginary audience that he so often seemed to be addressing. "I have tried to preserve some remnant of family atmosphere."

"And you have succeeded!" I exclaimed. "My point is precisely that what is left of it is still compatible with a larger school. You have to recognize, sir, that not only has Justin quadrupled since its beginning, but you yourself have changed.

You can't expect to be as intimate with the boys as when you were a younger man. You have become a rather awe-inspiring figure, like Arnold of Rugby. But the advantage of being on a pedestal is that more people can see you."

Of course, I was an idiot to have used such an image, but I was excited and nervous, and now that it was out, I could only bow my head to the angry storm.

"Then why not expand the school to a thousand or more?" he demanded, spreading his arms mockingly. "Why not build auditoriums throughout New England so that all the world may see me?"

"I doubt we could raise the money."

Prescott turned sullenly to the outline that I now placed on his desk. "But you think you could for this," he muttered. I must have sat for fifteen minutes in silence while he studied it. "Is this supposed to be final?" he asked at last.

"Oh, no, sir. It's simply a draft. A suggestion."

"A draft." His mood seemed to deepen dismally. "It would have to be changed, of course. But that's not the point. It *could* be changed. The point is that so could the headmaster. And I think that you may well need a new headmaster for this magnificent new academy of yours."

This struck me at last as a false note, and for the first time in my term as trustee I showed impatience. After all, I had worked for months on the project, and he had not even suggested that I might, however mistakenly, have the school's welfare in mind. "If you don't like the plan, Frank, the plan will be scrapped. The idea was not so much to sell Justin Martyr as it was to sell Francis Prescott. I'm sorry if you find the admiration of your board so offensive."

He looked up at me quizzically, taking in my change of mood and reflecting, perhaps, that there might be grounds for it. "I'm not acting, David, or putting on airs. You don't know what you ask of me. It's hard on the personality to be a headmaster."

He tightened his lips into the thin line that always marked his moments of peculiar candor. "It's particularly hard on mine. It develops all my tendencies to strut and bully. Here I am, covered with mud from the bottom of my own little puddle, and you want to pitch me into a larger one!"

"It wouldn't be like you, Frank, to deflate the school because you were afraid it might inflate your own ego."

He gave me a shrewd look, grunted and returned to the outline. After another long silence I realized that the conversation was over, at least for that day, and I left his study without even an interchange of farewells.

The following weekend I returned to the school, but Frank hardly spoke to me, and when he did, he was barely civil. At tea on Sunday afternoon, before leaving for my train, in Harriet Prescott's living room, which for all its clutter of books and family photographs and heavy, dark boy-proof furniture still managed to suggest some of its mistress's early New England austerity, I watched her fill my cup from the fine old silver urn that I remembered from "parlor night" in my own school days. Harriet was the bony kind of woman who begins to look old at thirty-five but after fifty seems younger than her contemporaries and more distinguished. At this point she had just started to dye her hair the chestnut color that it was always to remain. She did it, I am sure, not to seem young but to seem ageless, which, with her pale skin, her big, Emerson nose and dull brown dresses, she always succeeded in seeming. I told her that I feared Frank was put out with me.

"Oh, he is that," she agreed readily. "You should hear the catalogue of your iniquities. But don't worry. It will pass."

"Do you think I should not have brought the matter up?"

She considered this a moment, putting down the cup that she had half filled. "It's hard to say. If I thought that nobody else ever would have, I might say yes. You see, I like the school as it is. But now it can never be as it is again. If your plan is rejected, we'll always be a small school that *could* have been a big one. We'll always be justifying ourselves."

"You make me feel very badly."

"You shouldn't. You're probably quite right. If one goes in for education, one might as well educate as many as one can. It's up to Frank and myself to live up to your plan."

"You're laughing at me!"

"Far from it," she said very seriously. "One should never laugh at growth. It's like laughing at life."

"You resent me, anyway," I said gloomily. "Of course you do. Frank will never forgive me for interfering with his school."

"If he doesn't, it will be because he can't forgive himself for wanting what you want."

I stared in astonishment at those cool green eyes in which a glimmer of amusement was just discernible. "He wants a *bigger* Justin?"

"Oh, yes. Frank is ambitious, you know. For himself *and* the school, though they're sometimes confused. But don't imagine he'll admit it. On the contrary, he'll growl and grumble. He'll blame the whole thing on you. He'll talk about the vulgarity of size. Only he'll go along. At the last moment. He'll go along, fighting you every inch of the way. Don't fool yourself, David. It's going to be a bumpy road!"

Harriet was right. Prescott ultimately announced to the trustees his willingness to entertain the "Griscam" project, but only on condition that the plan be entirely revised and that the proposed fund for new masters' salaries be doubled. If Justin was going to increase in quantity, he argued, it would have to increase as well in quality. It would have to achieve the highest academic rating in all of New England. Similarly, the spiritual side of school life would have to be re-emphasized, and the project was again conditioned on funds to be raised for a new chapel designed by an architect of the headmaster's choosing. And finally he stipulated that the committee to go to the public for money under my chairmanship was to operate under his own constant review. It was the most dictatorial program ever presented to my knowledge by a headmaster to a board of trustees, yet the latter acceded to it without a protest or a dissenting vote. It established definitively the master-servant relationship which was to last for the remainder of his long tenure of office.

The principal burden of working under his conditions fell, of course, upon my shoulders. Prescott proved to be a remarkable, indeed an indispensable fund raiser, but I could never be sure that he would not undo six months' good work with a single burst of temper. When I organized dinners for friends of the school and asked him to speak, he would always comply so eloquently, so humorously, so winningly that I believe no tongue could have opened more purses. Yet behind the scenes no Italian tenor of the Metropolitan could have behaved more outrageously. He would fuss and fret over what he called the "Hippodrome" that I had prepared for him and demand in clipped, biting tones if his performance had been up to expectations, if his words had been converted into coin at as favorable an exchange as at the previous dinner. He would describe himself pathetically to friends as David Griscam's dancing bear, led by a ring through its nose from laughing village to smirking town.

Had it not been for Harriet I wonder if I might not have given the whole thing up. She preserved at all times her extraordinary equilibrium and helped me to understand the suffering even of the ambitious artist when he finds his work marketed on a national scale, and to see that Frank was having to learn to share his life's dream with every starched shirtfront that I had gathered in a dozen gilded halls. It must have sometimes seemed to him that the very soul of Justin Martyr would dissolve into the smoky air over the soiled plates and stained napkins and fade away with the waves of stale laughter evoked by his own jokes.

Far worse, however, than the private scenes between us, which had no effect on the fund raising, were his violent reactions to any gifts to which he chanced to see conditions, expressed or implied, attached. Sometimes he was perfectly right, as when he ushered to the door without further ceremony a man who had offered him fifty thousand dollars to admit his delinquent son to the school. At others he was too suspicious of interference, and I would have the devil's own time persuading him that a graduate's offer to build handball courts was not necessarily an improper attempt to add a new sport to the curriculum. But the episode that made him angriest of all was that of the two new dormitories. The donor of one had modestly left its naming to the headmaster, while the donor of the other, in order not to seem a lone egotist, had stipulated that *both* buildings be named for their contributors. Prescott's indignation at such meanness threatened to cost us not one but two dormitories, and only by the greatest diplomacy was I able to persuade the modest donor to allow his name to be used and to restrain the headmaster from mortally insulting the other. Yet for all our difficulties, the money poured in.

We had almost reached our goal, except for the chapel, and I thought I was close to a pledge for that from Shelley Tanager, a Chicago meat-packer who had a boy in the fifth form, when the episode occurred that was to detonate the mounting tension between Prescott and myself and nearly bring our whole project to the ground.

I was spending a week at Justin, where an office and secretary had now been assigned to me, and breakfasting with the Prescotts when Frank explained the troublesome business of the "trots." Apparently translations of Latin and Greek texts had been circulating among the boys, and the masters had been complaining of a growing uniformity in recitations. The sixth form had made raids on desks and studies and confiscated a number of trots, and severe penalties had been meted out, but the practice had stubbornly continued. It was particularly gall-ing to Prescott, himself an accomplished classicist, to be faced with so widespread a resistance to a proper study of the ancient tongues at just the moment when he was determined to raise academic standards in proportion to the contemplated new enrollment.

"It's the kind of thing one expects of little boys," he grumbled, "but it's most offensive to find it in the upper forms. I'm told it's particularly rank in the fifth. And here we are, almost at the end of the school year. Next fall those are the boys on whom I must lean to run the school!"

"Let us hope for good things of the summer."

"It's nothing to be facetious about, David. It's the kind of rot that can bring a school down."

"But, surely, all schools have trouble with trots," his wife put in. "I remember distinctly using one at Miss Yarnell's, in French class."

Prescott glared down the table while Harriet imperturbably continued to pour coffee. "I have announced to the fifth form," he continued, "that any member who is hereafter caught using a trot will not be welcome back next year."

"Isn't that rather stiff?" I asked.

"Perhaps it is. But I have given fair warning. It seems to be the only way to impress upon them that as sixth formers they will share with me and the masters the responsibility of administering the school."

I was faintly bored by the subject and said nothing more. I could not see that the use of a trot would necessarily disqualify a boy from being a good administrator, but I assumed that Prescott's warning, however fierce, would at least accomplish its purpose. I did not dream that any fifth former would be such a fool as to risk his school career for a dozen lines of Ovid.

Yet as early as the third day of my visit, when I was following the boys after morning chapel over the path, soft with spring mud, to the Schoolhouse, Prescott came up beside me with the bad news.

"You'll be sorry to hear, David, that a fifth former has not seen fit to heed my admonition. You'll be even sorrier to hear who it is."

The hope of spring vanished from that day, and the light blue of the sky faded to a dead winter's whiteness. "Shelley Tanager's boy?"

Prescott nodded and then shook his head roughly as if to confound the boy and his father and perhaps myself as troublemakers in an otherwise serene Justin. There was even a hint of something akin to triumph in his eye, almost of downright malevolence, which ended by exasperating me. When I thought back in later years on this scene I wondered if I could not date from it the first appearance of a new trait of hardness in Prescott, a hardness that was to grow, along with his great fame, in the coming decade and a half, culminating at last in the terrible episode of my own son, Jules. No one could write Prescott's biography without considering this side of him. It was a spasmodic, inconsistent hardness; a boy might spend six years at Justin without once encountering it, and I think most did. But those few who ran afoul of the headmaster in this period were apt to remember him for life with bitterness.

"Is there no doubt about it?"

"Well, he denies it." Prescott shrugged contemptuously. "He says the trot was put in his desk by his roommate, Max Totten. It seems sufficiently curious that Totten, a poor orphan whose tuition Tanager's father pays, should find it worth his while to 'frame' his benefactor."

"But not impossible."

"Ah, yes, wouldn't it be nice, David? And then we should not find ourselves in the uncomfortable position of having to expel the son of our potential benefactor, should we?" Prescott's voice rose in a cascade of sarcasm. We had reached the Schoolhouse and were standing outside the big windows of the assembly hall where some of the boys could see, but not hear us. "You must not be so anxious to save the hides of those who can be useful to us. Let us not gain the world and lose our souls!"

"Has it occurred to you," I demanded sharply, "that you may be condemning this boy for the glory of spitting in his rich father's eye?"

For once I saw that I had the upper hand; for once Frank Prescott was taken by surprise. It was part of his charm that he should not have made the smallest effort to conceal it. "Do you suppose that could be?" he asked soberly, raising his eyebrows. "That would be a very terrible thing, David."

"I'm only suggesting that you should not leap to conclusions."

"Would you care to be present when I see the boy? He and Mr. Mygatt, the master who made the charge, will be in my office after assembly."

"I should indeed be interested."

"You may act as his counsel if you wish," he said, and as he turned to go into the Schoolhouse, he gave me one of his slow, unsmiling winks. "I'm sure that Shelley Tanager's father can afford even the charges of a partner of Prime and Griscam."

I sat in a corner of Prescott's office, unintroduced and almost unnoticed, during the arraignment. The master, a rather oily, olive-complexioned fellow, told his story while Shelley Tanager, Junior, a tall, slight boy with curly blond hair and the pouting face, even at sixteen, of a spoiled child, sullenly listened.

The master had suspected Tanager of continuing to use a trot, although punished for it once already, and had been on the watch. He had searched the study which Tanager and Max Totten shared the night before while the school was at supper, and had found nothing. Half an hour later, during study period, he had knocked on their door, sent both boys on contrived errands and had then discovered the trot, open and face downward, as if hastily concealed, in the first drawer of Tanager's desk. Nobody but Tanager and his roommate had entered the study between the two searches.

"And you deny, Tanager, that you placed it there?" Prescott asked in the dry, melancholy tone that he used for such inquests.

"I do, sir."

"If you did not, I take it there's only one other person who could have."

"Only one, sir. That's correct." The boy's expression was certainly unendearing. He seemed totally unconcerned with the improbabilities of his accusation, as if his own malevolence should somehow be taken as ample evidence.

"Why should Totten have had a trot?" Prescott continued in a sterner voice. "He was a first-rate Latin scholar long before the first of these wretched books appeared on the campus."

"How do you know, sir, when the first one appeared?"

Prescott had to nod to acknowledge the unexpected justice of this. "But when do you suggest that he could have concealed the trot in your desk? When did he have time?"

"How should I know? It was *his* trot."

"His, you say. Yet you were caught with one yourself three weeks back, is that not so?"

"Yes, sir."

"And phrases from this trot, the one Mr. Mygatt discovered in your desk last night, have been found in your written exercises."

"If that's so, I got them from Totten. He sometimes helped me with my work."

"Surely, you know, Tanager, that's improper!"

"Yes, sir, but it's not using a trot."

And so it went, for a quarter of an hour, Prescott's questions, like those of a cross-examining lawyer, rising in vigor and hostility. He mercilessly pointed up the contrast between Max Totten the able student, brilliant athlete and natural leader and Shelley Tanager the dunce, the fumbler and lone wolf. Was it likely that the former would resort to a trot that he did not need and then use it to compromise a roommate for whom he had never shown anything but kindness and whose father was his own sole support? Was it not more likely that Tanager, jealous of the superiority of his friend both at home and at school, should have sought to cast his own blame on those stronger shoulders? But Tanager would concede nothing, even if he could explain nothing, and when he had been dismissed, I protested to Prescott against his roughness.

"But the boy not only obviously had the trot," he retorted angrily; "he's trying to get his friend expelled!"

"Aren't you begging the question?"

"Well, what more do you need to convince you, David? Do you have to eat the whole apple to tell it's rotten?"

"Perhaps you would allow me to ask Mr. Mygatt a few questions."

" 'Sir, a whole history,' " Prescott quoted impatiently and turned away in his swivel chair as I addressed myself to the master who had been listening with awe to our testy exchange. He had probably never heard the headmaster contradicted before.

"Tell me, Mr. Mygatt, when you asked Tanager to go on that fabricated errand, where exactly were you standing?"

"In the doorway to his study."

"How was he able to leave?"

"Why, I stepped aside, naturally."

"Did you step back, or did you step forward into the study?"

Mygatt, perplexed, considered this. "I stepped back into the corridor. Yes, I remember that because I saw Jimmie Dunn across the way reading a magazine, and I made a mental note to speak to him later about it."

"And when you returned to the study occupied by Totten and Tanager, Tanager was gone?"

"Gone? Oh, yes. He had gone to the library, as I told him."

"But Totten was still there?"

"Well, only for a second. I sent him off, too."

"How long had you been in the corridor?"

"Oh, two seconds maybe."

"Not more? Even in the exercise of your inspection of young Dunn's reading habits?"

Mygatt flushed. "No, sir. A few seconds at the most."

"But long enough for Totten to have placed that trot in Tanager's drawer?"

"Oh, not possibly, sir. Besides, I should have seen him."

"How? Through an eye in back of your head?"

"Please remember, David, that you're not in a courtroom," Prescott interrupted. "You happen to be in my office, addressing a member of my faculty."

"I'm very well aware of that, sir. I suggest that I am using no stronger language than you used to Tanager. A boy's whole life may be at stake here."

Prescott faced my stare for a moment and then nodded. "Proceed."

"I meant, sir," Mygatt volunteered, "that I would have been aware of the boy's movements. I was standing so close."

"But has the headmaster not just described Totten as a brilliant athlete?" I pursued. "And does not that imply physical coordination? What would be simpler for an agile boy, while your back was turned, to have crossed a small study, opened a drawer and pushed a book in?"

"But I would have heard him, Mr. Griscam!"

"If he did it stealthily? Come, Mr. Mygatt, all I'm asking you to concede is that it's not impossible."

Mygatt glanced at the headmaster in appeal, but the latter only scowled and grumbled: "Answer the question, Mygatt. It's a fair one."

"Very well, then, sir. I suppose it wasn't actually impossible. Only I can't see . . ."

"Thank you, Mr. Mygatt," I interrupted firmly. "And now to the matter of the trot itself. Where is it?"

"In the faculty room. The Latin masters have been examining it to see what phrases they can pick up in their exercises."

"You mean they've been handling it?"

"How do you mean, handling it?"

"I mean *touching* it. Putting their fingers on it."

"Well, inevitably."

I groaned aloud. "I suppose a print test would show half the fingers of the faculty."

"You don't mean you'd go in for fingerprinting *here?*" Prescott asked, shocked.

"I'd go in for anything to prove a boy's innocence!" I exclaimed. "Let me ask you, Mr. Mygatt, to lock the trot up until this investigation is over." I turned to Prescott. "Will you allow me to see Totten alone?"

He shrugged. "Most certainly. I shall see that he's sent directly to your office."

"Not for an hour, please. I'd like to study his file first."

At my own desk, with the door closed, I studied the contents of the manila folder marked "Totten, Max, Form of 1908." There was a passport-size snapshot of him, full face, showing a high forehead, a big jaw and nose, every feature giving the impression of strength and candor except for the small dark eyes. I learned that his father had been an impoverished cousin of Mr. Tanager's and that he had grown up an orphan in the millionaire's household, earning his keep by bolstering, morally and intellectually, his feebler cousin. He appeared to have the same facility for success that young Tanager had for failure, but despite what were evidently engaging manners he was not popular with his formmates. He was considered "political," according to one master's report and "insincere" according to another's. In each case, I noted, the reporting master disagreed with the boys whom he quoted. Max Totten was evidently a student who knew how to ingratiate himself with the faculty.

When he came in, he struck me as even bigger, darker and more attractive than I had visualized. Unlike his cousin and roommate, he was already a man.

"What can I do for you, Mr. Griscam?" he began, politely enough.

I explained, slowly and carefully, the accusation made against Shelley Tanager and the damning nature of the evidence. All this he knew already and shook his head with a very proper commiseration. I then proceeded to relate Mr. Mygatt's story, beginning with the search of the study during supper and taking it step by step to the discovery of the trot. Totten listened to me with close attention, but betrayed nothing. I was watching for the least reaction to his discovery from my recitation that if he *had* planted the trot in Tanager's desk, Tanager, and later Tanager's father, would necessarily know of it. For Mr. Mygatt's first search, of which Totten could not have previously known, had established that the trot had *not* been in the study before the boys had come in after supper. He did not so much as blink.

"Mr. Mygatt might have put it there himself," he suggested blandly when I asked for his comments.

"Why on earth would he do that?"

"To curry favor with the Rector. He's like that, you know."

"I can't believe it, Totten!"

He shrugged. "It was only an idea. I'd do anything to see poor Shelley cleared. He's the oldest friend I have in the world."

I had to pause here to reflect. The only thing I had not considered was that Totten might not have heard of Tanager's accusation. "That's not what Tanager seems to think."

His eyebrows rose. "It's not, sir? What does Shelley think?"

"He told Dr. Prescott that *you* had put that trot in his desk."

Totten looked at me steadily for a moment, but his expression struck me not so much as alarmed or shocked or even as very much surprised, but simply as interested, intensely interested.

"It must have been you or he," I pursued.

158

"Or Mr. Mygatt," Totten retorted with a smile that struck me suddenly as impudent. With a familiarity in marked contrast to his former deference, he rose from his chair and went to the window where he stood looking out, casually twirling the shade cord. He must have remained there in total silence for almost three minutes while I stared at his back. I assumed that he was concocting an alibi, and I was too interested in what it might be to interrupt him. "Or dear little mincing Mygatt," he said at last, repeating his obviously insincere accusation.

"Please remember, Totten, that Mr. Mygatt is a member of the faculty of this school and that I am a trustee."

"Oh, keep your shirt on, Griscam," he retorted with a cool, shocking insolence, turning back to me with a now brazen smile. "You and I don't have to kid ourselves, do we? You're scared shitless this little affair will do you out of old Tanager's dough, aren't you?"

"*Totten!* I shall have to report you to the headmaster."

"What the hell, lay off it, will you!" His barking tone startled me with its authority. "I knew when they put a shyster like you on my trail, the game was up. All right, so I put the goddam trot in little Shelley's desk. Is that enough for you? Can I go now? Or shall I give old Prescott other grounds to throw me out by kicking you first in the tail?"

As I stared, my dignity shattered, at that grinning, insinuating, oddly unhostile countenance, I found that for all my years at the bar, I had no idea what to do next. It was he who solved it. He walked slowly up to me, still smiling, and suddenly stuck out his hand. Hypnotized, I took it, at which he laughed aloud, winked and left the room. Certainly he had a kind of disgusting animal charm. There was an uncomfortable democracy in his total cynicism. I sighed, shuddered, shook my head and prepared to make my report to the headmaster.

Prescott took my news like a gentleman. He put his arm about my shoulders and gave me a hug. "You've saved me from an act of brutal injustice, David. I must learn a proper humility with regard to your profession. I confess to the ancient and unworthy prejudice against lawyers. I have always accused them of not seeing the forest for the trees. Yet *I* was the one who couldn't see those trees." He shook his head ruefully. "I would have torn up young Tanager, a tender sapling, roots and all. Yes, *there* was prejudice. Because the poor boy was unattractive and unathletic, I would have had him vicious, too. While the one who was clever enough to cast himself in the image that *I* set up was the real rotter. Oh, it's a lesson for me, David!"

Harriet Prescott, however, professed to find the whole thing incredible. "I'm not going to say it to anyone else," she told me as I circled the campus with her and her dogs before lunch. "Obviously, if Max Totten has confessed, I'm bound by it. But I will say to you, David, that it baffles me. I've watched that boy carefully. He always came to my parlor nights. I feel that I know him and that I like what I know. The boys may not, but I do. He's more mature than the others. He's had a bitter and humiliating childhood, and he's going to make up for it in life. Oh, yes, he's devious and sly and intriguing. He'd use a thousand trots and swear on the Bible he hadn't. But I can't believe that he'd have placed that trot in Shelley Tanager's desk. His one virtue is loyalty!"

I was greatly troubled, for I knew Harriet to be a shrewd judge of character, considerably shrewder, even, than her husband. Also, it occurred to me that it was odd that Totten, even if guilty, should have confessed to an action that would forever embroil him with his patron, Mr. Tanager. Why would he not have brazened it out? Might he not have convinced the father that the son was lying, or at least mistaken? And, after all, he had nothing to lose by trying, for this way he was both expelled from Justin and damned with the Tanagers. After our walk I went to the chapel, so soon, as I hoped, to be replaced by a new and greater one, and prayed earnestly for guidance, but I received none. I have never thought that the good Lord, like his servant, Frank Prescott, took a proper interest in lawyers.

That afternoon I made my way to Max Totten's dormitory in Lowell House. At the end of the long empty corridor between the varnished cubicles, each sheltered by a green curtain, I saw a trunk and standing before it, putting shirts in a drawer, was Max. His back was to me, and I could hear him humming "After the Ball." To my astonishment I saw that he was smoking a cigarette which he made no effort to conceal as he turned and saw me.

"Hello, Mr. Griscam," he called with the same cheerful impudence. "Is this the official farewell?"

I walked down the corridor and stood watching him as he continued his packing. "I came to tell you that you could drop the bluff. I know you didn't do it."

Totten looked up at me cagily but with his same smile. "Know? How do you *know?*"

"You wouldn't have had time to wipe your fingerprints off the trot."

His smile became fixed as he continued to stare at me. "What makes you think they weren't on it?"

"Because I sent it into Boston this morning, with prints of Tanager's and Mygatt's fingers. They were the only ones found on the cover. The detective just called me."

"And have you told the Rector?"

"As a matter of fact, I haven't told anybody. I thought I'd better come straight to you first. Why did you confess to something you hadn't done?"

I was a bit ashamed, watching those darkening eyes, of my own pleasure at outbluffing a mere boy, but the scene that morning still rankled. My pleasure, however, was not to be of any duration. Totten was a master at table turning.

"Look, Mr. Griscam, you strike me as a realistic guy. Can't you and I make a deal? We each have a hell of a lot at stake in this business. You want old Tanager's money for a greater Justin, isn't that it? In fact, your whole wagon cart may fall in if you don't get it, and you sure as hell won't get it if little Shelley is bounced. I, on the other hand, have my own deal with old Tanager. He knows all about Shelley and what poor stuff the kid is. He'll know who had that trot, never fear. But he's crazy to have the boy graduate, and it's my job to see that he does. If you will be kind enough to let me go through with my little plan, I'll see that you get through with yours."

I gaped at the boy, more stupefied than I had been that morning. "But you'll have given yourself a bad character!" I protested.

"For using a trot? Come off it. That's in the category of boyish pranks. And I'll have Mr. Tanager where I want him for life. Oh, I have great plans there. *Great* plans. Shelley's never going to be any use to his old man in the business. But *I* am. And his old man, deep down, prefers me to Shelley. He and I are the same type."

"Do you honestly expect me to make such a deal with you?"

"Why not? Isn't it for the glory of God? He gets his chapel, and you get your big school, and I get my benefactor. And otherwise we all get nothing."

I hesitated, which of course was fatal. "But you're too young to be allowed to take that responsibility on your own shoulders."

"Do you really believe that?"

I looked into those small glinting eyes, so full of premature worldly wisdom, and decided sadly that I did not. I imagined that the understanding between this boy and his patron was complete, and I felt a sudden certainty that the future would work out exactly as he saw it. I even wondered if he might not be a closer relation to Mr. Tanager than cousin. He had all the jauntiness, guile and charm of a papal bastard in the Renaissance.

"You won't mind leaving school?"

"*This* dump? Are you kidding?"

"Of course," I murmured sadly as I turned away, "it's just what I am doing. Kidding myself as well as others. God forgive me, Totten, but I'll go along with you."

"It's a deal then?" For a second time that day he held out his hand, and for a second time I took it.

"It's a deal." I walked back down the dormitory corridor and turned back at the end. "By the way," I called to him, "that business about the fingerprints was a bluff. The trot has never left the school grounds."

His roar of laughter filled the big empty chamber. "What a tricky old shyster you are, Griscam! When my ship comes in, I'll hire you for my lawyer."

I may as well put in here that as president of the Tanager Yards he remains to this day one of my most valued clients. But then, sick at heart with my own duplicity, I went to Prescott and pleaded with him to commute Totten's sentence to a month's suspension.

"How can I, my dear David?" he protested. "If it were simply the business of the trot, I might reconsider. But how do we get around the business of his trying to throw the blame on Shelley Tanager? That destroys all my sympathy. Doesn't it yours?"

What could I say? I had sealed my bargain with Max Totten in a handshake, and for all his scant sixteen years I knew that I had been dealing with my peer. I suddenly felt very tired, and I decided that I would return to New York that night. There was no telling of what indiscretion I might be guilty if I remained another day at Justin.

Mr. Tanager's pledge came in the following month for exactly double the amount I had requested, and the great job of fund raising was at last completed. In the next two years the new dormitories, the chapel, the gymnasium, the handball courts, the wings to the Schoolhouse, the infirmary and six new masters' houses were erected, and by 1910 Justin Martyr had assumed very much the external appearance that it wears today. The enrollment and the faculty were doubled, and Francis Prescott took a long stride towards the deanship of New England headmasters.

The new, larger school was more democratic than the old. Justin Martyr has never had the aura of snobbishness under which Groton and St. Mark's have suffered. Well endowed with scholarships, it has many boys of humble background as well as sons of the old and new rich. My own work in interesting some of the greatest of our new industrialists in the school has swollen its treasury beyond that of any other comparable private school. Justin's reputation is an aggressive one, both in sports and studies. It is known not to suffer fools gladly. Perhaps it has been a bit severe, but one can't have everything. The school was named for the early martyr and scholar who tried to reconcile the thinking of the Greek philosophers with the doctrines of Christ. Not for Prescott were the humble fishermen who had their faith and faith alone.

Shelley Tanager graduated the year after Max Totten's expulsion, but only by the blond hair of his head. He then proceeded to drink his way through Harvard to an early grave. But in his more drunken bouts before the end he was inclined to tell strange stories, and there was one in particular that came to my tensely listening ears about a self-sacrificing friend. It had two versions. In the first the friend was a sort of Sydney Carton who repaid his debt to his roommate's father by assuming his roommate's misdeed. In the other he was a sinister creature who used a seeming sacrifice to replace his roommate in the affections of a millionaire parent. I confess that my first reaction to the news of Tanager's death was one of relief that the source of these rumors was now dry.

I never got up the courage to ask Prescott if he had heard them, but I did once ask Harriet, on one of our walks after a trustees' meeting.

"Of course he heard them," she replied. "Frank hears everything. People say he's so formidable, but it doesn't seem to keep them from blabbing their secrets to him. It's unbelievable what they tell that man! Perhaps they want to shock him."

"But did he believe it? I mean, that Max Totten let himself be expelled to protect Tanager?"

She gave me the briefest glance. Oh, the briefest! Harriet knew how to do that. "Do you?"

"Not in the least!"

She nodded, apparently accepting it. "Well, I don't know what Frank thought. I suspect that he didn't really face it. In fact, I wonder if he didn't turn his back on it."

"That doesn't sound like him."

"It doesn't, does it? But, you know, David, every man has his moments of evasion. He wouldn't be human if he didn't. And you know how he cares about *that*." She turned and pointed with her umbrella to the great dark craggy tower of the new chapel that dominated the campus and even the countryside, the tower which had become already, on platters and seals and postcards, the very symbol of the school and of Frank Prescott's bold thrust into the infinity of ignorance. "How do you think," she demanded, facing me with her challenging stare, "he could live with it if he thought it had been built on a lie?"

II

NOVEMBER 15, 1941. On opening this neglected journal I find that there have been no entries since April. My only excuse is that when Dr. Prescott retired in June, the bottom fell out of my life. Before he left for the Cape to visit his daughter, Mrs. Homans, he arranged for my scholarship at Harvard Divinity in the fall and offered me the hospitality of Justin in July and August to do my preparatory reading. Nothing could have been more kindly meant, and nobody could have been more unworthy of his kindness. During the long hot summer in the deserted school, with too many books and too few people, my nerves went back on me.

Everything on the campus from the graceful elms to the great beetling chapel tower reminded me of Dr. Prescott and seemed to point up the contrast between us. Did I dare aspire to ordination in a church where such men as he were priests? As the turgid days wore on, his absence and his retirement combined to create in my fantasies the hallucination of his demise, and the heavy red and grey of the school's architecture seemed to enclose me in a granite mausoleum. Within the campus and all around me was the death of dignified and mighty things and without, borne in by black headlines, was the death of barbarians in the ghastly Russian struggle. I did not lose my faith — not quite — but I lost everything else. By September I was in no possible state to enter divinity school.

It was in this condition that Mr. Griscam found me when he stopped at the school on his way down from Northeast Harbor. He took me out for dinner at the New Paisley Inn, forced me to drink two strong cocktails and elicited the dreary story of my summer. He guessed at once that what most appalled me was the prospect of telling Dr. Prescott the small advantage I had taken of his goodwill.

"My dear fellow, leave that to me," he said blandly. "Frank will understand. He's the last person to push anyone into the ministry. Why, he had to go into the railroad business before he could make up his own mind. The only thing to do with a doubt, to paraphrase Oscar Wilde, is to give in to it. But afterwards one mustn't just mope. What are you going to do?"

I told him that my heart classified me as 4F, but that I hoped to get a Red Cross job that would send me overseas.

"So like a young man," he said with his tolerant smile, "to think first of his conscience and last of his utility. You'd all rather clean latrines than be Secretary of War, so long as you can get into something that looks like a uniform. But you should be above that, Brian. You should come and work in my 'Freedom First' Committee."

He explained that this had been organized to combat the "America First" movement and spread propaganda for immediate intervention in the war. If I believed, he argued, what I professed to believe: that every man and woman in the free world should join the fight against Hitler, then I ought to help to persuade them. When I protested in dismay that I would be urging other young men to shoulder arms in a struggle where I could take no active part, he pointed out that the moral comfort which I would thus be giving up might be precisely the sacrifice which the war demanded of me. When I insisted that I could never accept a salary for such work and could hardly live in New York without one, he offered me room and board in his own house and a chance to earn pocket money by cataloguing his Elizabethan collection.

I was no match, certainly in my nervous state, for the arguments of so persuasive a lawyer and diplomat. The very next day he bore me off, with my few chattels and the little portrait of Richardson, in the back seat of his big black Cadillac, and before I quite realized what had happened, I found myself in a long row of desks in a big office overlooking Fifth Avenue whose walls were covered with the banners of occupied nations, writing releases on what it was like to live under the Nazi boot. It has all been a bit of a nightmare, but I keep reminding myself of Mr. Griscam's injunction that I am sacrificing the only thing I could sacrifice: my own isolation and ease of conscience. It has been a consolation to think that in all likelihood we will soon be in the war, and then the offices of "Freedom Now" can be shut for good.

Life with the Griscams in Sixty-eighth Street is as comfortable, I'm sure, as money, servants and good management can make it, and it is only my self-consciousness that makes me suffer. I cannot convince myself that the maid who does my room in the morning does not regard my presence as an imposition and that the grave old butler in the dining hall below does not resent having to set an extra place at table. Yet their demeanor, I hasten to record, is perfect. Everything, in fact about this big yellow sandstone house is perfect. Perhaps that is just my trouble.

It is not, however unbecoming it may be in a guest to say so, that the "things" are good. Mr. Griscam himself is under no illusions about them. The mural of shepherds and shepherdesses in the yellow and pink "Louis XVI" parlor, he tells me, are copies of Hubert Robert, and the refectory table in the medieval dining room was manufactured to his measurements. Indeed, the oldest things in the house (outside of the folios in the library) are the big academic paintings of mountainous landscapes and rather fierce animals collected by Mrs. Griscam's late father. But what makes it all different, what makes it unique, is the "mint condition" (to borrow one of Mr. Griscam's bibliophilic terms) in which everything is kept, which ends by giving to the mansion a kind of museum glow that awes and dominates.

It is also noteworthy that Mr. Griscam does everything himself. It is to him that the servants look, and it is his eye that they fear if an ashtray goes more than five minutes unemptied. Mrs. Griscam seems to be above such matters. She is a "saint" who gives her time and energies to the Army of the Holy Word, an evangelical organization devoted to the intenser religious life. Some of the benignity of her cause seems to have washed over her person. She is tall, pale, lovely, with a high brow, soft grey hair and mild, undistinguishing blue eyes. I cannot help feeling that her love for the masses must have somewhat diluted her feeling for individuals and that her family may find her a bit impersonal as a wife and mother. But one's heart goes out to her when she walks. Nature meant her to be regal, and she limps awkwardly on a leg withered by childhood polio.

She was slightly put off the first night at dinner when Mr. Griscam told her of my abortive clerical career. Evidently she regards the church as inclined to be critical of evangelical movements. But when I turned the conversation to what I thought would be the more congenial subject of Dr. Prescott, I was surprised to discover that I would have done better to stay with her "army." Indeed, she was almost crisp.

"Frankly, Mr. Aspinwall, I have never entirely approved of Dr. Prescott's influence on my husband. It has always seemed to me that a private church school is a contradiction in terms. How can religion be packaged for the privileged and sold to the select?"

I was taken aback that *she*, in such "private" surroundings and the mother of two Justin boys, should take so sharp an attitude, but I reflected that the family as well as the household decisions were probably left to her husband. Mrs. Griscam seems to live as a kind of guest, however critical a one, in her own home.

"I suppose Dr. Prescott might answer that he would gladly build enough Justins to educate all America. He does what he can."

"Which I'm afraid is not enough," Mrs. Griscam rejoined with a touch of asperity. "I'm prepared to admit that Frank Prescott believes in God, but he's very fussy about how God is retailed. In my organization we believe in distributing God wholesale."

I sighed. "I wonder if that's not easier."

"Perhaps you would like to come to one of our meetings," she suggested with a flicker of interest, and when I told her that I would be glad to and when she saw that I meant it, we achieved a mild friendliness.

Yet if Dr. Prescott was not always a name enthusiastically received in Sixty-eighth Street, I discovered that it invariably hit some kind of nerve, in the children as well as the parents. There had been three of the former, two of whom, Sylvester and Amy, survive and live at home. I knew from Mr. Ives that the other son, Jules, had committed suicide after a disastrous career at Justin and Harvard. Sylvester, a long, gangling man with yellow-grey hair and Mrs. Griscam's blue eyes (except that his are watery) has recently been estranged from his second wife and has moved home, as he tells me frankly, because it's cheaper than his club. He professes a devotion to Dr. Prescott, but I wonder if the latter might not prefer his mother's more caustic attitude.

"I'm sorry my little son Davey won't have the old man when he goes to Justin," he told me one morning at breakfast. "You can say what you want about his being too rigid and behind the times, but you can't get away from the fact that he's a magnificent example."

"Of what?" I asked, in sincere curiosity.

"Why of anything!" Sylvester exclaimed in surprise. "Of the Christian ethic, if you like. I remember Sam Lovell at his Fly

Club initiation getting up on a table and shouting: 'Dr. Prescott is the nearest man to God on earth!' and Jim Copperly shouting back: 'God damn it, man, he *is* God!' No, you can't get away from it, Brian, it was a great thing to have been exposed to him."

I noted the repetition of the idea that I couldn't "get away" from such an allowance. It is one that I have heard before from Justin graduates, the concept that it is somehow desirable to be "exposed" to Dr. Prescott, as if he were a childhood malady like measles. Few of the old Justinians seem to have any feeling that his principles should have a continuing validity in their lives. I find it upsetting.

I could listen to Amy on the subject with less apprehension, for Amy did not represent any possible failure on Dr. Prescott's part. Amy lives for horses and horse shows. Thirty-seven and unwed, she is fair and bulky, with big, handsome features and a voice that carries to the furthest corners of the large stone house. She sets herself up to be her father's champion, but the bluntness of her partisanship must at times embarrass him.

"How do *you* feel about Dr. Prescott, Miss Griscam?" I made bold to ask her that same morning when Sylvester had left the table. "Do you like him, as your brother does, or do you feel, like your mother, that his influence on the Griscams is not altogether for the good?"

"It's never been a question of my liking him. I didn't have to like or dislike him. I wasn't a boy. But I certainly resented him."

"Because your father admired him?"

"No. Because he dwarfed Daddy. You know what they used to say of Teddy Roosevelt? That he was like a magnificent plane tree. That nothing grew in his shade. Well, Dr. Prescott is that way. Like a great Broadway star whom the people out front applaud. But as a child I was always in the wings. I could see the other people: the director, the stage manager, the electricians." Here she paused significantly. "I could even see the author of the play."

"But surely Dr. Prescott is the author of Justin Martyr," I protested.

"Only in the beginning. He had the initial idea, I grant. But who raised the endowment fund? Who doubled the enrollment? Who instituted the exchange masterships and brought the finest minds to the school? Who established the pension plan? Who bought the big neighboring estate and saved the school from finding itself in the center of a housing development? And, finally, who discovered Duncan Moore?"

"Your father, of course. Yet I imagine most people think of Justin as Dr. Prescott's school. The two names are almost synonymous."

"And who made them so?" she exclaimed triumphantly. "Whose idea was it that the school needed a prophet? Why, the legend of Frank Prescott is simply the pinnacle of Daddy's masterwork!"

I decided that it would be idle to press the point further and asked about her hunters in Westbury.

Mr. Griscam himself dwelt continually on the subject of the biography which he had now persuaded himself that I was actually writing. It was in vain that I kept telling him that I was not even positive that I would ever do so. He was determined that if he was not going to write the book himself, he would at least have a hand in its preparation. In similar fashion, as I knew from his notebooks, when he had seen that he would never teach at Justin, he had concentrated on being a trustee. Now he wanted me to interview graduates, and he was quite prepared to make all the necessary appointments. In desperation, I finally had to refuse point-blank.

"I must do things my own way, Mr. Griscam," I pleaded. "Please try to understand that."

"I would try to understand it if I could see that you were doing anything," he said in his patient, remorseless tone. "If you're too shy to talk to the Justin men, what about the women? Cordelia Turnbull lives right around the corner. She'd adore to see you any time. She *loves* to talk about her father!"

"If I'm going to talk to Dr. Prescott's daughters," I said evasively, "shouldn't I start with the oldest?"

"With Harriet Kidder?" He shook his head firmly. "You wouldn't get anywhere. I've tried. Harriet is that executive type of Manhattan matron to whom 'sweet charity' is synonymous with the speakers' dais at the Waldorf Astoria. Of course, she's very much admired — that sort of woman always is. 'Isn't Harriet wonderful?' people keep asking me. But when you've sat on as many committees with as many Harriets as I have, you know that their real genius lies in passing the buck."

"She wasn't interested in the book?"

"Oh, she was interested, all right. She considers herself 'Pa's favorite.' But every time she condescended to open the purse of her reminiscences out would tumble some tired old bit of folklore that any first former at Justin might know. You'll find that's apt to be so with the children of famous persons. Marie Antoinette's daughter will always tell you how her mother let the poor eat cake."

"What about the second daughter?" All that I knew about her was that she wasn't in New York, but that made me prefer her to Mrs. Turnbull.

"Evelyn Homans? She's worse. She married back into old Boston and believes that a man belongs exclusively to his descendants. She presumed to dictate to me what facts I could and could not use, even when they were facts that *I* knew at first hand and she didn't. She doesn't want a life of her father. She wants a floral tribute."

"But Mrs. Turnbull is different?"

"Oh, Cordelia is different from everyone. Cordelia is a 'character.' After she divorced Guy Turnbull and got her big settlement, she had the sense to convert herself from a bad artist to a good collector. You should go just to see the paintings in that duplex. Room after room full of Picassos, Braques and Kandinskys!"

"I'm sure she'd scare me to death."

"No, no. I tell you, there's nothing she likes so much as talking about herself and her family. I'll call and find out when she can see you."

Protest was futile, and I had to sit wretchedly by while he made the call. Of course he was right. Mrs. Turnbull was only too delighted to see me.

That afternoon, when I was ushered into the great white room, high above Park Avenue, I found her, dark-haired, pale-skinned, with square, stubborn face and luminous brown eyes, reclining in brilliant pink, with an amber necklace and ruby earrings, on a low, backless couch. It was as if Theda Bara were playing Madame Butterfly, or as if Dr. Prescott, in some fantastic masquerade, were playing Theda Bara. "I like your coming straight to me," she said with a half-mocking smile, not unlike her father's. "I like your not going first to Harriet or Evelyn. But, of course, that was David's tip."

I decided in my nervousness that the only way to cope with her tone was to be utterly serious. "You mean they wouldn't be able to help me?"

She shrugged. "I mean that their childhood resentments are too shallow a stream for a biographer to splash about in."

I took a breath. After all, what was I really afraid of? "But yours are deeper?"

"Well, let's put it this way, Mr. Aspinwall. *I* know they're resentments."

"And what do Mrs. Kidder and Mrs. Homans think that theirs are?"

"Why, true pictures of Pa, of course! They *seethe* with hate. They spend their lives trying to reconcile it with the love that 'nice' daughters are supposed to feel for their fathers."

"And to what do you owe your special insight?"

"Psychoanalysis. What else? Four long years of it. It's the only way left to grow up. Weren't you ever analyzed, Mr. Aspinwall?"

"No."

"A pity. You might have learned some interesting things. Why you're so obsessed with Pa, for example. Perhaps you have what Dr. Klaus calls 'Peter Panic.' You want to be a schoolboy again." As she exhaled blue smoke from her cigarette, she studied me carefully. "And why you fiddle with the Phi Beta Kappa key on your watch chain. Isn't that a form of psychic masturbation?"

I flushed crimson as I moved my hands to the black steel arms of the chair. Seeing she had now thoroughly shocked me, she was ready to turn to business. "What do you want to know about Pa?"

What indeed? After a few bewildered moments I found that my mind was empty of all subjects but her own terrible ones. "Would *he* have profited by analysis?" I asked.

"Not in the least." Her headshake seemed to dispose of this and of me. "If a man's lucky enough to be born a great artist, why should he seek to find out what made him that? The duds, like myself, have to, because otherwise they'd never have the sense to stop. But let the Leonardos just go on painting! No, if you want to learn about Pa, you can expect no help from analysts. You have to do the job yourself."

"Well, that lets me out," I said in relief. "I lack the equipment."

"Can't you even make a stab at it?" she demanded indignantly. "It shouldn't be *that* hard. Let's begin at the beginning. You're writing about a schoolmaster. Does he teach boys or girls? Boys. Very well, there's your first question. When did he begin to be attracted to his own sex?"

I hesitated. "I wonder if I'd put it quite that way."

"How else?"

"Surely you don't mean to imply . . . !"

"Oh, you non-analyzed," she interrupted impatiently. "You're so afraid of words. You're shocked to death for fear I'm going to call Pa a homosexual. I tell you, we're *all* homosexual! To one degree or another."

"I should think your father's degree was a very small one indeed," I protested, appalled.

"But still a degree," she insisted. "And if you want to understand human beings, you must jettison all that middle-class squeamishness about technical terms. There are certain very striking facts about Pa. As a handsome, popular young man, he married an exceedingly plain woman."

"But there were ladies before your mother," I pointed out, beginning, despite my agonized embarrassment, to wax hot. "Very beautiful ladies, too."

"Oh, yes. Before *and* after. That's still another story. But he married the plain one. Another striking fact is his horror of the very subject we're talking about. He was always suspicious of any more than casual friendship between two boys."

"But a headmaster, Mrs. Turnbull, . . ."

"Let me finish, dearie. Everyone knows that Pa had a bee in his bonnet about perversion. And naturally, we all know that a completely normal man does not fear that sort of thing. We only fear what *threatens.*"

"I thought there were no normal men. I thought we were all homosexuals."

Seeing she had at last made me angry, she smiled and proceeded to wax philosophic. "I'll tell you *my* theory about Pa. Actually, it's not Freudian, it's Jungian. I believe that Pa is an archaic type. A throwback to the ancient Greeks. He has always looked down on women. You have to have been his daughter to know how much. They don't really exist for him, except to satisfy a man's physical needs, bear his children and keep his house. Hence beauty in women is not essential, any more than it is essential to animals. Sex is divorced from love. Only men are worthy of love, platonic love, and this love among men is stimulated by beauty of mind, beauty of soul, even beauty of body. Do you see?"

I was dangerously close now to calling her a silly ass. It was too irritating to hear this cocksure woman, who had made a mess of two marriages, sneer at her parents', which had lasted half a century. But Mrs. Turnbull, if an ass, was no fool, and she was obviously dying to talk. I began to understand that Mr. Griscam might be right and that perhaps it was my duty to take it down. "Would you be willing to tell me more about it?" I asked. "I mean about you and your father?"

"Right now? On the couch? By free association?"

"Any way you want to."

"Let's have a drink and start!"

Actually, it took us only two sessions. Or rather two was all *I* could take. I have a suspicion that she would have been glad to prolong them indefinitely. I took no notes while she was talking, but each evening I confided my recollections to the typewriter as soon as I got back to Sixty-eighth Street. What follows is thus not a transcript of Cordelia's actual words, but my memory of them. Yet I venture to think that I have caught some of her flavor.

12

I WAS born in 1895, the baby of the family, the third of three girls, and because of complications attending my Caesarian birth it was decided that Mother should not be allowed to try again for the son whom she and Pa had so desperately wanted. Poor little fellow, I may have cost him his life, but when I think of the problems that any son of Pa would have had to face, it occurs to me that a wise providence may have known what it was about. Pa took his revenge on me by a gleeful exercise of his sardonic sense of humor in the choice of my name. Imagine the lifetime of bad jokes that I have had to endure, as a third daughter, with the name Cordelia!

But Shakespeare was a game that two could play, and there have been times, I'm sure, when poor Pa would have carried me across the stage, hanged and dead, with only mirth in his heart as he cried: "Howl, howl." I cannot imagine why Mother ever put up with such nonsense except that she had a rich aunt who was also named Cordelia. The aunt, incidentally, left me nothing.

Mother was acutely aware from the beginning of the difficulties of bringing up her daughters in the center of a boys' school. She was determined that we should not be petted and spoiled and grow up with silly notions of standing, like musical comedy princesses, on balconies while choruses of hussars sang our praises, and saw to it instead that we received instruction even tougher than that meted out to the boys. But however well she was able to teach me to read Greek at twelve and to understand Darwin at fourteen, she was less successful in coping with the strong strain of romantic melancholy that I inherited from Pa.

Mother was as rational as she was plain, as sensible as she was unimpressable. I think of her now as she was in her later years, tall, gaunt, a bit bent, with dyed brown hair and a great hook nose and small, darting eyes, walking around and around the campus, even on the wettest afternoons, dressed in brown tweed with a small brown ridiculous beret pulled tightly about her oval head. I am sure the boys called her a witch, but I hope they thought her a friendly one. She was sometimes formidable and sometimes almost scaringly detached as a parent, but she always tried to make her girls feel that they were as important as Pa's sacred boys.

I don't know how good a headmaster's wife she was, by ordinary standards. She wasn't gracious; she wasn't stately, and she made a poor enough show on the dais on Prize Day squinting nearsightedly at the titles of the volumes that she handed out. But she never forgot a boy's name, and she would argue with them over games of chance and in debates on "parlor night" as hotly as if they had been contemporaries. She was absolutely democratic, in an early Boston transcendentalist way, and she helped Pa to keep faculty feuds over precedence to a minimum. Above all, she could maintain Pa on an even keel when everyone else had failed. I think it must have been clear to all their intimates that she adored him (how that man was adored!) but she was never in the least a submissive wife.

I remember one summer at the Cape when Pa had been paying too much attention to a pretty neighbor (oh, yes, Mr. Aspinwall, that happened — you needn't look so shocked — maybe not actual infidelities, but cozy chats in windowseats and long, *long* walks on the beach) that Mother simply disappeared for three days. It turned out later that she had been in a hotel in Boston. When she came back, as seemingly cool and detached as ever, without offering the smallest excuse or explanation of where she had been, Pa, who had been frenzied by her absence, was a chastened man. He might have endured being left alone with his boys, but never with his girls.

We children grew up without ever feeling that we belonged to any particular group or class. Pa and Mother, of course, were supreme at Justin, but from the beginning we knew that Justin was not the real world. The real world was a summer world, seen on trips to Europe or at the Cape, and although it treated Pa and Mother with respect, it was the kind of respect that people might pay to the sovereigns of a small Pacific Island kingdom, more exotic than powerful, not quite to be taken seriously, perhaps even a bit ridiculous. I thought I could sense as a child among the graduates and the parents of the boys that curious half paternal, half protective, almost at times half contemptuous, attitude of men of affairs for academics, and I was determined that I should lead my own life in such a way as to be able ultimately to bid a plague on both kinds of houses. I would be neither sneered upon nor a sneerer. I would be an actress, a poet, a great artist and return to Justin only when Pa begged me, as a special treat, to come back and perform to the dazzled boys.

I should like to skip as quickly as possible over my first big mistake. Green as I then was, I still blush for it. I eloped with a young man whom I met at a tea dance given for me in Boston when I was seventeen by my great-aunt, Cordelia Hooper. His name was Cabell Willetts; he came of an old, devout Catholic family, and he had never in his life been away from his bigoted old mother, even to go to boarding school. He was mild and sweet and weak and ultimately stubborn. It's easy to see what he represented to me: he was the reverse in every respect of what Pa would have wanted a graduate of Justin to be.

I had hoped that my family would be shocked and by like token, impressed, by a daughter who had found her consolation in an older faith and in an older God, married to a husband who had always been above the juvenilities of football and "school spirit." I should have known better. The eloping couple were greeted back with smiles and open arms, and Pa told me, in a private conference, shaking his head in his gravest manner, that he, too, had had his doubts over the historic break with Rome. If I, like Cardinal Newman, had been losing my sleep over the idea of a church founded on a king's lust for Anne Boleyn, who was Frank Prescott, a simple, groping parson, to say I was a foolish worrier?

Really! Anyone who hadn't known Pa would have thought he was making fun of me. What was I to Anne Boleyn or she to me? The only queen who entered my mind in the wretched three years of my married life was Eleanor of Guienne who said of Louis VII that she had married a monk. But she, at least, got her divorce. Willetts and his mother adamantly refused me mine, and when I finally left the house in Dedham, with all its stucco virgins and gold crosses and jewel-studded missals, I felt lucky to be able to take the clothes on my back.

I could have established a residence in a state with easy divorce laws, but at that point I could not be bothered. I went to New York and to Greenwich Village and rented a studio and tried to paint. It was what I call my "Edna St. Vincent Millay period," and the less questions you ask about it, the better. What? You have none? How disappointing. But, of course, I must remember that you are interested only in Pa and that I exist simply in the biological fact that he sired me. It is a point of view to which I have become *very* accustomed.

I don't pride myself that my bohemian life scandalized Pa. I doubt if he wasted a serious thought upon it. Mother occasionally came to New York and insisted on staying at the studio and sleeping on a daybed; she shut her eyes to my men and opened them to my paintings. I think she was honest when she said that she liked them, and I have a suspicion that she envied me my independence. When we entered the war in 1917, I went abroad with the Red Cross, relieved and exalted to see the chaos of the world, and Pa, thoroughly approving of my adventurousness and jealous that I should be so near the Front and he so far, wrote me long, introspective letters to the effect that a lifetime's education was not the equivalent of a minute of Armageddon.

No, alas, I don't have those letters. I always destroy letters. It's a leftover from the days when they might have proved embarrassing. And, of course, I knew that Pa was not really writing to me; he was simply soliloquizing. We did not communicate, in the sense of his truly thinking of *me* and I of him, until more than a year after the war, in Paris where I had remained, an appropriate addition to the riffraff of Americans who could not face a return to a normalcy for which they tried to believe that the war had disabled them. Oh, Aspinwall, don't shake your head; I know they weren't *all* riffraff. But *I* was. And I was well aware that Charley Strong was not. It was over Charley that my first real bout with Pa began.

He was one of Pa's golden boys, Justin '11, senior prefect and football captain, a kind of American Rupert Brooke, at least in romantic appearance, blond, with sleepy grey eyes, a bit on the short side, but muscular and stocky, terribly serious and sincere, a savage tackle but gentle as a mother with children, honorable, naïve, charming, the kind of man who would protect his lady fair from a hundred wild Indians but whom *she* would have to protect from a swindling salesman — in short a magazine-cover hero, a Parsifal, Pa's ideal because the opposite of Pa.

What, you may ask, was such a man doing with such a gal as

me? Was not the chrism upon his head, on mine the dew? They were, indeed, but Mrs. Browning's next line applied also, for death *did* dig the level where these agreed. Poor Charley was a shrapnel victim in 1919, one of his lungs torn to shreds, and he had stayed on in Paris, because, as he put it, there wasn't enough of him to be worth taking home. He was condemned, but still beautiful in his decline, and the puzzled hurt look in those now desperately searching grey eyes was enough to turn to soapsuds a much harder heart than mine.

We had met, of course, at Justin in the early days, but he had been one of those athletic adolescents who will not so much as look at the other sex until complete maturity. And if he had been interested earlier, he would not have looked at me, a snappish, pigtailed, awkward girl who tried to conceal her sticks of legs in blue-stockings. "Billy Budd," I called him, in revenge for his indifference, but he was too unlettered to know what I meant. In Paris after the war, however, our physical positions had been reversed. I had "filled out," and Charley, poor darling, was a coughing shadow of the former football captain. He was dumfounded by the apparition in a city that symbolized to him the snatching of the day of a daughter of Francis Prescott.

We met at Horace Havistock's, that mean old friend of Pa's whose final decadence, after a lifetime of sipping tea in Walter Gay interiors, cackling gossip and collecting the most banal kind of impressionist canvases, was to assemble in his chaste halls the forlornly aging youth of the lost generation. You smile. Do you know him? Well, that's the way he is, isn't it? He wanted, the old vulture, to console himself for his own wasted life by surrounding himself with wasted youth.

Charley and I sat on his terrace till early morning, talking about what was real and what was sham. Charley had become very intense and passionate about finding what he called "some clean little rag of truth in the dirty laundry of the world."

What he wanted to know of me was whether or not the prewar Cordelia Prescott had been real. Had we actually existed, I and my sisters, in those quaint far-off Justin days? For if we had existed, then perhaps Justin had existed, and, of course, Pa, too, and how could he reconcile Pa and God (for Pa *was* God, I suppose) with what he had seen in the trenches?

He wanted dogma, whether from heaven or hell, and he certainly got it, for I was then at my most dogmatic. I told him that reality consisted of intensity of emotional experience and that we lived solely in our feelings. We had only the present, and very little of that; most people, in fact, never lived at all. The past existed only in remembered emotion: therefore the retained horror of the trenches was more real than the vague, sweet pastoral idyll that had been Justin. Charley listened to me carefully. I don't believe that anyone had ever spoken to him with such authority since the days when he had been under the spell of another Prescott. It was like a road company performance of *Tannhauser,* where the same soprano doubles for Elizabeth and Venus. Charley must have felt that he had heard that voice before.

"There is sensation," he kept muttering, "and there is Paris."

"And they're one and the same. Let's make the most of it!"

We became lovers, but not as soon as you might have thought in those easy days. I had first to overcome his scruples about Pa. It took me three months to erode the paralyzing vision of his old headmaster in the pulpit, a hand and forefinger outstretched. Poor Charley wanted to marry me, but I was still undivorced, and the absurdity of my legal position, shackled to a monk, was my trump card in persuading him that Pa himself would not wish me denied all sexual gratification. Yet for all my chatter, for all my efforts to liberalize his thinking, after our first night together Charley solemnly took my hand in his and told me that in the eyes of God, if there was a God, we were now man and wife.

We lived as such, anyway. Charley rented a beautiful studio in the Place des Vosges, embarrassingly grand for my inadequate oils but ideal for parties, and we soon became well-known hosts to the floating expatriate world that made a fetish of disillusionment. One begins to find references to us now in the journals and letters of the period that are being published. There is a tendency to sentimentalize the "lost generation" and its Paris refuge, and I suppose that it did include some important writers and painters. But for every man of talent in our group, there were three drunks, and a drunk is a drunk the world over.

One thing I will admit about old Havistock is that he was the first to recognize this. He early became disenchanted with the disillusioned. My liaison with Charley may have hastened the process. For all his vaunted freedom from prejudice he was shocked to the core and dropped us both. Perhaps he was afraid that Pa would hold him responsible. Or perhaps he simply made the old distinction of a nasty Victorian bachelor between the monde and the demimonde. A lady, at least one who had been born one, could not exist in both. Horace Havistock was a malevolent survival from an early Bourget novel.

You mustn't get the notion that Charley and I did nothing but carouse. He would have died even earlier had that been the case. On weekdays we led a very regular life. I painted in the mornings, and Charley wrote, and in the afternoons we went for a drive, for he tired too easily for walking. We went to bed early, as he woke up continually in the night, and sometimes I would find him at dawn, sitting by the big studio window, a pad in his hand, usually blank, for he wrote very sparingly. He was working, he told me, on a semi-fictional journal about his childhood and the war, a kind of literary free association. Charley had read with passionate interest the first of Proust's novels and had been taken by Mr. Havistock to visit the author in his cork-lined room. I suppose the journal was his own *recherche du temps perdu*.

I would not read it, at least then. I was too sure that it would be bad, and I did not want to discourage him in any enterprise that gave him an interest in living. Also, I was afraid of the effect of what I then imagined would be a turgid, childish prose on my image of the doomed Keatsian hero. I was sophisticated enough to know that the written word is no mirror of the writer's character, that the amateur, though a selfless angel, may show himself a pompous ass, while the professional, a monster of ego, can convince you in a phrase that he has the innocence of a child. I had in my mind's eye a likeness of Charley that, for all my would-be realism, might have been sketched by Rossetti or Burne-Jones. I did not want it blurred.

As I look back, I realize that I must have known him very little. Perhaps I talked too much. I always have. I thought he was conventionally neurotic, a standard case of postwar despair. I did not appreciate the difference between one like himself, who had lost a real faith, and one like me who had never had one. I wore the mood of Yankee Paris in 1920 as if it had been a new hat; he wore it in his soul. Charley was not content, like the rest of us, to bask picturesquely in the cemetery of his hopes, a shaker of martinis on one headstone, a pipe of hasheesh on another. He was desperately and earnestly fighting the chaos which I wanted to cut up into colorful strips to use for studio decorations. If he resented me, he was too much of a gentleman ever to say so. Besides, he needed a friend, a companion and, increasingly, a nurse. In the latter capacity my war training stood me in good stead. It gives me a bit of consolation now, in view of how often I failed him, to remind myself that at least I ministered to his physical comfort.

One late June day at noon, while I was working on a still life, a glass of red wine on a table by my easel, and while Charley, still in a kimono and pajamas, was lounging on a sofa, pad in lap, gazing moodily out the window, there was a loud rap at our door. As I went to open it, I heard Pa's unmistakable deep basso, singing, in perfect key, the theme of the students from the first act of *Bohème*. For one horror-stricken moment I debated not opening. Then I turned to warn Charley who fled to our bedroom. When Pa stepped over the threshold, his arms loaded with packages, he was at his most ebullient, his most awful.

"Cordelia, my dear child! May the mild bright sky that shone on Vigée-le-Brun and Rosa Bonheur shine upon your palette! Give me a hug! Your mother and I docked last night at Le Havre. She's unpacking at the Vendôme."

Once he had embraced me, he went straight to my canvas, taking in the wineglass with a flicker of the eye, as hard to miss as it was ostensibly tactful, that would have done credit to a veteran performer at the Française. "And is this what the French call a dead nature?" He nodded slowly as he gazed at my poor effort. "Ah yes, my child, I can see that you have made strides, and with seven-league boots! Only I wonder if that lemon couldn't do with a little perking up."

It was just what it did need, damn him. "Look, Pa," I said sourly, "if you and Mother have sprung this surprise visit to make an honest woman of me, you can save your breath. Charley and I are quite happy with things as they are."

"Can't an old couple come to Europe on their vacation without being accused of interfering?" Pa rolled his eyes in a graphic parody of reproach. "Do you realize we haven't crossed the Atlantic since 1912? Do you and Charley *own* Paris? Should I have gone to you for a visa?"

"You know perfectly well what I mean."

"I'm blessed if I do. How *is* poor Charley?"

"Why don't you ask him?"

Pa turned to face Charley who had just emerged from our bedroom, in grey flannels and a red sweater. He was pale as I had never seen him, and his eyes had a dull glitter.

"Charley, my boy!" Pa approached him with outstretched arms, but Charley stepped quickly back.

"No, Dr. Prescott," he said in a strangled voice, "I cannot take your hand until I know that you respect me."

"Respect you? Of course I respect you! What on earth are you thinking of?"

"I mean, respect Cordelia and me as man and wife."

Pa's pursed lips and soaring eyebrows, his immediate grave headshake and the suppressed whistle that one could almost hear would again have been worthy of French classical comedy. "But, my dear fellow, isn't that precisely what you're not? Isn't it, so to speak, the point?"

"The point of what?"

"Why, the point of your being so prickly and defensive. The point of your not taking my hand." Here Pa turned suddenly and shrewdly back to me. "Do *you*, Cordie, consider that you and Charley are married?"

"Legally, no, of course not."

"Religiously, then?"

"I don't happen to be religious."

"Alas, poor child, you have suffered from an overdose of Rome." He returned his full attention to Charley. "But of course I see what you mean. You mean that your relationship with Cordelia is a serious one. That neither of you would be unfaithful to the other. That you *would*, indeed, be married were it not for Cabell Willetts' arbitrary refusal to give Cordelia a divorce. But I must still insist, all that does not make a marriage. It does not even make what is called a common-law marriage. Now, wait, wait, Charley, before you blow up."

Pa placed two heavy hands on Charley's trembling shoulders and shook him gently. "I haven't come to call down anathemas on you and Cordie. I'm not the old blood and thunder type of parson. It's a wonder those old men didn't drive their flocks straight back to the Pope. Perhaps some of them did. Try to remember that I, too, was young once and that there was a Paris even then."

"Oh, young," Charley muttered with a searing bitterness. "You'll never be as old as I am now, sir." And he pulled himself free of Pa's grip and sat down morosely on the sofa, plunging his face in his hands.

Pa interpreted his action as at least accepting his own continued presence. He took a seat by the sofa and continued to address himself exclusively to Charley. "I'm not pretending that I'm pleased to have you and Cordie living as you are. You wouldn't believe it if I said I was. But I love you both, and I want to help you. Don't throw me out, Charley. Don't hurt me. I've tried not to hurt you."

"Oh, Dr. P," Charley moaned, his face still covered. "It's too crazy to have you in Paris like this. Don't you see my position? It's impossible, utterly impossible!"

"Don't you see mine? Nothing is impossible if we both try."

"But I'd ceased to believe you existed!" Charley exclaimed, half hysterically now, looking up at Pa in agony. "Cordie had persuaded me that you weren't real!"

Pa shot a glance in my direction. Just a glance, but it would have convinced a total stranger which of the two of us he had come to save. "Really, Charley," I protested, annoyed, "I didn't mean Pa personally. I meant Justin, or rather what Justin stood for in your mind."

"Cordie has her motives for not wanting me to be real," Pa said with a hint of grimness. "Every child has. But parents are not that easily destroyed. We continue to exist, if for no other reason than that we may be able to help our children's friends."

It was evident at this point that Pa was going to stay and that he and Charley wanted to be alone, but I had no intention of leaving them. Unfortunately, as it was our cook's day off, I had eventually to go to the kitchen to fix lunch, and brief as I was when I returned with a tray of lettuce salad and cold chicken, they were on intimate terms again.

"No, you're wrong, Charley," Pa was saying earnestly. "I

can see that death might become the only reality. Of course, I've never been in a war. I've never been wounded or hungry or even particularly uncomfortable. But I have always been acutely conscious that such things existed. My father, you may remember, was killed in the Civil War when I was an infant, and I grew up in a world from which I thought all valor had departed. You would be astonished if you knew how many times in my life I have longed for the test of battle. How else could I know that I was a man? Or 'real,' as you would put it?"

"You wouldn't have longed for a war if you'd ever seen one," Charley muttered.

"Don't be too sure. Have we not all imaginations? Can one not visualize, at least to some degree, how it would feel to be cold and wet and hungry, smelling a mountain of rotting flesh, and knowing that any moment one might be added to it?"

"Please, Pa," I protested, "you'll only upset Charley."

"Don't interrupt, Cordie!" Charlie barked at me with a rudeness that he had never shown before, and I flushed angrily that Pa should be the witness of my humiliation.

"Oh, yes, my boy," Pa went on, heedless of the interruption, "we, too, have our nightmares, we who are left at home, haunted by never knowing how we would have measured up. They say that if the old men who made the wars had to fight them, we'd have eternal peace. I am not so sure. They might rush into battle! Here is reality, at last, at last. When I think of the nights that I have lain awake, imagining myself with limbs blown off in a trench, or burnt alive in the engine room of a sinking battleship or starving in a freezing prison camp, I sometimes wonder if I have not suffered as much from fancy in peace as I might have from reality in war. If so, it has served me right, for morbidness is a kind of vanity. My final punishment will probably be to die painlessly in bed."

Charley looked at him with wondering eyes. "Is courage so important? I should have thought courage mattered very little."

"That's because you have it. And *know* you have it."

Charley was too interested now to waste time in modesty. "And it is *that* you envy me? How curious. I should not give it a pin's fee alongside your faith. What can courage do? As Falstaff said of honor, can it set an arm? Can it take away the grief of a wound? But one *can* eat faith. One can live on faith." He stared at Pa for a moment and then, with a curious gesture of appeal, a faltering extension of his right arm, he asked: "*You* do, don't you?"

Pa's eyes glittered as he shook his head sadly. "If I had real faith, Charley, I should not worry about courage. For my fear would be cast out, would it not? And without fear, there would be no need of courage."

"But you *have* faith, do you not?" Charley persisted, with a stubborn, childish literalness. "You must have. For, after all, you do have courage, everyone knows that. It's just that you *think* you may not. You had the faith on which you built Justin. You did build it, didn't you?" He glanced now at me with what was beginning to seem like actual hostility. "I mean Cordie isn't right, is she? There *is* a school there, isn't there?"

"If I can convince you of that, then I haven't come to Paris in vain!" Pa exclaimed, slapping the little table on which I had lain his plate. "I don't care how you rate Justin. I don't care if you call it, as one graduate did, 'a motley derivative pile of red brick, shrouded in the fog of its headmaster's platitudes.' All I care is that you should admit it exists. Exists at least as much as that slithery rat that tried to eat your rations at Château-Thierry!"

Charley rose to his feet, trembling. "What do you know about that rat?" he cried hoarsely. "How could you know about that rat?"

"My dear fellow, don't look at me as if I were a magician. You wrote me about it."

"*I did?* And you got my letter?"

"Why should I not have got it?"

"Oh, I don't know." Charley collapsed again into the sofa. "I suppose because I doubted there was a world beyond the trenches."

"But I wrote you, too. Didn't you get my letters?"

"Yes, I suppose I did." Charley had a fit of coughing now which lasted until tears appeared in his eyes. "Yes, of course, I got your letters, Dr. P. Bless you for them. A fine return I've made for your kindness."

I rose at this, too suffocated by the sentiment in the room to remain there longer, and went to our bedroom to await Pa's leaving. Later that afternoon, alone with Charley, I tried to reason with him. I told him that he was not well enough to subject himself to the strain of further visits and that we both knew all that Pa would have to say. That under whatever guise of tolerance Pa chose to travel, his only purpose could be to separate us. That he was a wily old fox working subtly for the forces of superstition and bigotry. I suggested that I should make an appropriate number of filial visits to the Vendôme and leave Charley out of it.

"But you don't understand!" he shouted at me. "Your father doesn't care about *us*. He's trying to save my soul!"

"And he's given up on mine?"

"Of course not. But he has time for yours!"

"Really, Charley," I protested, "this isn't like you. I want you to have peace and quiet —"

"Peace and quiet!" he retorted brutally. "What do you know of peace and quiet? A woman like you can kid herself into believing that simple distraction is a philosophy of life. But I can't! I tell you, Cordie, stay out of this!"

I was so hurt that for a moment I was almost frightened. I would not have dreamed that Charley could have been so rough. I stood in the middle of the studio, a hand over my lips, staring at him like a little girl who has been unexpectedly and viciously slapped in the face. But he would not even look at me; he went to his post by the window and stared gloomily down into the street. I think I would have left him on the spot had I not known that he was dying. Even I was not such an egotist as to abandon a dying man.

Pa called every day at the studio in a rented touring car with a chauffeur and took Charley for a drive. They usually ended up sitting on a bench by the Seine where they had long religious discussions. At home Charley grew more and more taciturn. Sometimes he would hardly speak to me at all. He looked grey and haggard, and his coughing was much worse. Twice I found blood on his pillow in the morning, but when I begged him to go to the doctor he simply stared at me and shrugged. He was like a dope addict for whom the real world has ceased to exist. Pa, of course, was feeding him the dope, and I found myself as much ignored as some old ranting peasant mother whose boy had discovered urban amusements. If I dined at the Vendôme with Pa and Mother, Charley would refuse to accompany me. He had reached the point where he could no longer share my father. He had to have him all to himself.

I suppose it was jealousy, as well as frustration, that made me read the manuscript of Charley's book. He had often offered it to me, and I had always refused to look at it. Now, as I dipped surreptitiously into its pages while he was out with Pa, sitting by the window so that I would see him if he should come home early, I felt horribly guilty. For I wanted to find something in the book that would shock Pa if I should ever show it to him. Not that I had any intention of showing it — I had not dropped that low. But I wanted to feel that there was a part of Charley that would never belong to Pa, even if it never belonged to me. Alas, if there was such a part, I did not find it. The book was as pure as its author. Charley was that rarest of creatures: an innocent who was able to convey a sense of his own innocence.

Certainly it was a curious manuscript. A chapter might start with a list of the things that Charley had observed from the studio window, described in the plainest, flattest terms. This list would continue until his mind took off, like an airplane on a runway, and then there might follow panoramic pictures of Justin days, boating on the river and football and then more intimate ones, of Pa in chapel, of myself in Paris at a restaurant, or painting, or even in bed. The manuscript was candid without being in the least salacious. It had some of the quality of an amateur film. At times the characters seemed to be moving at a frenzied pace, jumping up and down and jabbering; at others the inaction and repetition became cloying. The most unusual aspect of the book was its jumbling of dates, so that a walk with me and a lyric description of rowing at Justin and the death of a sergeant in the trenches seemed simultaneous. And not only simultaneous but of equal value. Charley was intent on breaking down his experience into units of the same size, a procedure that enabled him to introduce a dreary, at times a rather frightening order into his chaos.

It embarrasses me to confess, even at this late date, that my first reaction was one of pique. Charley, whom, in matters of art, I had treated with such condescension, had produced a more interesting work than any of my *natures mortes!* The shallow artist is apt to make the best critic, and I was a shallow artist. My second reaction was equally egotistical, but less painful — I imagined that I saw the manuscript already published and heard my name on every tongue. I saw it printed on thick parchment by a private Paris press (the kind that Harry and Caresse Crosby later started) with heavy black script and drawings by Derain or Picasso. If Pa was taking Charley away from me, he at least had left me his book.

He had also left me Mother, with whom I spent my afternoons. She adored Paris and was trying to make up for the lost years of summer travel which the war has cost her. She could spend hours at the book counters along the Quai Conti where bargains were still to be had, and she was indefatigable at poking into back alleys in search of some surviving fragment of a medieval wall or keep. As her Paris seemed to end with Louis XI while mine began with Degas, it was all sufficiently boring for me, but I had not the heart to begrudge her the obvious pleasure of these peregrinations.

It would have been difficult to imagine a more un-Gallic figure than she cut, with her dull Boston clothes, her big nose and long unpowdered face, her total indifference to the preoccupations of Paris women, even to food and drink, yet at the same time I had to admit that she fitted into the city quite as easily as I did. There was a distinction about her, made up of her total honesty, her probing curiosity and her wonderfully good manners, to which the French immediately responded.

"The thing about your mother," a young French novelist told me, "is that the Atlantic doesn't exist for her. Most of you Americans are either absurdly proud or absurdly ashamed of living on the wrong side of it. But your ma's a genuine internationalist."

Of course, I took this to mean that *I* wasn't. Mother not only was making me feel a Philistine in the Paris to which I thought I had fled for Art's sake; now she was taking over my friends. At a party of painters and writers, she became the storm center of a discussion that raged over Henry Adams' study of Mont St. Michel and Chartres. She attacked him as a staunch medievalist for sentimentalizing, if not actually inventing, the cult of the virgin, and her loud driving syllables seemed to lay flat every distinction of age and class in the room so that we were all students together.

I decided that I would have to get out of Paris. The midsummer heat was becoming unbearable, and Mother made matters worse, the old lizard, by showing no effects of it while I unbecomingly sweated. I suggested that she and I go to Venice while Pa and Charley worked on the latter's soul and then down the

Dalmatian coast to Spalato where I knew she would want to see the noble remnants of Diocletian's palace. The idea intrigued her, and we went off; we spent two weeks in Venice and two in Spalato. In the middle of our visit to the latter, where conditions were primitive, we changed hotels, and Mother made a mistake in forwarding our new address to Paris. A total suspension of communications resulted, and when we finally got Pa's telegram, Charley had been dead two days.

We went straight from the train to the American Cathedral where Pa was to conduct the funeral, and we had no chance to speak to him before the service began. Never had I heard him read the comfortable words in a more beautiful or resonant tone, but in my numbed state, where feelings of bitter grief and abandonment loomed like dead monsters under the dark ice of my despair, he might have been declaiming a paean of triumph.

We sat in a pew behind Charley's widowed mother and spinster sister who lived on the Riviera and whom I had never met. After the service Pa walked with them to a waiting limousine to drive to the Protestant cemetery, and Mother persuaded me to return with her to the hotel. Only later did I learn that this had been at the request of Mrs. Strong. She had been afraid that if we met at the edge of the grave, an introduction would have been unavoidable, and she would have had to touch the hand of the woman who had debauched her dying boy.

I shall never forget my last glimpse of those two ladies sitting primly on either side of Pa as their car drove away from the cathedral. He did not, of course, have his arms around their shoulders, but I felt that he might as well have. He had an air of having taken them, as well as Charley, under his big wings, of hugging to his benevolent chest all creatures but his own Cordelia. King Lear had not been content to deny me my share of his kingdom; he had seized the little principality that I had gained on my own. Obviously he felt that he had little to fear from filial ingratitude.

13

I CAN SEE from your face, Brian, that I must sound very cold and unfeeling. I assure you I did not sound so at the time. Charley's death turned me inside out, and I could not get through a day without at least one fit of tears bordering on hysteria. I had to close the studio, as I could not possibly spend a night there alone, and move to the Vendôme, in a room next to my parents, where I plagued them by calling Mother at least twice during each night to come and sit by my bed and hold my hand.

All that, however, was a long time ago, and I have since been psychoanalyzed, so that if I sound detached today it is because I have faced up to the fact that I was really more detached then. What I fundamentally minded about Charley's death, as I now more honestly see it, was that he had departed in peace, owing none of that peace to me. Or to put it more baldly, he had owed it to my absence. On my analyst's couch I plumbed the humiliating depths of the egotism and possessiveness of love. But at the time I thought myself an inconsolable widow, which must have been hard for my parents to bear.

Pa, in fact, did not bear it. Two weeks after Charley's death we had our first big row when he told me that he had destroyed the manuscript of Charley's book. He insisted that he had done so in obedience to Charley's dying instructions, but I denied that this was an excuse.

"It was a work of art!" I kept shouting at him. "No one has the right to destroy a work of art, not even the artist. Supposing Lavinia Dickinson had burnt all her sister Emily's poems? Think of the loss to civilization!"

"Charley's manuscript was hardly the equivalent," Pa said dryly. "He had read parts of it aloud to me. But even if it had been, I should have felt constrained to do as he had asked. I cannot admit that works of art, any more than artists themselves, are outside the moral law."

"We don't have so much beauty in the world that we can afford to go about destroying it!"

"The beautiful thing about Charley was the way he met his death," Pa said gravely. "His little book was simply one of the steps that led to it. Of course, *you're* all excited about it, because it was a book. Communication is everything to you artists. You can't look at a landscape or a bowl of fruit without thinking how you will put it on a canvas so that somebody else will see it as *your* landscape or *your* bowl of fruit. That is the inescapable vulgarity of art."

"And why I'm proud to be an artist!"

"What you are, my dear girl, is not in question. It's what Charley was. He used his pen to try to see God. When he had seen him, his papers were no more use than autumn leaves."

"Might they not help someone else?"

Pa shook his head firmly. "They were too personal. Besides, they contained references to living people which would have been very painful."

"You mean references to *me*," I cried, aflame now with indignation. "References to me that in print would have been painful to *you*. You couldn't face the idea of letting the world see that I was Charley's mistress!"

"It would be nearer the point to say that I couldn't face your pride in letting the world see it," Pa retorted.

"That's a vile thing to say. Just because I wanted the one

beautiful unique thing that Charley created in his short, unhappy life to survive as his memorial!"

"Ah, uniqueness," Pa muttered with a gesture of impatience. "There it is again. That's all you care about. To stand out. To have people say: look, look, look. See me with my little pen or paint brush or chisel. I did it all myself!"

"What else is there but death and annihilation?" I cried desperately. "Can't you let us poor mortals live a bit first? *Your* trouble, Pa, is that you hate what happened to Charley in Paris. You had to tear up the record of his accomplishment and turn him back to an adolescent robot on the playing fields of Justin! You and his old bitch of a mother had to burn up everything but your own juvenile image of him." I was now completely out of control. "I believe you killed Charley! Killed him with the dope of your nihilistic religion. And if he came to life, I believe you'd happily do it again!"

Never shall I forget the look that Pa gave me then! Those great brown eyes glowered at me for what must have been half a minute, and then I saw a strange glint of yellow in their irises. I had the sudden terrible feeling that Pa was looking at me as a magistrate might have looked at a screaming, muddy street urchin caught in a bestial act and dragged before his bench.

"You use the word 'bitch' very easily, Cordelia," he said icily, as he turned away. "Take care you don't give others cause to."

At this I had my first attack of real hysterics, and Mother had to sit up with me all night as I sobbed and screamed. By morning an equally violent reaction had set in, and my anger melted down with exhaustion to a murky cesspool of remorse. I insisted now that I was indeed a bitch and that a lifetime of penance and good works would hardly suffice to redeem me. I acknowledged, over and over again that I had sinned in distracting Charley from his one true path to consolation. And finally I announced solemnly that I would go home with my parents and assist them in their duties at Justin Martyr.

Mother, who distrusted the durability of my mood, advised against it, but Pa, who for all his scorn of artists was inclined to see penitence in the light of a colorful drama of oils by Veronese or Tintoretto, insisted that I be taken at my word. When we sailed from Cherbourg I brought only three dresses from all my Paris stock. The rest I gave away, determined to select a new kind of wardrobe in Boston. I might have been taking the veil.

Oh, that winter at Justin! Even my own powers of self-dramatization were barely enough to get me through it. I helped Mother with "parlor night," Tuesdays and Fridays, when boys having the required grades were invited to our house from eight o'clock until nine to play games. Mother had a large and venerable collection of parlor games and puzzles, in all of which she used to participate with a passionate interest and competitiveness. I can still see her wonderful old witch's profile over the parcheesi board and those glassy eyes intent upon a little boy counting out the steps for his disks. But I was bored by the games and played them badly and could never keep order at my table which was always in an uproar, to Pa's extreme disapproval. In the mornings I earned a little money by tutoring boys in French, and in the afternoons I walked with Mother or trudged around the slushy campus by myself. As part of my penance I had given up painting; it was also the perfect way out of an artistic career for which I had little aptitude. I never went out to meals, and on the evenings when there was no parlor I would sullenly read Proust and Joyce by the fire and dream of the lives I had given up and of the lives I had never had. By early spring I was on the edge of a full nervous collapse.

Mother, however, had been watching me. She knew well my habits of self-mortification and understood that to try to rescue me from my own stubbornness too early would only make matters worse. She also knew that when she did move, it would have to be decisively. One morning at breakfast she announced that I was to spend the spring vacation with my sister Harriet in New York.

"Your father's going to the ecclesiastical council at Hartford, and I'm going to stay with your Aunt Maud at Pride's. The whole house is going to be painted, and I want everyone out. Harriest feels you've neglected her, so I took it upon myself to tell her you'd go."

I pretended to be angry and sulked for a day, but actually I appreciated Mother's tact in getting me out of my own prison. I had had my fill of Justin and self-pity, for a while anyway. It is always a tricky business for a grown-up child to live with parents, particularly at her own request. She is in no position to throw bricks. Pa was little interested in advice as to how to run his school from anyone, let alone a daughter, and I had before me, night and day, the frustrating image of that educating machine that I could not even criticize. I do not mean to imply that Pa was not kind to me, for he was. We walked together at least one afternoon a week, and we breakfasted together every morning. But he took it painfully for granted that I had nothing better in which to interest myself than his school. He even expected me to know the names of the sixth formers and who were the prefects.

Pa had the advantage over me in that he had been able to create a monster to which he could transfer an egotism that must in his youth have been even worse than mine, a monster of red brick and Romanesque arches, of varnished, carpetless halls and dreary stained glass windows, a monster that howled with the carnivorous howl of its four hundred and fifty cubs. I knew that if I did not get away, it would ultimately break me, as it had broken the plain, smiling, creeping, softly speaking wives of the masters.

My sister, Harriet Kidder, "Goneril" as we called her in the family, had married to advantage in New York and lived in considerable state. She was ten years my senior, fifty pounds heavier and hundreds of times richer, but for all her disapproval of my bohemianism, she has too many of the basic Prescott doubts to enjoy a really comfortable sense of superiority. In fact, Harriet's insecurity has often manifested itself in the crudest kind of boasting about the Kidder possessions, so that people meeting her for the first time are often surprised to discover that she was born a Boston Prescott.

She and Evelyn and I seem to have in common a fatal incapacity ever to put anything quite behind us. In the library we tend to gaze out the window at the garden party which we have passed up and deplore an afternoon wasted on mere musty books, but the moment we have changed our minds and joined the garden party we turn from its trivia to stare back in at those abandoned tomes that now seem to contain the only true richness. We have the minds of scholars (oh, yes, we're as bright as Pa, each one of us!) and the hearts of Pompadours. We would have done much better had we favored Mother.

It was at Harriet's that I met Guy Turnbull. Of course, it was not a coincidence. I was still married to Cabell Willetts, but Harriet insisted that getting a divorce was simply a matter of getting the right lawyer and that she would get him for me when the time came. Guy, a widower some fifteen years older than myself, was a great friend and business associate of my brother-in-law and constantly at the house. It was really very generous of Harriet to offer him to her erring sister. He was big and stout and loud and still blond, but he could have regained what must have been strikingly good looks by taking off sixty pounds — which he never did. He had that odd, almost ladylike fastidiousness in taste and speech which so often goes with strong, self-made men and which whets the appetite of jaded creatures like myself who are titillated by a sense of the crudeness that must be so concealed.

Guy wore silk shirts with jeweled cuff links and ordered his suits and boots from London; at restaurants he was always sending back dishes and examining the silverware for spots. Yet he thrilled me when he shouted at a taxi driver or snarled at an offensive drunk. He could be terrifying in his sudden animal loudness and his obvious hankering for a fight. And his laugh was frankly vulgar; he seemed in his hilarity to be recklessly trying to rip down all the illusions that one supposed him to have been at such pains to build up. Had Guy been less of a sentimentalist, had he not talked quite so much about his poor dear dead wife, I might have fallen seriously in love with him.

As it was, there was only one place where Guy and I really belonged, and we soon got to it. Do you guess where that was? Really, Brian, don't try so hard not to look shocked. Be natural. Of course you disapprove of my having gone to bed with Guy. He disapproved of it himself. There has always been something about me that has made my lovers want to keep me straight. With Charley it was the image of Pa, pursuing us to the most intimate recesses, but Guy had never met Pa, nor had his background been one to bring him under the shadow of the Prescott legend. Guy lumped Mother and Pa in a group that he loosely described as "society," a term that he by no means used slightingly. On the contrary, he thought that "society," like the Philharmonic and the opera, was something which ought to receive every self-made man's support. And he was not at all sure that he was properly supporting it by making me his mistress.

Harriet was furious. She accused me of a neurotic compulsion to become *déclassée*. She pointed out that it was just as easy to marry a man as to seduce him, and that, after all, I owed *something* to our parents. She explained at length her subtle maneuvers in convincing Guy that a wife of Prescott lineage was the one jewel missing in the crown of his material triumph. When I simply laughed at her, she sent me packing back to Justin and dispatched a long letter to Mother in which she suggested that Pa should summon up his heaviest battalions to combat my moral delinquency. I went back north, very pleased with myself. Guy and I had arranged to meet in Boston on the weekends to carry on what Harriet called our "intrigue." Fortunately, it was convenient for him as he had to make periodic inspections of one of his textile mills in Lowell.

Pa and Mother said nothing on my return, and I was divided between relief at being let alone and resentment at the idea that they had given me up. I consoled myself with the prospect of my weekends, and on early spring afternoons, circling the campus behind Mother and her two old beagles, I would look up defiantly at the great craggy oversized chapel tower, as ugly as Pa's deity, and think that I, at least, enjoyed a real relation with a real man, that Guy and I gave each other the pleasure of our bodies without the cant of religious fantasy. And what was Justin Martyr to a man like Guy? Had he gone to such a school? Had he needed to? Could he have made any more money if he had? Might it not even have paralyzed some of his initiative? Schools like Justin, I decided, were endowed with the excess funds of patrons like Guy, and headmasters, like the big-hatted, black-robed tutors and pedants of seventeenth century comedy, had to perform grotesque antics in their benefactors' audience chambers.

But, indeed, I had not been given up. The coils of Justin had actually been tightening around me. One evening after supper in the school dining room Pa asked me to come to his study, and there, as I faced him across the huge square desk, like a boy about to be disciplined, he told me that he had finally persuaded Cabell Willetts to seek an ecclesiastical annulment of our marriage. I was so surprised that for a moment I could only stare.

"It appears that he desires another union," Pa added dryly.

"With a nun?"

"With a widow who shares his own deep faith." Pa was not one to spoil his sarcasm with even a glint of the eye. His gravity was perfect. "Those of the Roman persuasion will not admit that a marriage has existed when there has been no matrimonial intent. If you will testify to a priest from the Rota that you never intended to be bound by your oath or to have children . . ."

"But I did!"

Pa surveyed me for a moment. Then without twitching a muscle in his face, without in the least compromising his solemn mien, he slowly lowered and retracted his left eyelid in a wink uncannily like that of a chicken. I was not amused.

"A Catholic priest doesn't count, is that it?" I demanded scornfully. "It's all right to tell a lie to a Hottentot? Well, having no church, I can't afford to dispense with my few principles so sweepingly. We agnostics, thank you very much, *do* have principles. If Cabell wants his annulment, let him tell his own lies. Even a Jesuit is entitled to the truth!"

Pa nodded, but sighed. "It seems a pity. I have thought deeply in the matter, and I could not help wondering if it *was* a real marriage. You were so young and so determined to shock the old folks."

"I wasn't as young as all that! And I had every intention of having a child. Thank God I failed!"

"Amen," Pa replied, with a sincerity that annoyed me. "Very well, my child, that is all there is to it. I thought it my duty to put the matter before you. But, of course, I shall never counsel you to go against your conscience."

When Mother heard about my stand, she was angrier than I had ever seen her. She could be terrible in her tempers, cold, articulate and biting. She seemed to lose all sense of her relationship with the person at whom she was angry, and she would strike at her own flesh and blood as if we were thieves in the night. The occasions were rare, but feared by all, even by Pa, or perhaps I should say particularly by Pa.

"Even from you such gall astounds me!" she exclaimed. "To

give your poor father a cheap sermon on intellectual honesty. After all he's done for you. Do you think it was easy for him to go to the Willetts? Do you think it was pleasant for him to have to stick his arms into the mud of a Catholic annulment? Do you think he *enjoyed* having to root out all the facts of Cabell's sanctimonious little love affair? I tell you it made him sick! But he did it because he thought that his daughter, who's made such a stinking mess of her life, was entitled to another chance. And he did it, too, against his own conscience, after days of prayer and tortured reflections, to keep *you* from turning into the complete tramp that you show every sign of wanting to be. Well I tell you here and now, my girl, if you don't go through with this annulment, you've seen the last of me. And I mean it!"

As in Paris I had collapsed before Pa, so now did I collapse before Mother. None of us girls had anything like the force of personality of our parents. I could sneer at Pa and sulk with Mother, but I was no match for them in their real tempers. Without even talking to Pa I went to Boston and saw Cabell's lawyer and prepared my testimony. The Willetts had great connections in the church, and in three months the annulment was procured. During the following summer I went to Reno and obtained my civil divorce. I then did a thing of which I am still ashamed. I wrote Cabell a letter in which I told him that my testimony was perjured and that the annulment was void in the eyes of God. He never answered, but I have often speculated about the effect of my message on his marital relations with the holy widow. Oh, yes, it was a bitchy thing to do, but you must remember that if he had given me my divorce when I had first wanted it, I could have married Charley and brought peace to the last months of his life.

Everybody was pleased with the new, compliant Cordelia, even Guy, who after formally proposing to me at lunch in the Boston Ritz, announced that our other relationship would have to be suspended until marriage. Evidently the future Mrs. Turnbull — and he took it for granted, quite correctly, that despite my refusal to commit myself, I would ultimately become such — had to be beyond suspicion, even if it was a whitewash job. Guy was much more at his ease in the status of fiancé to a Prescott than of lover. I suspected that he had another mistress, on a lower social level, to take care of his physical needs, and that this explained his preference to have me chaste. Guy was enough of a bull to be fairly indiscriminate about his cows. I was a "lady," and, to change the simile, he liked his pigeons to stay in their pigeonholes.

Of course, he was enchanted with Pa. On the weekend when he was first invited to Justin, Pa took him over every nook and cranny of the school, and Guy thoroughly berated me afterwards for my past irreverence.

"I realize, Cordie," he told me, "that it must have been hard for a girl to be brought up in a boys' school. But the fact remains that you're prejudiced. Your father has created an extraordinary thing in Justin. He'd have made a tremendous businessman!"

This was actually an idea that had often occurred to Pa himself. He had his moments, not so much when he regretted the fortune that he had not made as when he begrudged fortunes to those who had made them with less than his own capabilities. I remember a rich visitor to the school, who arrived in a long yellow Hispano-Suiza with glittering accessories, saying to Pa after lunch: "I'd give up all my corporations to have been the founder of Justin," and Pa snapping back at him without a grin or a wink: "I'd give up Justin for your car."

But if nothing made Pa more scornful than wealthy men who sighed after the spiritual life, wealthy men who gloried in the bitter competition of the marketplace and in a creed that put the profit motive ahead of all intrigued him. Perhaps, he felt that like soldiers, they were nearer the basic male than himself.

For all Pa's faith and for all his accomplishments there was a side of him that tended to identify the priest's cassock with a woman's skirt and to sneer at the world of education as an ivory tower. He was in it himself, to be sure, but he had the vanity to want you to know that, unlike most of the inmates, he had not fled to it for refuge. He *could* have survived on the ringing plain. And he liked Guy for promptly recognizing this.

"He's a natural, that fellow Turnbull," he told me. "Hang on to him, Cordie. I sometimes wonder if we don't send forth our graduates to a holocaust in which they must try their tinfoil swords against the steel of men like that. I wonder if he'd consider teaching a seminar course to the sixth form in business competition?"

"He'd crave it!"

And do you know, he did? He taught every Saturday morning during the fall term. Guy and Pa became the most devoted friends. They inspected Guy's big mill at Lowell together as carefully as they had inspected the school, and Pa put me in mind of Boswell's description of Dr. Johnson at the sale of the deceased Mr. Thrale's brewery, bustling about amid the boilers and vats like an excise man, with an inkhorn and pen in his buttonhole, and talking pompously of the duties of his executorial office. Back at school he diverted the prefects' table with an account of his excursion, including a graphic description of the chairman's office.

"I paused at the threshold, dazzled by the scene in front of me. As far as the eye could reach stretched grey sofas, mahogany tables, murals, shining appurtenances. I took a step forward; I lost my foothold; I cried out." Here Pa stretched his arms wide. "Gentlemen, I solemnly assure you, I had sunk knee-deep in carpet!"

Perhaps you can see what he was doing already, the old rascal. It was soon to become a pattern. He was undermining Guy with ridicule. Oh, yes, I realize that I sound inconsistent, and

I repeat that he admired Guy. But he was also jealous of him. He envied Guy his business success, as he had envied Charley his war career. The only way that he had been able to reassure himself that he was as much of a man as Charley had been by asserting his religious leadership. He was smart enough to see that this would never work with Guy. For Guy he had to put into action his own superior intellect and erode with little sarcasms the uncomfortable image of the tycoon who could build a dozen Justins by signing detachable pieces of paper from a little black book that had nothing to do with hymns or prayers.

I don't want to sound too Freudian, but I was certainly in basic competition with Pa. My two men were men, after all, and they had looked to me for something that Pa could not offer. But Pa, the old magician, had ways of recovering distracted attention. He could prove to them that he, too, was a man, that he was more than a man; he could show them a heavenly kingdom where women and wars and moneymaking did not exist. And when Pa decided to be a prophet, he did so on a Cecil B. De Mille scale. He ended by making even Guy suspect that business was not all.

My second marriage lasted seven years, but it was a failure from the start. Guy was carnal to a degree that even I had not believed possible. I learned to be glad every time he took a new mistress. He had some disgusting practices with which I need not shock you, and the foulness of his language in our bedroom was an education in vice. When he realized at last that there were certain things to which I was never going to submit, that I was not titillated but genuinely revolted, he began to hate me and to humiliate me whenever he could. Fortunately his large means and multiple business trips made it easy for us to live apart, and when we finally agreed upon a divorce he surprised everybody by the big alimony that he allowed me. I suppose he wanted even an ex-Mrs. Turnbull to live grandly and be a credit to him, for he provided that the payments would cease on my remarriage. However, I have fooled him, for I have arranged my life quite satisfactorily without marrying again. He should have remembered that I had learned the trick before.

During the years of our marriage and despite its deterioration, Guy's relations with Pa and Mother went from good to perfect. He frequently stayed with them at Justin without me. I would have thought that some of the crudity of the man would have repelled Mother, but she seemed immune to it. There was a worshiping little-boy quality about Guy as a son-in-law that was apparently irresistible. The line that he drew in his own mind between me and my parents was the line between the flesh and the spirit. All his reverence for the Prescotts as a symbol of what he called "distinguished living" went to Pa and Mother, while I became increasingly a mere physical convenience to him, and when I ceased to be convenient, I became nothing. Basically he must have always regarded me as a tramp with a lineage that was detachable and could be acquired by himself. Even after our divorce he continued to be on as good terms at Justin as ever.

I resented it, of course. I resented Pa's and Mother's whole attitude about my marital troubles. It was only too obvious that they believed that any nice reasonable girl could have got along with Guy. When in desperation I told Pa a few of the true facts, he listened with an interest that I was sure did not stem entirely from sympathy with his daughter. Part of it was the natural lubricity that exists in even the holiest mortals and part was perhaps his feeling that such activity as I described was characteristic, however unfortunately, of any real male. Or perhaps he simply thought that I was making it up, and his attention was a mask for the horror that he felt at having sired so morbid and malevolent a daughter. In all events he never referred to it, but continued to see Guy as before.

I fumed at such disloyalty, but I fumed in vain. Pa stimulated Guy's interest in the school to the point where he did something that was in direct contradiction to every principle in his self-aggrandizing nature. He made an anonymous gift. Yes, I see how big your eyes are, Brian. You can't believe that the man I have described would forego the glory of a public presentation. But do you know why? Because his money was allocated to the erection of that grey sweeping temple dedicated to the god of sport and named for the dead hero whose beautiful statue by Malvina Hoffman, so radiantly evocative of golden youth cut short, stands before its portals. Charley Strong and Guy Turnbull had more in common at last than the physical possession of Cordelia Prescott.

14

APRIL 3, 1942. It seems like a miracle (and how do I know it's not?) that I can open this journal and record that I am living in Cambridge, enrolled at last in divinity school!

I can hardly take in that only four months have elapsed since my last entry. It has been, anyway, a period long enough to go to hell and back, and I say this fully and humbly recognizing that during every minute of it I have been safe and sound while American boys were dying in the Pacific. But I have learned that safety and soundness can have their own hellish twist.

It started with Pearl Harbor, which was greeted by the Gris-cams with the hysteria that children might show to a premature Santa Claus. War seemed the extra dimension that had been needed in their lives. To Mrs. Griscam it was the ultimate opportunity for her "army," through military recreation centers, to reach American youth; to Amy it was escape into glamour through the Red Cross; to Sylvester it was the dignity, after domestic scandal, of a naval officer's uniform and a desk in Church Street where his father could not check up on him, as opposed to one in Wall, where he could. And to Mr. Griscam, happiest of all, it meant secret trips to the State Department, even the White House, and the rumor of a diplomatic post to the governments in exile. In the bustle of those days it seemed to my saddened eyes that nobody over five and thirty could possibly want peace.

Not that I was left out in the division of spoils. Mr. Griscam spoke of taking me abroad as his private secretary. "Freedom First" had been officially closed, and I was helping to liquidate the office. But I felt a violent and unreasonable aversion to clambering on the Griscam band wagon. I wanted *my* war to be a grimmer, obscurer business. As I could not continue to accept Mr. Griscam's bread and shelter under the circumstances, I quietly decamped during one of his absences in Washington, leaving four polite and grateful letters to my hosts, and moved to a boardinghouse on West 90th Street. I then took a volunteer job, suggested by one of my fellow workers at "Freedom First," from midnight to eight in the dispatcher's office of the Fire Department at Central Park. I figured that I could just subsist on my own small income and make this token contribution to the defense of the city.

I moved through the cold, dreary winter like a man who has been drugged. I performed my almost mechanical tasks at the dispatcher's office with adequate efficiency; I enrolled as an air raid warden, and I contributed my services as a dishwasher to a stage door canteen. There still remained a goodly number of hours in each week when I would sit on the bed in my little room and read Trollope. Only after I had done everything for the war that I could think of doing did I permit this escape to the world of Plantaganet Palliser and Lady Glencora.

I would have seen nobody at all had it not been for Mrs. Turnbull. She tracked me down through the Griscams and insisted that I dine with her on my night off from the Fire Department. When I went there, unable to think of an excuse, I found a large party of artists and dealers who did much drinking and talking. Nobody but my hostess, who insisted that I call her "Cordelia," paid the least attention to me, but I found it diverting for a change to hear talk that was not about the war, and I went again on several occasions.

I suppose I should have suspected that Cordelia had her own

plans for me. After all, it was obvious that I was not being asked because I could paint or talk, and she was very put out once when I refused to linger after the others had risen to go. But she must have been fifteen years my senior, and I have suffered all my life from a feeling that I am unattractive to women, a feeling which has survived (I may say at least to my journal without fatuity) a certain amount of evidence to the contrary.

My naïveté in this case let me in for an appalling scene. One night I went to the duplex to find myself the only guest. Cordelia, reclining in a pink negligee before a pitcher of martinis in which she had obviously been imbibing prior to my arrival, might have scared me to instant flight had not her voice been so gruff and matter-of-fact.

"Yes, sweetie, we're all alone," she said as she took in my apprehensive glance at the table set cozily for two by the window. "After dinner I'll play soft music and show you my etchings. Don't look so scared. It won't hurt. Here, give yourself a drink." But when she abruptly changed the subject, I decided in a flutter of relief that she must be joking. "This damn war," she continued. "I'm sick of it already. The last one was bad enough, but at least there was all that Wilsonian idealism. Oh, I grant you, it nauseated me at the time, but now I find it's worse without it. All you young people are so terrified that anyone will think *you* think you're making the world safe for democracy that of course you won't. Not a chance of it."

She continued morosely in this vein all during a lengthy cocktail period and a much shorter dinner. I wondered hopefully if the amount of gin that she was consuming might not end by disposing of my problem, but her capacity seemed unlimited. Only her temper was affected, for it grew shorter and shorter. After the meal she blew up at me for suggesting that we listen to *The Magic Flute*.

"Everyone likes Mozart now," she grumbled. "Tinkle, tinkle,

tinkle, that's all you youngsters want. Give me Beethoven. He's obvious, but God knows, so am I. At least, he was a *man*."

We listened to the Seventh, I constrainedly, she moodily. I noted that she had shifted to bourbon.

"I said I was obvious, honey," she repeated in a more ominous tone. "What did you think I meant by that?"

"Simply that you liked loud, emphatic music."

"And not loud, emphatic men?"

"Perhaps them, too." I managed a shrug. "What a pity they're all away."

"Isn't it just?" she took me up sarcastically. "Isn't it hard on poor Cordelia? But it luckily happens that she also has a taste for quiet little boys of milder emphasis. Like you, bunny. Yes, dear, I fancy *you*. Can you bear it?"

"I'm glad you like me."

"Oh, come off it, bunny!" she exclaimed sharply. "I didn't say I liked you. I'm not at all sure I do. I said I *fancied* you. Don't pretend you don't know what that means. Don't you think you could fancy me for a bit?" Her tone was of mock cajolery. "Just for a wee bit, bunny?"

"I'm sorry, Mrs. Turnbull . . ." I began in an agony of embarrassment.

"Cordelia!"

"I'm sorry, Cordelia, but I don't think I could ever . . . well, I don't think I could ever feel that way about you. I respect you very much, but I'm not . . ." I braced myself. "Well, I'm not in love with you."

Her shriek of laughter was shocking. "I should hope not! I'm not in love with you. But you have a scared littly bunny look that I find intriguing. Don't you think it might be fun to pretend we were in love just for tonight?" She looked at me with bold, penetrating, still laughing eyes. "Are you a virgin, bunny? I'll bet you are."

"Please, Cordelia!"

"Well, why be ashamed of it? All would-be ministers should be virgins till they marry, shouldn't they? I *like* the idea of your being a virgin!"

I rose, trembling with embarrassment and indignation. "I think I'd better go now."

She reached out and caught my arm and pulled me down on the sofa beside her. "Is it Pa you're worried about? Forget him. He understands a lot more things than you think. Come on, bunny, relax. It's a great big lonely war, and Cordelia's all warm and nice and huggy."

"No!" I tore myself away and jumped up.

"Oh, but yes, bunny." She rose and threw her strong left arm about my neck and implanted a sticky, whiskeyed kiss on my shrinking lips while with her free hand . . . !

I cannot write what she did with her free hand.

Again I ripped myself from her embrace and made a frantic dash for the hall. In the foyer I kept my finger on the elevator bell as if I were escaping a fiend. As the doors swung open and I plunged into the car I could hear through the open front door behind me, her mocking farewell: "Good night, Joseph Andrews!"

All that night in my rented room that cry sounded in my ears. Joseph Andrews! Did that shameless hussy know that poor Joseph Andrews who saves his virtue from the brazen Lady Booby, naked under her sheet, was a caricature of my adored Mr. Richardson's Pamela? Was it not enough that Cordelia had confused the image of her sainted father in my mind with that of a leering vamp? Did she have as well to make the father of the English novel, whose little portrait by my bed had been a consolation in war and peace, ridiculous? It seemed to me as I lay tossing that Cordelia had fouled not only her nest but the universe, that the very war was hardly worth winning if *she* was what our boys would come home to.

Things went from bad to worse. I could not recapture in the

days that followed even the flitting sense of utility that my frenzied war activities had briefly given me. It seemed to me now that I was only a fool and, like all fools, thinking only of myself. Had I not allowed an unchristian prejudice against Mr. Griscam to keep me from assisting him in what was perhaps an important diplomatic post? Wasn't my whole attitude about the war simply a demonstration of my need to appease the ego? I found I could not even read Trollope and took to going to the movies in the afternoon.

One night, going to work, I had a distressing experience in the subway. It was raining, and the car was very crowded and stuffy. When the doors opened at Seventy-second Street a group of rather rowdy Negro boys, in red and yellow jackets, shoved their way in, jostling and pushing the other passengers, laughing loudly and using rough language. This in itself was nothing, and the passengers hardly noticed the intrusion. The boys, after all, if rude were not bad-tempered. They were even in a rather pleasant mood. But what distressed me was that in the heat and closeness, listening to the high laughs and the crude remarks, I momentarily lost my faith.

I thought: how could God want all the creatures in that car, including myself (oh, yes, including myself) to enter into eternal life? It was not that those cackling boys were wicked, but whatever they were, good or bad, the point struck at me that a mortal lifetime seemed quite as long as one could want for them. A long happy lifetime — to be sure, one wished them that — but *immortality?* Were they up to it? I thought of Calvin and his answer to my problem in the doctrine of elected souls, but wasn't it worse to have *some* saved than none? That was the horror of Calvin, like the horror of the Inquisition and the horror of Hitler, and where these horrors did not exist, I faced the horror of the empty grins and silly laughs in the underground of Manhattan.

I suppose it was inevitable that in this mood and with my

odd hours of work I should have sickened and that a feverish cold should have turned into pneumonia. My landlady behaved with the greatest consideration, and the doctor whom she called pulled me through, but for a day I was delirious. It seemed to my darkened mind that the only thing to dread was recovery.

And then, just as I passed the crisis, he came. I heard the rich, deep voice from far away:

"I am going to take care of you, Brian. As soon as you're feeling better I shall move you to my daughter Harriet's apartment. She and her husband have gone to Washington. It will be a good place for your recuperation."

"But how . . . how . . . ?"

"How did I know? You put my name down as the person to notify in emergency on the form that you filled out at the Fire Department. It touched me very much, dear boy."

Had I? It all seemed a dream but a wonderful one. If I had died, I had gone to heaven, and wasn't that just the place I would expect to meet Dr. Prescott?

But I had not died. Sitting in Mrs. Kidder's beautiful Georgian living room overlooking the East River, we spent our mornings with books and games and puzzles, and often just gazing down at the tugs and naval vessels and the big squawking gulls that flew low over the thick grey eddying fullness of that rapid water. I would not have believed it possible to be so relaxed with him. When I started once to make a murmuring effort to articulate my gratitude, he pulled me firmly up:

"Let us settle the question of thanks once and for all, Brian, and then it needn't bother us again. I am an old man, and I have nothing else to do. I like you, and I want to help you. You may show your gratitude, if you must, by allowing me to finish up the job I've started."

In a week's time we were taking little walks in Carl Schurz Park to take advantage of the brief new sunshine. I was feeling now the beginnings of a restoration not only of my body but of my mind. I still had the sense that I had had since Pearl Harbor of suspended animation — of existing in an echoing void — but the sense had ceased to be disagreeable. The echoes were softer, almost at times consolatory. As soon as Dr. Prescott felt that I was strong enough, he began to talk to me about the ministry.

"I see now that I made a mistake when David Griscam told me about your decision not to go to Harvard. I should have left the Cape and gone to you at once. But I hesitated to use any pressure. I thought that if your call was not clear enough, that might be a warning that the church was not your true vocation. What I failed to see was that you are the exception to an otherwise valid rule. I am now confident, my boy, that your call is a true one and that the impediments in your way have been simple nervous afflictions that will disappear once you have learned to face them. That is why I want you to go to divinity school as soon as you are well. I do not even want you to wait until next fall. The sooner you are actually taking courses the better."

"But won't I have to wait for the beginning of the school year?" I protested, drawing back instinctively from the prospect of decision.

"For credit, yes. But I have arranged with the Dean that you may be admitted now as an auditor."

"I'm afraid, sir, I'm not ready!"

"You never will be if you wait. With you and me faith will always be a matter of exercise. But the faith that you work for is just as fine as the faith that is conferred. Perhaps finer!"

I told him now of my dismal experience with the Negro boys in the subway and asked him if one of such visceral reactions had any right to become a minister.

"We all have such reactions," he replied. "I am besieged with them myself. Moments of vacuum, I call them. I'm sorry to say they do not disappear with age. Nobody can believe in a life hereafter *all* the time. What you must do is accept your moods of doubt, as you have just accepted your illness. You must say to yourself: 'Here I am, a believer who is doubting.' Then you will find that, although alone with yourself in that terrible vacuum, you still can see yourself. See yourself doubting. Instead of self-revilement, there may be calm. Instead of blame, there may be sadness. And if you will wait quietly enough and long enough, that vacuum may suddenly and thrillingly begin to throb again with your awareness of the presence of God."

"But isn't it a terrible thing to think so little of one's fellow humans? I had no *right* to be put off by those colored boys."

"No right, of course. But you were. You have to accept the fact that there is that in you. But why does it matter?" Here he stopped and turned on me and smote his fist into the palm of his other hand. "You *know* God exists, and you *know* those boys have immortal souls! That you didn't believe it for a time is simply a fact. A little fact that, like so many others, is of little importance."

"I pray that may be so, sir."

"It *is* so, Brian, believe me." He pricked his brows and became sunk in reverie. "We can overcome a great many things by the simple expedient of accepting them. I used to worry that I did not sufficiently love my daughters. You see, dear boy, I am taking you into my deepest confidence. But now I see that loving them inadequately was part of me and part of the condition into which they were born. God did not expect me to love them more. I couldn't. He expected me to tend them devotedly. Ah, love." He grunted suddenly. "Those who merely love get too much credit from a world of geese. It isn't love children need. It is devotion."

As I came gradually to accept his theory that I should stop fretting about faith, a wonderful peace began to creep over me. One by one he disposed of my remaining objections.

"You've tried to fight, and they wouldn't have you," he retorted to my protest that I should do war work. "That's all that can be expected of a man. Now your place is back in the church. Do you think God's work must stop in wartime? Do you think ministers won't be needed when peace comes?"

I asked him if it was fair to take up a place in divinity school, particularly on a scholarship, when I still had doubts if I would ever be ordained.

"But ordained or not ordained *you* are always going to be a minister," he insisted. "Personally, I think you will come back to Justin and teach. There is no real distinction between the pulpit and the classroom. I tried to put God into every book and sport in Justin. That was my ideal, to spread a sense of his presence so that it would not be confined to prayers and sacred studies and to spread it in such a way as to make the school *joyful.*" He shook his head ruefully. "Oh, if I could have done *that,* Brian, Justin would have been a perfect thing. It would have been the model for all preparatory schools!"

"It is, sir."

"It is *not,* my boy, but I'm counting on you to help make it so."

There was no resisting this. Besides, I no longer wanted to. I had a new conviction now that I would be able to stick it at Cambridge. I even wondered if I might not like it. And I have. Of course, I know that he is only thirty miles away at the Andrews cottage at Justin, and that thought helps to sustain me. But I do not run to his side every time I feel giddy. It has been agreed between us that I must learn to stand on my own feet.

Before we left New York he discovered something that I had not dreamed he would ever discover. On our last day he suggested that I come and lunch at Cordelia's, and I declined, saying that I did not wish to intrude on a family party. When he insisted, and I continued to refuse, flushing deeply, he grunted.

"She told me you wouldn't come. What's it all about? Has something happened between you and Cordie?"

"Oh, no!" I cried in dismay. "Nothing, I assure you!"

"Nothing, eh?" He gave me a shrewd stare. "Well, I daresay it wasn't her fault. But I see she must have given you a scare. You've got to learn not to worry about women like Cordie. They're basically simple creatures. She says she told you about her marriages." His smile was faintly grim. "Poor Cordie. Harriet used to say it was all our fault. That we didn't cuddle her enough when she was little. I'm afraid she's made up for that since. Did she tell you about Charley Strong?"

"A bit."

"I loved Charley, and it was my sad duty to have to rescue him from Cordie. Of course, she could never forgive that."

"She says you destroyed his book."

"Yes, I told her so. At the time she was very distraught, and I thought the truth would upset her more. Actually, Charley destroyed it himself for fear she would publish it. All but one chapter which he gave to me. I still have it." He stared for a minute down at the river, and when he looked up at me there was a gleam of amusement in his eyes. It was a sarcastic, an almost impish gleam. "I'll send it to you, if you like. When you're safely ensconced in Harvard. It mightn't be a bad thing for you to read. You'll see the terrible consequences of sex. Or, perhaps I should say, the consequences of brooding about sex."

He took no chances with me as he did last summer, but accompanied me, when the doctor pronounced me recovered, to Boston, where his daughter Evelyn put us both up in Arlington Street. There we stayed until Dr. Prescott had introduced me to the faculty at the divinity school, enrolled me as an auditor in the courses and even helped to find me a room in Cambridge. I was thoroughly settled, almost, one might say, hammered down, by the time he returned to Justin. It has been an awesome experience to have found myself the beneficiary of all the energies of the ex-headmaster, but my ultimate reaction has been one of bursting pride. The uneasy feeling that I *must* make good has been ameliorated by the growing suspicion that I really may.

Two weeks after his departure he sent me the surviving chapter of Charley Strong's book. I happened to read it just after attending Dr. Vane's famous lecture on gnosticism, and the comparison was stimulating. Certainly poor Charley must have been a curious study in heresy. It is a pity that he could not have written the final chapter of his story and told how Dr. Prescott, in their talks by the Seine, had lifted his eyes from the mortal headmaster to the God in and behind them both. But at least the few pages that he did not destroy show that this ending was possible.

15

IT HAPPENED in Southampton in the summer after my fifth form year. Claude is a cousin of Mummy's, halfway between our ages, a giddy, discontented old maid who is always trying to put her hands on me and stares in provoking, smiling silence during family meals. When she asked me to come to her bedroom to tell me a "secret," I went, to find her naked and still smiling. She was shameless and shrill, and the white puffy flesh on her buttocks gave way under my groping fingers as if it had been cotton on sticks. I took it for granted that she would be pregnant and that I would get syphilis. Neither event occurred, but when war came, and mud, they seemed a natural consequence.

There is very little purity in Paris, and yet the air is pure. There is very little cleanliness about the French, and yet their minds are clean. How the visiting Sunday preachers at Justin dwelt on purity: clean young men and clean young women offering each other unstained bodies in a marriage of true sacrament! Harry Nolan tells me that he and Libby wake up sometimes at night and find themselves consummating the act. I think that in the greenish light of the chapel I must have visualized the wedding night like that. A love that transcends embarrassment, an orgasm that explodes as the Grail is raised to the altar, a naked odorless copulation, passionate but unsweating, before a white surpliced choir, witnessing without concupiscence and bursting into song. Is it not thus that Henry Esmond would copulate? And Prince Albert and the Chevalier Bayard? And even the preachers themselves, old as they are, if they still do it, and my Latin master, Mr. Van Wormser, sitting in the back with his big bony wife in the little straw hat with the silly peonies? Imagine how much of it there is and how blessed!

People always think me innocent, naïve, good. They whisper things they think I shouldn't hear. Oh, Charley, sweetie, no, she's not for you, I'm not for you, you need a nice girl. I am cream chicken and green peas at a children's party; I am spun sugar and ice cream; I am the peck of a kiss after a subscription dance at the Plaza on a spring vacation. I am confusion and hot, slow tears after a wet dream. Little do they know, giggling by the shoe lockers in the cellar of Lowell House or hiding under the beds while the old women clean the cubicles to look under their skirts, that Charley, who blushes at their stories, Charley whom they delight to shock, pretending to be doing things that even *they* wouldn't really do in the showers, Charley who falls asleep at lights and dreams of sports and Mother, this same Charley has no bottom to his voluptuousness. Nay, your wives, your daughters, your matrons and your maids could not fill up the cistern of my lust.

Hope for redemption can lie only in casting myself at the feet of him whom I have betrayed. For it is he, I know, who made me senior prefect; the upper school's election is merely advisory, and it is by no means clear that I had a majority. I enjoy the transient popularity of looks and football prowess, and I have no avowed enemies. But I am deemed too much a Christer to be a real leader, and when he told me of my appointment, I trembled and wept at such an act of trust. He it was who baptized and confirmed me, he who talked to me of my doubts and miseries, he who gave me a love that made the shallow, prattling love of shallow, prattling parents seem like the spray on one's face in a speedboat at sea.

Yes, hope is only in him. Redemption is only in him. He prefers Saint Augustine to Saint Francis, the Magdalene to Saint Cecilia. He knows that purity is not to be confused with inexperience. Those also are saved who flee from Alexandria to the desert and raise long grey El Greco arms and roll wide white El Greco eyes to a God who glares fiercely over their heads at the flickering light of the about-to-be consumed city revels which they have shrewdly abandoned. I must go to the Cape and leave Southampton; I must abandon Father, Mother and Cousin Claude; I must flee to the Cape to confess and kiss his feet, wash his feet, sit at his feet.

Daddy cannot understand my leaving in the middle of the season. When I tell him that the Rugby fifth esteemed it the greatest of honors to be asked to Dr. Arnold's in the summer holidays, he says it is nonsense. Daddy thinks everything is nonsense. There is something eternal about people who think this, and I find it hard to believe when I visualize the gay striped summer waistcoat over the round little belly, the shivering pince-nez, the coughs as he taps his egg at breakfast, a Dickensian Yankee, that Daddy is as dead as ever I shall be, that Mother is a widow on the Riviera and that my sister Alice is an older maid than Claude.

Daddy concedes that Dr. Prescott may be a great headmaster, but doubts that he is quite a gentleman. Old Boston family? What has that to do with it? King Edward is not a gentleman. The Kaiser is not a gentleman. Very few royalties, indeed, are gentlemen. But Delancey Parker *is* a gentleman; so is Emlen Rutherfurd. It takes Harvard on top of Justin to make a gentleman. A club on top of God. Never forget that, my boy.

At Lola's last week on the Rue de Peur, under a window through which I could see at dawn the flèche of the Sainte-Chapelle, two young men in red silk shirts huddled side by side, arms about each other's necks. Lola, in one of her moods, had gone to an inner room with a Russian who had parked his taxi below, and outside the door Leo, cigarette dangling, dispassionately waited. These are the innocents. What do they know of the flickering sky over El Greco's deserts? What do they know of damnation? They were not taught by a master.

"I am sorry, Charley, for what transpired, particularly that it should have happened in your home, but I suspect there was an element of seduction. Stay up here, my boy, until your cousin has left Southampton. And do not think that life is over because of this. *I* was not pure when I married. You see how I honor you with my confidence. You could make a good tale of this next term, but you won't. No, boy, don't weep. Get up and go out. Walk down the beach and breathe in the Atlantic. Recite *Dover Beach* if you must. It will go well with your present sentiments. But don't be late for dinner. Mr. Depew is coming, and I want my senior prefect to entertain him."

Had I fornicated only that I might be forgiven?

When Madame de Genlis returned to Paris after an exile that had lasted a quarter of a century, a period which had encompassed the revolution, the directorate, the consulate and the empire, what struck her most was that ladies who received their callers on the chaise-longue no longer covered their ankles. The *couvre-pied* had fled with democracy; France had wanted neither one nor the other, and are there grades of importance in the junk pile? Seduction by Claude, forgiveness for seduction by Claude, the love of Prescott and shrapnel in the Argonne.

Sixth form year! With the sixth behind him Dr. Arnold wouldn't have traded his job for any in England. I see the blond senior prefect standing on the dais with eye on wristwatch and finger pressing the assembly bell; I see him dashing down the football field, one arm stiffly out, for an eighty-yard gain; I see him singing loudest in the song fest, laughing loudest at the headmaster's reading of Leacock. He keeps exhorting the lower forms to a greater showing of school spirit and the upper to a greater cooperation with the prefects, until at last he fades through innumerable examples of example giving into a kind of cinema poster of Tom Brown, a puppet to jig about the stage and prattle in a disguised voice, manipulated by five strong fingers behind the curtain, a Faust who has sold his soul to God.

In the whole process of non-living it is the least lived year, waiting for the emerald green of June with the creamy white parchment and prize books rebound in morocco leather, thinking of graduation first as a day to be dreaded, then as a release and finally as an extinction, not because there is no life after school (though that may be) but because school has sucked out one's life, and the holy vampire with the arching eyebrows who loves to read Lucretius and Epictetus has taken one's blood and bones for the cause (as of course one had begged him to!) and spread upon his green, green campus a fragment of one's translucent skin, a lock of yellow damp hair.

That was the life one made love to, was it not; that was the sacrifice one sought, to let the middle-aged god return to his earth and his boys in the guise of one of them, to rejuvenate and redeem his school through the medium of a captive senior prefect? What does it matter that there is nothing left of one when the great spirit moves out of one's body? Is the process not ecstasy? Or as near it as one would ever come?

When I think of early communion I always think of it as being in the spring, and I feel the sweet sad tug of a pointless melancholy and the light, exhilarating caress of a warm zephyr against my cheeks as I cross an empty campus to what I hope will be an almost empty chapel. And then I remember the sting of the sour cheap wine on its passage to my empty stomach and the wonderful rumble of the comfortable words. How he could say that word "comfortable"! It seemed to have more syllables than four and to be filled with the biggest of pillows; it suggested a great dark cool leathery gentlemen's club with discreet silent attendants, visible only because of their white raiment, passing between the half-sleeping members with delectables. And I would close my eyes, kneeling at the altar rail, so tightly that I would see explosions of light and spots of blue, and when the service was over I would go back, faithful hound, to help him with his disrobing and listen mutely to the flow of the day's instruction.

"I have noticed, Charley, that Mr. Taylor's dormitory is habitually late for morning roll call. I have noticed that there are more books overdue in the library, that the back row in the schoolroom was giggling last night at prayers, that there was a fight with tin basins in Mr. Dugdale's lavatory, that shoes are not always shined, that tongues are not always clean, that minds are spotted and flesh is vile (at least as second formers may conceive it), that virtue has departed from the campus and the great veil in the temple is rent in twain. Do you know who rent it?"

How could I think I would survive being his boy, his son, his victim? My formmates keep their respectful distance; the faculty step gingerly by me. The Rector's hound is safe only when the Rector is present, to allay with a finger's touch the bristling hair on his neck. But if I give him youth, he gives me redemption. I enter into him and become but a pulse of a mighty being. With what dawdling sentiment do I see myself as an aide-de-camp standing on a hilltop over the battle, absorbed in my general's tactics and mindless of the shells and bullets over my head! But there will be other battles in which such things may receive their due consideration.

The war has been a godsend for people who like to blame things on things. My virgin sister Alice and my virgin-in-heart mother at Cannes, on terrace after terrace, nibbling macaroons under a macaroon sun, tell of me and my vices in subdued tones that throb with pride. A total wreck, so much promise, such a tragedy, such a loss. Oh, yes, it might have been better had he been killed outright. There are worse things than death, far worse, and it is I, his mother, who tell you that. I hope when I go, I go quickly, like dear Mr. Popley, at eighty-eight, on his tennis court at Hyères last Sunday. I should never wish to survive my faculties or live to be a burden to Alice. I want to live just so long as I'm useful, not a minute longer. Well, it's kind of you to say so, but if I *do* look young for my years, it's because I try to take an interest in what the young people do and say. After all, the future depends on them. And that's what I mind about Charley. He doesn't seem to care what's happening in the world today outside of that woman (I won't mention her name!) and her trashy crowd. Well, of course, I can't imagine *what* Dr. Prescott thinks about it! When Alice was last in Paris, she ran into her right smack in the Rue de la Paix. Naturally, she cut her. Oh, yes, she cut her dead. Alice is one of the few of her generation who remembers how to do that. It's another of the arts that was lost in the war.

I can hear the rumble of Dr. Prescott's laugh in the rustle of autumn leaves on the Champs Elysées as I sip my cointreau. I can hear it in taxi horns. I heard it in the exchange of artillery in the Argonne; I heard it in the slush of boots through the oozing mud of the terrible spring of 1918. He was always bigger or smaller than life, louder or softer than any sound. At times he was as silly as a letter from Mother; at times he seemed to bear as little relation to my present as the memory of one of Alice's big marquise dolls. And at times he loomed over the war-lit battlefield like a leering caricature of the Kaiser, exulting in Armageddon, or exulting that he had predicted it, flitting back and forth across the beam streaked firmament with Cardinal Richelieu in a grotesque game of tag, now the pursued, now the pursuer, like a dog and cat in a jerky animated cartoon.

Ridiculous? The only faith of Marlowe and Webster was that the grinning skull was less ridiculous than the jeweled crown that it wore askew. But can naught be funnier than zero?

16

DECEMBER 7, 1942. I am a bit shamefaced to enter in this journal, on the first anniversary of Pearl Harbor, that I am happier than ever before in my life, but I am beginning to understand that happiness is a state of which God approves. A man who has attained spiritual union with him could be happy in the Roman arena; indeed, we read of saints who were. Dr. Prescott used to quote Phillips Brooks who, when asked if he was happy, would reply: "Yes, perfectly." Well, I have not achieved any such state of grace, but I think I can safely say I have attained peace of mind. I believe that I am doing what I ought to be doing and that if I live and graduate I will be ordained in the spring of 1945.

I would go every weekend to visit Dr. Prescott, to whom I owe it all, if he would allow me, but he says that it is unpatriotic to take up train space. Actually, the train to New Paisley is never full, and what he really wants is to have me learn to stand on my own feet. He realizes the effect of his personality on mine. There are those who say that his continued presence so near the school is evidence that he doesn't realize its effect on Mr. Moore's, but they are wrong. There is no such effect. Duncan Moore is totally independent of Dr. Prescott, and Dr. Prescott is well aware of it.

Which does not, of course, mean that Dr. Prescott likes it. That is another story.

Last weekend he let me come to Justin because he was preaching in chapel. I arrived at the start of morning service and slipped into a back pew as the choir was passing down the aisle singing "Ten Thousand Times Ten Thousand," followed by the two headmasters, acting and emeritus, Moore towering over his predecessor, his firm bass voice clearly distinguishable above the sopranos and tenors, and Dr. Prescott, very grave and majestic, his lips moving but emitting no audible note, his eyes fixed on the great altar window of St. Justin before Rusticus. For all Moore's height and noisiness he might have been a schoolboy walking beside his principal.

Divinity school has made me more aware of Dr. Prescott as a clergyman. Mr. Griscam told me once, in his half denigrating way, that as long as the headmaster had to be a minister only an hour a week, his conscience required him to put on a good show for at least those sixty minutes. There was a small degree of truth in this, for Dr. Prescott at times felt guilty, not at having no parish duties (for, obviously, he had no time for them), but at never having wanted them. His principal reason, however, for giving so much care and devotion to the chapel service was that he regarded it as the keystone of his educational plan. God might indeed be everywhere, but he was particularly in chapel when masters and boys worshiped together.

As Mr. Havistock had once pointed out, there might have been a touch of the theatrical in Dr. Prescott's one-time practice of reciting the service by heart, but I think almost everyone agrees that he is a great preacher. Mood follows rapidly upon mood; pathos, humor; the rich, resonant tones soar into serenity and dip into raking sarcasm. He can be funny; he can be awesome; he can be sublime. Only the envious could begrudge him the pleasure that it so obviously gives him. It is the pleasure, after all, of a great artist.

That morning he took his text from the parable of the laborers in the vineyard, and he described amusingly the natural exasperation of those who had borne the heat and burden of the day only to receive the same wage as the Johnny-come-latelies of the afternoon. But then suddenly the note of levity fell away; a pucker appeared in his brow and the tone deepened.

"What then in all seriousness, my boys, should be our attitude to the blessed of this earth? To those who have better looks, better bank accounts, better health? Or even better character, or better faith in God? Should we not pray (and this can be hard!) that they may be as happy as they *seem?* And should we not confess to ourselves that the ease of their circumstances does not necessarily mean that God loves them less? Indeed, he may love them more. For the blessed of this earth can be very lovable indeed. And none of us is a Christian until he has accepted the parable of the laborer in the vineyard. Until he is willing to share the kingdom of God equally with those who have toiled but a fraction of his working day. Until he has recognized that it would not be the kingdom of God if there were any differences in it."

After chapel, as I was greeting Dr. Prescott on the steps, Mr. Moore came up to ask me very cordially to lunch at the head table. To my surprise Dr. Prescott intervened impatiently.

"No, no, Duncan, I'm taking him to lunch at my house. I want to find out how he's doing at school."

"Perhaps then you will both come over afterwards?"

"He has to get back to Cambridge. I'm going to put him on an early train."

I had known nothing about either lunch or my train, but obviously my role was silence. It occurred to me that Dr. Prescott was treating his successor with much the same testiness that he had used to show Mr. Griscam. Was it the treatment that he meted out to those who disputed his absolute control of Justin? Feeling sorry for a headmaster who had to operate under such a handicap, I felt impelled to observe, when we had left Mr. Moore: "Everyone tells me he's doing a splendid job."

Dr. Prescott stopped short and plunged his walking stick into the earth. "Are you trying to bait me, Aspinwall?"

"No, sir!"

"Well, you're behaving as if you were. Every Tom, Dick and Harry makes a point of seeking me out to tell me what a great job Moore's doing. They want to see if the old lion can still roar. They're trying to goad me into breaking the sacred rule that condemns the retired to silence."

"Surely, sir, you can't think that of *me?*"

He gave me a sharp, hard look, pulled up his stick, grunted and continued his way across the grass. "Well, I grant that you've always seemed a particularly fulsome admirer of mine. Keep it up, my boy, keep it up. If it's not sincere, tell me it is. The old live on flattery, you know."

Happily I knew him well enough now to discount some of the seeming malevolence of his mood. "Wherein has Moore been so deficient?" I asked as I caught up with him.

He stopped again abruptly and once more stuck his walking stick in the ground. "Have you noticed how the boys go into the dining room? Always in my day they were dismissed by forms from assembly and passed to their places at table in a double line. Now they all push in together in a crush that jams up in the doorway like a New Year's Eve crowd in Times Square!"

I was too surprised for a minute to say anything. Was this the man who twenty minutes before had transported me to a vineyard in Palestine, who had given me fresh insight into what could be accomplished from the pulpit? Could one descend from so spiritual a sublime to so earthy a ridiculous?

"I suppose they still manage to get into the dining room," I said wonderingly.

"Of course they get *in*. But does appearance mean nothing to you? When you've been a schoolteacher as long as I have you'll know that appearances are three-quarters of the battle." He pulled his stick up. "No, nine-tenths!"

"I am surprised to hear it from one so steeped in fundamentals."

"Oh, I know, you think I'm an old fusspot," he muttered crossly as he walked on. "But that's just because I happen to *be* old. If I were twenty years younger and said the same thing, people would say I was profound. That's the hell of old age. You'll find out, Brian!"

"I doubt it, sir. With my heart I shall not make old bones."

He gave me a swift appraising glance. "You seem very accepting."

"Oh, but I am. I don't mind at all. I shall probably have much more time than I need to make the small contribution that I'm likely to make."

We talked now of more cheerful things, of the beautiful clear winter weather and the prospect of snow. I had spoken designedly of my heart because I had wanted to interrupt his own inclinations to self-pity. We went to the little cottage that he had rented and ate Mrs. Midge's good roast beef. He lives very simply, waited on by his devoted housekeeper and one maid. I have heard that Mrs. Prescott's trust went to the daughters on her death and that he has refused any contribution from them. But he has no interest in worldly things. All he wants is a seat from which to watch the continuation of his school. I am only sorry that he watches it quite so closely.

April 6, 1943. The Dean preached at Justin this morning, and knowing that I always like to go back to the school he very kindly asked me to drive over and back with him. I was surprised not to see Dr. Prescott in chapel, but Mr. Moore explained at lunch that he had a slight cold and had been told to stay in.

"Go see him if you have a minute," he admonished me, as if such a visit were a charity and not a privilege. "He's all cut up about the news we got yesterday of Martin Day. You remember Martin, don't you? He was senior prefect in '37. Shot down in the Pacific. A wonderful boy. But tragedy's all we hear these days, isn't it?"

The Dean said he would not be leaving for Cambridge for an hour, and as soon as the meal was over I hurried to Dr. Prescott's house. I found him alone in the living room by a fire, very morose and rather remote, but obviously glad to have someone to talk to. I sat in the chair opposite and occasionally poked the fire, allowing him to ramble on at will about Martin Day.

"He was the kind of boy you couldn't fault, Brian. Straight as they come, hardworking, hard-playing, devoted to a widowed mother, the inspiration of younger brothers and sisters. Yet he seemed to look at life with an impassive resignation, a kind of contained bitterness, as if he were saying: 'Oh, yes, I'll do my best; I'll even make it a good best, spit on me though you may.' He was the best senior prefect I ever had; he took infinite burdens off my shoulders — and yet, do you know, Brian? I never warmed to him as I should have. He was charmless. Totally charmless. Can you imagine a priest of God caring about such a trifle as charm?" In disgust he smashed his fist down on the table beside him and made the lamp and ashtrays jump. "Can you imagine a supposedly serious headmaster caring about a smile, a trick of expression, a way of joking? Yet *I* did. Charley Strong, whom you know all about, had extraordinary charm. But he was no finer than Martin Day. Less so. Oh, yes, less so." He sighed and shook his head regretfully. "And poor Day *wanted* my affection and knew he wasn't getting it, and he accepted this just as he accepted everything else. Just as I'm sure he accepted that last horrible dive into the blue of the Pacific!"

"Oh, come, sir," I interrupted at last. "Surely you're making things worse than they are. I was with you once when Day joined us for a walk, down on a visit from Harvard. You were exceedingly nice to him. I remember it distinctly."

"If I was, it was because I was making up for what I didn't feel. A man who sets himself up to be a headmaster should distribute his affections equally."

"You mean he should *appear* to," I corrected him. "Even our Lord preferred John to the other disciples."

He gave me a testy stare. "Will you tell me why you are always so bent on excusing me, Brian?" he demanded. "Is it because of that work of hagiography on which you are embarked? Do you object to my departing an inch from the role of saint to which you have so ruthlessly condemned me?"

I remembered how he had torn into Mr. Griscam for his proposed biography and could only suppose that it was my turn now. He had never before mentioned my habit of making notes about him, but I had known, of course, that he must be aware of it. Cordelia, if no one else, would have told him.

"I wouldn't really call it a work of anything," I answered humbly. "It is true that I collect stories about you. Would you care to see what I've got? I'll burn them all if you wish."

I had not expected that so little oil would settle such troubled waters. Dr. Prescott looked suddenly almost sheepish. "No, no, dear boy, you're very welcome to what you've got. If anyone is going to 'collect' me, I had as soon it be you." He looked again into the fire for several silent moments. "As a matter of fact I have a prize bit of 'Prescottiana' for you that I was looking over this morning. When one is past eighty one doesn't wish to have papers in one's possession that one would not be willing to have anyone see in case of a sudden demise. This document must decidedly be either burned or placed in trusted hands. Would you take it subject to two conditions?"

"What would they be?"

"To be sure that David Griscam never sees it. It was written by his son, Jules, who died twenty years ago, and it would pain him."

"I promise."

"Wait. That's not all. You will also promise me that if you ever publish anything about me, you will incorporate the gist of this document. Of course, you need mention no names."

I hesitated. "May I ask why?"

"Because it is the record of my greatest failure. That's why I got it out yesterday when the news came about Martin Day. Martin was not so great a failure of mine as Jules. The Japs killed Martin, but I killed Jules. Or, not to be melodramatic, I sent him down the path that ended in his death."

It was my turn now to stare into the dying fire as I debated my next remark. "I thought he committed suicide."

"I have always dreaded to think so, for if it was suicide, it was also murder. Jules' car, a Bugatti sports model, left the highway between Nice and Cannes and crashed into a rock pile. It was traveling at eighty miles an hour, and Jules, as usual, had been drinking. But Jules was not the only person killed. There was a girl in the car. Why should he have made that poor little Riviera tart pay the price of his own mad follies?"

"Maybe she wanted to die with him."

"And maybe somebody has a taste for cheap cinema," Dr. Prescott retorted crisply. "Two months before his death he sent me — out of the blue, for we hadn't met in three years — an extraordinary document. So far as I know, nobody but myself has ever seen it — except, of course, the French psychoanalyst for whom it was apparently written. He must have been trying to get Jules to exorcise me by writing me up. I have heard of such therapies. One dredges up the old guilty incidents and reduces them to impotence by simple articulation. I suppose Jules was so proud of the finished composition that he wanted to show it to his old headmaster." His smile was very wry. "Or maybe he just wanted revenge."

"Did he get it?"

"He got it when he died."

He rose and went slowly to his desk from which he took a

thick pile of white papers held together by a rubber band. When he handed it to me I saw that the top page bore the letterhead HOTEL DU PARC and was closely covered by a thin, spidery handwriting.

"You accept my conditions?" he pursued.

Again I hesitated. But, after all, I had only not to publish. "Without reservation."

"Then it's yours. Along with whatever you got from poor old Horace Havistock. He died, you know."

"Oh, no, I — didn't."

"Yes. Two weeks ago." He nodded gloomily. "High time, too. His mind was going. And I believe David Griscam gave you something?"

"He did."

"We're always in David's debt, aren't we?" He continued to nod, but more in distraction now. "It's amazing how many people are and how much they mind it. Yet David doesn't rattle the keys of his prison. I have never figured out if he has deserved much more of life or if he has got all that he had coming to him. But tell me, Brian. You think you'll stick it now? You think you'll be ordained?"

"God willing, sir."

"Good boy." He put a hand on my shoulder. "I'm sure of it. Work hard, and don't come back here. I may go to Florida, anyway, next winter. The point is that I don't want you to see me. Or rather I don't want you to see what I'm turning into. I hate old age, and I'm becoming a nasty, cantankerous old man. No, I mean it! I'm put off by the merest trifles. I can still see that they're trifles, but the time may be coming when I won't. I want you to remember me as I was."

"But, sir," I pleaded, "don't you see that I need you?"

"I do not," he said firmly. "I see that you're on the verge of becoming a man and that you must go the rest of the way alone. There, isn't that the Dean's car calling for you now?"

I tried to console myself on the ride back to Cambridge with the thought that he did not really mean his interdict, and I was mortified to discover that the weight of the unread manuscript in my lap helped to soften my depression. Is it possible that the acquisitiveness of the collector has reached such a pitch in me that I would rather have the relic than the saint? It has happened before to those who have tried too hard to persuade themselves that they are divinely inspired. Help me, dear Lord, to be moderate.

17

WHEN Father named me Jules, after my grandfather Griscam, the black sheep whose evil doings had blotted our escutcheon, he must have felt that he could close the books at last on the dreary tale of the performance of his filial duties. I suppose he had reason to pride himself on having been a good son, but there was no reason for his being so tiresome about it. If I heard the story of those paid debts once, I must have heard it a hundred times! I naturally felt sorry for poor old Grandpa Griscam, whose magnificently delinquent obligations should have been so ignominiously satisfied, and modeled myself from boyhood on a romantic misconception of him. For all the mess I have since made of things I am still glad that I did not do as my brother Sylvester. He modeled himself on Grandpa Prime and became a prize stuffed shirt.

I have never been in the least congenial with Father. Our philosophies, if either can really be said to have one, are at opposite poles. Yet I will admit that he is a hard man to dislike steadily. He is so damnably reasonable. He has an infinite faith that there is no problem in the world that can't be solved by sitting down and talking it out. Oh, those talks! He would have talked the heart out of Keats and the sublime gaiety out of Mozart.

Some basic instinct of self-preservation always made me resist him, as country dwellers resist the intrusion of signposts and hot dog stands into the beauty of the landscape. It is true that he professed to care about art and beauty, but if they ever got through to him at all, it could have been only by the written word. He had no real response to his physical surroundings, in painting or sculpture or even in natural scenery (though he did keep a bird list) and in music he was deaf to all but the noisiest Verdi choruses. Indeed, his worst danger as a Philistine consisted in his efforts not to be one. He was so determined that culture, like calisthenics and tennis lessons, should have its proper place in our lives. The epicurean had to keep step with the puritan down the long aisle to the altar of the well-adjusted God.

But what Father could never comprehend and what ultimately destroyed his system was that if you put things in pairs, the cruder twin is bound to predominate. I think that he and Mother must have had a subconscious belief that it was all right to be grand if you were uncomfortable, all right to be social if your parties were dull, all right to be extravagant if you bought the second-best. And so we lived in large, drafty stone houses, filled with dubious period furniture, and did a great deal of pointless entertaining of ostensibly "important" citizens.

The fear that we children would be spoiled was a constant obsession. Sylvester and I slept in a cold gymnasium on top of the city house, and in Northeast Harbor summers, while all our friends were sailing or playing tennis, we had to work on Father's mainland farm, purchased for the sole purpose of keeping us occupied. Amy, even in her coming-out year, could not dance after midnight on Saturday because Father, an agnostic, saw fit to borrow from the church its disciplines if not its consolations. Similarly, although an active opponent of the Eighteenth Amendment, he welcomed the excuse of its passage to ban all liquor from the house.

As a family we were un-American to the extent that Father

ruled the roost. There was no aspect of our education too trivial for his interminable planning. Mother accepted it all passively, not because she was weak but because she was not interested. She was a terrible disappointment to me, for she would not even pretend to need my passionately professed championship. She was beautiful (or so I thought), stately, remote and lame, the perfect combination for a fanciful boy who wanted to be a knight-errant to a princess in distress. On the rare occasions when Father was unable to control his temper, and it exploded at Mother with a force all the greater for its long suppression, how gladly would I have leaped to her defense had I thought she was in the least affected by the ranting little man at the end of the table!

But Mother needed nobody's help; she had her causes: woman suffrage, birth control, the Army of the Holy Word, and she knew that in the period of abject apology that inevitably followed Father's outbursts she would be offered a large and useful check for her current favorite. She loved humanity, but she looked with a misty, faintly bored benignity towards its individual specimens, even when that specimen happened to be her oldest son. Father was officious and irritating, but at least he cared.

The romance of his life — and this may explain some of Mother's domestic apathy — was Dr. Prescott. I am not well enough versed in the new theories of Freud to be able to determine how much of this attraction was sexual; all I know is that his worship of the headmaster was of a jealous, proprietary kind and that it provided him with the only emotional excitement and quickening of the heart that I suspect his dry nature was ever to know. At least, I am sure he did not find such things with his wife and children. I imagine that in his subconscious he must have played at every possible relationship with Prescott: as son, as brother, as lover, as wife. We children naturally resented Father's hero, not only for the affection lavished upon him at what we felt was our own expense, but for the smallness of its return. For it was obvious that however indebted Prescott was to Father, however even fond of him he might be, Father was still not a "man" as Prescott conceived of one. Sylvester and I as boys in Northeast Harbor, on the great man's summer visits, shifting restlessly under his deep brown stare and whimsical, rhetorical questions (he was uneasy with children, for like a dictator visiting a free country, he knew that his power was suspended), brooded with a dark foreboding of the great disciplinary factory to which our infatuated father had irrevocably destined us. Dr. Prescott had only to bide his hour, and we would be his.

Nor was there anything about Justin Martyr, when the hour came, to falsify my apprehension. A handy case of tonsilitis delayed my going for one year, and jaundice for another, cutting my prison term from six to four, but in the fall of 1918 I was duly entered as a third former, and my long duel with Dr. Prescott began. To an egotist of fourteen the mighty events across the Atlantic hardly existed. The holocaust that was ending in Europe was dwarfed by the difficulties of adjusting to the school hierarchy. I was the only "new kid" in my form and ranked socially with those in the two below. What was the agony of the trenches, sublimated as it must have been, according to my wishfully thinking mother, by the wonderful comradeship engendered by shared dangers, to one of my Byronic pride who had to endure alone the indignities of hazing? The ultimate humiliation was my family's assumption that I was homesick. There was surely a difference between homesickness, to which morbid malady I was always a stranger, and a natural, healthy detestation of Justin Martyr!

My first important discovery was that Dr. Prescott was a master and my father a mere amateur in the great nineteenth century art of making life uncomfortable. "Fun" was defined in terms of group activity, such as football or singing or even praying; the devil lay in wait for the boy alone, or worse, for two boys alone. The headmaster believed that adolescence should be passed in an organized crowd, that authority should never avert its eyes unless the boys were engaged in fighting or hazing or some other activity savage enough to be classified as "manly." Life beyond the campus was universally suspect: the drugstores, with their sodas and lurid magazines, the slatternly country girls, the very woods and streams that encouraged boys to take long walks and wax sentimental about nature and perhaps each other.

Where Prescott excelled above all was in his intuition as to where temptation lay. As a young man and an Oxford dandy, he had strolled by the Thames reading Baudelaire and Rossetti. He was widely, and I think justly, reputed to have a perfect ear for music and a fine tongue for wine, and he could actually speak Greek and Latin. Had it not been for the perverted violence of his puritan conscience, he might have been a great artist or at least a great voluptuary. But he had crushed the joy in his own nature, and so far as he could, in those of others, pleading with his angry God to help him, his hands tightly clasped, his eyes squeezed tightly shut, waiting as much as thirty seconds between the prayer that he recited at the end of chapel, and his own thundering "Amen," knowing, the old ham, that the congregation was reverently watching his silent communion. He would have been a glorious repertory actor of the Henry Irving school, playing Iago one night and Tamburlaine the next.

Yet he got away with it. My own father is proof of that. If you want to be taken seriously in this life, you must start by taking yourself seriously. Prescott was surrounded with an atmosphere of almost incredible awe, to which the parents, trustees and faculty all contributed. I do not think that many of the boys liked him, but they respected and feared him, which was much more fun, both for them and for him. At least a quarter of the student body, like myself, were sons of graduates and had grown up in his legend. They were proud of his fame, excited by the rumble of his leadership and diverted by his wit, his inconsistencies, even by his sermons. As I have said, he was basically a ham actor, and the school was a captured but still admiring audience.

I got off to an immediately bad start with everybody by resisting the hazing. The rules of hazing, like those of all activities not protected by law, were exact. One was meant to fight back, but not too hard. One had to resist just the right amount (immediate surrender would have been "flabby") and then submit, and then, after a fixed period, the hazing ceased. Violent resistance, like violent hazing, was bad form because it brought the masters into an unconstitutional area which by tacit consent had been left to the boys. But I failed to appreciate such delicacies. I fought like a cat with nails and teeth and was so badly beaten up that I had to spend two days in the infirmary. Dr. Prescott, who had hitherto ignored me — afraid, perhaps, that I would presume on his friendship with Father — came to see me and was gruffly sympathetic, but I suspect that he had already spotted me as one of those who would never fit in. Had I deliberately incited my formmates to mayhem to give his school a bad reputation? Perhaps Father had warned him that I was capable of it.

The hazing came ultimately to an end, burnt out by its very intensity, and I found myself suddenly and blessedly left alone, ignored now by boys who believed that the silent treatment was the hardest of all to endure. They did not comprehend that they had left me a New England sky and ultimately a New England spring, a library with all the poetry I could want, woods to hike in and occasionally another maverick to befriend. It was thus that I came to know Chanler Winslow, a strange, blond, lazy, quiet boy who, although handsome and athletically competent, was shunned by the others as "crazy." Chanler was very slow and had abominable grades; he was surly and unsociable, and he had a murderous temper that, unlike my own, was widely feared. He would not, for example, have hesitated to use a knife if attacked. He liked me because I asked nothing of him and because we shared a passion for the out-of-doors.

It was still the era when boys were allowed to have huts in the woods, and there were a number of these along the Lawrence River, two miles from the school, made of timber and old shingles and used on Sunday afternoons and holidays. The privilege dated from one of Dr. Prescott's rare sabbatical leaves in the tenure of an indulgent substitute, and it was known that the headmaster was waiting for the first infringement of his many regulations of the huts to abolish them. For what were they but a challenge to his theory of moral protection in crowded living, a defiant community of independent Thoreaus camped on the very border of his village of robots? Chanler and I built the biggest hut of all and furnished it with an old rug and some wicker chairs purchased from a local junk shop. Had we been allowed to keep it I think I might have finished my career at Justin Martyr without ignominy.

For the hut was helping me to become a man by absorbing and dignifying my resentment of the school. When Chanler and I sat on the banks of the turgid Lawrence, chewing grass and watching the kingfishers plunge for their prey, or when we fished ourselves or climbed trees looking for eggs, or even when we lay on our backs and watched the clouds and the triangles of ducks and geese, far from the nervous atmosphere of ringing bells and hurrying feet, I could pity rather than despise the old man who thought that boys went to the woods only to smoke or drink or masturbate.

But that old man and I were not to be allowed to pass each other like ships in the night. An officious young master, the kind of twisted sadist that is the bane of secondary school education, hoping to curry favor with the Rector, spent a weekday afternoon searching the empty huts and discovered three cigarette butts. It was flimsy evidence of illicit smoking, for there were always tramps in the neighborhood, but Dr. Prescott had waited a long time, and he must have decided that it was as good as he was likely to get. The next morning at roll call he announced that the huts were to be dismantled before the end of the week.

For the first and last time in my life I tried honestly to reason with him. That night after supper I asked for an interview and was told to go to his study at nine. When I knocked at the appointed hour and heard his deep, weary "Come in, boy," and, coming in, saw him leaning over the great square desk so that the one burning light illuminated his broad gleaming forehead and rich crop of gray hair, I knew that the stage had been set on which only his victories could be played. Was it a coincidence that the corners of the room and the big busts of the Roman emperors in the surrounding book cases were shrouded in darkness, so that Prescott was the center of what dim light there was? Was it chance that the stillness was in such dramatic contrast to the noises of the school? Was it unintentional that the few objects on that expanse of mahogany surface should have been of heavy gold: a cross, a fish, a miter and a paperweight that was a crude replica of Trinity Church in Boston?

I told him, as he gravely listened, that I thought it unjust that all the huts should have to pay for the sin, if sin it was, of one. I insisted that our activities had been innocent. I protested that even my father encouraged us to stay out-of-doors.

"Out-of-doors, exactly," Dr. Prescott interrupted with a whimsical smile. "I am not interfering with the out-of-doors. In fact, by removing the roof of your hut I am removing a bar between you and heaven."

I returned at this to the safer ground of the injustice of making many pay the fault of one.

"But, my dear boy, that is exactly the injustice of life," he pointed out. "All the German people are now paying for the fault of the Kaiser and his advisers. All members of a football team are penalized if one is offside. But more fundamentally — yes, Jules, much more fundamentally — we all share in original sin. And why not? Why should we pay only for our own little crimes? Isn't there something petty and avaricious in such a plea?" Here Dr. Prescott looked up and seemingly through me, in the pose of one alone, struggling with his despised mortality. "Why should another man be hanged for a murder that *I* was never tempted to commit? Is it anything but coincidence that I am not a thief? Or a perjurer? I sometimes think it would be impossible for any of us to suffer injustice. That our greatest blessing lies in the sins we have *not* been led to commit."

"But, surely, sir, you would not walk into the schoolroom and give a black mark to the first boy you saw on the ground that he might smoke if he had the opportunity!"

Dr. Prescott smiled, and his smile, I admit, was charming. "No. But I might remove the opportunity. And that is why the huts must go."

"You mean Winslow and I must really tear down our hut? Ourselves?"

The smile faded, and the brown eyes searched me gravely. He had taken in my note of desperation, and he knew that he could either allow me a dignified retreat or provoke me to a stand that would involve my expulsion from the school. Did he wish to lance the ulcer that I represented? Or let it naturally disappear? His eyes became for a moment quizzical, and then he glanced away.

"I understand, Jules, that you and Winslow have exercised much industry and imagination in the adornment of your hut. I appreciate that it would be distressing for you to carry out the work of demolition personally. I am not, whatever you boys may think, totally devoid of delicate feeling. I will make arrangements for your hut to be taken down by others. Good night, Jules. Please remember me to your parents when next you write. They are well, I trust?"

"Perfectly well, sir."

It was not until I was out of his study that I realized how cleverly I had been handled. By accepting my complaint about the method of demolition, he had obliged me to accept its fact. It was a formidable matter for a schoolboy to be up against a diplomat as well as a general.

In the year that followed this incident I brooded much over my wrongs, but my overt resistance was confined to sniping in sacred studies class. This was Dr. Prescott's one vulnerable period, for if there was anything sincere in his vaudeville nature it was his belief in his mission to persuade boys to join the company of Jesus Christ. He would, no doubt, have liked to have ordered them to sign up and to have damned the recalcitrant, but he knew that his God was as mean as himself and would never let him get away with anything as easy as that. He could order a boy to play football or to take a cold shower or to destroy a hut, but he could not order a boy to love God. This was a matter of propaganda, and sacred studies was its allotted time. He and I would have dialogues in class such as the following:

"Please, sir, we always seem to take for granted that monotheism is superior to polytheism. But is it so? Why should it not be just as good to have many gods as to have one?"

"That is a good question, Griscam. I'm glad you asked it. It seems to me that a faith diffused in many gods must lose much of its efficacy. Which one, for example, do you pray to? And after you have chosen, can you be sure that your god will not be thwarted by the jealousy of another god? That is why, in great cultures that have practiced polytheism, like the Roman and Greek, there is always a high degree of fatalism. The believing man tends to regard himself as a mere plaything of gods absorbed in their own internecine conflicts. There is nothing like the magnificent strength and consolation of knowing that there is *one* God, here and everywhere, in you and in every particle of nature."

"That may be, sir. But the fact that it might be nicer if there were only one God doesn't mean that there *is*, does it?"

There was an ominous blink of those brown eyes, a twitch of those shaggy eyebrows. The word "nicer" had been a dangerous touch. "Of course, it doesn't, Griscam. That is a matter of faith. And in this school, which is a church school, we are dedicated to the sustenance of that faith. We hope that every graduate will know the joy of believing, but it is only a hope."

In church history I was always ready with questions about the mercenary motives of the Crusades, the jealous destruction of pagan literature by priests, the burning of heretics, the religious wars. Dr. Prescott would shake his head heavily and agree that terrible things had been done in the sign of the cross, but when I suggested that we at Justin Martyr could avoid the guilt of these associations by dating our religion from the ordainment of Phillips Brooks, whom he was always quoting, I had finally gone too far.

"You are not sincere, Griscam," he told me wrathfully after class. "You are making mock of sacred things. Doubt I allow. Intellectual curiosity I encourage. But there is no place in this classroom for cheap cynicism."

"But I only want to learn, sir," I protested in a tone so earnest that I almost convinced myself. "I only want to be sure that the church has not done more harm than good. How can I be confirmed until I have answered that question?"

"I am sorry to say that I doubt you."

"Oh, sir, I mean it!"

"If you do, then I have made an error to speak to you so. Perhaps a grave one." He sighed heavily. "But I make them. Oh, yes, I make them. You will be excused from sacred studies for the rest of the term, Griscam. You may spend that hour with extra lines of Virgil. We may as well derive *some* benefit from your preference for the pagan authors."

Once again I was worsted by the old charlatan, but this time with more dramatic consequences. It was apparently unique in school history for a boy to be suspended from sacred studies, and I was made to feel like a Lutheran priest imprisoned in the somber courtyards of the Escorial. The absorbent powers of the school were strong and could in time embrace most mavericks, but there were limits to the permissible period of dissent, and Chanler Winslow and I had let ours expire. We came to be permanently regarded as "outsiders," and my only answer (for Chanler was far too inert and indifferent to have one) was to win an occasional recruit to our isolated fraternity.

The picking was not good. By fifth form year our group consisted of only two besides Chanler and myself: Gus Crane, a snippety, effeminate, crabby old maid of a boy who had at last given up a fawning cultivation of the form leaders, and Sandy McKim, a small, dull, gentle, inarticulate lad who worshiped Chanler because the latter, traditional for once, had pulled him out of the Lawrence on a school holiday when his canoe had capsized. They all followed my lead, not because of the strength of my personality but because I alone had the will and imagination to clothe our mere unpopularity in the robes of a creed.

For I gloried in standing for art and the individual against football and the mass. I did not realize that my revolt was as hackneyed as the conformity of the majority. I had not then read the dreary heap of English and American fiction that deals with unhappy boyhoods. I thought my independence wonderfully unique, my hate fresh and pure. When I walked by the river on glorious October Saturday afternoons, I reveled less in the golden brown of the foliage and in the cold melancholy of the fall breeze than in the smug knowledge that I was *not* attending the football game and that I would attend none for the entire season, not even the final one with Chelton that marked the climax of the athletic year, the great patriotic event of the school calendar. I realized my project, but the sixth form decided that I should be "pumped."

Pumping was a penalty that fell in a semi-official zone between the boys and faculty. It was given for "bad school spirit," a crime that subjected the offender to no official penalty, but that was particularly odious to the headmaster. On a pumping day the whole school was assembled for roll call by the senior prefect, and no master was present. The sixth form stood about, their arms tightly folded, glaring at us and frowning. "Wipe it off, Jones!" one of them would bark if Jones dared, in his tension, to let his lip crease into a nervous smile. It was well done, on the whole. It was a bit of a nightmare even to me. But on the terrible day of my ordeal I was borne up by the ecstasy of my passionate sense of wrong and the idea that, like the Count of Monte Cristo, I might have a lifetime for my revenge.

I had decided in advance how I would act. When the senior prefect shouted: "Griscam, go to the cellar! On the double!" I would not jump up like a scared rabbit and scamper from the room followed by a line of six executioners, ponderously, ridiculously, pacing in step. This would be no Mexican sacrificial ballet with a cooperating victim, decked in flowers, swaying up the steps of the altar to bare his throat to the obsidian knife. No, if they wanted me, they could come and get me.

When I heard, through the haze of my brave resolution, as if from another, meaner world, the rasp of my name and the well-known order, I simply folded my arms, in mocking parody of the sixth formers, and remained at my desk. They had to come and lift me and carry me out, and when in retaliation they nearly drowned me, ducking me in the big sink of the laundry below, as I gasped for my breath, I made myself remember the laughter that had broken out in the schoolroom over my act, the laughter that could blow away the sixth form like chaff.

They had at last gone too far. The old man had gone too far. There was a deep reaction in my favor, and in the days that followed I felt surrounded by nods of sympathy. Never again was it suggested that I attend an athletic event. If I had lost one hut, I had gained another, built with the bricks of rebellion on the very grass of the campus, and I was to be allowed to occupy it thenceforth unmolested. The sixth form and the faculty might surround it by a *cordon sanitaire,* but they would not again try to level it.

My own sixth form year, when it came, was something of a triumph. I made independence almost the fashion. By submitting a poem which had been rejected by the *Justinian* to Frank Crowninshield and having it published in *Vanity Fair* I won a glory that even Dr. Prescott could not ignore.

"You have put us on the map, Griscam," he told me gruffly one morning after chapel. "There may be a question in some minds if that is where we wish to be, but nobody can belittle the feat of getting us there."

So it seemed that my school career might be ending on an actually pleasant note, that my long duel with the headmaster might conclude in the banality of exchanged salutes. And so it might have had I not, by the simple act of turning a small piece of metal in a three hundred and sixty degree arc, brought about a series of catastrophic events that were to shake the school to its very foundations. Nothing could illustrate more graphically the shifting sands on which the whole absurd structure had been jerry-built than the fact that my act was the simple physical one just described, that it hurt nobody and that it had not been designed to hurt anybody. But Prescott, like all the great idiots of history, was always willing to burn the world for a toy, a prayer, a cross, a thimble.

18

IT HAPPENED, like all bad things at school, at the end of the winter term. Spring was coy that year, and the cold season had a long and fretful death. We blotted out the days, one by one, with elaborate inkings on the calendars in our sixth form studies and talked interminably of girls and Easter dances. And beyond the lagging spring loomed graduation and the unbelievable prospect of liberty. The once formidable school was shrinking around us to the dimensions of a small provincial village, as quaint as Cranford, and poor boys on scholarships, who had once scorned me as a nonconformist, began to show unlovable signs of awakening to the values of a world beyond the campus where the friendship of families like mine might count more than the silver plate trophies of the athletic field. Only the figure of Dr. Prescott remained the same, and it may have been his failure to fade, along with an institution that was proving less durable than himself, into the backyard of discarded childhood things that made me try to push him there.

One morning after classes, just before the bell announcing the roll call that preceded lunch, I was standing with Chanler Winslow, Gus Crane and Sandy McKim in the Audubon Corridor by the main schoolroom where all the forms were about to assemble. The headmaster's study, from which he would shortly emerge, after the bell had ceased ringing, to proceed to the schoolroom for the midday announcements, was just adjacent, and the door was closed. I happened to notice that the key was in the lock. The study was never locked from the inside, only from the out when it was unoccupied.

"Do you know what would be fun?"

The other three glanced at me curiously, for my tone had been sharp. I suddenly remembered the windmill on Granny Prime's place in Long Island. It had a shaky wooden ladder leading up to the platform under the vanes, and Sylvester used to dare me to climb it. I always did, hating it, because anything was better than to be afraid.

"What would be fun?" Gus demanded suspiciously.

"To turn the key and lock the old bastard in!"

Three pair of eyes followed mine to the door, and in a sudden tense exchange of looks, I understood that my friends had seized the feasability of the project. There must have been forty boys moving up and down the corridor, talking or reading their mail which had just been distributed. Detection would be almost impossible.

"Shall I?" I asked.

It was the terrible moment of the first rung in the windmill ladder. I read assent in their eyes, even in Gus's, and I walked quickly past Prescott's door, pausing just long enough to turn the key and pull it out. In three steps I was back, smiling at the horror in Gus's eyes as they took in that key.

"Jesus God!" he whispered. "Put it back, you fool!"

"Put it back?" I sneered. "When all I need do is this?" I rubbed it quickly with my handkerchief and dropped it out the open window. "Now move on, all of you. Move quietly. Be natural."

Twenty seconds later the bell for assembly shrieked through the building, and we walked to our places on the back benches for the upper school behind the desks of the lower. Mr. Coogan, the master in charge, stood on the dais until all were seated and then nodded to the prefect at the door who took his hand from the bell. He then turned to the other door through which Dr. Prescott always emerged and waited.

He waited for a full minute. I stared at him, careful not to look to either side to catch the eyes of my friends. Then he scurried down the steps from the dais, crossed the floor to the hall and stood before the headmaster's door. We heard first the rap and then the sound of a knob being violently turned.

"Are you all right, sir?" Mr. Coogan shouted, and we heard a muffled angry, indistinguishable sound from the other side of the door. "Did you say it was locked, sir?" Coogan inquired. "No, there is no key on this side. Are you sure it's not on the floor in there, sir?" There was another incoherent rumbling from behind the door, implying both a negative and an angry reproach for the question. "Shall I get a ladder to the window?" The answer to this put Mr. Coogan in a real flurry, for he hurried off, and a little group of masters began to gather about the door, until they, too, were dispersed by another muffled roar.

At last Mr. Ives, the senior master, appeared. He ignored the commotion about the headmaster's door, sauntered to the schoolroom dais, read out the announcements with his usual imperturbability and dismissed the school to Lawrence House for lunch. As I looked back across the campus ten minutes later I saw a ladder by the headmaster's window supported by a group of prefects with heads raised. Then I saw the large familiar figure, like a great beetle, move slowly out the window and slowly down. When Gus Crane poked me, I gave him an aloof stare and passed before him into the washroom.

I had figured that no boy could have seen me except my co-mates, and I had figured correctly. But there was someone whom *I* had not seen. That amateur sleuth, Mr. Ives, a man who always looked at his watch if he heard an unusual sound to be prepared, if necessary, to testify in court as to the exact time of its occurrence, had left Dr. Prescott's study just four minutes before the assembly bell, closing the door behind him. He had observed — for he observed everything — the proximity of my group to the headmaster's threshold. At four o'clock that afternoon he had found the key under the window near which we had been standing. This, plus our bad reputation, was all he needed. We were summoned to Dr. Prescott's study after supper, where Ives, in his passionless, singsong tone, recited his findings and his deadly conclusion. One of us four must have done it.

Dr. Prescott glanced up from his brooding pose as his junior finished. We were standing in a row before his desk. "Which?" he asked, in a weary, seemingly bored tone.

We were silent. We exchanged no glances.

"Let me tell you something," he went on somberly. "You are sixth formers. As such you are officers of the school. You are, or should be, above the code of little boys who will not 'snitch.' To tell on a fellow officer who has tried publicly to humiliate his commander-in-chief is a simple duty. If that fellow officer is too cowardly to confess, seeking to implicate you in his contemptible conduct, why should you protect him? I ask you again: which did it? Was it you, Griscam?"

"No, sir."

"Was it one of you?"

"I couldn't say, sir."

"You couldn't or you wouldn't?"

"I couldn't, sir. I didn't see it."

He turned to Chanler. "And you, Winslow? Was it one of you?"

"I didn't see, sir."

"And you, McKim?"

"I didn't see, sir."

"And you, Crane?"

"I saw who did it, sir, but I don't think I should be asked to tell. It wasn't me."

How I despised Gus Crane! Until then the old man had

evidence, good evidence, but no proof. We could have bluffed it out. But now!

"It wasn't 'I,'" the headmaster corrected him without a smile. "If you will not tell me who it was, you must share in his punishment."

"But that's most unfair, sir!"

"It would be, if you were not a sixth former." Prescott now stared slowly from one to the other of us. "Very well, gentlemen. I will give you twenty-four hours. If within that time one of you has not given me the name of the culprit, I shall not consider that any of you has the right to protest whatever penalty I may see fit to impose." He paused again, for he was a master of dramatic emphasis. "No matter how heavy that penalty may be. You are all excused from classes tomorrow morning. I wish you to have full time to reflect. Or to telephone your families for their advice."

It was a curious twenty-four hours that ensued. In the morning the four of us trudged through the mud to the river and sat on the crew dock, chewing grass and watching the sluggish, eddying Lawrence. Dirty patches of melting snow under the stark trees and the bleak sunlight emphasized the belt of void that surrounded the little shrill idealism of the marooned school. I had stepped to the perimeter and was ready and willing to fall into that void. So was Chanler, whose truculent defiance of the universe I tried to interpret as loyalty to myself. So was Sandy McKim, whose loyalty to Chanler was impervious to any test that a mere Prescott might impose. Only Gus showed any inclination to consider the value of what we might be turning our backs upon, and as the morning drew on he became strident and vindictive.

"Why should we all be punished for what you did, Jules?"

"We all did it," Chanler retorted. "We all agreed."

"I *never* agreed!" Gus spouted. "Jules said it would be fun, and before I knew what he was talking about, he went over and turned that key. Nobody could say it was my fault."

"Why don't you go and tell, then?" Chanler jeered. "Why don't you go to Dr. P, like a good little girl, and tell him what a naughty boy Jules was?"

"Because I don't want to be a snitcher, of course! Who wants to be a snitcher and have the whole school know? That's why Jules has got us so neatly on the spot. I'd be as infamous as Benedict Arnold. But why doesn't Jules confess? Why, if he's going to be kicked out anyway, does it do him any good to have the rest of us kicked out with him?"

"Because we're in this thing together," Sandy McKim answered unexpectedly. "We've been in everything together. If Jules confesses, I'll say we put him up to it."

I was touched, for I would not have anticipated such fineness of feeling from one as passive as Sandy. "Look," I pointed out. "Nobody's going to be kicked out. The old boy wouldn't dare. Four sixth formers, three months before graduation, because none of them would snitch? Think of it! The trustees, all the graduates would be up in arms. No, mark my words, the old boy's bluffing, and it's up to us to call his bluff. Besides, what a triumph!"

"But supposing he's not bluffing?" Gus insisted.

"Then if he's not, I can always confess. That much I promise. He certainly can't expel you after he has his culprit."

Gus had to be satisfied with this or shoulder the terrible onus of snitching, and he gloomily elected silence. He refused to speak any more to any of us, and when we filed into Dr. Prescott's study that night, he stood sullenly to the side. The headmaster looked grey and grim; his lips were a pale thin line. But his eyes were tired, and there was something faintly quizzical in their expression, as if he wondered where we had come from, four imps whose very existence seemed designed to plague him.

"Well, this is your last chance," he announced quietly. "Will one of you tell me now who turned that key?" There was a silence in which we all listened to Gus's panting. "Will you, Crane?" Gus caught his breath, and I clenched my fists. "No? I will count out a minute." He pulled out his thin gold watch, a gift, as I remembered, from my father, and waited while the second hand spun a circle. "Very well, gentlemen," he said in a voice now of infinite sadness, putting the watch away. "You have given me no recourse. You will proceed to your dormitories to pack your clothes. You will spend this night in the infirmary annex. I will telegraph your families to make arrangements for your departure tomorrow. For I must inform you that you are no longer members of our school community and that you will not graduate from Justin Martyr. That will be all, gentlemen."

So great was the lingering spell of his authority that I had dumbly followed the file of the other three to the door before I recollected what it was I had to do. Quickly I closed the door after them and returned to stand alone before the headmaster's desk.

"Of course you know it was I who did it."

There was no flicker of the lids over those great gravely staring brown eyes. "I had my suspicions, yes. What a grief this will be for your poor father."

"Shall I call the others back now?"

"What for?"

"So you can tell them they're not expelled."

"But they are." The rich voice had become metallic. "I see no cause for revision."

"You mean you'll make them pay for what *I've* done?"

"No. For what they have done. By their deliberate silence they have associated themselves with your deed. Now they may associate themselves with your punishment."

Had it not been for my despair I would have laughed aloud at such hypocrisy. As it was I uttered a kind of strangled groan. "Do you think I don't see through your game?"

"You forget yourself, Griscam."

"Forget myself! When have I seen myself more clearly? Or you, sir? Why it's as open as daylight. By rejecting my confession, you brand me for life as the boy who got his pals fired to save his own hide! Oh, it's beautiful. It's diabolic. To think that *I*, who thought I was so smart, should have heaped up my own faggots and handed you the torch!"

Dr. Prescott leaned back in his chair and folded his arms magisterially across his chest. He raised his eyes to the ceiling and did not shift his gaze for several seconds. He might have been seeking in that dirty plaster some hole through which his deity might vouchsafe him an explanation of my conduct. He was no longer angry or even reproachful. He pursed his lips as he looked back at me as though he and I together had a theological problem to unravel.

"Tell me, Jules," he said at last in a milder tone. "Why do you ascribe to me so violent an animosity? Why should I wish to apply a torch to your faggots, as you put it?"

"Because my will was stronger than yours! Because you asked those three to tell on me, and I asked them not to! And they obeyed *me*, at the cost of being expelled."

In my exultation I was not in the least put off by the sudden concern in his eyes. Obviously, he would have to take the position that I was deranged. What alternative had I left him?

"I think you've been under a great strain, Jules," he began. "I think I had better talk to your father . . ."

"Never mind about Father." I cried. "Everyone knows that he's your rubber stamp. You've hated me from the beginning because you were shrewd enough to know that I saw through you. You had to get me before I got you!"

"And when you saw through me, what did you see?"

I was not taken in by his almost conversational tone of curiosity. I paused, but only to spit out the words more offensively. "I saw you weren't God. I saw that you don't even believe in

God. Even in yourself as God. I saw you were only a cardboard dragon."

"I will pray for you, Jules," he said in a very soft tone, almost a whisper. "And for your father."

"And I, dear Doctor Prescott, will pray for you. Till we meet in hell!"

This time his eyes really sparkled, and I knew it was my moment to turn about and march from the room. If he had won, I had had the last word. And a pretty magnificent last word, at that.

Two days later Father and I walked on the banks of the Lawrence in the damp exhilarating air of what seemed at last to be spring. From time to time he paused to identify a bird, and once he expressed surprise at seeing a chewink so early in the season. There were no sermons or recriminations. Father knew when milk had been spilt, and he was not one to try to scoop it back in the bottle. Even I had a dim appreciation of what it must have meant to him to have a son expelled from Justin, and for once in my life I made an effort to be diplomatic. I told him that I was sorry for what had happened and that I accepted my punishment, but that I hoped he would be able to use his good offices to obtain a pardon for the unoffending three.

"I have already tried that, Jules," he told me in his dry, matter-of-fact tone. "I first made it clear to Dr. Prescott that I was not asking for any reconsideration of your own case. That would have been hopeless. But I begged him only to suspend your friends and allow them to return for graduation. Unfortunately, their parents have already organized a group of graduates into a noisy campaign of telegrams. This, of course, will be fatal to their case. However, they didn't consult me."

He shrugged in that way I knew so well, the shrug of the foreign minister who moves disdainfully aside when militarists or radicals take over the government. Father had only contempt for stupidity. I think he believed that the stupid deserved to suffer, unless they had the inspiration to take their problems to David Griscam.

"You mean there's no chance he'll change his mind?"

"Not *now*," Father emphasized. "Dr. Prescott was never a man to be stampeded."

"But can't the trustees overrule him?"

"And have him resign?" Father gave me a pitying glance. "Do you really think they'd be willing to lose the greatest figure in American secondary education to save the scalps of your three little friends? You don't know the world, my boy."

"I don't want to know the world," I said bitterly, "if the world admires a man like Dr. Prescott."

"You're not to criticize him to me," Father retorted with sudden sharpness. "It comes most ungraciously from you, who have caused this whole sorry mess. I have not reproved you, Jules, because I feel you have suffered enough and, alas, that you are going to suffer more. Our job, yours and mine, is to work out a future for you."

"How can we? The old man's done me in. I'll always be known as the boy who wouldn't own up to save his buddies."

"For 'always' read 'six months,'" Father said with a brisk little headshake. "You won't believe how soon this will pass. No, you won't," he repeated sternly, raising his hand as I was about to protest. "Don't let's discuss it. Youth is hopelessly astigmatic. All I ask is that you cooperate with me in getting yourself and your friends into Harvard."

Harvard! I had not dreamed that such a horror was still possible. Was there to be *no* end of the New England experiment? Had I climbed the windmill ladder only to have to do it again and again? "Father," I pleaded in sudden desperation, "I don't think Harvard is the place for me. Couldn't I go abroad for a year? With Chanler? Or off somewhere on a tramp steamer? Please, Father," I went on, even more earnestly, as I saw him stiffen, "I think it might be the making of me. I think it might be the only way!"

"I thought you would have something like that in mind, Jules. But don't you see, that to run off to Europe would be to stamp yourself forever with this wretched business? No, my boy, you must make a go of Harvard and then it will be forgotten. Or if remembered at all, it will seem a boyhood prank."

I knew from his tone that the case was hopeless. I was being "handled," and there was no appeal from that. "It's one thing to get me into Harvard," I said sullenly. "It's another thing to make me go."

"I think you will make yourself go," Father retorted blandly. "For the simple reason that if you don't, I shall not speak to President Lowell about your three friends. You have been instrumental in their losing their Justin degrees. Will you wish to be involved in the loss of their Harvard ones?"

"But that's blackmail!"

"It is no such thing. It is a fair exchange. I do something for you, and you do something for me. You're a difficult young man to bring up, Jules. One has to fight you for your own good all the way." He stepped suddenly to the side of the path and peered down the slope into a clearing. Then he snapped his fingers. "Dammit all!" he exclaimed, forgetting the proximity of the Justin campus. "I should have brought my field glasses. I could swear that was a great northern shrike."

19

FATHER, in his usual fashion, did an efficient job, and it was arranged that all four of us would be admitted to Harvard, provided that we passed the entrance examinations. Unhappily, he could not take these for us, and Sandy McKim failed. Gus Crane, who now hated me with all the vindictive force of his womanly nature, told everybody that Sandy had failed because of a nervous crackup brought on by our expulsion from Justin. It may have been partly true, and it was certainly widely believed, and I found that the smudge of that black eye which Dr. Prescott had dealt me, for all of Father's patient scrubbing, was never entirely going to come off.

Father was good to his word and did not give me any formal punishment, as I had "suffered enough," but he suggested that it might be more "appropriate" that summer if, instead of joining the family on their stately tour of first-class hotels in European capitals, I should work as a counselor in a camp for city boys of which he was a trustee. I agreed to do this, seeing in it the opportunity to square my accounts with him, and when I entered Harvard in the fall I felt no longer under the least obligation for what he had done — or tried to do — for my fellow delinquents. It was a curious thing, considering how little Father expected to be thanked, that nobody could ever bear to be indebted to him.

The only thing that Harvard seemed to offer me was freedom: freedom from home and freedom from Justin Martyr, and Chanler and I, as roommates, determined to drink as deeply of it as we could. We avoided our old school classmates and spent our evenings and our money in the areas of Boston from which it had been a goodly part of Dr. Prescott's ambition to exclude his graduates. Chanler was really interested only in low women and I in booze, and we made a gloomy enough couple for two young men who wanted to revel in their new-found liberty.

Father had given me a very large allowance on which, in accordance with his usual "responsibility" theories, I was expected to support myself and two indigent old maid Griscam cousins, and I reduced the poor dears to a lamentable state of need, promising them golden things in the future. I knew that they would ultimately complain to Father, but the moment was mine, and the moment was all I wanted. I did not really believe in Harvard or in Father or in his dreary theories. Reality was gin and whiskey and poetry and fast driving and the evil memory of Justin Martyr.

For the maddening thing about Dr. Prescott was that he still refused to shrink into the past. It sometimes seemed to me that his shadow was actually broader at Harvard than it had been at school and that we had not so much gained our freedom as he had enlarged his jurisdiction. My faculty counselor was always asking about him. He prided himself on being a liberal and opposed to private schools, but he liked to describe Prescott as the only intellectual who had ever been a New England headmaster. Men whom I met in classes, on the campus, on Boston evenings, when they heard I'd been to Justin would immediately identify it with Prescott and make some inquiry such as: "Is the old boy the ogre they say he is?" But there was usually a note of respect in the question. Even Chanler's tarts had heard of him. And certainly the evidences of his whip were still around me, in the proximity of poor Sandy McKim working unhappily in a Boston insurance company, in the bitter glances of his older brother, Bert, a sophomore, in the dozen little weekly reminders, by chance allusions or semi-snubs, of my own still fetid reputation.

It was as if Dr. Prescott had challenged me to a game of proving which of us was real and was now laughing in his triumph. "You thought you'd find *your* world after Justin, didn't you? But, my dear boy, you woefully underestimated your old prestidigitator. See where the universe has become a school!" Of course, it hadn't — I knew that. He knew it, too, the old devil. But he could make it *look* that way. He knew that if men cared little about faith, they still yearned to be hypocrites. The single lunatic in a world of timid sanity, he made his fellow beings pretend they were in an asylum.

I think it was my feeling of helplessness in defeat that made me drink. I doubt that I was ever really alcoholic. For after I had conceived my great idea, after I had felt with loving fingers in the pocket of my soul the long sharp secret weapon that I was going to use, I lived more on exhilaration than on gin, reverting to the latter only when my weapon seemed dull or in the desperate moments when my clutching hand could not find it at all.

My idea was born in the unlikely delivery room of a party that Chanler Winslow and I gave after the Yale game. Half the people who came we did not know. Some of them had simply happened upon the wrong party. Chanler's tart friends from Boston did not improve the tone, and after a couple of hours I retired to a window seat, in fuzzy isolation, with a glass and a bottle of whiskey, to consider sardonically the scene before me as it might appear to my solicitous father's eye.

"Well, if it isn't our Jules! The spunky little guy who wouldn't squeal — on himself."

I contemplated thoughtfully the tall rangy figure of Sandy's brother, Bert McKim, that sprouted into a small, spotty head with small features and sticky blond hair. "How charming," I replied. "In the stuffy old days people used to feel they shouldn't go to parties of people they disapproved of. Now, with their inhibitions removed by their host's liquor, they feel free to vent their spleen on him."

Bert stared down at me with troubled irresolution. "Party? Whose party? Not *yours*."

"Oh, but it is, my dear fellow. And please don't misunderstand me. You are very welcome. You hate me, because of Sandy. I hate the world, because of Sandy. We have more in common than you think."

"Sandy's as good as they make 'em," Bert said in a slow, sullen suspicious tone, "and what happened to him shouldn't have happened to a dog."

"I quite agree. But you seem very solicitous for an older brother. I cannot pride myself that I would share a similar concern over my brother Sylvester. Though I hope, at least, I would have the decency to show it."

"Sandy and I have always done things together." Bert sat down unsteadily on the window seat, and I was astonished to see what appeared to be tears in his eyes. Was he simply drunk and maudlin? Acting on a sudden prick of inspiration, I began piecing together what I knew of him. I knew that he and Sandy were the children of their father's first marriage and that they had the bond of a lost mother and an unsympathetic successor. Bert had not gone to Justin because of a sinus condition, since cured, but he had frequently visited the school with his father and certainly knew the grounds. As I caught the first glimmer of my idea I was so dazzled by its beauty that I threw back my head and laughed.

"Laertes," I exclaimed, in jubilant paraphrase, "was your brother dear to you? 'Or are you like the painting of a sorrow, a face without a heart?' "

"What are you talking about?"

"About Sandy. About what really happened to Sandy. About you and me. And what we can do about it."

"Don't you think you've done enough?"

"Bless you, my boy, I haven't even started!"

"Oh?"

Bert seemed totally confused, and I saw it was the moment to take a firm position. "I care for Sandy as much as you do, Bert. Make no mistake over that. But I don't propose just to moan. I propose to act. If I can find the right partner."

"Act?"

"I want to get back at the mean old man who did him in," I said bluntly. "But now is not the time to discuss it. You and I must meet alone, if you're interested. I will let you know when. And where. What I want you to do now is leave the party in a big huff, telling people you didn't know I was giving it and that you won't stay another minute. Lay it on thick. Do you want me to help you?"

As he stared at me blankly I arose and cried out for all to hear: "Well, if you feel that way, why don't you get the hell out?"

Bert rose slowly. "I'll get out all right," he said sullenly. "I'd never have come if I'd known whose room it was." He was so convincing that I thought my plan was ruined until, as he turned to go, I noticed that the eye away from the room was closed in a long wink.

Two nights later I sat in Bert McKim's room and watched his small, glittering eyes as I told him the story, or rather *a* story, of what had happened to Sandy. I started with the episode of the overturned canoe on the Lawrence River when Chanler Winslow had swum out to rescue Sandy, and I made much of the docile devotion with which Sandy had affixed himself thereafter to the bumpy course of Chanler's school career. But the beautiful little twist that I added and that made Bert's sullen breathing come suddenly in gasps was to suggest that

Dr. Prescott, who had a notorious aversion to "sentimentality," had diagnosed Sandy's affection for Chanler as being of that nature and had surveyed them from afar with brooding eyes.

What under this interpretation had been the whole ridiculous episode of the turned key in the door but the old man's long awaited chance to get rid of Sandy and Chanler on the shallow pretext of a failure in their duties as sixth formers? Had not the indignation of the parents and trustees, nay, of the whole graduate body, sufficiently testified that the official story was too flimsy? And now that I was giving to Bert, and only to Bert, this more convincing explanation, I could reflect with exhilaration that he would never be able to check on it without the danger of starting up the very rumor whose accuracy he was testing. Oh, how it fitted. How it all fitted.

The effect on Bert was almost too great. He could hardly speak for several minutes. "And is such a man to get away with that?" he finally stuttered. "Is the old fiend to go on from glory to glory? With his praises sung by every idiot in Massachusetts? Is he to croak without knowing what I think of him?"

I stared at him sternly until he was calmer. Then I smiled and crossed my legs. "I have given the matter the most careful thought, and I think I have found a way to get at Prescott. I believe I have discovered the chink in his armor through which we can jab the burning needle."

"Where? Tell me."

"Patience, my friend." I held up a restraining hand. "And listen. To comprehend requires a bit of philosophy. The old man is wily and quick and crooked as a corkscrew. He can persuade you and even himself that Christ came down to earth to found a boys' academy under the tuition of Francis Prescott. But one thing he *must* believe, and that is the 'mystique' of his school."

"What are you leading to?"

"You will see. To strike Dr. Prescott where he can be hurt one must commit an act of desecration on the school grounds.

The act must be clearly that of a Justinian, and it must be anonymous, so the old man will never know again, in shaking a graduate's hand, whether or not he is shaking the hand of the desecrator."

Bert nodded slowly as my idea settled in his mind. "You think that would really hurt him?"

"I think it might even destroy him."

"How would you perform this . . . this desecration?"

"Ah, that is the crux. After much thought, I have decided on three things. The face must be cut out of the portrait of Phillips Brooks in the school dining room." I smiled grimly as I heard the click of Bert's closed teeth. "The manuscript of the school hymn by Richard Watson Gilder in the library must be torn to shreds. And a hole must be poked through the figure of Justin Martyr in the altar window in chapel."

"Oh, no!" Bert protested, shocked. "What do the saints have to do with Prescott? Can't we leave the chapel out of it?"

I shook my head very firmly. "There is a mystical significance in these three things. Any one or two is useless. All *three* must be perpetrated. If it makes you feel any better, my father gave that window, so I have a quasi right to its disposition."

Bert looked at me suspiciously, but a bit in awe. "When would we do this?"

"You mean when would *you* do it, my dear Bert."

"Me? Me alone?"

"I'm afraid so. I will plan the operation in such a way as to be practically devoid of all risk. But I cannot go myself. In fact, I must have an airtight alibi the night it's done, for I will obviously be the first suspected. Nobody, on the other hand, would ever think of you. You didn't even go to the school, so how would you know its symbolism?"

Bert was silent and motionless for at least two minutes. Then he got up to get a bottle of whiskey out of his desk. "Tell me your plan," he said tersely.

"You will hire a car in Boston. I have the place and the money. The school is forty minutes' drive. I have a map that will show you just where to park. The buildings are open at night. You can enter the dining hall easily and cut the portrait. The library, as you know, is in the adjoining wing, and the key to the glass manuscript case hangs on a hook by the librarian's desk. Finally the chapel. I will give you a bamboo pole with a steel head that will reach to the window. This is the only act that will make any noise, but it need make very little, and the chapel is far enough from the nearest dormitory so that it shouldn't be heard."

"Is there no watchman?"

"There's old Pete, but he reads newspapers and drinks coffee in the housekeeper's kitchen. He makes a tour of the campus every hour on the hour. You can start at a quarter past, and you should be finished in twenty minutes."

"How do you know some of these things haven't changed? You haver 't been at the school since last year."

"Nothing changes at Justin. At least nothing sacred does."

"We hope! Supposing I'm caught? Do I take the rap alone?"

"I will give you a letter setting forth our scheme. All you will have to do to inculpate me is deliver it to the authorities."

Bert was silent again and then nodded. "I'll think it over," he conceded grimly. "I admit it doesn't sound so bad."

Only two days later I received a laconic note in the mail saying "Okay" and fixing our next appointment in Bert's room. From then on our plan raced ahead, for Bert wanted it executed while his enthusiasm was at its peak. He studied my map that showed the exact locations of the picture and manuscript and selected a night of half-moon. We agreed not to meet the next day which would be a Wednesday, but that on Thursday, when we both had a class in Adams Hall, we would meet briefly in the washroom at eleven.

*

I decided that I would spend the night of the great deed with Chanler in the flat of two of his tart friends. When the detectives reported to the headmaster and to my distinguished father the whereabouts of Jules Griscam, they would have an added shock to the one already inflicted. Yet in point of fact I was too excited to do anything but drink and sit up late, reciting poetry and talking wildly about school days to the disgust of Chanler and the boredom of the girls. All the next day I kept looking in the faces of my classmates, of my professors, of people in the street for some indication that the deed was done. I even kept turning my eyes in the direction of the distant school as if I expected to see a red glow in that portion of the sky. But nothing, of course, occurred to distinguish the day from other days.

On Thursday at eleven I waited tensely in the Adams washroom until Bert, astonishingly self-possessed, swung the door open. He glanced about to be sure that we were alone and then took a brown manila envelope from under his jacket.

"Here's the portrait face. Do you want to see it before I burn it?"

"Yes! And the poem?"

"That's destroyed."

"Oh, Bert! My Achilles! And the window?"

He shook his head curtly. "I couldn't do it. At the last moment. After all, God damn it, it's a church. This is enough."

I winced as if he had drawn a razor across my cheek. "Let me see the portrait, anyway," I hissed.

He pulled a piece of canvas out of the envelope and flashed it before my unbelieving eye. What I saw was a part of the cheek, oddly cream-colored, the hooked nose, oddly red, and one great eye and one great, fatally familiar, bushy eyebrow.

"But that's not Brooks," I gasped in horror. "That's Prescott. It's the Laszlo portrait!"

"Yes, I thought it would be better to cut up the old bastard himself than Bishop What's-his-name. I thought perhaps you hadn't remembered that his portrait was there. Sst! Someone's coming." And Bert snatched back the bit of canvas and left me to the explosion of the heavens and the downpour of despair.

I don't remember how I got back to my room. My next memory is of lying on my bed and biting my pillow between angry sobs. Macbeth was no more frustrated by the escape of Fleance than I by this grisly chance that had turned the beautifully conceived eagle of my revenge into a croaking blackbird. For what would Prescott care about such petty vandalism? That some embittered Justin boy should have attacked *his* likeness — how small, how puerile, how like a cashiered servant, a disgruntled janitor! And, indeed, if suspicion were to fall on me, either as principal or agent in the deed, how easily could he not shrug his shoulders and say: "After all, what more could one expect from a boy who got his friends fired in an effort to save his own skin?" It was too much, after everything, too much for my hate, for my pride, for my love of self to bear. I sat up and drank from a bottle of gin until I was full of fire.

Somehow I was not killed in my wild drive in Chanler's car to the school. Somehow I stumbled from the road to the shadowy hulk of the chapel, clutching a rock that I had carried all the way from Cambridge, and made my way to the back where I could see by the moonlight the high, black arched panes of the great Justin Martyr window over the altar. And somehow, even more miraculously, I was able to spot the two figures scurrying towards me from each side and was able to heave the rock and hear that soul-satisfying crash of glass before I was pinioned and hurled to the ground by detectives.

I had plenty of time the next morning, lying on the cot in my cell at the New Paisley jail and feeling the long, shuddering throbs of my hangover, to contemplate the nadir of my short and unhappy career. Here I was at last, sin incarnate. At least I could hope that the rock through the altar window had elevated me to the dignity of sin. Sin, the real sin, in the eyes of our society is almost always a symbolic act. For what, after all, had I done? Had I killed anybody? Had I even hurt anybody? Did a single mortal ache in any joint or go thirsty or hungry because of me?

All I had done from the beginning was to turn a piece of metal in a full circle and toss that piece of metal out a window to the grass where it had ultimately been recovered. Then I had caused the destruction of a piece of paper on which were traced the lines of a very bad poem, of which, unfortunately, thousands of other copies existed. More seriously, perhaps, my agent had slashed a painting and I had broken a window, both inferior artifacts and one of which was easily reparable. Had all my little damages been accidents, nobody would have been in the least concerned. It was my intent that made the sole difference, my contempt for the little jumble of lares and penates, in short, my desecration of the holy things of our superstitious Christian society. Could I hope, in a lifetime, to do a fraction of the more real harm to others that was accomplished by "good" men like Prescott and approved by "good" men like Father? If Satan was not a headmaster, he was at least a parent. Where in the world was there room for anyone as wicked and harmless as myself?

Dr. Prescott came to my cell late that afternoon in the guise of the weary philosopher who has tried all, lost all and accepted all. It was a superb performance, enhanced by his beautiful, rumpled, cashmere grey suit and black vest and by the melancholy modulations of his address.

"When I leave, Jules, you will be free to go yourself," he told me. "The school will press no charges. Unhappily, Harvard has been less forgiving. You may not return there. But it may perhaps interest you to hear that I interceded on your behalf with President Lowell. Alas, to no avail. He is quite adamant. One night's bad work might have been forgiven. Not two."

"Two?" I demanded sharply. "What do you mean by two?"

"A copy of your letter to Bert McKim was found in your rooms this morning," he replied dryly. "It cleared up the mystery of your having been with Winslow at a place of ill repute last Tuesday night. Once again, Jules, you have managed to implicate another. I am glad to tell you, however, that President Lowell may reconsider McKim's case."

I shrugged. I cared very little about Bert McKim. Perhaps I had hardened since my sixth form year. Perhaps I was simply disgusted at the way he had bungled the job. "Where am I to go when I go?" I asked. "Does Father know?"

"Your father is here. I asked him to let me see you first. He is talking now with Mr. Ives about the possibility of your continuing your education abroad."

"Good old Father!" I exclaimed with a mocking laugh. "Always at work over a piece of broken crockery. If he can put this one together, he should be in line for a commission on Humpty-Dumpty."

The dark line down the center of Dr. Prescott's forehead deepened as he sighed windily. "Tell me, Jules, have you no remorse?"

"Remorse? For what you've done to *me?*"

"There was a time when people were considered as being possessed. Possessed by the devil." He shook his head to and fro vigorously. "I sometimes wonder if we have not too easily flung it away as superstition. How else can I explain the extraordinary malevolence that you have evinced against the school and myself from the very beginning?"

"Mightn't we *both* be possessed? Mightn't our devils have recognized each other?"

As he stared back, it seemed to me that I could make out in

those big eyes a mixture of apprehension, curiosity and something like awe. "Tell me what you mean by that."

"Don't people with devils feel them early?" I exclaimed. "I'm sure I've always been aware of mine. Like a lazy tapeworm, all warm and comfortable, feeding on the jumble of my cerebrations. But yours, I suspect, had a harder time. For when you first became aware of his coiled presence, you saw instantly all the possibility of staging a great drama about your conflict with him. You built the school as your amphitheatre where through the decades generations of wondering boys could watch your Laocoon act. Oh, it was something! Until the devil peered out and saw his supposed victim strutting about on the rostrum, praying and preaching and exhorting, and realized that a new Barnum had put him on the boards and was making a fortune as a snake charmer!"

"And then what did he do?" Prescott's question came almost in a whisper.

"Well, devils have a way of having the last word, you know," I said, looking at him hard, "particularly with those who are making a peepshow of God's mercy. Who are using God's things as props in vaudeville. And so it was that your beautiful academy, your palace of lies, should have at last a graduate — a moral graduate, shall we say — who carries your act to its ultimate degree and shatters for a gaping multitude the great glass window of your idolatry."

Prescott dropped his big head into his hands and groaned: "Jules, Jules, my boy, what have I done to you?"

When he looked up and gazed at me wretchedly there were actually tears in those great brown eyes! Tears, while mine were dry! The tears of his defeat, of his collapse, tears that would fall and splash until the very tower of the school with its clanging bell would crack and be submerged. He wept, ah, yes he wept at last, but what was there left for me in a world of water?

20

OCTOBER 8, 1945. It seems unbelievable to be back at a Justin Martyr of which Dr. Prescott is no longer head. Of course I have come here, since his retirement, as a visitor, but it doesn't really hit you until you return, as I do now, once more a master. Not that Mr. Moore is doing such a bad job. Far from it. He is big and cheerful and forceful and probably more popular with the boys than Dr. Prescott ever was. But what one cannot imagine is how he can have the courage (perhaps some would say the nerve) to move so jauntily along paths hallowed by his great predecessor, particularly when that predecessor is watching from so close at hand. For every brick of Justin, every fountain and porch, every structure from the glorious dark struggling chapel, a drama in stone of the Protestant soul, to the old green bleachers by the football field are impregnated with the Prescott personality. It is as if God had paused and withdrawn to a misty mountain-top to see how man will manage his creation.

Only in the afternoons now does the familiar figure with the long blue coat and stick appear, on the still daily round of the campus and grounds: once about the lawn, thence to the garth for ten minutes' meditation on a memorial bench, thence to the football practice, thence to the river and back. It is quite a stint for one of eighty-five. He stops to speak to boys and masters; he smiles and sometimes laughs his high-pitched laugh. He seems with his every gesture and syllable to defer to the new order, but how I would hate to be that new order under that glassy eye!

October 12. As a clergyman, I have been relieved of even the most formal athletic duties, and I have taken to walking of an afternoon. I watch from my study window until Dr. Prescott has passed before going out and taking the opposite direction. I do not wish to intrude upon him, for I still feel constraint about working for his successor. It is not, God knows, any feeling that I am being disloyal, for Dr. Prescott was the person who championed my return to Justin, but as a minister I am more identified with the new order than others of the old faculty. I assist the headmaster in chapel, and I mark his term papers in sacred studies. No doubt I am unduly sensitive, but I will wait for Dr. Prescott to make the first move in resuming our old intimacy. So far he has not done so.

My clerical status does not seem to have improved my disciplinary powers. In fact, I am almost back where I was when I first started. I fear that my reversed collar (unlike Mr. Moore's or Dr. Prescott's — oh, so unlike!) is taken for a symbol of weakness. I am again aware of whisperings and giggles in the back row of my classroom and odd noises in my dormitory after lights. The boys know that it is painful for me to give black marks and, all too naturally, they take advantage of this. Yet I have qualms about penalizing them for my own failure to be obeyed. If I were interesting, my classroom would be silent, and if I had a shadow of "command presence" (instead of its opposite) there would be no moving between the cubicles at night.

My fourth form English class (for I am to teach that as well as sacred studies) is reading *Persuasion,* and I am disheartened by my utter incapacity to make them see what an exquisite thing it is. I feel woefully inadequate when I contemplate all the delights which Jane Austen might offer them if only *I* had the ability to get her across. I know that Mr. Dahlgren, the head of mathematics, would call me absurdly naïve. He believes that only a tiny number can be expected to see the light. But to me this is Calvinism. Why should only a few, arbitrarily chosen, be saved?

October 21. Dr. Prescott came up behind me this afternoon as I was leaving the garth and grabbed me by the arm. "Won't you walk with me, Brian? Have you been avoiding me, dear fellow? We seem to be the sole pedestrians in an autumn world prostrate before the idol of football. Can we not unite our forces?" I stammered that I had thought he might wish to be alone. "Alone? Wait till you're an octogenarian widower. You'll find you have your fill of solitude." And holding my arm he walked beside me, asking me questions about my classes and the boys and whether I was satisfied at having become a minister. There was a warmth and a kindness and an interest that made me tremble like an idiot and want to fall down on my knees and kiss his hand. How the richness of his loving nature fills in the crannies of the somber buildings and acts as a great red Romanesque arch over the bleak fall sky! One cannot understand the architecture of Justin without its necessary complement in Dr. Prescott's personality. And what bliss to have back our old friendship again!

I told him of my troubles, of my worries in English class, and he nodded gravely. "If you could transmit some of the beauty of Jane Austen, you would be transmitting a small vision of God. But don't blame yourself too much. It is desperately hard work. Perhaps with that particular novel and those particular boys, it is impossible. I wonder you don't try Melville. I sometimes wish we didn't divide our curriculum into subjects. An equation, a Keats ode, a Gothic Cathedral, a Mozart aria, the explosion of gases in a laboratory, they should be seen by boys as related — and divine. I tried in this campus to convey a sense of oneness and Godliness. Now *that*, for example, is plural and non-God." He pointed with a frown to a white refrigerator truck passing the Schoolhouse to park by the football field.

"I would never have allowed it in my day," he continued more somberly. "You may ask, can soda pop be sinful, if consumed in moderation? Perhaps not. But that truck is sinful *here*." And watching the truck as it passed the chapel, white against dark, a flash of absurdity against the seeming permanence of our place of worship, it appeared in the instant of its silhouette to symbolize the transiency of our commercial mores. I could only agree with Dr. Prescott that so discordant a note was somehow meretricious. Perhaps, as he said, even sinful. As it would be sinful to insert a chapter of John O'Hara into the chaste pages of *Persuasion*.

November 2. I was having a particularly bad time with fourth form English this morning when Dr. Prescott appeared suddenly in the doorway, put his hand to his lips in a gesture that indicated the class was not to be disturbed and noiselessly took a seat in the back. None of the boys who were facing me saw him, so their bad behavior continued. The poem under discussion was Browning's "Meeting at Night: Parting at Morning," and the little devils were pretending that they did not understand what had happened during the night to make the narrator need "a world of men" the next day. Of course, they knew that I blushed easily. Sloane, a dreadful, tall, thin, slick New Yorker was the ringleader.

"But tell me, sir, if he had been with a woman and yearned for a world of men, mustn't there have been something unsatisfactory about the woman?"

"Not necessarily, Sloane." I dared not glance in Dr. Prescott's direction. "He simply needed action after so much emotion. That's understandable, isn't it?"

"You mean there had been no action during the night?" The class tittered, and I felt my cheeks burning. "You don't think, sir," Sloane continued in a false tone of intellectual curiosity, "that he was what is known as a 'queer'?"

"You may leave the room, Sloane."

"But, sir, I was only asking a question!"

"Leave the room, please."

"But, my God, sir, it's not fair when I've just asked a question . . ."

"Sloane!" Dr. Prescott's deep voice filled every cubic inch of the room, and the whole class jumped. Though he had retired before any of them had come to Justin, he was still an awesome campus figure. "Stand up, Sloane, and turn around!"

Sloane leaped to his feet and spun about. "I'm sorry, Dr. Prescott, sir, I didn't see you."

"That is neither here nor there. Your language should not be regulated according to who is present."

"But, sir, it was a word I've heard my own father use. I did not know it was so bad."

"It is not a bad word, Sloane. It was your use of it that was bad."

Sloane looked utterly at a loss. "Queer?" he mumbled.

"No, not *that* word!" Dr. Prescott thundered, rising now himself, and the class rose with him. "I admit, I never expected to hear such a term used in a classroom in this school, but that's a relatively minor matter. The important thing, and the one that you do not even seem to recognize, is that you used the name of God in vain!"

Sloane's face cleared as he recognized at last what must have struck him as a minor misdeed. "Oh, that's true, sir. I did, didn't I? It must have slipped out. I'm very sorry, sir."

"Slipped out? And you're merely sorry? We'll see what

the headmaster has to say. You will proceed, Sloane, to Mr. Moore's study where you will report to him exactly what you said. If he is not there, you will wait till he comes."

Sloane hastily left the room, and Dr. Prescott nodded to me. "You may proceed with your class, Mr. Aspinwall. Pray forgive my intrusion."

When he had gone, and the class was seated I enjoyed for the first time the undivided attention of the boys as we turned with subdued monotones to a discussion of "My Last Duchess."

After school, as I was walking to Lawrence House for lunch, I was touched on the shoulder, and Mr. Moore, holding a black velvet bag with the Justin arms on it, where he kept his papers, adjusted his long legs in step with mine.

"Tell me, Brian," he began in his vigorous, amiable fashion, "how did Dr. Prescott happen to be in your classroom today?"

"He just dropped in, sir."

"You had suggested that he pay you a visit?"

"No, sir. Except that I had confided in him some of my teaching problems. I think he wished to help me."

"I see. It's unfortunate that he should have been there when Sloane said what he did. Obviously, we cannot allow swearing on the campus, but neither can we treat it as quite so grave an offense as Dr. Prescott would wish. The boys simply use the expressions they pick up from their fathers, and I fear, even their mothers."

"It was my fault, sir, for allowing the discussion to get out of hand."

"Well, we won't worry about it," Mr. Moore said with a rather forced smile. "These little hitches are bound to occur with the old gentleman being around so much. But if you have teaching problems, Brian, you can always confide them in me, you know. I am never too busy to talk to one of my masters."

"Thank you, sir," I said in a voice chastened enough to acknowledge the mild rebuke in his tone. "I happened to mention them to Dr. Prescott because we walk together."

"Naturally, naturally. And an enviable experience to know the great man. I wish I had more time to see him. I do, indeed."

When I joined Dr. Prescott that afternoon, I found him silent and moody. I dared not apologize or even mention the lamentable scene of that morning, and we walked without exchanging a word. Yet Dr. Prescott's silences, like those of royalty, are not embarrassing. One simply understands that his mind is closed to audiences. On our way back from watching the football practice we passed the headmaster's house and saw Sloane under the porte-cochère washing Mr. Moore's Buick. Dr. Prescott paused.

"We meet again, Sloane," he said gravely.

"Yes, sir," Sloane replied ruefully. "I guess I've learned my lesson this time. I had to miss football practice which means I won't be able to play in the game on Saturday."

"Is your punishment confined to these ablutions?"

"You mean to washing this car? Oh, no, sir, I have to do Mr. Langborne's as well."

"Indeed? We live under a stern regime, Sloane."

"You can say that again, sir!"

Dr. Prescott moved on, and I accompanied him to the door of his house. As I took my leave, he stared down at the flagstone path, and I lingered, unsure whether or not I had been dismissed. At last he muttered sadly: "To have to wash two cars, Brian. For taking God's name in vain. Think of it! In my day he'd have been lucky not to be suspended for the rest of the term!"

November 4. Pierre Dahlgren has taken a fancy to me, which improves my position a bit, not only in the faculty but with the boys. For Pierre, as head of the mathematics department and master of Lowell House, is number three, after the head and senior masters. Indeed, he should by rights have become senior master when Mr. Ives retired, but it was felt that a younger man was needed. No doubt he resents this.

Pierre, at fifty-three, is a tubby, white-haired, mincing, round-eyed, baby-faced bachelor who loves to sit up late and gossip in his beautiful study hung with eighteenth century French and Italian drawings (Pierre is rich, at least for a Justin master). He is a perfect example of what unlikely material Justin can assimilate and turn to its own profit. For all his silliness, he has a lucid, beautiful mind which enables him to teach mathematics as I would love to teach poetry, and his stentorian dignity counteracts his plump softness, so the boys know he is not one to be trifled with. And then he has a passion for the school which for twenty-five years has been his entire life. Dr. Prescott (whom he worships) must have seen from the beginning that there was a place on his faculty for at least one Pierre.

My dormitory is near Pierre's bedroom and study, and he has taken to asking me in after lights for coffee. This is his best time, enthroned in a great armchair covered in blue velvet, before a silver tray and coffee urn, a cigarette always dangling from his lips, an ash always on his silk tie, his eyes snapping as he chews up the juciest bits of gossip of the school day. Nothing is sacred to Pierre: neither the boys, nor their demanding parents, nor the poor faculty wives who try so hard to look well at lunch, nor even Mr. and Mrs. Moore. He will burst into dry gusts of laughter and then hold his fat hands to his thin lips as the coughing overcomes him. Sometimes he even serves brandy, which is against the rules, but he has a dispensation because of a weak heart.

I told him of the Sloane episode and of Dr. Prescott's reaction to the punishment.

"Well, at least there's one boon," he commented with a

wicked chuckle, "and that is we've finally got that jalopy of Mr. Moore's cleaned. I had been on the verge of paying the local garage to do it. Only if I were Moore and had the disposition of Sloane's services I would employ them indoors." Here he smiled nastily. "My maid Ida tells me the girls at the headmaster's house sweep everything under the rugs." Here Pierre went through a pantomime of glancing to his left and right and then leaned forward to hiss at me: "And she says their kitchen's a *sight*."

It seemed to me that we had got a long way from blasphemy. "I'm afraid Dr. Prescott was very upset. Of course, to him swearing is as bad as lying."

"And he's quite right, the poor old superseded darling." Pierre startled me with his sudden stern tone which meant that no sarcasm was intended. It was remarkable how quickly that magistrate could emerge from the dotted garb of the clown. "Dr. Prescott has forgotten more about running a school than Moore will ever learn! He knows that everything is interrelated: the clean collar, the shined shoes, the hard-played game, the deeply felt prayer." Pierre might now have been Dr. Prescott himself; I quailed before his flashing eye. "It is reverence that must be taught, day and night, if boys are not to be apes. When I think what a beautiful thing a disciplined boy can be, I feel a positive hatred for those who allow him to wallow in his native grossness. It's as if some thug had wandered through a gallery of Caravaggios and smeared the faces of his charming youths with brown paint!"

"Perhaps it would be better if Dr. Prescott moved away," I suggested, a bit embarrassed by this outbreak.

"Perhaps it would be better if Dr. Prescott had never retired. He can do a lot more going downhill before he meets Moore coming up."

Even such an admirer of Dr. Prescott as myself was taken aback by the idea that he should still be in office at eighty-five.

"He keeps complaining that his memory is going," was all I could think to say.

"He only *thinks* his memory is going. Because he's old. You, for example, Brian, are presumably not worried about yours. Yet you forgot to read out the detention list before dismissing schoolroom yesterday, and you left your term papers on the desk in faculty hall."

I reflected that it was small wonder that Pierre could control the boys. "I'm sorry. How stupid of me."

"It's quite all right, I put them in your locker," he continued, brushing the ashes from his waistcoat and tie. "You had neglected to lock it."

November 7. Eric Langborne was at Pierre's last night after lights. He is Pierre's age, or a bit younger, and also a bachelor, but in other respects they are opposites. He is skinny and bald, with a long oblong face and white perfect teeth that he likes to show as he articulates his syllables in a dry, superior tone. He is head of the Latin department, and being English born and a Rugby graduate, he obviously considers himself Justin's leading intellectual. Listening to him and Pierre hold forth gravely on such "dangerous" innovations as Moore's suspension of the requirement of blue suits for Sunday wear, one begins to wonder if Dr. Prescott's faculty was not an orchestra that only Dr. Prescott could conduct.

November 10. Eric was particularly lugubrious last night. After a silence of some moments he announced: "Obviously neither of you has heard."

"What?" I asked.

"You haven't heard what he's done today?"

"No, what?"

"Latin is to be made optional after the fourth form!"

Pierre and I exchanged glances. We knew what a blow this

must be to Eric's pride. "And what is to be put in its place?" Pierre demanded. "Jujitsu? The history of vaudeville? Or needlepoint?"

"Art appreciation," Eric answered grimly. "The mother of languages must veil her eyes in a darkened room where smirking boys will gape at slides of Dufy and Matisse."

"But they can still *choose* Latin," I murmured consolingly.

"Few boys will choose a difficult subject," Eric retorted. "They will choose you, Brian, where they can read *Jane Eyre* and *Lorna Doone.*"

"Eric, the time has come!" Pierre announced abruptly.

"What?"

"The time has come," he repeated solemnly.

Eric now nodded, but as I continued to stare, Pierre explained: "The time has come to ask Dr. Prescott to join our little meetings. He has wanted to come, I know, but he has been restrained by delicacy of feeling. Now we must tell him that it is his duty. His duty to save the school!"

I had not realized that our "little meetings" had such significance or that we constituted a nucleus of organized dissent. I see now that I must have been cultivated by Pierre because of my intimacy with Dr. Prescott. I have a horror of disloyalty, but it still does not seem possible to me that any gathering could be stained with that quality at which Dr. Prescott is present. Pierre, for a soft man, talks a great deal about the softness of our age. Dr. Prescott may convince him that it did not all originate with Duncan Moore.

November 15. Dr. Prescott came to Pierre's last night, but the meeting did not go off very well. In the first place the great man was in an obviously sour and despondent mood, and in the second Pierre, very foolishly, had placed four brandy glasses on the silver tray by the decanter. Dr. Prescott glared at these before sitting down and pursed his lips disapprovingly.

"I was aware that *you* had a dispensation, Dahlgren, from the rule about liquor on school premises," he began in the dry, bleak, weary tone that he used to school offenders. "I was not aware that it had been extended to your visitors. Or is that another of the new regulations?"

"Indeed not, sir," Pierre replied heartily, whisking away the offending tray. "I think my poor old Ida must have set them out in your honor."

Dr. Prescott chose to ignore this transparent falsehood. "I shall certainly not break Mr. Moore's rules while I am criticizing his administration."

The discussion went very slowly after this. Dr. Prescott held forth in a melancholy voice about the importance of Latin in the curriculum. It seemed to me that he stressed it much more than he had in the past, and he was obviously tired. Pierre spoke of the importance of daily calisthenics at noon, and Eric deplored the fact that the boys no longer had to wear stiff collars at supper. I had nothing to add and was surprised, when we broke up, to hear Dr. Prescott suggest that we meet again the following week. I had thought he would be through with the Dahlgren circle. I hope to be myself, but so long as Dr. Prescott goes, I will go with him.

December 1. I have not made an entry now for two weeks. I have been troubled, and my mind has not been clear as to which of two is the real reason. Is it that I feel that our Wednesday night sessions are dangerous to the welfare of the school or is it that I feel they are not? In other words, am I worried for the school or for us? Wouldn't I rather see Dr. Prescott, if he *must* play an active role, howl like the anguished Lear in the tempest and ultimately bring ruin to all, so that the usurpers and the dethroned perish in a single fifth act cataclysm? Wouldn't that be better than to have him preside, like an addled old field marshal, over a council of disgruntled royalists who have dragged him from retirement to envelop their shabby plans in the musty glory of his ribbons and banners? Yes, in the last analysis, do I not care for Dr. Prescott far more than for his school? Would I not rather have him lethal than absurd? I cannot bear the picture of his gravely nodding head as Pierre discusses the iniquities of Mr. Moore's new project of having the boys wait on table.

Yet what can I do? I tried on one of our walks to hint that Pierre and Eric were carping critics. "Oh, yes, of course," he muttered impatiently, "but their hearts are in the right place. That's the great thing."

He would not go on with the topic, and when I left him, he remarked dryly that I did not have to come to Pierre's unless I chose to. I assured him that I did so choose, and that is true. For I love Dr. Prescott, if that is not too presumptuous a term, more than anyone in the world. I cannot bear to be away from his side in time of trouble, even if I can only observe. All my life I have been an observer, and now, when I crave to act, to interfere, to *stop* something, it is ironical that I am compelled to go on in my old role.

December 3. Mr. Moore came up behind me on our way from morning chapel to the Schoolhouse and put his long arm around my shoulders. He is always very friendly, but one feels that he is constantly having to overcome a naturally cold nature. Still he tries, and I believe that he tries sincerely.

"I hear you've been having some interesting sessions at Pierre's," he said cheerily. "I bet I wouldn't have been a very happy fly had I found myself on *that* wall!"

I was so mortified that I could only stammer something completely inarticulate, and Mr. Moore's smile became tighter as did his grasp on my shoulder. "Don't get mixed up in something you're going to regret, Brian," he warned me in a lower voice. "I'm hoping you'll go far at Justin. Leave campus politics alone, my boy. Believe me, that's good advice."

I was paralyzed by his kindness. What could I possibly say?

That our little meetings were not conspiratorial? That I attended them only with reluctance? I was too embroiled in disloyalty to be able to affirm my allegiance without seeming to betray my cohorts. And how could I betray Dr. Prescott?

It was an impossible situation, and on our walk that afternoon I was almost able to tell Dr. Prescott so. I finally found the courage to suggest that he did not fully assess the effect of his own personality on others and that he might be pushing Pierre and Eric into an overt opposition of the headmaster. He was very upset and paused to pound the earth with his walking stick.

"I tell you, Brian, you're a fusspot!" he exclaimed. "We're only trying to devise a way to save what is best in Justin. This is not disloyalty. If I make a report, it will be to the trustees of the school, of whom, as ex-headmaster, I am one."

"But your prestige is such that a report might ruin Mr. Moore," I protested. "The trustees and the graduates would be behind you. Too much behind you."

"I don't know about that," Dr. Prescott said gloomily. "The old are soon forgotten. But even if it were so, I must take my chances. What you must learn, Brian, if you are to be an effective priest, is that you belong to the church militant and that means you have to fight! I think I could have put up with anything from Mr. Moore but the depreciation of Justin Martyr as a church school. Do you know, there are six Roman Catholic boys in the present first form? And that they are excused from chapel!"

"They go to mass in the village."

"But we're a *church* school, Brian, that's what you forget. That's what all of you forget today."

"Yet you took Catholic boys yourself, sir."

"Reluctantly. And only on strict conditions." Dr. Prescott set his jaw in a new way to which I was beginning to become accustomed. "When some infatuated graduate, forgetting his manhood, signed away the right to bring up his sons in his own faith and then in sober afterthought came to beg me with tears in his eyes — yes, tears, Brian — to take his boy in Justin . . . well, I relented and took the boy. I let the graduate have his cake and eat it. But the boy had to attend every chapel service and every sacred studies class!"

"And Jewish boys?"

"They were offered the same conditions. But I'll say this for *them*. The conditions were never accepted."

"Then all your Jewish boys were converts?"

"They were *Christians*, Brian!" Dr. Prescott thundered. "I have never admitted the word 'Jew' as any but a religious term. Of course, you'll ask me about Negroes next. That, I admit, is a tougher problem. But I can tell you this. If I found Negro boys who could really profit from Justin and Justin from them, I'd take them. But I'd never take just one, or maybe two, to wear as feathers in my liberal cap!"

It was known on the campus that Mr. Moore was considering a Negro boy for next year's first form. I was afraid of provoking Dr. Prescott into an even more open denunciation of his successor and drew his attention hastily to the fact that it was beginning to snow. He shook his head moodily and plodded on ahead of me towards his house.

December 10. I have had a vicious flu and been a week in the infirmary. Everyone has been very nice about it, though it plays havoc with the curriculum. But what has set me back much more than my own sense of physical unworthiness was a visit that I received from Pierre Dahlgren. He sat by my bed and gave me the gossip of the week, filling the stuffy air of my room with smoke and chuckles, and I lay back on my pillows, my eyes half closed, murmuring positives or negatives as required until he said something that made me sit up.

He was discussing the great plans for the school's diamond

jubilee that is to be celebrated in the early spring, an event that is expected to bring to the campus a great troup of graduates. Dr. Prescott, of course, is to be the last speaker at the principal banquet, and of his speech Pierre had the following to say, after leaning forward to see that no one was listening in the corridor:

"I wish you could have been at our last Wednesday meeting. I think that Dr. Prescott's address will come as a bit of a bombshell."

"A bombshell? Oh, Pierre, *should* it be?"

Pierre placed his fingers on his lips as we heard the sound of the nurse's heels in the corridor. "It is the perfect, perhaps the last chance," he whispered gravely, "for the affirmation of our ancient faith!"

It was a relief to have the nurse come in and stick the thermometer abruptly between my lips so I did not have to answer. All that I can do now is to go to Mr. Griscam. For he, thank God, is my opposite. He knows when and how to act.

21

JANUARY 22, 1946. I have told Mr. Griscam everything, and he has promised, as I knew he would, to take the needed steps to head off Pierre Dahlgren's little plot. But my visit to the Griscams in the Christmas holidays has produced another and much more extraordinary result: I have been instrumental in raising a great sum of money for Justin Martyr. Among the various small services that I have hoped to do for the school I never dreamed of a financial one. Life is certainly bizarre.

My visit has also had a private significance, being the first time that I have felt accepted by adults as a minister. I had gone straight from divinity school back to Justin where I had to do only with the boys, who made little distinction between ministers and masters, and with the faculty, who continued to see me as the same old Brian Aspinwall with a quixotically reversed collar. But in Sixty-eighth Street the Griscams treated me as a figure of more stature, and I hope I did not let them down too badly. I have a terrible tendency to think of myself as a minister in a play. Please, God, help me to lower that curtain!

They were much the same as in 1941 and greeted me with much the same enthusiasm. Mrs. Griscam was deeper than ever in the affairs of her "army" and was now giving it (I gathered from one of her husband's dry asides) every dollar that he had not hidden away in trust. Amy was still vociferous and firm in her opinions; Sylvester, still separated but undivorced from his second wife. And their father was still wearing the same patient air of the man who has to unravel the knotted affairs of an ungrateful universe. Only, like the gods of Valhalla after the abduction of Freia, they all seemed a bit graver and older. I am afraid that the war must have provided their spirit of youth.

Sylvester was particularly friendly and made me, early in my visit, the embarrassed confidant of his matrimonial troubles.

"When I married Faith — that was my first wife — I was really only a kid. You won't believe me, Brian, but I'd never even kissed another girl."

"Why shouldn't I believe you?"

Sylvester's pause was only momentary. "Well, I suppose you were always religious, even as a boy. Not that it isn't a very fine thing to be. But as a minister you'll have to hear all kinds of things. We may as well start making you a man of the world." He laughed in his loud, cheerful, rather forced fashion. "Take it from me, my friend, it's extremely unusual for a lad of twenty to have kissed only one girl. You see, I'd been engaged to Faith since I was fourteen."

"But you were only a child! Surely, your parents didn't countenance such a thing?"

"Oh, they thought it was cute. Faith's parents were their best friends and all that kind of thing. We were trapped in a family valentine. Not really trapped, of course. But that's how kids are. We thought it was expected of us. Dad and Mother didn't see that I needed anything more than Faith. They've never had any interest in sex themselves."

"That's what we tend to think about our parents," I cautioned him. "But it's not always true."

"Oh, I suppose they were normal for their generation." Sylvester shrugged and poured himself more brandy. We were sitting in the dining room alone after a long Sunday lunch. Mrs. Griscam had retired to the parlor, and Mr. Griscam and

Amy were playing backgammon in the library. "Though how normal was Dad, I sometimes wonder, when he proposed to a lame girl who happened to be the boss's daughter?"

"Sylvester," I protested, "please remember I'm his guest!"

Sylvester smiled complacently into his brandy glass and sniffed its contents with a heavy sniff. He was obviously delighted to have shocked me. People, I am learning, like to shock ministers. "A little realism implies no lack of respect, Brian. I still obey the fifth commandment. All I'm saying is that Dad and Mother have sublimated their sexual urges to higher things. Dad has Justin Martyr. Mother has the Army of the Holy Word. Fine. But poor little Sylvester didn't have either, and he had some pretty basic needs. After fifteen years of tepid wedlock, when he suddenly met a secretary at the bank called Estelle . . . !" Sylvester leaned over to put a hand on my shoulder and whisper in my shrinking ear: "Brian, my boy, I tell you I woke up to sex like a giggling freshman on his first visit to a whorehouse!"

"I suppose that's the trouble with young marriages," I murmured uncomfortably.

Sylvester nodded his solemn agreement as he sat back to continue his brandy. "Well, I admit Dad was a trump about it. He didn't like Estelle. Nobody liked Estelle. Only I was blind enough not to see what a bitch she was. Yes, Brian," he repeated gravely as he saw me wince, "my second wife was a bitch. But Dad put up my alimony and made it possible for me to marry her. It wasn't a year before I had to walk out."

"*Had* to?"

"If I wanted to preserve my sanity, that is. You could never conceive in your wildest dreams, Brian, what things went on."

"You mean she was . . . unfaithful to you?"

"A word like 'unfaithful' is a cataclysmic understatement to describe the activities of a woman like Estelle." Sylvester almost smacked his lips as he said this. I couldn't help wishing that it wasn't quite so much fun to impress the innocent. "But don't think I can prove it — not a single act! She's as smart as Satan and can smell a detective ten miles off. No, she's still Mrs. Sylvester Griscam, five years later, and will be until I ante up a million bucks."

"A million!" I gasped. I had read of such settlements, but only in the tabloids.

"Don't worry, she won't get it. She's got herself a shyster lawyer who likes the sound of big sums. She'll settle for a quarter of that amount. But the point is: where do I get the quarter?"

I could not imagine that Sylvester had come to me for financial advice, but as he continued to stare at me expectantly, I finally asked him why he needed a divorce at all.

"Because I want to marry Doris Drinker!" he exclaimed, as if it were the most obvious thing in the world.

"Perhaps you'd better tell me about Doris Drinker," I suggested with a sigh. "That is, if I'm to be any help. Though I don't see how I can."

"You'll see." Once again his hand was on my shoulder, and once again his voice sank confidentially. "Brian, this little Doris of mine is the wonder of wonders. She was a Wave at Fifty Church Street where I did my stint in the war and the brightest one in the whole office. She didn't know a thing about the Griscams or Dad being an ambassador or any of that rot. To her I was just plain Lieutenant Commander Griscam, another guy in the service. And there hasn't been any rinky-dink, either. No sirree. One good-night kiss on the doorstep has been my ration from the beginning."

Looking at poor Sylvester, so thin and plain and lanky, so heavy of breath and emphasis, so clumsily sincere, I thought of Mr. Griscam's passion for perfection and felt sorry for both of them.

"Maybe when your father understands about Doris, he'll be willing to put up Estelle's settlement."

"Not a chance. He put up for Faith, and he's sworn he won't do it again. The only hope is Mother. There's a way she can get at her trust with my consent. I'm the trustee, you see. She always wants money for her holy army. Very well, then." Here he suddenly gave me a conspiratorial wink. "Do you sniff a way that I can give the old girl what she wants if I get what I need?"

"But, Sylvester, is that honest?"

"Oh, it's honest enough. As trustee I have what is called a power to invade principal for her benefit. But Dad will regard any exercise of that power as highway robbery. He thinks that to let principal out of the family is to be . . . well . . ."

"Unprincipled," I finished for him. "Yes, I'm sure he'll be angry, but what can he do?"

"Oh, there's always something *he* can do. That's why I want you to talk to him." Sylvester's tone became eager again. "Please do it, Brian. You have a way with him. He'll take anything from you."

"Me?"

"Yes. Why he even gave up his plan of writing a life of Dr. Prescott because he saw you'd do it better! What more proof do you need?"

"But, Sylvester, there were other reasons for that."

"Come and talk to Mother, then."

We found Mrs. Griscam in the parlor, sitting straight and apparently serene on a pink bergère against a tapestry of blues and greens that depicted an eighteenth century French hunting scene. But there was something about her straightness, even in the flowing silks that enveloped her (she dressed exquisitely, but as women who dress for a cause) that seemed to repudiate, to shoo away as idle and silly any suggestion of a Pompadour or even of a Lespinasse. As she talked I noted for the first time a slight tremor in her tone.

"I don't want you to think, Brian, that we'd be doing anything wrong. It was my money that went into that trust, and it will be my money that comes out. Sylvester's father can have no just cause for complaint."

"I suppose he cares very deeply that you should be well provided for."

"But I *am* well provided for, that's just the point! My husband has very grand standards. We could all live on a fraction of what he's got. Do you think I need this big house? Why, I'd be happier in three rooms."

Yes, I saw them, those three little rooms, dusky and elegant, polished and neat and efficient, with a small residue of the best bibelots, and Mrs. Griscam writing checks on the cash saved at her slender-legged escritoire. And I saw Sylvester and Doris, happy in a Tudor cottage in Rye and Amy traveling from horse show to horse show. They needed money — oh, yes, they needed plenty of money, more money than I could even visualize — but they didn't need the heavy minted coin in which Mr. Griscam sought to entomb them. They didn't need, or in the least want, the big solid stone house, the shiny town car with the spoked wheels, the thick glass-grilled doors, the pompous porte-cochere, all the external paraphernalia of wealth without which men of Mr. Griscam's generation couldn't quite believe it existed. Poor Mr. Griscam, he had provided all the things that nobody wanted because, as the child of a bankrupt, he couldn't even take in the fact that everybody did not need, like himself, the constant consolation of marble pillars!

The only thing I could do for them, I concluded, was to bring the inevitable to a head. I had to find in my pity the courage for that. "Let me talk to him, then."

"Tell him it is God's will."

What sort of lives were these? Yet over their dryness and desolation Mrs. Griscam's fanaticism (if I can call it that) seemed to rise with the pale radiance of a Ryder moon.

Sylvester, like a little boy, had to bring any projected act to immediate fruition. As I had been dragged to the parlor, so now was I dragged to the library. Amy was induced to leave the backgammon table as she finished a game on the excuse that her mother wanted her, and Sylvester hurried out of the room on her heels.

"What on earth is Sylvester up to?" Mr. Griscam grumbled. "Can't he let me enjoy a game of backgammon? Do you play?" I confessed I did not. "What is it, Brian? You look as guilty as if you'd smashed my best Lowestoft."

"It's not what I *have* smashed. It's what I may be going to. I came to New York to ask your help, and here I am meddling already in your family affairs." I paused uncomfortably. "Sylvester asked me to talk to you about this girl he wants to marry."

Mr. Griscam's expression became impatient. "The Wave? Fine. I'm not stopping him."

"No, sir, but it seems he needs a divorce from his second wife."

"Why doesn't he get it, then? I shan't stand in his way. I never could abide Estelle."

"But it's the settlement he wants."

"Let me ask you something, Brian." Mr. Griscam's tone was very sharp. "If you were a father in my position, would you allow a substantial block of capital to go out of the family to a woman whom your own son describes as a bitch?"

But his very sharpness gave me the spirit I needed. "Yes, sir, I would. If my son's happiness depended on it."

"His happiness! Even if his happiness depended on a *third* marriage? How many times would you make it possible for him to marry? *You,* a minister of God?"

"Three times, sir."

He paused and laughed dryly. "A good answer. But I tell you, I won't do it. No, I won't, Brian. You probably think a father will always weaken, but not I. As I feel at the moment, the only way of having a satisfactory son is to adopt one fully grown, like the Romans!"

"Do you stop to consider that you may be sending him to other sources?"

"What other sources?" he demanded contemptuously, and then as, staring at me with a narrowing fixity, he took in my continued silence and gravity, he slowly reddened. "The trust!" he suddenly shouted. "Emmaline's trust! I knew it! *That's* what he's after, is it?" When I continued silent he seized me by the wrist and shook my arm. "Is it?"

"Mrs. Griscam needs money for her cause . . ."

"Oh, the crook!" He let me go abruptly and hurried out of the room. When I followed him to the parlor, I found the whole family in a state of great agitation. Sylvester had jumped to his feet, and his mother was very pale. Amy, watching her livid father, gave a low whistle.

"Hey, there, take it easy, old man. Do you want to have a stroke?"

Mr. Griscam ignored her as he faced his wife. "Emmaline, is it true? Is it your trust he's after?"

"I believe, David, that is a matter that concerns only Sylvester and myself," Mrs. Griscam retorted firmly. "Isn't that so, Sylvester?"

"Most assuredly." But Sylvester's grey cheeks and shifting eyes belied the confidence of his words.

"It concerns the head of the family, I think," his father said furiously. "Even in today's matriarchy I suppose a husband has something to say when his wife proposes to dump her money in the river!"

"Oh, Father," Amy protested, "must we talk business even on Sunday?"

"If you will let me speak, Amy, I think I can guarantee that even you won't regret it. Some years ago your mother and I agreed to make Sylvester the trustee of her trust. It was a delicate position as the trustee has power to give her principal. However, your brother in those days seemed the exemplification of all my hopes and theories. But love has come to erode the standards of that stern fiduciary." Here he looked with a scowl at Sylvester who continued to stare stubbornly at the Aubusson carpet. "In short, my dear Amy, your loving brother, finding that his sainted mother wants money for her cause, has made a deal with her. He will invade the trust for God, if God will divvy up with Venus."

"You mean, Sylvester," Amy called harshly across the room, "that you're going to blow Mother's money so you can marry that little Wave of yours?"

"She's no longer a Wave, Amy," he retorted bitingly. "If you'd read the papers, you'd know the war was over. But at least she served her nation while it was on."

"I'm sure you'd rather have me call her a Wave than what I'm really thinking!"

"Amy, my *dear!*" cautioned her mother. "Your father has not explained things fully. The money coming out of my trust will be divided three ways. One part will go to me, one to Sylvester and one to you."

"What's so terrible about that, then, Father?" Amy demanded immediately. "Why shouldn't Sylvester have his share so long as I get mine?"

Mr. Griscam turned impatiently from her to his son. "Have you considered, Sylvester, that I may take you to court for looting your trust?"

"What's the use, Dad?" Sylvester, still nervous but with the resolve of desperation, folded his hands on his stomach and peered down at them. "If you go to court, you'll lose. You drew that trust deed yourself, and you know my discretion is absolute."

"Sylvester!" his father exhorted him suddenly. "Leave your mother's trust alone. I'll give you the money you need!"

"I'm sorry, Dad. It's too late. I've given Mother my word."

Mr. Griscam looked from one to the other of his family helplessly. "Emmaline," he appealed to his wife, "tell me you won't give all that money to your ridiculous organization."

"I shall do as I am called to do, David."

"If you'd earned it yourself, if you'd saved it, if you'd even so much as watered it and let it grow as I have, you might have some right to fling it away. But how can you justify taking money that your father made and that I salvaged and increased, money that you've never lifted a finger about, and leave it away from your posterity?"

"If I give it to God," she answered in her stately tone, "God will give it back to them in his own way."

Her husband raised his hands to his temples with a moan of despair. "You ought to be committed!"

Mrs. Griscam and the children exchanged glances.

"I wonder if Mother's the one who should be committed," Amy murmured.

"David, dear, do take it easy."

"Oh, go away, all of you, please go!" Mr. Griscam groaned, leaning forward, his face covered with his hands. "Throw away your money, do anything you like. Nothing ever makes a dent on you. You take everything for granted. That I should spend a lifetime nursing you all, making you rich, why of course. Why not? What else am I good for? Nothing will teach you anything but starvation, and then it will be too late. May the god of money treat you as you have treated me!"

It was a highly embarrassing scene, and when the others had silently left the room I remained alone with my host. It was now that my real job began.

That afternoon Mr. Griscam and I went to Central Park and slowly circled the Reservoir. It was a cold, damp melancholy day, very much like his mood, and even the sea gulls on the ice in the middle of the water seemed to huddle together. The oblong of distant buildings which surrounded us and the circle whose circumference we were traversing seemed to reduce the great city under the starkness of a pale winter sky to two of the simplest geometric forms and Mr. Griscam's life to the simplest of failures.

The burden of his monologue was disillusionment. It seemed to him now, he related, that he had lived for no use, that every person whose life he had thought to have influenced would have done as well without him, that all of his supposed good deeds had been hidden from others, not by what he had proudly regarded as his diplomatic camouflage but by their own innate unimportance. The money that he had made and saved, who wanted it, except for foolish purposes? The clients and relatives whose bad tempers and destructive tendencies he had controlled, the school whose headmaster and board he had kept in harmony, the lawsuits he had settled, even the crisis in Panamanian-American relations that he had smoothed over, what did it all add up to but the fact that he had stood between his fellow beings and the dogfights for which they spoiled? Who cared for the peacemaker, the conservator? To spend, to throw away, to fight, to avenge — wasn't that what they called living? "Well, they'll get enough living one of these days," he concluded bitterly. "They'll all be blown up in a nuclear war, and good enough for them."

For the first time I found myself really liking Mr. Griscam. His mood of self-pity was more genuine than the old role of the vigilant fiduciary. As soon as he turned petulantly on life for what it had done to David Griscam, as soon as he had allowed the gates of his self-sufficiency to be forced, one's compassion could at last come in.

"I had a son, Jules, who died many years ago," he continued. "You've heard of him at Justin. He left a bad enough name there. Poor Jules was one of those tragic souls who make a mess of everything they touch, who bring unhappiness to everyone they meet. And yet he is still talked of with fascination by his friends. Almost with admiration. Why is it, Brian? Why is the world that way?"

At just that moment I had my inspiration. The idea and its articulation were almost simultaneous. "Why have you never put up a memorial for Jules in Justin Martyr?"

"Don't you know what he did there?"

"Of course I know. But it was so long ago. Time harmonizes the most disparate things. You and Jules and Dr. Prescott are all parts of the essential legend of the school. Why should only the happy boys be memorialized? Why not the failures, too? If I were you, I would build a library there and name it after him?"

Mr. Griscam gave me a quick look. "You're pretty free with other people's money, young man. It must be Sylvester's influence. Have you the smallest conception of what a library would cost these days?"

The biting cold suddenly pierced my coat, and I took a few quick steps in advance of him, hugging myself and breathing hard. I think the idea that now irradiated my mind must have chilled me as much as the weather. It was a brilliant idea, perhaps even an inspired one, but I was not used to such things, and I trembled. Had it been heresy to think of Mrs. Griscam as a fanatic? Might she not have been called to give away her money? And might not her husband be similarly called? Why should Justin Martyr which had provided the only home for his unhappy boyhood, which had been the lifelong outlet for his emotional needs, not give him the consolation that he needed in his old age? Oh, how it came to me!

"What does it matter how much it costs?" I asked in an ultimate burst of courage, turning back to him. "Haven't you just been telling me that nobody wants your money except for foolish purposes? Haven't your family already got more than they

need? Why shouldn't you take some of the fortune that you've
earned by your own sweat and toil and spend it on the things
you care about? Why should you build just a library? Why
not a new infirmary, too? They need one."

"Whoa, there, young man! Who do you think you're talking
to? A Rockefeller?"

"Yes! At least to me you are. Is it so terrible to suggest that
you spend your own money in your own lifetime on your own
projects? I know one's not supposed to talk to rich men about
their fortunes — or even to describe them to their faces as rich
— but you have confided in me and I care about you. I want to
help!"

Mr. Griscam stood still. We were facing west, and he was
staring intently at the great yellow towers of the Beresford that
rose into the bare sky with the heavy placidity of an Aztec temple. His breath, I noticed, was short. "I can see why people
like you, Brian," he said at last. "You speak straight to the
heart. Go on, young man, go on."

In the excited dialogue that followed, his spirits seemed to
soar. It must have been true that Justin Martyr supplied the
fuel to his being, the very blood to his veins, for his color returned and with it his normal confidence. I even suspected that
I had stumbled upon — or been guided to — a project that he
had long kept buried in his own mind, but that he had hardly
dared mention even to himself. Oh, of course, he had given
things to the school before, a window, a fountain, a dormitory
wing, but not on *this* scale. As he talked on, I had a dazzling
vision of the gleaming glass edifice that might be the Jules
Griscam Library and of the sober grey one that might be the
Infirmary. When we had completed our tour of the Reservoir,
he paused again to look over the grey water. His dark mood
was completely gone.

"No, I'm not just an old man yet, Brian. Not yet for a bit.
And think of what a glorious moment to announce a big grant.

On the diamond anniversary dinner!" He pinned my arm under his as we walked forward in the rapidly chilling air of the darkening afternoon. "It will be a good substitute, will it not, for the naughty speech that poor old Frank is plotting? My God, will it not!"

22

APRIL 1, 1946. The great diamond jubilee has exploded and gone, and I sit, so to speak, in a litter of paper hats and cigar butts and reach for my pen to describe its high events.

I have entered nothing since Christmas, for it has been a dull winter term, and Dr. Prescott has been in Florida for most of it. He came back only two weeks before the jubilee, and when I went over to call on him I found there was still constraint between us. He was very critical about everything, even the news of Mr. Griscam's proposed grant.

"But surely," I protested, "it's a princely gesture for a man to offer a new library and a new infirmary at one swoop."

"Princely?" he grumbled. "Why do you call it princely? Princes don't make gifts. David Griscam has always tried to turn Justin Martyr into a thing of his own. He couldn't do it by policy, so now he's trying to do it by bricks and mortar, that's all."

I thought this was pretty grudging, but I said nothing. The only thing that worried me about the Griscam gift was that it threatened to rob Dr. Prescott of some of the glory of a jubilee which I felt should be exclusively his. But, of course, I should not have worried about anyone stealing a show from Dr. Prescott. When the great anniversary came and the graduates descended upon the school at the beginning of the spring vacation, filling up the empty dormitories and giving to the place a comic atmosphere of middle-aged men, cigars in mouth and flasks in pockets, playing at schoolboys, the whole occasion, without its having been in the least so planned, moved about the short, broad-shouldered, plodding figure of the ex-head-master. He seemed the constant center of revolving circles, a piece of cork helpless on the surface of an eddying stream. For the tide of the jubilee was a rough one for the staid school; it swamped it and covered it with an affection as violent as it was ultimately undiscriminating. Justin over that weekend began to seem to me like Paris occupied by German soldiers. Could the City of Light survive it?

Mr. Griscam asked me to lunch with him at the inn in New Paisley on his arrival and drove me back to the school after-wards. As his car turned in the school gates and started up the drive that wound around the campus, we saw Dr. Prescott com-ing across the grass followed by a crowd of some thirty gradu-ates. He seemed to be leading them on an inspection tour of recent improvements, but the group conveyed a distinct sense of hilarity, and I was put in mind of the celebrating procession that traditionally followed a victory over Chelton, when the whole school would parade around the campus, following the headmaster in a chair strapped to two poles and borne on the shoulders of eight prefects, stopping to cheer each object or person encountered: the Schoolhouse, the aged oak tree, a mas-ter's wife, the fives courts, a dump truck.

Mr. Griscam told his chauffeur to stop, and we got out of the car as the group approached. For just a moment I had the irra-tional feeling that Mr. Griscam was a threatened symbol of authority about to take his chances with an unruly mob. Dr. Prescott had never struck me before as a revolutionary, but now he might have been a wily old Danton, ready, for the mere excitement of the gesture, to consign the chairman of the board and his limousine to the fury of his followers. Was it my imagi-

nation that made me wonder, as he came closer, if he had cast a
mocking glance through the open door of the car at the tumbled fur rug upon the floor?

"David, my boy!" he exclaimed, clasping Mr. Griscam's hand.
"Now that you're here the jubilee can begin! It's a superb
thing you're doing. The gesture of a Medici prince." Was that
dry eye upon me? I could not tell. "I trust your family will
not be impoverished by this unexampled generosity?"

"Oh, no, Frank. In these days, you know, taxes are everything. They'll hardly feel it."

"Pray don't tell me about taxes," Dr. Prescott protested
warmly. "Everything gets so twisted up that there's danger the
very concept of gratitude may be lost. I *want* to be grateful.
I want to be grateful to David Griscam for his princeliness to
his school."

Certainly nobody could turn on the charm better than the
old man when he wanted to.

That night the dinner was informal, with only one brief
speech of welcome from Duncan Moore, and afterwards we all
watched a movie of school activities in the assembly hall. When
this was over, I accompanied Dr. Prescott to Mr. Griscam's
suite at the Parents' House for a drink with some of the trustees.
Mr. Griscam had asked me to this little party at lunch and had
told me that he had a particular reason for wanting me to be
present. He had a fire going, for it was a cold spring night,
and a silver tray with an assortment of whiskeys and liqueurs.
After ninety minutes of boys on the screen it was a cheerful
sight.

The group was small and, I assumed, carefully selected, for
Mr. Griscam always had a purpose for the things he did. Besides our host, there were only three trustees. I knew them all
fairly well, for they were frequent visitors to the school. There
was Sam Storey, president of Boston City Investors' Trust, a
round red shrewd cotton-haired financier, whose mammoth,

puffy build contained somewhere the muscular embryo that had made him one of Harvard's greatest quarterbacks. There was Gavin Glenway, like Mr. Griscam a New York attorney, the senior partner of a great corporation law firm, a dry, caustic, brilliant man, as gaunt as Storey was stout, with all the biting conservatism of a representative of industry and the high temper of a litigator. And finally there was Ira Hitt, a younger man, in his early forties, who had been a scholarship boy at Justin and who had made a fortune during the war, the type of new speculator, dry, bone-headed, sharp-eyed, prematurely balding, with a remarkably strong personality for one of such thin shoulders and unprepossessing appearance. They were all good drinkers, and they had all started early in the festive atmosphere of the day. Dr. Prescott himself had had a few cocktails in the long period before dinner. He was by no means a regular drinker, but he had a great capacity, whenever he chose to use it. The only effect of liquor was to make him at once gentler and more sardonic.

Mr. Griscam led the discussion into the question of what sort of boys the future Justin Martyr should seek to educate, thus placing in issue Duncan Moore's policy of "broadening the base." Dr. Prescott asked if this was compatible with his concept of the school as a family.

"It's a curious sort of family that can turn down Jack Gregg's grandson," Gavin Glenway suggested, with his deep lawyer's throat-clearing, as he packed his pipe.

"*Has* he been turned down?" Dr. Prescott asked in concern. "Has he indeed?"

"Perhaps we shouldn't be too shocked," Glenway continued, in a tone of weighted sarcasm. "Perhaps we should endeavor to take the modern view. What if Jack Gregg raised a half million dollars for the pension plan? What if no fewer than ten Greggs have graduated from Justin? What if Jack's father was one of the first trustees? What is all that against simple merit? Let Justin Martyr be as stern as Justice!"

"But, Gavin," Dr. Prescott protested, "to admit Jack Gregg's grandson, would we have to consider what he has *given* the school? Is it not enough that he is an old *friend* of the school? And what is so wrong with making an exception for the grandson of an old friend? Would it have to mean that one was truckling to wealth?"

"I'm afraid it would, Dr. P. Because it's hard for a man to become a well-known friend of the school unless he gives to the school. And it's the wealthy who give. However, I am not so scrupulous as you. I most assuredly would manage to find room for any grandson of Jack Gregg who wasn't a Mongolian idiot."

"You mean *because* of his wealth?" Dr. Prescott persisted, shocked.

"I'd never answer that question. Why should I? I'm a practical man."

"And I'm not?" Here Dr. Prescott rose slowly to return to the drink tray, and Mr. Griscam moved to help him. "No, no, sit down, David," he grumbled. "I'm just putting another drop of whiskey in this. You made it too light. Sit down," he repeated irritably, "you're getting old yourself. A practical man!" he exclaimed, his back to the rest of us as he poured his drink. "How many times a schoolmaster has to hear that term! All you graduates like to believe that you have been buffeted by hard realities whereas we at Justin have lived unspotted by the world. You return here lovingly perhaps, but certainly condescendingly. There's dear little old quaint Dr. P. Was he the demon who scared us so as boys? Why, he's as soft as sawdust!" He turned now to face the trustees as they protested and raised his hand to check them. "Now, stop it, all of you. You know it's true. It's one of the functions of a school to make even the softest graduate feel hard-boiled."

As we laughed, he sat down again, stirring his drink slowly and gazing into it as if unsure whether it were friend or foe. "You want to protect me, so be it. We agree, anyway, about taking the Gregg boy, if for different reasons. You, Gavin, because of your experience in the law, believe that the most discreditable reason must be the governing one. I am not so sure of that. I believe that we could make an exception for Gregg boys simply because we like them and because they belong at Justin."

"Well, we can all agree that there's room in life for exceptions," Gavin Glenway said placatingly. "I'm sure David will agree with me that a lifetime in the law makes one suspicious of rules."

"Perhaps the exception should *be* the rule," Dr. Prescott said so mildly that Glenway did not realize that he was being laughed at. "Perhaps that would be a lawyer's paradise."

"Of course, if Jack Gregg had changed the boy's name to Kowalski, he'd have gotten in fast enough," Sam Storey intervened explosively. He had followed Dr. Prescott's example in fortifying his drink. "Next year's first form might have been garnered at Ellis Island. Now I like to think I'm as democratic as the next guy, but where do we stop? Do we want to jettison altogether the principle of a Protestant school for boys of Anglo-Saxon descent?"

"But there was never any such principle!" Dr. Prescott protested, shocked again.

"Not in your eyes, sir, I admit. But in the eyes of most of the country Justin, along with the other New England prep schools, has that reputation. And why should we be ashamed of it? Haven't our boys come of the families that made America great? Isn't there something in traditions of honor and responsibility handed down from generation to generation? Look at the aristocratic tradition in England!"

"I know a bit about that, Sam," Dr. Prescott replied, still, I thought, with astonishing mildness. "Don't forget that I went to Oxford. But in England the upper classes used to give something in return for their privileges. They went into government and into the army and the church. It was a tradition of public service."

"Well, Groton produced Franklin Roosevelt," I volunteered. I had been silent so far, respecting the presence of my elders and betters, but I could not resist this opportunity. The reaction was immediate.

"Ugh!"

"Groton should be ashamed of it."

"Groton *is* ashamed of it!"

"Gentlemen, gentlemen!" Dr. Prescott exclaimed, raising both hands now, a glimmer of amusement in his eye. "You forget that David Griscam was one of our late president's diplomatic appointees." There was a murmur of perfunctory apology. "It has always been my chief regret," he continued in a sadder tone, "that Justin has sent so few men into public service. When the English nobility began to turn to the stock market, it seemed to me there was no further justification for an upper house."

"Yet it's just what saved it!" protested Ira Hitt. "That's the only way any of your old families survive. By adapting themselves to the new. Ask Dave here." I had never heard anyone call Mr. Griscam "Dave" before, but no doubt excitement made him intimate. "He's the expert. Would families like the Griscams occupy the position they occupy today if they'd gone into the army or navy or wasted their time in politics? Hell, no! I beg your pardon, Dr. Prescott."

"It's quite all right, dear boy," the old man replied blandly, waving his arm. "Hell no, as you say. Pray go on about the Griscams." He cocked a mocking eye in Mr. Griscam's direction. "I find it most instructive."

"They stayed in the market. They put their money where the new people were putting their money. They even married the new people. Isn't it so, Dave?" He pressed on, ignoring Mr. Griscam's irritated shrug. "Because business is our aristocracy. Finance is our aristocracy. Even after thirteen years of creeping socialism! You should be proud, Dr. Prescott, that you have sent your boys to take their places in the front ranks of American progress. And until the day we go Commy — which may not be far off — business will continue to be the front ranks. I believe Justin Martyr *should* educate the sons of our business and banking leaders. And, of course, a certain percentage of the new people, too. *I* was a new person. I made my way, but I got my start at Justin!"

We were all a bit embarrassed by this outburst, but Dr. Prescott knew just how to deal with it. "That's very gratifying to hear, Ira," he said smoothly. "I remember when you were a third former and wanted to put the school store on a paying basis. You even had a plan to issue stock. We suspected then that you would go far." The rest of us laughed, and Ira flushed with pleasure. "I take it, then, that in broadening our base you would select, in addition to the Cabots and Lowells, boys who look as if they might grow up into Cabots and Lowells?"

"Well . . . yes. As a matter of fact, I rather like that way of putting it."

"I am glad that my phrase was so felicitous. I think I begin to put together the opposition that you gentlemen feel to my successor's program. Gavin would favor the sons of the rich, and Sam, more in the tradition of John Adams, would lean to the well-born."

"Now, Dr. P, it's not that simple."

"Ah, but it's an old man's privilege to oversimplify. And Ira would lean to both while keeping a wary eye on the hordes from which new recruits for the Social Register must be periodically selected. I must say, gentlemen, you make me feel like the patron saint of the Chamber of Commerce. Or should it be the Society of the Cincinnati? My likeness should be raised upon a pedestal at the foot of Wall Street."

"You may laugh at us, Dr. P," Gavin Glenway rejoined, "but

in sober truth you should be proud. It is the moral tone of the business community that sets the moral tone of the nation. And you have done your share of elevating it."

"Good, good," the old man muttered.

"Of course, I don't say Mr. Moore is entirely off base," Ira Hitt conceded. "In these days a school must keep an eye on its tax exemption. The time may be coming when it will be politic to have a couple of coons to show the Revenue boys. Just to keep the record straight."

Dr. Prescott's face was drawn to an expression of the tightest fascination. "Coons?" he asked softly.

"Negroes. We may come to that. Oh, a couple would do the trick. And some of them, you know, could pass for whites."

"So?" Dr. Prescott pursued. "Is there an agency that supplies them? Can we write and ask for a Negro with a white face and a Jew with a straight nose and a Japanese who's hardly yellow at all? Ah, the wonders of your liberal world, Ira!"

"I didn't make the world, sir," Ira said sulkily. "You can make fun of me, of course, if you like."

The pause that followed this was a bit weighted with constraint, and Gavin Glenway ended it by asking: "What does David think? He hasn't expressed an opinion."

"Oh, David believes in everything," Dr. Prescott answered in a strong voice tinged with bitterness. "David would have the old families and the new, the bright and the stupid. The Jew and the Gentile. And somehow, when David was through with them, they'd all be the same. They'd all be Davids. Isn't that the American dream?"

As he rose to bring his drink again to the bar table, the trustees exchanged uneasy glances.

"I wonder if it isn't my bedtime," Gavin Glenway suggested.

"I think perhaps it's everybody's," Sam Storey agreed, and we all rose.

"Can I see you home, sir?" Glenway asked Dr. Prescott.

"No, no, I'm going to stay and have a nightcap with David and Brian," Dr. Prescott said without turning from the bottle that he was carefully pouring. "Don't worry about me. I shall be fine. Good night, gentlemen. And thank you for your ideas."

As I watched the departing trustees one by one take Dr. Prescott's hand to bid him good night, adding further stories and opinions to what had already been said, a great light flashed on in the attic of my mind, illuminating suddenly what had been only a dusky doubt. I had been disturbed about something obscurely but unpleasantly at hand in our meeting, a something that seemed to amount to a small sense of surprise that trustees of Justin could be so ordinary, so angular, so predictable. But if predictable, whence the surprise? It was just the answer to this that I now saw: if they seemed predictable it was because they had been predicted, because Mr. Griscam had picked them out and turned them on. He had stacked his hand with the men on whom he could count to persuade Dr. Prescott that Duncan Moore, with all his faults, was an idealist compared to the average graduate. To warn him that if he ever *did* unseat Moore, his successor might be worse!

I saw Mr. Griscam nod to the others as he shut them out, to reassure them, perhaps, that he would take care of the old man, and then return to his seat. Dr. Prescott took his drink back to his armchair. He sat for several minutes staring moodily into the fire, and when he spoke it was clear that he had been thinking my thoughts.

"Did you plan it that way, David?" he asked, and when Mr. Griscam did not answer at once, he pursued: "Did you plan that little discussion to open my long-sealed eyes?"

"I thought you might find it interesting."

"Then you must answer me something. Truthfully."

"When have I not?"

"Oh, many times, David. You are like a Jesuit with truth. You believe in meting it out according to the recipient's capacity to take it. Mine you have always rated very low. But I am learning — oh, yes, I am making strides. I sometimes think my education began with my retirement. I can take most anything now. Tell me truthfully." Here he paused and held up a finger to warn Mr. Griscam that he was in earnest. "Are those three men — Sam and Gavin and Ira — representative of graduate opinion?"

As I opened my lips to protest, I saw Mr. Griscam's eyes fixed upon me in what, surprisingly enough, seemed a rather mild stare. "All right," he appeared to be telling me, "rush in and break things up, go on, impetuous youth. But, remember who came whining down to New York last Christmas for help and tell me afterwards who will keep the old man from making a fool of himself tomorrow night." He continued so to look at me, perfectly patient, ignoring Dr. Prescott's question, throwing me, so to speak, the ball, until in silence and confusion I could only bow my head.

"I believe they *are* typical, Frank," he answered gravely.

"I see." Dr. Prescott gave one of his deep sighs. "I don't, but does it matter? If even *some* are that way! Of course, none of them is actually young."

"The young don't make the decisions. You know that, Frank."

"No. They simply die for those who do. So be it." He was silent again, and there was no sound but the crackling of the fire and the sipping of his drink.

"Don't finish that, Frank," Mr. Griscam suggested softly. "You have a long day tomorrow."

"Don't be impertinent to your elders, David. I know exactly what I can drink, and I have every intention of finishing this one."

We sat for a few minutes more until suddenly Dr. Prescott started talking, in a low, somber tone, gazing into the fire. "I took my daughter Evelyn's youngest child to the circus in Boston last week. There was a clown in it who kept trying to escape from a round bright spotlight trained on him from the top of the house. He ran all about; he tried to escape into the audience. Everywhere the bright circle remorselessly pursued him. Now I see that *I* was that clown. And the spotlight was the effort of all the rest of you to keep the truth from me."

"The truth?" I burst out in dismay. "What truth?"

Dr. Prescott looked at me as if he had forgotten my presence. But his tone was perfectly kind. "The truth about Justin Martyr, Brian. I was to see only the bright light of the circle in which *I* was to perform. Beyond it was the darkness which was no affair of mine. Oh yes, *you* saw it, David, you and the others. You were used to the darkness. But it was not for clowns. Clowns had to keep clowning so that the rest of you could forget the darkness in which you sat."

"But now you see it," Mr. Griscam said impassively.

"As if it were light."

"And what exactly do you see?"

Dr. Prescott jerked his head around to give his interrogator a cold stare. "I see that Justin Martyr is like the other schools. Only *I*, of course, ever thought it was different. Only I failed to see that snobbishness and materialism were intrinsic in its make-up. Only I was naïve enough to think I could play with that kind of fire and not get my hands burnt. But you, David, of course, understood all that. You even saw how to make a selling point out of my naïveté. You persuaded the world that the gospel of Prescott of Justin was the passport to good society. And the world believed it! When I urged the boys to go into politics or the ministry, they accepted it as Prescottism, so many lines of a lesson to be learned that had no relation to the real world at home. They learned their lines, yes. Some of them even enjoyed learning them. They had been told by their parents that to be a graduate of Justin would be a material aid in that real world. Ah, yes, reality." He grunted here and paused. "Reality was the brokerage house, the corporation law firm, the place on Long Island, the yacht, the right people. The obvious things. One can't be too obvious about them. I was simply added to their list."

"Why, Frank," Mr. Griscam demanded, "must you assume that nobody but you has any idealism?"

"I assume there was no idealism in this room tonight!" Dr. Prescott exclaimed in a loud barking tone. "I listened to those men. I listened carefully. Your unhappy boy Jules thought I was a devil. Had he lived, he would have learned that I was only a fool. Perhaps Jules and I had more in common than either of us suspected. Perhaps we were both clowns imprisoned in our spotlights."

"But you've always been a realist," Mr. Griscam protested, "ever since I've known you. A rather bitter realist, too. There are those who've even called you a cynic. You've professed to understand the worldly motive, the power of snobbery, the dollar. Why suddenly is it so appalling to face those things in Justin?"

"Because I created Justin!" Dr. Prescott cried out. "And I created it precisely because I saw the world as you say. Because of the carpetbaggers who sold out the victory in my boyhood! And now I see that Justin is only another tap for the world's materialism. For *you*, David. Oh, rot!" He rose suddenly and disgustedly to go. "I may be a maudlin old man, but I'm not a complete idiot. I see your game. You've had wind of my speech tomorrow night, and you're trying to head it off. Well, sleep well, old boy. You've succeeded. As you've always succeeded in everything you've tried to do here."

"Please, Frank." Mr. Griscam followed him to the door. "It breaks my heart to hear you talk that way."

"You should know how to mend hearts, David. Isn't it your trade?"

"That's not fair!" Mr. Griscam was suddenly angry himself. "Do you think you're the only one who's ever been disillusioned? Do you think the rest of us have experienced nothing in life? How do you think I felt when Jules pitched that rock through the chapel window that *I* had given?"

Dr. Prescott turned at once and placed his hand sympathetically on the other's arm. "Poor Davey."

"You haven't called me 'Davey' since I was a schoolboy!"

"Then it's time I did. Good night, my friend."

I picked up Dr. Prescott's cloak and put it over his shoulders. "Let me see you home, sir," I murmured.

"Thank you, Brian, I will. These old eyes aren't what they used to be in the dark." He turned now to shake hands with Mr. Griscam. "We've put young Brian through quite a scene tonight, haven't we?"

Mr. Griscam glanced at me in his old, half-suspicious fashion and shrugged. "Oh, Brian is used to them by now, I guess," he said as he closed the door behind us.

The following night, at the big dinner, Dr. Prescott sat at the head table on the dais between Duncan Moore and the Bishop of Massachusetts, looking down over four hundred men in evening jackets at long tables decorated with silver candelabra and red candlesticks. It was a good show. The big portraits were lit, and I happened to be facing the magnificent canvas that Ellen Emmet Rand had painted of the former headmaster under Mr. Griscam's commission to replace the Laszlo portrait which his son Jules had destroyed. Gavin Glenway had already announced Mr. Griscam's proposed gift, and he had received, as anticipated, a standing ovation. Duncan Moore was now concluding his speech with a eulogy to his predecessor.

"Whatever we do at Justin Martyr, whatever we keep of the past, whatever we change, whatever our mistakes and whatever our strivings, in happy moments and in times of discouragement, we are always in the tradition of Dr. Prescott, for the simple reason that there is no other tradition that we can be in. No matter how good a job I may be lucky enough to accomplish, and no matter how brilliant my successors, we will always be the disciples of Francis Prescott. Justin Martyr is his school, his child, his ideal. And whatever he may think of our fumbling, I hope that he will always have his renowned tolerance for those whose best, after all, is only of his own creating."

The whole room arose again in a spontaneous roar of applause, and when they were seated I noticed that Dr. Prescott had remained on his feet. He stood for several seconds until the room was silent. Never had he looked more sage, more beautiful, and only the twitching of the muscles of his left cheek betrayed his conflicting emotions.

"Bishop, Mr. Moore, fellow trustees and Justinians," he began in his grave, slow, carrying tone, and then he paused again.

I could not bear to look at him. I decided it would be less painful to watch the drama that must ensue in the theatre of Pierre Dahlgren's round face, and I fixed my eyes on him and saw his lips open and close.

"You have all heard much fine oratory this evening, much moving oratory. I had hoped that I could add to it, but I find that I cannot. When I think of sixty years of school my heart is too full for comment. Let an old man say one thing and then step back into the shadows where he belongs. May all of you know the joy one day that *I* have now, the greatest joy that can befall a man of my years, the joy of knowing that his work is carried on. To you, Duncan Moore, my more than worthy successor, I lift my glass." Solemnly, slowly, he did this and turned back to his audience. "God bless you, gentlemen."

We all rose for the third ovation of that evening, but this one was far greater than its predecessors. We must have stood clapping and cheering for five full minutes. Poor Pierre Dahlgren! He clapped the hardest of anybody and looked as ashy as if he had had a stroke.

*

I did not see Dr. Prescott again that weekend. When I called at his house the following afternoon, Mrs. Midge met me at the door and told me with obvious apprehension that he was very tired after the celebrations and was resting in bed. Over her shoulder I saw Duncan Moore coming down the stairs, and I turned away, ashamed of the sudden prick of childish jealousy. I went to Parents' House to bid farewell to Mr. Griscam and found him on the porch. The chauffeur was already putting his bags in the car.

"Frank is tired, I hear," he said as I came up.

"Yes, last night took a lot out of him."

"Heroic deeds are apt to."

"What I don't see, sir, is how you could have been so sure that everything would work out as it did."

"I wasn't sure. I took my chances. A lawyer learns that."

"And if I hadn't come to visit you last Christmas you wouldn't have done anything?"

"Naturally not. How would I have known?"

"I see." I nodded stupidly. "I suppose you had to do it. Only somehow I didn't anticipate that you would disillusion him so."

"You must learn, as a minister, Brian," Mr. Griscam reminded me severely, "to bear the consequences of conduct that you believe to be right."

"Yes, of course." I plunged my hands in my pockets and continued to stare at the floor. "Only if I'd known that you would find it necessary to hurt him so deeply, I wonder if I wouldn't have let the whole thing alone. That's always been my trouble. I care more for him than for the school. You don't. You're right, of course."

"Hurt him so deeply?" he queried, and I knew by the exasperation in his tone that he was fighting to stem his own concern. "But surely that's nonsense. Frank has great resilience. You'll see. In a day or two he'll be smiling at the whole thing."

I shook my head. "He's old now, sir. Suddenly very old. That's the difference. And he thinks his life has been a failure."

"But that's absurd!" In his sudden impatience I thought Mr. Griscam was going to shake me. "One doesn't decide one's life has been a failure because one happens to disapprove of the point of view of a handful of trustees!"

"Let's hope not, sir."

"Well, *does* one?"

"I'm sure you wouldn't."

He stood there, biting his lip, frustrated by his inability to convince me. Or to convince himself. "Is there anything I can do?"

I tried not to show in my tone how much more than enough I thought he had already done. "No, I don't think so, sir."

He saw that it was hopeless and shrugged. "Just remember, young man, that you can't make an omelet without breaking eggs." He went briskly down the steps to his car and turned before getting in. "Keep me posted. You know how much I care."

I waved mechanically as the big limousine drove off, remembering my fantasy of its seeming the threatened symbol of authority. I continued to wave, as foolishly as a child, until it was out of sight.

23

OCTOBER 10, 1946. Shortly after commencement last spring I was asked by the Bishop of Massachusetts to take a six months' leave of absence to prepare a report on church schools and church education in the diocese, and Mr. Moore thought it advisable that I should accept. I have been living in Boston since June, and only yesterday on my first visit back to school, did I receive the bad news.

I had driven down for the day, as I now have a car for my researches, and after Sunday chapel Mr. Moore came up to me and led me aside from the throng.

"Have you seen Dr. Prescott?" he asked gravely.

"No, I'm just on my way now."

"Good. But you must expect to find him much weaker. We had the diagnosis yesterday."

The bell in the tower above us struck the quarter hour, and the air throbbed with its note and my apprehension. "I didn't even know he was ill!"

"None of us did, though he's been looking poorly and didn't make his usual trip to the Cape this summer. Evelyn Homans finally took him into Boston for a complete test at Massachusetts General."

"What is it, for God's sake?"

Mr. Moore put his hand firmly on my shoulder. "Take it

easy, old boy," he said as I shivered. "It's what you'd want at his age. It's what he wants himself. Cancer of the lung. Dr. Larkin says it will be very fast and almost painless." His grip tightened as I suddenly sobbed. "Try to remember, Brian, that he's had a very long and a very happy life."

I nodded, but I couldn't look at him. "Does he know?"

"Oh, yes. You'll find him actually cheerful about it."

"And how long does he have? I mean, is it weeks or months?"

"Weeks, probably. But one never knows. He's so strong. I'm glad you've come, Brian. Go to him now."

I stumbled like a drunkard across the garth to Dr. Prescott's house and found him as cheerful as Moore had said.

"I see you've heard my news," he exclaimed in the tone he might have used to tell me of another honorary degree. "I must say it's not kind of you to look so downcast. A speedy, efficient little killer, isn't that what we all want?" We were sitting on the tiny front porch from which we looked out at the back of the school chapel and up at its great rambling dark tower. Dr. Prescott's little house seemed to squat happily in its shadow like a reverend toad stool. "Think of it. Could any old fogy of eighty-six ask for more? I used to have a dim little hope that my seeming immunity from pain would run out and that one day I would suffer a bit of what other humans have suffered. Well, that hope is apparently going to be a vain one, and it's just as well. Only vanity asks for a test when none is offered."

When he saw the tears start to my eyes and that I was about to blurt something out, he raised a warning hand. "I don't want to talk about it any more. It is very awkward. I have always deplored the selfishness of old people who embarrass the young with unnecessary references to their demises. I have told my daughters and Moore, and I told him to tell you. You are a minister and you must learn to take death in your stride. It is another fact to a professional, that is all."

He then had the kindness to send me away until I should have collected myself. "Go for a walk, dear boy. Go to the river and back. Consider my years and that my career is over. Consider that Harriet has gone before me. Consider what a gentle exit, laced with dope, awaits me. And then ask yourself how much more time you would want for an old man who wants none for himself. You see? It's not so bad. Then come back, and we'll talk about other things."

I did as I was told, and when we had tea together, later that afternoon, I was under control. When I left, I asked him if I could make a habit of driving down to see him every Saturday afternoon, and he consented provided only it did not interfere with my church report. And then in a burst of gratitude and because I had been overwrought by his news, I subjected him to one of my silly fits of conscience. Oh, the egotism of the neurotic!

"Unless you think I'm only coming to collect your last words!" I exclaimed. "Perhaps I am. Perhaps, God help me, I am!"

"Coming to see me is a good deed, Brian," Dr. Prescott replied gently. "It gives me pleasure, therefore it is good. You worry too much about motives. Suppose your motive *is* selfish. Very well. But now suppose yourself an inquisitor of the Middle Ages who would burn my living body to save my soul. The *motive* might be good. But what about poor me at the stake! Do you imagine the good Lord will reward the inquisitor more than you? Of course not. Some of the intrinsic goodness of a good deed must seep into the motive, and some of the bad of a bad deed. Keep doing good deeds long enough, and you'll probably turn out a good man. In spite of yourself."

October 17. I was much ashamed of my outburst of last week, and I resolved not to daub my sick little worries again on the serene canvas of his departure. When I went down yesterday I was able to behave more like a man. I stayed the night in Dr. Prescott's guest room, and the next morning we went to chapel together. The disease is as rapid as he hoped, and his strength is failing fast. He had to pause to rest every few steps of the brief distance.

"I made a foolish resolution last spring," he told me. "I wanted to teach myself a lesson for having interfered with Duncan Moore's administration, and I made a vow that I would never set foot on the campus again. But that, of course, was making poor Moore pay for my mistake. That was sulking in my tent! When I understood this, I decided to make certain regular appearances at the school. On Sunday chapel. At Sunday lunch. At football games with visiting teams. On Prize Day, and so forth. Now I am obliged to cut it down to Sunday chapel, but I shall continue that as long as I am able."

October 24. Alas, he was not long able, for when I arrived this afternoon, I found him in bed and in a very despondent state of mind. He was sitting, hunched up on three big pillows, looking unexpectedly forlorn in a rather ragged old dressing gown. He seemed hardly to mind what I was saying, shaking his head gloomily. As I was about to leave, he told me a story that seemed relevant to nothing but his mood.

"When I was a little boy I used to visit my maternal grandmother in Dedham, and I attended a Sunday school there. The minister, a long, lanky, dour-looking fellow, opened each class by making us hold out our hands with the index fingers pointed upwards. 'Consider, children,' he would tell us in a sepulchral tone, 'the pain of touching the tip of your finger to your mother's stove, even for a fraction of a second. That is an experience which most of you must have suffered. Now try to imagine that pain, not simply on a fingertip but spread over the whole surface of your body, and not for a mere second, but everlastingly. *That,* children, is hellfire."

I shuddered. "And did you believe it?"

"At seven? Of course I believed it!"

"But you don't believe it now?"

"Oh, now." He shrugged. "I suppose not. But I think of it sometimes when I lie awake in the early morning!"

October 31. Today, thank God, he was in an easier mood. I found him sitting in an armchair in his bedroom, dressed in a beautiful blue silk kimono that Cordelia Turnbull had sent him. It looked a bit curious on him, but one forgot about it as soon as he began to talk. I have never heard his voice softer or more melodious.

"Do you know, Brian, that retirement was the making of me? It taught me some elementary lessons in humility. It taught me, for example, that I should have retired ten years ago. For my own good, as well as the school's."

"Surely not for the school's, sir."

"Well, you know what people are saying. 'Old Prescott, he was picturesque, in his way — of his generation, you know. A bit theatrical, a bit violent, but he got away with it. Now, however, one needs a different type. A more accommodating head. One like Moore who knows how to get on with the parents and trustees.' " He turned on me suddenly with some of his old presence. "Do you *dare* deny, Brian, that they're saying that?"

"Some say it, I suppose, sir."

"And they're right, too," he said emphatically. "The crowd has a way of being right, of flaring the ego under the noble ambition. Who was I to think I could change the face of American education?"

"But why, sir, must you always be looking to the high goal you haven't totally achieved? Could anyone have come any closer to it? Why can't you ever consider instead the smaller goals that you *have* reached? The individual boys you've helped?"

"That's all a man should look to, isn't it?" His smile was

melancholy. "Yes, Brian, I have asked too much. I have been greedy. I *have* helped a few boys, and I should be grateful for that." He closed his eyes as he cast his mind back. "I think I helped Charley Strong a bit. At the end, anyway. And Gates Appleton, when his parents had that terrible divorce. And Christian Villard when he lost his arm." Then he opened his eyes and shook his head wistfully. "But think of the others, Brian. The ones I hurt. Or killed, even. Like Jules Griscam."

"You didn't mean to. God will know."

"God will know I hated that boy!" he exclaimed violently. "A headmaster should have no hates. Poor Jules. He has had his revenge in my remorse." He shuddered. "Yes, it was terrible, my remorse. For I had allowed him to bring me down to his level, and he *knew* it. When his father tore the scales off my eyes last spring and made me see my lifework for the poor thing it was, I wondered if I couldn't hear Jules' high, screeching laugh. How he would have crowed!"

"Jules was only one of thousands of boys, sir. How could you succeed with them all?"

"I couldn't," he said abruptly. "I'm getting maudlin. You'd better go."

November 8. Today he told me not to come again. He is in bed and likely never to leave it. For the first time he seemed like a dying man. He was lying on his back, staring up at the ceiling.

"There comes a time when the doors should be closed," he said, "when the family takes over. My daughters are coming. Harriet, in fact, is here. It is a rather pleasant atavism, the priority that blood takes over friendship in the end. It is a ceremony in which each participant knows just what to do. I shall say goodbye, Brian. You must be a fine minister and cast out fear. I love you, my boy." He turned now, and the dark eyes seemed to stare through me. "Do you know what my old master at Balliol, Jowett, said at the end? 'I bless God for my life.' It's all one can say. Bless God for my life, Brian. And for yours."

In tears I fell to my knees and kissed his hand, as I kissed his wife's seven years ago. I then remained by the bedside praying. I do not know how long, until I felt a touch on my shoulder. It was Mrs. Kidder, who with a brief but friendly smile indicated that I was to go. I took my last look at my dear old friend, whose eyes were closed, and tiptoed out of the room.

December 10. Duncan Moore telephoned to say that Dr. Prescott died in his sleep this morning. God was merciful to the very end in sparing him the pain he had sometimes wanted and that I have no doubt he would have borne like a hero. He died in peace, and I believe that we should be in peace. But the very sky looks darker to me, and the Boston streets where I walked today seemed dreary and woebegone. He would have scoffed at me and told me not to be a fool. And, God helping, tomorrow I shan't be. But today all is dust within me, and I can write no more.

24

APRIL 2, 1947. I returned to my post at Justin in January, and the winter term has been crowded with catching up. I determined, however, that I would spend the two weeks of the spring vacation alone at school and review my thoughts and notes on Dr. Prescott. Ten precious days have now gone by, and I am still in a quandary.

What do I do with these papers?

How can I use them so as to convey the smallest hint of his greatness, bound as I am to include the essence of Jules Griscam's story? Not that I regard Dr. Prescott's condition as a wholly unreasonable one. I agree with him that his failure with Jules was an important part of his record as a headmaster, and with Mr. Griscam that there was a "hard" period in Dr. Prescott's life.

But my trouble is precisely that I am not interested in writing a biography. I am interested only in *inspiring* my reader, and I am much at odds with my century in believing that to demonstrate the best by itself is more inspiring than the best with the worst. I want to reveal Dr. Prescott resplendent in the pulpit with his arms, so to speak, outstretched and his great eyebrows arched. I want the little figures like myself who might turn up on preliminary drafts washed out of the final picture. I know that we live in an age where the homely or psychological detail is considered all-important. We like heroes in shirt-sleeves, or, in other words, we don't like heroes. But things were not always that way, and today is not forever.

The Francis Prescott who was Charley Strong's boyhood hero certainly existed, and existed more vividly, to my thinking, than the Francis Prescott who failed to sympathize with Jules Griscam. I say more "vividly" because Charley Strong's vision of God coincided, at least at moments, with Dr. Prescott's own, and it was this kind of bridge, this kind of communication of the ideal, that seems to me the only part of the Justin story worth memorializing. To tell it otherwise is to record a failure, and why do that? Something remarkable happened on that campus, and there is no profit in dwelling on the unremarkable.

Of course, nobody knows better than I that in the end Dr. Prescott deemed himself a failure, but a contrary view seemed to be overwhelmingly borne out when the great coffin, draped in the school colors of red and gold, was carried by the prefects from the packed chapel through a double row of hundreds of graduates, for whom there had been no room inside, all singing at the top of their lungs: "The Son of God goes forth to war." Behind came the Governor, the Bishop, four senators, eight judges and the headmasters of every boys' school in New England. Was it simply, as he himself might have put it, that the survivors of his organization, now that he was dead and harmless, wanted to build a bonfire of glory in which they could warm their trembling fingers and forget their relief?

I think not. I think the demonstration came from the depth of many hearts. For I believe that Dr. Prescott's true greatness lay less in his school than in his impact on individual boys. I even believe that he knew this himself, for he knew himself thoroughly, good and bad. He knew his capacity to be petty, vain, tyrannical, vindictive, even cruel. He fully recognized his propensity to self-dramatization and his habit of sacrificing individuals to the imagined good of his school. Yet he also saw at all times and with perfect clarity that his own peculiar genius was for persuading his fellow men that life could be exciting and that God wanted them to find it so. And having once seen and understood the good that he was thus destined to accomplish, how could he ever stop? How could he ever, even in moments of doubt, switch off his genius and leave his audience before a darkened stage?

Justin Martyr remains to us, as does the legend of Francis Prescott. In this early spring the awakening elms seem more glorious than ever and the brown craggy chapel tower more massive against a white sky streaked with blue. I walked through the empty dining room this morning to look at the Rand portrait. His hands folded uncharacteristically in his lap, Dr. Prescott gazed serenely over my head at the campus, which appeared in its entirety through the wide south windows. Listening to the purr of the lawnmower outside I had a funny feeling in that silent chamber that he might have been dead a hundred years.

Perhaps that is because I am less concerned now with the man than with the legend. Dr. Prescott was greater than the school which he created and by which he was ultimately disillusioned, and it is my ambition to distill for future generations of Justin boys some bit of the essence of that greatness. To those who would claim that I am contemplating a novel and not a history, I can only respond that the stories of all great men have been in some part works of fiction.

But I must stop rambling. I must cease my everlasting speculations. If I am ever to write anything, even if I give it my whole lifetime, I must still make a beginning. I must still make a mark on the acres of white paper that seem to unroll before me like arctic snows. And I must shut with a man's firmness a journal which seems the softest of self-indulgences in contrast to the austerely empty notebook that now I open.

Made in the USA
Middletown, DE
18 July 2021